Love and the Monroes

Suzanne Power has been writing since she was seven years old. At eight she received her first pay cheque – a princely three pounds – for contributing to an anthology of children's poetry. Now, a millennium later, her novels, *Lost Souls' Reunion* and *The Virgo Club*, have been published to critical acclaim and as far afield as Russia, Holland, Germany, Greece, Australia and the US. Suzanne also works as a columnist for two leading Irish publications. She has twin boys and lives with her partner in Wexford. *Love and the Monroes* is her third novel.

Love and
the Monroes

SUZANNE POWER

Hodder Headline Ireland
A division of Hodder Headline
335 Euston Road
London NW1 3BH

HODDER
HEADLINE
IRELAND

First published in 2005 by Hodder Headline Ireland
8 Castlecourt Centre, Castleknock, Dublin 15, Ireland

A Hodder Headline Ireland paperback original

1 3 5 7 9 10 8 6 4 2

A CIP catalogue record for this title is available from the
British Library.

ISBN 0340 75203 3

Typeset in Plantin Light by Hodder Headline Ireland
Printed and bound in Great Britain by Clays Ltd, St Ives plc

*For James and Marina,
my mother and father*

1

A bird's-eye view of 51 Verbena Avenue is of any purchased council dwelling, but for the lost Eden that is the back garden. It's a story authored by one who knows and loves plants. Any bird would consider it paradise and nest there forever, if it weren't for the presence of a Persian cat.

If the bird was given half a chance to peer through the window, aluminium framed by the poem of a Chinese lantern plant, it would see poetry give way to practicality. A three-two-one sofa and chair arrangement in the living room, television in the corner. At this time of year an Advent calendar is opened on the second window.

The bird's-eye view will not reveal what is different about this house. You have to let yourself in to a hallway with an Axminster carpet, a plastic runner on it to preserve what younger members of the household would throw out. But the old ruler is yet to be deposed.

The door to the sitting room opens, the first place where you get the sense of something being amiss, in the framed photographs. But the content appears the same as any other family's.

On the kitchen worktop, three cups hang from a wooden tree – one porcelain butterflies, one white designer glaze, one chipped china with a faint rim of shell-pink lipstick, washed by hand by someone with fading eyesight.

In the utility room there's a shelf with potted plants, all grown from garden clippings. Lemon verbena scent fills the space as if to compensate for the complete absence of it on Verbena Avenue. There's something about the shoe rack that doesn't fit, though the six pairs of outdoor casuals and one pair of Wellingtons yield no immediate clue.

Upstairs there are four doors off a small landing, with a stained-glass window featuring cornflowers. A resurrection of the garden's magic. The Axminster fan didn't approve of its installation. Now she smiles each time she passes.

Each bedroom now. The dark veneer furniture in the largest was purchased in the late forties. The candlewick bedspread dips in the centre to follow the shape of a hollowed mattress. The one who sleeps here, in patches, likes the comfort of that hollow in the empty hours. It's similar to that offered by another body.

The second bedroom is the only one that faces south and is scented with essential oils. An antique brass bed covered with a cerise satin throw faces the window, the view of the back garden. Her canvas. Books spill from the shelves, clothes pour from the wardrobe. The Persian cat lies here for most winter days, a comma curl on the end of the bed.

The smallest bedroom has a mattress on a step platform made of the same beech the floor is laid with and the wardrobe doors are made of. The walls are white. A near-death-experience bedroom. A cream linen blind diffuses light, offers privacy. Sliding doors open to reveal a ceiling-to-floor music selection and computer workstation. Everything perfect, in place, modern. No display of attachment or personality.

You walk downstairs piecing details together, one of which is the picture on the bedside locker of the second bedroom. A tangle-haired mother and child, walking through a summer meadow as if on the way to heaven, or at least Woodstock.

How could you not have noticed? The shoes on the rack fit the feet of three Cinderellas. There is no prince. No razor in the bathroom, no photographs, no presence of a man anywhere in number 51. There hasn't been for almost the same number of years that hang on the door.

The woman who has the semi-d next door, number 50, won't let her husband near the house, even in an emergency, like the downstairs flooding. He's five feet and bald. The occupants, the Monroes, have seen bigger eggs. This is why they christened him Humpty.

You haven't seen the photograph wrapped in a linen cloth, hidden in the bedside locker of the first bedroom. In it a man clutches a girl's waist, his smile corners the cigarette in his mouth. He greets the camera with a raised eyebrow that says: I will never do what you expect. And the girl loving that, for now. Their child in his arms, laughing.

Each night someone takes out the photograph and adds another kiss to over half a century of them. Each night she falls asleep with regret and dreams. For what they could have been, for what they were in that moment.

Love and the Monroes are oil and water, never to mix – that's why the owner of the second bedroom, Elizabeth Monroe, loves lava lamps. And her daughter hates them. Her daughter's room, naturally, is the smallest one. A place to misplace her passion, since she's never been in love. Nothing extraordinary in that, but for being named after the century's most desired woman – Marilyn Monroe.

She was born in 1968 when love was free and her mother, Elizabeth, paid the price, being single and only nineteen years old. Elizabeth's mother, Brigid, also had Elizabeth when she was only nineteen. They held their breath when Marilyn reached the same age in the fear that she might make it a hat trick. But she's thirty-two and childless.

It's 2000. Marilyn always thought she would be ancient, far different, at the millennium's dawn, but she sleeps in the same room, lives the same life. Except now she can afford minimalism. Thirty-eight years separate her from her grandmother, but there's not much difference between them. Brigid's always telling Marilyn not to waste her choices and chances, quoting Yeats: 'Never give all the heart.'

Marilyn's grandfather left Brigid on 2 December, forty-eight years ago, taking most of her with him. Marilyn's listened to Brigid's advice too well, Elizabeth not enough.

They are a close-knit family shrub, since half their branches are missing. Aunty Theresa is the man in the house, but she's seventy and the days of her climbing up ladders are numbered. This evening, if you're around, call again and you'll see Grace. She's Theresa's wife and Brigid's lifelong bête noire. Her eyes are pale blue and far-reaching. Brigid throws verbal and eye darts, which Grace treats like feathers brushing her peaches-and-cream skin.

Grace wears off-the-rack clothes like they're haute couture. Her home, six doors down from number 51, is the kind of place featured in magazines, and it was once. Grace is a writer. She knows about the arts, human nature, can hem curtains and is as accomplished as her looks. When Theresa came home from London to be near Brigid, Grace followed. Were she not a lesbian she would be arranging a rich man's flowers, entertaining the influential, as she is one herself.

'How acclaimed I might be,' she sighs, 'and how dull. I'd rather have Theresa in my future.'

The future, an after-dinner subject she now brings up for the Monroes by reading the leaves in their teacups. A 2 December tradition. It's Elizabeth's fifty-second birthday.

'I'm one year older than the number on the door today,' she laughs. 'Maybe I'm grown up enough to walk out of it.' They doubt it as much as she does. Marilyn's hopes in this regard are confined to herself.

Elizabeth's birthday is the only day in the year when Brigid or Marilyn subscribes to 'fortune-telling nonsense'.

'Go on, for the day that's in it. We'll have no more of this nonsense tomorrow,' Brigid offers, like it's a penance to do so. Her tendencies are like Marilyn's – although she loves this ritual, she would never show it. The anticipation in watching Grace line up the porcelain, chipped china and designer cups, examining, pausing. Elizabeth's eyes widen, as if she were consulting the Delphi oracle in person. Tonight Grace chooses to say one thing only.

'Men are on their way to the Monroe house.'

Marilyn Monroe didn't see a pair of male underpants until she lost her virginity, in cloudy circumstances, to a dull man at the age of twenty-two. She used to wander around the menswear department longing to have a dad to buy boring socks and jocks for, with things like 'Golf is Life' on them.

She's had one relationship lasting two months and twenty-seven days, with another actuary. When he left her for a traffic warden, he explained. 'You just won't take risks. You can't go through life like that.'

There are reasons why. The first is how she came into the world in the first place.

Elizabeth Monroe left her father after about five minutes. Marilyn was conceived in the fourth. Elizabeth is resigned to the fact that love is not realisable on this mortal plane and plans to indulge herself on the astral. On terra firma the main object of her affections is Persuasion, the Persian cat that sleeps on her bed. Marilyn bought Persuasion for herself, to go with her fabulous lifestyle that can only be so in two places – her box bedroom or her designer office. Everything that happens outside of those places has a horrible touch of chaos to it.

When Marilyn brought the cat home she leapt straight into her mother's arms. Elizabeth once joined the Temple of Isis in Clonegal Castle and they worship cats, so Persuasion has come to expect full and unadulterated adoration. Elizabeth will do anything for the cat, including handling meat, something she's never been prepared to do for Marilyn.

Over the years Brigid would dish up traditional dinners piled to Everest height with a dramatic thump on the table, glaring at Elizabeth. She thinks all vegetarians grow up with buck teeth and long ears and she lights candles in thanks that Marilyn turned out carnivore.

Sixteen years ago Misty came from the Disturbed Dogs Who Ought to Be Shot charity, via Elizabeth, and the first person she attached herself to was the one eating the bacon sandwich when she arrived like the Tasmanian Devil into the house. In return for half of it she never leaves Marilyn's side.

As you can see, even the animals in number 51 are female. Twice they tried to get a dog, and twice the dogs ran away. No male survives their house. Once Brigid had a budgie, George, but it died, falling under the Monroe gender curse. Marilyn's room is next to Brigid's. She heard sniffs that night, and a muttering: 'I'm not doing that again, all that cage-cleaning.'

You can see why they should be overjoyed by Grace's pronouncement, but it falls on ears flattened by lifelong disappointment. Besides, she said the same thing last year about men coming to and for the Monroes. They tell her so. She pulls off her pearlescent glasses.

'They were delayed. No doubt by your expert defences in this regard. But you're not going to keep them out this time.' She points to the leaves like the heaps and swirls are obvious, biblical in their truth. 'This time the men come armed.'

'What were they wearing all the other occasions?' Brigid narrows her eyes.

'Nighties.' Elizabeth shakes hair longer than decent for a woman her age and waves a turquoise-and silver-laden hand to dismiss the prophecy.

'Elizabeth, I expect more from you.' Grace is regal in her rebuff, but not cold to the daughter of her soul. Brigid looks at their confidences, the flow between them, out of the corner of her eye.

'Fleck off, Grace, this kind of talk creates trouble, and expectations,' she blusters. They hate the way Brigid says 'fleck' instead of 'feck'. If she abandoned herself to a swear word the world might end. It's one of a million things that make them frustrated and tight inside this house. At that moment, Marilyn thinks, I don't want him to break in if he's coming for me – I want him to break me out.

'Oh, you can expect trouble,' Grace smiles. 'You should increase expectation, darlings, that's half the problem. You expect so little from men, they've behaved accordingly.'

The hint of aristocracy in Grace's tone has always made Brigid bristle. Theresa steps in and guides Grace to the doorway, talking to her sister at the same time. 'Brigid, it's Elizabeth's day. Let's keep the disagreements for tomorrow.'

'She has precious few days to call her own in this house,' Grace says in the hallway. After one too many glasses of Chardonnay, her refinement has slipped.

'Now, Gracie, we're going and we're taking our talk with us.'

The comment still shapes the air. Elizabeth ignores it as she loads the dishwasher. Brigid puts things in presses, muttering under her breath. Marilyn watches her mother, wondering what she really thinks of the tracker bond she bought for her birthday. Her eyes glazed at Marilyn's explanation of how it worked. Her mother has no pension plan – her faith in providence extends to that. When they had builders in doing the roof and central heating she bonded with them, and gave them all dream-catchers, while Brigid made sure she got itemised receipts and Marilyn double-checked the figures.

Elizabeth studies law at night in a bid to convince them she is present to the real world, but in her personal life all laws are karmic. She is a reincarnation of a pre-Raphaelite muse. Ethereally beautiful, eternally tragic, addicted to laudanum and the adoration of artists. The pedestal of beauty is a draughty one, and makes you all the more noticeable to the wrong kind of man. Marilyn considers herself better off being plain and tough.

Elizabeth talks to her flowers in the garden, listens to opera with misted eyes, lights candles instead of flicking a switch, burns oils, sings in her room, whispers as she writes thoughts and intentions in velvet-backed notebooks. Her hands are always occupied – tasks prevent arguments. Most of her conversations are with herself and the past she lost, which her family knows nothing about.

With Brigid and Marilyn she is unsure, having no natural ally. Her voice heightens, her breath constricts. Brigid and Marilyn as a combined force would intimidate God. Being male, He wouldn't last long in their house either.

The truth of it is that Elizabeth isn't meant for the life she leads, as much as her mother and daughter are tailor-made for it. If Marilyn had Elizabeth's looks and Brigid's balls, she'd be made. Instead she got her looks from a stranger she has never met and her creativity, inherited from her mother, is well hidden and never discussed.

'Pipe dreams,' Marilyn occasionally whispers as she passes pictures of herself with her proud mother and piano tutor, holding up certificates, medals, trophies. Too many competitions for a child to enjoy what she was doing. She thinks she should have specialised in the oboe – oblong, weird, never a star attraction in an orchestra.

'Would you be too tired to play the piano a little?' Elizabeth asks when the kitchen is nearly cleared, her back turned. The loss of Marilyn's music has been for her the worst thing to contend with. She wishes she had handled it differently, had done everything differently. She only asks on special occasions and for years Marilyn has almost always refused.

'Yes, sorry. Night.'

The word 'wistful' was invented for the way Elizabeth looks at her daughter's retreat.

Marilyn's shoulders are small for the weight of expectation placed upon them, not least of which is possessing the biggest female name in recent history. In the queue for the bathroom that night she goes last and wishes she could go second, as always, since Elizabeth takes ages more than both the other Monroes put together. There's a small corner of her wanting to believe Grace. She leans against the doorway and lets herself imagine men coming armed to the Monroes. If love came. When Elizabeth opens the door Marilyn lurches into it and gets on with the business of brushing and flossing for fifteen minutes a night, without fail. She's been doing it since she was five and doesn't have a single filling. Her smile is Ultrabrite, but it never reaches her eyes.

'Come on,' she whispers to her reflection, 'it could be true. Finding a man's not rocket science.' She pauses and spits into the sink. 'No, it's harder, for this family.'

As she falls asleep, she hears Brigid through the wall speak in a manner she would never use outside her bedroom.

'Do you think she's right, John Joe? If I'd thought more of you, would I have got more? God knows if love had done the trick, you'd have been saved.'

As Brigid gets older her private ruminations get louder, and Marilyn's ears are well trained. It keeps her briefed on the current state of battle. She falls asleep, her body as tense as when she's awake. It's only in the dead of night that relaxation comes on her, that she breathes as if she is herself, her dreams full of what she is not, laced with colour and music.

If she could dream of outcomes, of Grace's tea-leaf reading, of Brigid's whisperings, if she knew about the photograph and the visitations, if she knew Elizabeth and what lay behind her secrecy, it might not be a good thing. Marilyn is a slow learner when it comes to all things outside of numbers. Her mind is as thin as her frame, a straight line in all ways, sharing a name but not a fate with the most celebrated curves in history.

2

The name has been the cause of multiple bruisings, mostly verbal, over the years. She's skinny, wears glasses, has mousy hair, no reason to wear a bra and she's Marilyn Monroe.

Elizabeth had given up pushing in labour until Marilyn the midwife grabbed her by the shoulders and, in the kind of tone you hear actors addressing each other with in *ER*, roared, 'You can do this!'

Immediately after the hot lump of new life was placed in Elizabeth's arms, she wept, 'I'm calling this baby after you.' Elizabeth swears she didn't make the association until the birth certificate was issued.

'I was trying hard enough to cope with other things, like feeding myself so I could feed you,' she pleads with her teenager, who has just sat through her first viewing of *Gentlemen Prefer Blondes*.

'You named me after a slut showgirl,' she whispers.

'I did not, I named you after a kind woman who was the only kind woman I knew at the time.' Brigid wasn't part of their lives then.

In the early days of Marilyn's realisation of what she had been saddled with, Elizabeth attempted to make it better. 'You'll grow up to be a siren.' She dropped the line when Marilyn turned seventeen and still looked twelve.

There would be no standing on hot air vents with her pleated white skirt billowing up round her thighs. The one compensation was that she graduated with straight As. What does a nerd with no friends do? Study. Marilyn's brain is the biggest part of her. She would give anything for a J-Lo bum, but she's more J-cloth.

She officially learned in college about risk assessment, but it was only putting into theory what she'd practised and abided by since birth. When she first came up with The Scale, which she uses to judge the suitability of men in order to prevent, in her words, 'foolish pregnancy and the kind of desperation that makes you call your child after the nearest health professional', she ran straight to her best friend Julie's house with a flip chart to demonstrate.

'Appearance, for me, counts for fifteen per cent. Ability to open up: five per cent. Interest in you: twenty-five per cent. Following so far?'

Julie looked amused, but Marilyn ploughed on. 'Look, here's the main one for you to consider in your own customised calculation, which I took the liberty of drawing up for you: solvency: thirty per cent. I'm not talking rich, just ability to make a living. If he's idle he's useless. Granny had one of those in granddad and it made for disharmony. Okay, where were we?' she asked.

'I'm sure you know better than me, Mari.'

'Ah yes, ownership of an animal: five per cent. Mother affiliation: five per cent. Abnormal mother affiliation: minus twenty-five per cent. We don't need two in the same relationship. We'd end up being seventy, sleeping in boxrooms, seeing each other for tea and buns before going on to ballroom dancing. On the walk home we'd ask ourselves, "Why did we never move out of home and marry?" Our epitaphs would read the same. Julie, are you listening?

'Granny affiliation: five per cent. Abnormal granny affiliation: minus twenty-five per cent. Belief in Supreme Being: five per cent. Atheists are always so depressed. There's got to be something out there, doesn't there?' Julie silently agreed. 'Please don't let it be the Catholic God, though. I'm a bit scared of Him. The fact that He requires a capital H says a lot. Elizabeth hates Him. Brigid thinks there's no one like Him, she's the head of His fan club.

'Interest in alternative lifestyle: minus ten per cent. Sorry, I know you love Elizabeth, but the actual children of hippies grow up Tory. Psychoanalysed: plus five per cent. Over-analysed: minus ten per cent.

'Here's another one designed with you in mind. The ability to buy a present without hint: seven point five per cent. If he knows what you like, he knows who you are. There are plenty of other smaller percentages than the ones I've listed, such as you can always trust a man in a bad jumper. Two point five per cent for that.'

This is how she puts it across, as fast as machine-gun fire. They're in their twenties, and so far Julie's had countless failed relationships. Marilyn hasn't even got to the failed relationships stage. A date would be nice.

'What do you think? Isn't this the way to make sure we never get stuck with anyone unsuitable?' Marilyn is eager. Marilyn is rarely eager.

Julie twists her lips.

'Come on, out with it!'

'It could be described as anal, Mari, that's what I think.'

'It's not! It's calculated not to be − there's room for discretion in there with the fourteen individual percentage points − you can decide on those categories for yourself. That's a lot of room for personal taste. The rest are rules that have to be applied.'

'The bad jumper one? You consider that to be essential?'

'Yes! It's a universal truth. Look, I've just gone too fast for you. I'll have a laminate done and you'll be able to take it at your own speed. You'll never be heartbroken again.'

★

If life were a colour-by-numbers picture, Marilyn would be long finished by now. Numbers are her life. With all the oestrogen storms in her house, she likes to think her dad was an accountant taking time out in Israel on a kibbutz when he copulated with Elizabeth on his last night. She says the only thing she can remember was that he was Irish too. They'd drunk a lot of Israeli wine and the stars were involved in their coupling, though not enough to make them a match.

Result? Father Unknown. Nothing romantic about that. Elizabeth had Marilyn's astrological chart done for her eighteenth birthday, as if to compensate. To Elizabeth it's an official document. It says Marilyn's father is a strong, single-minded type and that she takes after him. Brigid threw it in the bin. 'Heresy has no place in this house.' Marilyn fished it out and wiped off the stains, put it into her beside locker with other treasures and locked it against prying eyes. The bedside locker theme runs in the family.

Marilyn has conversations with him, at least as best she can for someone unblessed with imagination. He's getting older now, thicker round his middle. He's kind to her, has bear hands and arms and a soft voice. He says, 'Don't you love them like no one else?'

'Yes, Dad, that's the problem. I want to love someone male. After I'm finished loving Ma and Granny, there's nothing left over for anyone else. And Julie's as much trouble.'

'I'd have thought what with the way she looks, she'd help you in attracting men's interest.' Even fictitious fathers can't help being men.

'Dad, please, less of the *American Beauty* plotline. The kind of men Julie gets aren't interested in me, and before you go telling me otherwise, I'm glad. Lately they're getting sleazier, just like you.'

'I see.' He pushes his glasses up his nose. All known relatives have reasonable eyesight, though they wear reading glasses, except Marilyn, who wears glasses all the time, or contacts. So she figures he has a similar long-sighted problem. 'I won't mention it again.'

'Dad, would you have called me Marilyn?'

He smiles, won't answer. He doesn't want to upset her mother.

'Am I like him?' Marilyn asked Elizabeth once.

'Who?' Elizabeth was potting plants and drew a blank on an-out-of-the-blue question.

'The man who helped you to create me.'

'Not in the slightest. Theresa says you're like my father.' Elizabeth doesn't have a clue what her dad is like either. From her first three years she has only two memories. One is of the day he left, as her third birthday was taking place. No wonder Brigid's crotchety on 2 December. There are no photographs but for the one in Brigid's locker, which at this point no one has any idea exists. Their wedding was not the sort you took photos at, being shotgun.

John Joe Monroe left them with only his surname. If he'd taken that as well Marilyn would have been delighted to be Marilyn Downes. On meeting her, no man would have reason to say, 'I want to be loved by you', 'Are diamonds your best friend?' or 'Come up an' see me sometime.' She tells them they've got the wrong sex kitten.

'I can see that,' one nodded. 'You're more of a mouse.'

'Is it any wonder I never find the perfect man? I've met men who scored more than ninety only once or twice,' she tells Julie in one of her more vulnerable moments. She has very few of those, in public.

'You know, you didn't quite work out the maths right on this.' Julie has been waiting a long time for the right opportunity to say this, to voice again that The Scale sucks and is more a way of avoiding men than allowing them to approach.

'It adds up to a hundred twenty-five, Marilyn. It should have only been a hundred per cent. You must've gone wrong somewhere.'

'Julie, please.' Marilyn fixes her friend's eye. 'I got As in physics, applied maths, maths and computer science. Numbers do what I tell them. For me, perfection represents a hundred twenty-five per cent, unachievable and also implausible mathematically. But not if you're an actuary – we work things out in terms of risk and benefit and for us a hundred per cent is never what it seems. If you apply for insurances as a self-perceived safe bet – teacher, lives with mother, world tiddlywinks champion, non-smoker, Olympian fitness, Finnish origin – we load you for all the things you never thought of. Finland presents possible risk of death by avalanche or sauna asphyxiation. Also injury potential. If you're world champion everyone else is worse than you.

'When you work in the world of attaching maths to such indefinable and flighty things as horses, as I do, you'll come off worst if you believe a one hundred per cent success rate – i.e. wall-to-wall wins from maiden race onwards – means a sure thing. Sure things bankrupt. Actuaries look for more than perfection, and that's why we never lose, once we're dealing with figures. So I use calculation where and if possible.'

'Oh,' is Julie's reply. She stopped listening after the word 'tiddlywinks'.

The sliding scale doesn't apply to women friends. If it did, Marilyn considers for a brief second, Julie would be a no grade. But she's the best Marilyn has. Still, she won't listen, she just chews the corner of The Scale laminate, going to auditions for acting jobs she never gets.

Julie's had her heart broken once every three months for the past sixteen years. Her idea of the right man is The One.

There are almost seven billion people on this planet, forty-nine per cent of them male. Of those, roughly a million have enormous income, flash job, connections in high places. But they also need access to endless patience to meet her copious insecurities. This, Marilyn has calculated, hones it down to sixty-four subjects spread out over a planet whose circumference is twenty-four thousand miles.

But her chances are 251 per cent greater than Marilyn's, Marilyn has also calculated. Julie is like Elizabeth, with youth just about on her side. Voluptuous breasts, vulnerably thin and, this has to be whispered, not a good actress. Outside all a woman should be, inside all the things a woman can't afford to be. Julie would love to have Marilyn's name, envies it.

'Imagine the publicity I'd get out of being called after her. It's wasted on you.'

'We could always swap identities. What use is a name like I've got with a body like mine? It belongs to someone like you,' Marilyn offered in jest once, but the light in Julie's eyes frightened her enough never to say it again, especially when Marilyn realised she'd have to take on Julie's parents, who represent far more of a challenge than the single one she has to cope with. Julie's parents cling to her and neglect her at the same time, a balance only the most determined can achieve.

Since they've left school Marilyn has done for Julie what she did for Marilyn in allowing her to be her best friend. The boys round Julie were the alpha plus variety. That's why the multiple bruisings for Marilyn, her sidekick, were strictly verbal. They welcomed the opportunity to beat people up in front of Julie.

Marilyn remembers putting stuff into her locker one day, third from the top and she didn't even have to bend down. You couldn't see her head when the door was open. Julie was walking down the corridor with some of the prize bitch fraternity, the kind that file their nails in class, then claw you with them afterwards. They were petitioning her to dump Marilyn, on Marilyn's birthday, and join them for a groping session with the jocks at their house on the coming Saturday.

'Sorry, Mari's ma is cooking a special meal. Maybe we can come along later on, yeah?'

'What's with the "we"?' Chief Meow asked. 'It's you or no one.'

'Well, looks like it's no one.'

'But if you don't come, Alan Blaine won't come, and if he doesn't come, Noel Furlong won't come, and there's a chance that—'

'Okay, so invite Mari and I'll come.'

'If she comes, none of them'll come.'

'Why?'

'She has a hygiene problem, wears pebble glasses and dresses like a spa.'

'Her only hygiene problem is that she has two showers a day and threatens to rub her skin off. One more word from you, and I'll fuck you out the window.' Julie was tall, and a thump in that overeager way of hers could knock your teeth out – and that's if you were her friend.

The Meows walked by Marilyn, leaving Julie behind, asking themselves why someone so stupid got to be the best-looking girl in the school.

'It's not fair,' one of them moaned. 'She should be with us.'

Julie never believed she was as beautiful as she was. She never acted superior because she never felt good enough to be even average. Marilyn, however, didn't return the favour. When they left school and brains actually mattered, Marilyn was way ahead of any game. Colleges fought for her. Industry wanted her.

Julie never got on after school. Outside the glasshouse environment, life started to throw stones at her. Where were all the people to look at her? At work, doing something called a job. She took up modelling and acting to try and win back the adoration, but they only ever offered her top-off jobs. In her late teens and early twenties she was naïve enough to be shocked. These days she's too old to be offered. Marilyn has to pay for her holidays, her pizzas, her cinema tickets, her therapy when she had that panic-attack stage, her outfits if they're for auditions. She is Julie's Sugar Buddy. But they've been sisters since they were six.

'But what I need is a brother,' Marilyn often says to herself.

What Marilyn is is an actuary with a huge salary in her thirties, living at home. To move out would hurt her mother and grandmother, who won't let her pay for anything. It could be why she's decorated the boxroom out of existence, to resemble purgatory, since it's where she lives, waiting for life to start.

'You need your money, for the future,' Brigid and Elizabeth both insist.

What future? she used to think. Soon she will almost have too much of it. Be careful what you wish for outside bathroom doors on your mother's birthday.

3

3 December, 2000. Marilyn tried to leave for work and found her Saab wouldn't start. Saabs are supposed to, but it didn't know the measure of its dysfunction and Marilyn couldn't bear to part with it, referring to it as 'her'. She adored her mother's description of it as the pearl-green goddess, which for much of its life chose to remain stationary – another reason why the people at number 50 had little to do with those in number 51. It was frequently parked outside their property, since Marilyn found parking a mystery she couldn't solve.

'Those kind of cars should be owned by mechanics,' the man of the house, known to the Monroes as Humpty, often barked to his wife.

Marilyn's provisional driver's insurance cost more than the car was worth. Still, she defended it and spoke to her father often on this subject. 'It's my fault as much as hers. I won't say how many tests I sat. Okay, five, but the inspector got out of the car only once. I have that to be proud of! If you were around I'd have lessons from you, instead of from my mother. I'd have passed by now.'

For some reason the car breaking down again was pushing Marilyn to an edge she wasn't used to reaching, being so disciplined in her emotions. She had to wipe tears of frustration from her eyes – Marilyn only ever cried twice a year and then in solitary confinement – as she walked down to knock Theresa out of bed.

'You know, you've got to go to the car maintenance class,' Theresa grouched as she fiddled under the bonnet.

'Yes, yes, I will,' Marilyn said, knowing she wouldn't. She did Italian at evening classes because she loved music and Italian is the language of music, of opera. Marilyn played the piano, you already know, but it would have been hard to see she still had one, tucked under the stairs and covered with a dust sheet, trying not to draw attention to itself. Brigid kept threatening to sell it, as it was breaking a cardinal rule by Taking up Space. Brigid's cardinal rules, like the old version of the Commandments, all start with Don't:

Don't Get Up to Anything.

Don't Have Ideas Above Your Station.

Don't Develop Notions.

Don't Expect Too Much.

Don't Invite Disappointment.

Don't Live Beyond Your Means.

Don't Gush.

Don't Enjoy Yourself.

Don't Do Anything You Will Regret.

Don't Think You Are Indispensable, That's God's Job (which Brigid did for Him when he was busy).

But when selling the piano was suggested, Elizabeth reared up. 'It's not yours to sell, it's mine. I bought it for my daughter, who would have been a pianist only you got on to her.'

Each knew what was best for Marilyn, and their best was the other's version of worst.

'It's true, though, Dad.' Marilyn spoke to her father after a particularly vicious dispute had broken out. 'I was as good at music as I was at maths, maybe even better, if I do a comparison chart. When I said I wanted to be a musician, Brigid said, "Huh, your mother will love that." I wonder what you'd've said if you were around?'

The answer came that he would have urged her to listen more to her mother.

'But you don't know what she's like! You haven't lived with her! And no daughter wants to turn out like her mother, especially when she's the kind to smudge the television set after the news. Why is it spiritual types are never organised? If she just showed half of a clue, maybe I'd take notice.'

'She's organised enough to have studied law at night for seven years.'

After saying this Marilyn's father shrugged, sighed and chose no comment, which only made her feel worse about what she knew was her biggest mistake. It was awful that even imaginary figures stood up to her on this subject.

Elizabeth didn't help herself. Her timekeeping bore no relevance to the clock's. Five minutes late was the earliest she'd ever managed. Her morning entrances were all flurry and apologies and 'look at the time'. The morning of 3 December was no different. Theresa had adjusted the starting motor and got the Saab ticking over by the time she emerged, even more of a hurricane than usual.

'I'm sorry, I had to make a call, something important.'

'Elizabeth' – Marilyn mostly called her by her Christian name to soften the fact that she had once lived in her womb – 'what can be more important than getting to work on time? Brigid's going to be here soon.' Brigid didn't like Marilyn calling her Brigid either, though this was a more recent development, started when Marilyn was about twenty-five, in a bid to glean some kind of independence.

Brigid appeared on cue, barrelling up the road having done four hours of office cleaning. Elizabeth knocked on the passenger window to get into the car. Marilyn had control of the central locking and didn't press the button, punishing her into a scene with Brigid.

'There you are, you two, late again. If I was as late as you we'd have starved over the years. I'll get inside and clean up the mess ye've left with your breakfast.' Brigid said 'breakfast' like it was a dirty word. She didn't believe in it. She had six cups of tea between five a.m. and midday, when she had her big dinner, leaving theirs on a pot of water. No microwave would threaten an appearance in 51. 'Where would you be without me and Theresa to do your dirty work?'

'You don't have to clean, Mother, I told you I'll look after it when I get back,' Elizabeth hissed. There was no longer a need for Brigid to be on her hands and knees before dawn, doing floors, at seventy years of age. Still, she couldn't give it up because she didn't know how to stop after years of having to. If you took the 'have' out of Brigid's existence you took everything. She would have done well in two places – Stalinist Russia and an ascetic monastic order. She refused all of life's pleasures, but for tea and Judge Judy. Judge Judy was Brigid's hero, talking plain and tough to reprobates, putting order on slobs.

'She's the one to sort our curs out.' That's what Brigid called elected representatives, a view that filtered down through the generations. 'Why did you not run for councillor, Marilyn? You'd have done well at it, with that brain.'

'A politician called Marilyn Monroe? I don't think so. Think of the ridicule.' I always have to, she thought.

'I couldn't see her doing it either,' Elizabeth intervened at the time.

'You were political once, if you remember.' Brigid eyed her.

'Well, I stopped.' The way Elizabeth said it put an end to questions.

'Backing horses, after all that education,' Brigid said. It was one of her favourite lines. Both Brigid and Elizabeth were disappointed with Marilyn's choice of career. Elizabeth believed racehorses were treated cruelly. When Marilyn first got the job, Elizabeth was happy to hear she wouldn't have to attend meets. 'It'd be like watching blood sports at the Colosseum,' she'd said.

Brigid's reason was closer to home. John Joe lost the house putting it all on a horse, and only for Theresa they'd have been on the side of the road.

At the same time as Marilyn took her new post she was offered a directorship in her former company, but she still took the job as risk manager of Larry Leahy Bookmakers, believing it would lead her to some actual risk, and men. It soon became apparent that her new position was about avoiding both, like the plague. Still, in five minutes she could earn what Brigid did in one morning of backbreaking work.

She allowed Marilyn and Elizabeth one single opportunity to spoil her. Each year they took her on a holiday, though it was Nowhere Fancy, a sub-clause of the cardinal rules. It was always Trabolgan, a Butlins-style camp that catered for all tastes except Marilyn and Elizabeth's. Brigid loved the ballroom dancing but would only do it because she Had To, it'd been Paid For. For one week a year, the last in May, they saw her as Brigid could have been if responsibility hadn't been so heavy – happy. They always went then because any other time might have been Too Hot, another Brigid no-no. In Ireland, August is freezing.

'Do you think that girl will ever learn to drive properly?' Brigid asked as she and Theresa watched Marilyn drive away. She'd reason to fail five driving tests.

'I don't imagine so. She's clever enough to have got it by now if she was any good at it.' Theresa, hungry and cold, was putting her tools away quickly.

'How's your friend?'

'Are you referring to my wife, Brigid?'

'If that's what you call her.'

'I have done for nearly fifty years, Brigid. She's sleeping on, having drunk and said too much last night.'

'She said the men were on the way to the house.'

'She did.' – Theresa looked at Brigid – 'and you never put pass on anything Grace said before.'

'True enough for you. Do you think Marilyn is as bad at courting men as she is at driving?'

'From what I know, I'd say she's worse at it.'

'I agree. What about Elizabeth?'

'Worse again.' Theresa Downes, like her sister, never minced her words.

'Would you think that had a lot to do with me? The way I brought them both up?'

'You didn't bring up Marilyn on your own; her mother had more than a hand in it. I can't answer your question on the side of the road, you'll have to invite me in for a rasher.' Theresa combed calloused fingers through waves of grey hair, watching Brigid, but Brigid seemed reluctant to leave the pavement. Her eyes were still trained on the top of the avenue, where the Saab had disappeared.

'Where will the younger ones be without us when we go, Theresa? They know nothing compared to us, of getting on with things.'

'Can you get on with putting a bit of breakfast on for me, sister? It's not a summer morning.'

Brigid had to push the door to get it over the Axminster. 'Flecking carpet.'

'If the other two heard you say that they'd pull it up here and now,' Theresa laughed.

'I'd never give them the satisfaction. What do you want with the bacon – batch loaf, is it?'

*

'Will you have a rasher?' Theresa said, expecting the stock refusal from Brigid – you know my ways, don't be on at me.

'I will.' Brigid reached across for the plate.

Theresa put her knife and fork down. 'You might as well get on and tell me, I can't take another bite until I hear.'

'What?' Brigid snapped. 'What are you on about?'

'Something's up, Brigid. You're asking me big questions, you're eating, all at this hour of the morning. You even referred to Grace.'

'I didn't refer to her by name.'

'You acknowledged her, rare coming from you. I want to know what it is.'

'I've had another weakness.' 'Weakness' was Brigid's word for cancer. Ill health was an attitude, pneumonia was a cold, cancer was a weakness. She had beaten it five years previously. Brigid now had the expression Theresa used to see when they were hiding from their parents. 'It has me again.'

'Stop it, nothing'll get the better of you unless you let it.' Theresa's voice was harsh. The Downeses did not cry. 'When did you get the tests done?'

'They haven't found it as yet, but I know it's there, all the feelings are back from before. I couldn't go through that again, Theresa. I'd have to give up.'

'Give up, she says! Brigid Downes give up! Will you give me an example where you ever did that?'

Brigid's hands were white from clasping them together. 'I've a lot to do, so don't go soft on me. When John Joe left, giving all we had to drink and the horses, it put hate into me for men, it really did. Especially when the priest said it was my fault he left. I did think twice about church then, if the man who said Mass could say such a thing to me.'

Theresa nodded agreement, but Brigid held up her hand. 'The priest was wrong in the way he put it, but he was right, Theresa.'

'Was John Joe right to drink and gamble? Was he right to leave you homeless with a child?'

'He was my choice.' Brigid folded her hands into her lap and her voice softened. 'And if I wasn't happy with it, it was because I didn't make a good one. At the back of it, I didn't expect any more from life than a drunk, it's what our parents were, it's what I was used to. Falling off his legs even on the day I dragged him to the side altar.' It had been a time when no pregnant woman was allowed to marry at the main one.

'I gave way to him. It's what the modern would call psychology, Theresa. I turned the other two into the same as me, afraid of men. Your friend said it last night, which is why I'm acknowledging her. She's hit the button, and it's me at fault.

'Every young man who called to the door for Elizabeth got the run, for not being good enough. And there were plenty of them, in her heyday. One or two for Marilyn there were, too. I never made men welcome, Theresa, and you weren't much use for that either, in your condition.'

Theresa rolled her eyes. 'What about the weakness?' She used Brigid's word.

'Not yet. What's come with it is more important. Come with me.'

They walked upstairs to the first bedroom and from the locker Brigid produced the photograph. Theresa sat down on the bed, looking at a scene she never knew existed.

'This must be near to the time when he left?'

'Trabolgan.' Brigid stood behind her. 'I thought if I got him away from the drink for a while it'd make him see how much he had in the way of me and Elizabeth. He never touched a drop that I saw, all the long weekend, never wanted for it even. We had so much to be getting on with. Did you know that Trabolgan is Irish for "the place of the big wave"? I never saw waves like it. There were a hundred chalets, and full of families like us, though better off, it has to be said. They were going to be there the whole week. The sun never left the sky. Even though it was only May, we could stay on the beach all day. At night we went dancing, tea-time dances, Elizabeth watching us.

'I paid for that holiday out of saved and borrowed money, and all it proved to him was that he couldn't ever be right for the family life. He was gone by the autumn. I found him after he left, in some pub, and gave a fishwife performance. At the end of it he said the one thing: "I'd never be enough for you, Brigid, it's as well I'm gone." At the back of my roaring and shouting all I wanted was for that man to come home. But I never asked, I had the curse of pride all my life, as you well know. And then a few weeks later the bailiff called and told me about him having used the house as collateral for one of his notions.

'What I never realised, until recently, was he was trying to get Trabolgan for me, a full week, like the normal families. He was trying to get more in the way of opportunities, in his drunken, lazy way. He was all you think of him, Theresa, and he was more, because he loved me like that one down the road loves you.'

'Don't compare my wife to him,' Theresa warned.

'Please.' Brigid touched Theresa's arm. Theresa pulled back – the Downes never employed physical demonstration. 'I never said he was as good as her.'

'Well, you'd be right. Will I tell you how I came to be able to help you that time? Grace made it possible.'

Brigid took the photograph back. 'You had no right not to tell me that.'

'We had no option. We know about your pride as well as you do. And how was she thanked? Ignored like a second-class citizen by the woman who could have made her feel like family.'

Brigid put her face in her hands. She wasn't accustomed to the noises from the back of her throat. Theresa pressed her chin into her palm.

'I'm sorry, such a thing to say, and you the way you are. I'm upset with your news, I'm not myself, forgive me. I never meant for you to know that, ever.'

'It's me looking for forgiveness. I'd have been a fool not to know it was her did the helping.'

'You paid it back to her. Every penny.'

'Without thanks, and I've the same problem about most things. I'm even apologising in my dreams now, for not abiding by them. I've never loved others as I have wished to be loved, and it's my God's first law. Those I've looked down on He's sent to give me lessons – a drunken husband and a lady lesbian.'

'All lesbians are ladies,' Theresa pointed out, 'and I don't have the faith you do, but any God that takes you down a peg or two is doing a good thing.'

Brigid looked in that moment all her seventy years. It frightened Theresa.

'It's more than a peg or two I've lost, it's a footing. Did I tell you about the dreams, Theresa, the last time? The last weakness? After all the sessions' – Brigid never called it what it was, chemotherapy – 'I'd go off somewhere, to a picture in my head of a beach like Trabolgan, with big waves, and a lady watching me, John Joe alongside her.'

'Probably the next one he swindled didn't get over it as well as you, Brigid. He's bound to be dead by now, the way he was, and took her with him.'

'This woman wasn't to do with John Joe, this woman was all for me leaving him behind, or the idea of him. That's all that's kept me going in lonely times, my notions of him coming back home to me, sober, reformed.'

'Hah!' Theresa couldn't help exclaiming.

'Hah is right. He's my husband, and I've kept my vows.'

'Don't tell me you had contact with him?'

'I'm no fool. There are people who know of him. It's their job to help the likes of him. I give to them.'

'I can't believe you would, after all he did to you.'

'He's not what I want to talk about, he's my own private business. I want to talk to you about the lady, what she meant. I'm not one for talking. I'm one for getting on with things.'

Theresa leaned forward, resting her elbows on her knees. Brigid pulled out the stool from under her dressing table, sat down with a sigh, and began again. 'She was a very peaceful lady, foreign-looking, and she always had a scarf knotted about her head, like the old mantillas it was, black. She had the kind of smile that warms you.'

'Right, and she was with John Joe?'

'Yes, but Joe turns away, and she comes right beside me. She takes my hand, takes me up a path. It's that steep.' – Brigid held her hand at right angles – 'but I feel full of energy. She shows me into a narrow, low little house at the top of the way, and it's a blue door. She gets me to sit on a little stool, like they used to have, long ago, and the house is a country cottage, only it's not Ireland, and she gets all her things out of a chest that she's collected up over the years and shows them to me, smiling all the time.

'They're lovely things, they're things only those with a good eye have. I never recognised them at all. They're nothing I've ever seen.'

'Then how would you know they're lovely?'

'They're not alien things, you stupid woman, they're glasses, plates, embroidery and the like, all different colours and things. And she lays them out before me, and the way she's waving her hands, she's saying they're for me. Only I wouldn't take them on her. Then she gets up, knocks on a door and points for me to go through it. But I know I'm going through it alone, she's not coming.'

'And what's there?'

Brigid's eyes filled with tears at the question. Theresa had to look elsewhere, embarrassed. 'I never had the courage to find out.'

'But what's there to have courage for? You walked up the hill with the woman and into her house, why wouldn't you go through the door?'

'Well, at first I thought it was death and she was there to take me to it, and I wasn't ready. Then the dream kept coming back, and the same thing kept happening over and over, so I knew that whatever it was inside that door would change me, and I had no wish, or courage, to be altered. I'm set in my ways.'

'Set? You're cemented! I want to know about the doctors now, Brigid, you have to tell me more about that.'

'Theresa, I'm telling you, for the second time, this is more important.'

'Okay, okay, I've no wish to upset you. Carry on with the story.'

'It's no story, it's a visitation. When I left the hospital and got well, that lady went and took all her lovely things with her. She was telling me I had to leave the beach with the big waves, John Joe, and go on after something else. And what do I do? Get on with things exactly as they were. And what happens? The weakness comes back.'

'Brigid, don't be tying yourself to the Catholic whipping post!'

'There's nothing Catholic about it. The lady turned up after almost five years gone only a few weeks ago. And as soon as she came, I knew to get to the doctor. The doctor says it's not there, but I know it is. Her coming back confirms it. I'm sick, and there's no getting away from it.'

'Now I'm telling you, Brigid, your head is what's weak. There's nothing wrong with you a good holiday at Trabolgan won't fix.'

'It's not what it was, they closed it as it was shortly after John Joe and I left. When I read in the paper it was to open again I saved up, brought the girls. I thought it'd be a treat for them, something they'd thank me for. They endured it. Nothing's ever the same, is it? You should never go back anywhere that has true meaning for you.'

'You're right there, Brigid.'

'And every year since then they take me. I can see it's a test for them. I can't help liking the dancing, but as for the rest, I endure it too. My life's never had a summer since.'

'You didn't allow one, did you?'

'I didn't.'

'And you don't have to go to Trabolgan for holidays.'

'If I don't go, they'd book somewhere foreign, and I never wanted to go abroad. And after my weakness I was afraid to, in case I bumped into the lady, in case God put me on a plane to her place.'

'You hold God responsible for a lot, Brigid.'

'I do not, I hold myself.'

'Well, you're worked to the bone is all. Even the strong need a rest.'

'I'm being guided, to death or to difference of some kind. I don't know which I'm more terrified of. Leaving the world completely, or staying in it changed. And I'm scared. When Grace' – Brigid said the name like it was one she'd never heard – 'said last night the men are on their way, I can't tell you what it meant to me.'

'She said it last year as well and you never thought anything of it then.'

'I hadn't the sickness back. I took great stock last night. Even her accusations. Ah, Theresa Downes' – Brigid held up a hand to ward off complaint – 'you would defend that woman in a murder trial having seen her do it. I'm not disagreeing. What I want now, more than I've wanted anything my whole life, is to see my girls happy and settled. It's all I've ever wanted, but I just went the wrong way about it.'

'Marilyn's not your girl, she's Elizabeth's. You'd do well to remember that more than you do. And secondly, Grace is reading tea leaves out of the bottom of a cup. I love her, but I don't for one minute think there's a blind bit of truth in that.'

'Ah, you, you're just like me, but we're wrong in what we are. I've come to realise it's never too late for magic. We learn until the day we die, and I've more learning to do than most. Had I been a shade more like Elizabeth I'd have been a sight happier, and the rest of my descendants the same. It's as much as I can do not to cry, and I've no wish for tears. So help me to get things done.'

Theresa stood and nodded.

'Good, so. That woman is back in my dreams, and this time she's impatient with me, she's tapping at her wrist.'

Theresa's eyes were narrowed in her reply. 'What's your plan?'

'I've to get those two fixed up. With men and that. Stop the nonsense, and I've got a way, but you've got to help me with it. I read in the *Evening Herald* about computers that match you up with men.' She took the clipping out of her handbag. The article was on Internet dating. 'Do you know how to work a computer?'

'I know how to work most things, but not a computer. There's only one person who can help us,' Theresa said.

Brigid rose from the bed. 'I was afraid you'd say that. Will she be up?'

'She will.' Theresa followed Brigid down the stairs, pausing to look at the cornflower window, which she'd fitted and found to be the most beautiful thing about number 51. 'Grace will do all she can.'

'Then she's a better woman than me,' Brigid said,

slipping on her coat. 'It's time I found a way of saying it to her. I know there's a need for an apology.'

'Do you now?' Theresa watched her. 'Even after you cutting the head off her last night?'

'Old habits die hard, Theresa. Just because I'm not saying how sorry I am doesn't mean I don't feel it. She's bound to make a big meal out of any "sorry" I give her, after all that I've said over the years.'

'Grace will make light of it, I can assure you. But it won't mean it won't be appreciated, by both her and me. The hurtful comments cut me too, you know.'

'Then I'll say I'm sorry to you first,' Brigid rasped. 'It's as well to get the practice in.'

4

'Happy birthday to me,' Elizabeth whispered, having shut the door on Mr Dickey's rant that there was no loyalty in the world any more. It was the morning of her fifty-second birthday. When she'd resigned, he laughed first.

'Where else would you go after nearly thirty years?'

'That's my concern, Mr Dickey. I've no need for a reference.'

He'd played the flattery, persuasion, loyalty, disbelief, indignation, anger and threat cards in that order. It had been a half-hour conversation, almost a minute for each year. The last one was the worst: 'Who else would employ a woman of your years, when there are younger, prettier, cheaper women to do your kind of job?'

For a moment she couldn't breathe. The tragedy of lost youth and looks didn't always come home to her, since she had never lived by them, but Dickey was a man who had watched her age in the way no husband had, and his face showed she was not half what she had been.

'That's just as well, because I'm going to be doing your kind of job,' she informed him. 'You're more than aware of my training.'

'That's not a completed training. You can leave at the end of today.'

Elizabeth shook her head. 'You don't know where you are with the clients, I brief you on everything.'

'I'm a professional, and qualified, unlike some,' he pointed out. 'And I know how to hang onto the clients. I've one or two stories to tell them that will ruin your reputation

41

before you even start. Your sudden departure will only con-firm them.'

'You'd be making up stories, Mr Dickey.'

'And who's to disbelieve me, after thirty-five years in reliable practice?'

'The only thing reliable about this practice was me.' She was shaking as she shut the door.

'I'd have missed out on that office space. And if I'd expected him to act otherwise, I'd have been a fool. Now get yourself together and take his "today" to mean right now,' she coached herself as she cleared her desk. She left fifteen minutes later to pay her deposit on her future, taking Dickey's client list with her. She'd have to inform them of her dismissal on her own time and expense. Most of them didn't even realise she was just his secretary. On the street outside, the contents of her desk in two bin-bags, she phoned for a taxi on the mobile she rarely even switched on.

'It's busy, could be a while. On account, is it?'

'No, cash.'

'You're Elizabeth from Dickey and Co., aren't you?' The controller recognised her voice, the upset in it.

'Yes. I don't suppose you could do anything?'

'Okay, last name so, Monroe? Okay, hold on.' There was a silence that filled with her panic. She'd done this, she'd really done this. 'It'll be twenty-five minutes. Do you want us to buzz you when we're outside?' the controller asked.

'No. I'm outside on the pavement with two bin-bags, in dire need of transport to Commercial Lettings on Thomas Street.'

'What? Did the old shite sack you?'

'In a manner of speaking . . .' Elizabeth was disorientated.

'So there's no chance of him paying up the last account, then, it's always you writes the cheque. Hang on again. I'll see if I can get you anyone there quicker. It's freezing out.

Christmas rush already.' He checked it out. 'You're in luck, love. One will be there in five minutes.'

'Must be fate,' Elizabeth smiled, but her belief was serious. Her stock phrase was 'fate finds no friends in the cynical'. Now was a moment where she had to acknowledge the human being's bad design – fear and intuition operate from the same place. Elizabeth was never sure which one was making her do the things she did. She hoped it was intuition that had told her she just had to resign.

'Well, heavens,' Elizabeth looked up to address the sky, 'please make this right for me.'

The mention over the airwaves of the name 'Elizabeth Monroe, damsel in distress on Dame Street, just sacked by that shite Ian Dickey, the solicitor' by an atypically concerned cab controller at five minutes to ten o'clock on the morning of 2 December 2000 caused Tony Devereux, a man who'd never had a parking ticket and never broken a speed limit, to lie about his position, U-turn on a dual carriageway, head back into the city and do a three-mile journey in seven minutes.

'Are you sure you're up to it, forty-seven?' the controller asked. 'You've been on since ten last night.'

'I know her,' Tony radioed back, 'it's on my way home.'

'She's not going home, she's going to that new block on Thomas Street, property letting place, you'll be all day getting there.'

'Then I have all day. This is my job. Anyone else wants it has to fight me.'

5

'Brigid, asking Grace for help on a computer is like asking me for the loan of a spanner, she'll think nothing of it. She's been using them for years. And she had one of the first e-mail accounts in Ireland. They featured her in *Senior Citizen* magazine. In fact, I think she's their Internet correspondent now. Come on, will you? Act your age.' Theresa's key was in the lock.

'Don't, ring the doorbell instead.'

'If she's writing she won't answer it.'

'I know. I always want to look presentable before I show my face. You're not one for the make-up,' Brigid warned.

Theresa stuck her thumb on the bell. Two minutes later Grace came to it.

'I'm sorry, you've caught me unprepared.' She put a hand to her uncombed hair and skin that looked thinner without her perfect foundation base. Brigid had never seen her flawed in this way.

'I shouldn't be calling at this hour, and when you haven't had a chance to get yourself together. It's rude of me,' Brigid apologised. Grace took a full minute to recover before answering. They had known each other for almost fifty years. During that time Brigid had never been anything but rude.

'Wouldn't it be simply marvellous if your sister was woman enough to see that? She thinks nothing of appear-ances and the time it takes to make a good one. Had you not rung the doorbell you'd have seen me in total disgrace.' Grace stood aside to let Brigid in. Brigid glanced back at Theresa with a triumphant smile.

44

They had tea, which Brigid was grateful for, and scones, which Theresa was grateful for, having left her bacon uneaten.

'It's lovely to have you in my kitchen two mornings in a row, Brigid, and both visits impromptu. This is what I call progress between us,' Grace said as she made a second appearance, this time as herself rather than a lacklustre impression.

'You mean you were here yesterday as well?' Theresa couldn't stop herself from asking. Brigid ignored her before answering Grace.

'I have a purpose, as I had yesterday.' Whatever the reason, Brigid was not about to disclose more. It didn't satisfy Theresa's curiosity, but Grace seemed happy to let it go at that.

'I never thought otherwise, and it's still lovely to see you. You came to use my computer?'

Brigid gave Theresa a look. 'Did she read that in the cups?'

'No, darling, I didn't,' Grace answered. She was too polite to say that she'd noticed Brigid's preoccupation of late. Her bursting in on Elizabeth yesterday, in a place she viewed as enemy territory, had only confirmed something was wrong. True to Monroe fashion, Grace had received a flustered Elizabeth, then a flustered Brigid, without being given an explanation. Having observed both women for over half a century, she knew better than to look for one. 'But it's nice that you might think so. The sceptic is only a step away from believing. Unfortunately I do realise I have only one skill you would ever need to call on me for.'

'We need you to tell us how to get onto the places where men meet women,' Theresa explained.

'Are you sure you know what you're doing? And who you're doing it for?' Grace quizzed them.

'Not for me, if that's what you think.' Brigid flushed. 'For the girls.'

'You did believe me! You believed in my reading!'

Brigid fingered her collar. 'I have to believe it, whether I like to or not. They've been long enough on their own, I want them sorted.'

'My skills are accurate.' Grace held her head high. 'I know Theresa has no regard for them, but my dear Nanny had gypsy in her, and she taught me.'

'So,' Theresa couldn't stop herself from saying, 'it follows that everything you say is gospel.'

'What kind of men did you see, Grace? You never elaborated.' Brigid glared at Theresa for interrupting.

'I'm not at liberty to say.'

'That means she doesn't know,' Theresa pointed out, afraid of how seriously Brigid was taking this.

'It most certainly does not mean that.' Grace flushed. 'I'm not in the habit of lacing things up to look pretty. But I've no intention of raising concern with less-than-favourable predictions, especially at Elizabeth's own birthday dinner.'

'You'd better explain yourself,' Brigid said. 'My girls aren't going to get hurt in this, I won't allow it!'

'Brigid, as you well know, you can't prevent nature from taking its course. Any romantic involvement causes up–heaval. It's what makes love so interesting, such a challenge. All developments should be welcomed and hiccups expected. There. As much as I can say.'

'And I'll say this,' Brigid thundered. 'If they get damaged, I'll—'

'Now, Brigid,' Theresa intervened, but Grace interrupted.

'Please, Brigid, don't shoot the messenger. You're only thinking of your loved ones, and so am I when I say this is something you must allow, rather than prevent, as you've traditionally done. Avoiding life hurts more than living it. I'm happy to help you look for these men, and I know how to do it, but you must let the men look for them. Fine? As long as we all realise that, come up to my office, and we'll begin what should have begun years before now.'

Grace's pianist fingers were at work on the keyboard. Brigid and Theresa were impatient with the time it was taking, with what they couldn't understand.

'Now who will we look for first, Marilyn or Elizabeth?'

'Elizabeth, her situation is the more desperate,' Brigid instructed.

'No wonder, for all the encouragement you gave, you were hard as a steel brush on her,' Theresa broke in. Grace's fingers clicked harder on the keyboard in agreement. 'We can call her Elizabethan Beauty in our replies, she'd like that,' Grace suggested.

'Beauty, is it? I suppose she's not bad for her age,' Brigid conceded.

An hour later, Brigid turned to Grace. 'Is that all there is on offer?'

'I know,' Grace sighed. 'It's like choosing a husband from a psychiatrist's waiting room.'

'I wouldn't let Elizabeth's cat go out with one of these gentlemen.'

'Look at this one.' Grace scrolled down. 'Calls himself Lear Jet. No. She hates flashy people. And Semi-Detached has to go, for the same reason. A flourishing estate agent with a "Dublin Four address and no one to share it with".'

'What about this lad, Old-Fashioned?' Theresa pointed. 'He'd be able to handle a dinosaur for a mother-in-law. "Yes, I am old-fashioned, believing as I do in old-style values – good manners/courtesy, civility, discretion".'

'I think he sounds perfect.' Brigid leaned forward. 'Where's his photo?'

'No photo, just a blurb and then you have to e-mail him.'

'But how can you do that if you don't have the e-mail?'

'I can set it up for you now. Just think of a name you want to be called.'

'Brigid, it's the name I was born with.'

'Okay.' Grace worked away. 'Now, here you are, BrigidM@airwave.net. If you want we can mail now and set up a meeting. But he uses capitals a lot, which means he shouts. If he shouts Elizabeth will hate him.'

'Would you mind not telling me what my daughter will or will not like? The fact she doesn't know what she wants is what has her a spinster, and consulting with the likes of you has her no better.'

'I'm entitled to my view,' Grace sniffed, 'and if your daughter responds to me as I do to her, then it might have to do with the fact her mother has never understood her.'

'Right, that's it,' Theresa said, putting a stop to it. 'We're here to help Elizabeth.'

'Next one, then,' Brigid ordered.

'"I have all my own teeth and faculties" – and men wonder what I don't see in them?' Grace shook her head as she read.

'Does that mean the rest of them don't?' Brigid looked like she was about to keel over.

'Let's make up our own advertisement, shall we?' Grace suggested. 'Someone might reply to it who wouldn't dream of advertising themselves. There's a chance.'

'We can't leave anything to chance.' Brigid stood up. 'There isn't enough time.'

'I'm glad you take my tea leaves seriously, Brigid, but really, Elizabeth's been on her own a long time. I told you last year men were coming, and you nearly threw me out of the house,' Grace said, turning around from the screen.

'I know, sorry for it' – the apology sounded strangled but it was a start – 'but her loneliness has gone on long enough.

This won't do. We have to find someone who wants to look after her, properly. Then get them up the aisle, and they're not getting near her till they do that, not after last time,' Brigid insisted.

Last time. Elizabeth had stood in the porch she hadn't darkened for five years. Marilyn was almost three years old, fast asleep on her shoulder.

'I'm only here because I've nowhere else to go. If you won't take me, at least take her. We won't stay long.'

'You need no bribes to come back to your own house.' Brigid had held open the door.

Later, as she served sandwiches, Brigid asked, 'If you couldn't have told me, could you at least not have told Theresa and that woman?' They hadn't spoken a word to each other. Marilyn was up on Elizabeth's bed, which Brigid had made up with fresh sheets each week since her departure.

'No.' Elizabeth spoke quietly, addressing the table more than her mother. 'It wouldn't have been fair to make them keep something like this from you.'

'Fair, she says! Is it fair to keep my own granddaughter a secret?'

'Your illegitimate granddaughter. I know your views, Mother.'

'I wouldn't care if she had two heads! She's family, she should be cared for as such!'

For a moment, Elizabeth had felt relief. This was the right thing to have done. How right it was would become all too apparent, as her mother assumed control to the point where she imagined sometimes that she didn't exist.

'Do you know where her father is?' Brigid asked that evening.

'I don't even know who her father is.'

'In that case,' Brigid had said, 'I think you might consider stopping here. What's her name?' Elizabeth told her. 'Now why did you call the poor thing that?'

'When you're done dreaming, Brigid, any suggestions?' Theresa looked at her watch. 'Grace's got the dinner ready shortly.' Theresa ate hers in the middle of the day too.

'Grace this, Grace that!' Brigid was pressing the space bar like it was a crowbar. The information kept slipping off the screen before she could read it.

'I've just put the chicken in, it'll be twenty minutes, and you're welcome to join us for luncheon,' Grace said.

'Am I now?' The formality of Grace's invitations often made Brigid turn them down. Grace had never come to terms with the Irish code that the more informal you are, the more welcoming. She also considered it rude to give people more food than made them comfortable, whereas Brigid considered it rude not to observe the national custom of filling you to bursting point.

'The problem with these men is they're all Irish,' Theresa said, looking at the screen.

'Greece!' Grace said suddenly. 'She spent a few weeks there before she had Marilyn. She loved it.'

'I never knew that,' Brigid said.

'Well, she wouldn't think to tell you, would she? You don't like foreign, you're always saying.' Theresa was brusque.

'You can imagine her floating through olive groves,' Grace said, sitting at the computer again. 'And you don't have to go to Greece, Greece comes to you. Here's Hellenic Introductions, to put us in touch with "Homer and his followers". This, ladies, is much more like it.'

Three minutes later they were surfing what Grace was calling 'a site for sore eyes', with what even Brigid had to call Lovely-Looking Men. 'Mind you, they all want to get in here to work is all.'

'Brigid, Greece is a member of the European Union. They can come here any time they like, and you don't exactly see them flocking to this miserable rainy shore, do you now?' Grace pointed out.

'Look, it's all written funny.'

'That's Greek to you, Brigid, one of the oldest and purest languages in the world. The English we speak is a mongrel tongue.'

'Can you make it proper, so I can read it?'

'I can.' Grace brought up the English version before going down to the kitchen to check the potatoes – Dauphinoise for her, boiled with butter and salt for the Downes sisters.

'Isn't it a new world that you can bring anyone in it into your bedroom? I'm glad I'm dying, Theresa. The world frightens me,' Brigid whispered.

'Don't.'

'I'm not going soft. I'm only saying—' Brigid stopped talking.

They'd found him. But it wasn't Elizabeth he was looking for. Brigid realised she'd known this all along. Theirs would be a meeting five years overdue. Thanks to her reticence, a woman who had never been late for anything.

51

6

Elizabeth was embarrassed to be on the pavement with bin-bags, her coat too thin. It wasn't the normal one she wore to work, but she wanted to be stylish for her birthday. It was turquoise-blue velvet that she'd found in a period clothes shop. The day she came home with it Brigid said it made her look pregnant and Marilyn made no comment. For Marilyn and Brigid, clothes were a uniform. For Elizabeth, they were expression.

Most of the time she didn't worry about being seen as an individual, but even she felt a fool in the sub-zero wind in what would have been evening wear over fifty years ago.

Tony saw the turquoise from the bottom of the street and knew it was her.

'Sorry I'm later than the five minutes, traffic's terrible,' he said calmly, which wasn't how he felt.

'So your controller said. I'm just grateful that you're here at all,' she said, shivering.

'I'll put those in the boot, you get in and get warm.' From the first he was looking after her. 'Where to, madam?'

'It's not madam,' she laughed, 'it's Elizabeth. I need you to get me to Thomas Street as quick as possible.'

Brigid and Marilyn would have winced at the lack of formality. Elizabeth was open to the point of bleeding, unable to turn a Jehovah's Witness away from the door. 'You can be interested in people without being converted,' she defended herself.

'It's the Hare Krishnas you need to join. They're for vegetarian food and non-judgement. Brigid doesn't like any old dog or divil coming in. Remember when I was younger and she found the tramp tucking into the stew she'd put on? You were upstairs running a bath for him and I was in the kitchen making sure he didn't steal anything,' Marilyn reminded her all too often.

'Will I ever be allowed to forget it?' Elizabeth sighed. Brigid's reaction had been loud and swift. He was gone in one minute and Elizabeth was advised if she wanted to run a soup kitchen, she could find her own.

'You can't see beyond the dirt, you can't see the humanity, can you? He was telling me and Marilyn about what causes the Aurora Borealis.'

'I can see too well beyond the dirt. Never let anyone like him into the house again – we may never get rid of him.'

'Oh, we will, if he's male, you can be sure of that,' Elizabeth had said.

Later, in quiet moments, she wondered about his eyes, if he might have been John Joe, but their brilliance, a cornflower blue her daughter had inherited, had long faded. He was no longer recognisable as such, even to himself.

'In this traffic,' Tony said, trying hard to keep his voice level at being on first-name terms with Elizabeth, 'Thomas Street will be three quarters of an hour.'

'Will it? I'd walk quicker,' she said, but she couldn't contemplate getting out of the car into that cold again. The meter was at €7.50. She reminded herself it was her birthday as well as the first day of a new life. 'So long as we're there before noon. They're keeping the place on a first-come-first-served basis.'

'A new flat, is it?' Tony asked.

'No, a new office. You know the way the economy is, it's hard to get anywhere and impossible to get city centre. You can't swing a cat in it, but they've got a waiting list of four if I don't turn up with the deposit.'

'Good for you, we'll get you there. Have you worked for Dickey's for long?'

'Almost thirty years.'

'If you don't mind me saying, I imagine he was very hard to work for.' To think I ran that miserable man home at least ten times a year and never saw you once, Tony finished off in his head.

'I never took taxis anywhere working for him. And I had a daughter to support. The economy wasn't always like this.'

'So, what are you going to be? What's your new venture?' He seemed interested, so she told him. There was no reason not to. Elizabeth was setting up as a family law consultant, her fees one-sixth of the average solicitor's. By summer she would have taken her final exams and would be fully qualified.

'I admire you.' Tony turned right. He knew going right was quicker than straight on and couldn't prevent himself from doing the honest thing. 'I haven't found what I want to do when I grow up, and I'm forty-seven.'

'Oh, you needn't worry, you will. I'm fifty-one, sorry, fifty-two, and I only just got there.' What are you telling him all this for? Elizabeth asked herself.

'You strike me as the kind of person would always get to where she wanted in the end,' his said, his eyes meeting hers in the rear-view mirror.

'Oh, I'm not so sure.' Elizabeth felt the first pinprick of awareness that he might be too interested in her. She assumed she was being paranoid, so she said too much, as kind women tend to do in awkward moments. 'I've made more mistakes than you, I bet you.'

'I wouldn't bank on it.' Tony's eyes had a shadow of his story in them.

Your turn to be wrong, Elizabeth thought. My sins are considerable. Particularly of omission.

Elizabeth had always planned to tell her as soon as Marilyn turned eighteen and was legally an adult. She wanted to give her the gift of an astrological chart and her father's identity, so she wrote a letter to Niall, asking if he wished to know his daughter, and had it delivered by special courier, with the sender's name marked clearly on the back of the envelope. It would be read only by him. He never replied to the box number she had set up specially.

When Marilyn was born her father had wanted sole custody. Had he got that, Marilyn might have been a pianist instead of a number-crunching neurotic with a teenage desire to hide in her bedroom. A daughter of Niall Tormey would have had all the opportunity life could offer.

'Is it the new block we're going to?' Tony asked.

'I think so. I've never been to the actual office.'

'It's the one they're still working on,' he said, 'as you can see.'

She could see a workman up a ladder, putting a sign across the entrance. It was eleven o'clock, four minutes earlier than Tony had predicted they would get there. The meter read €23, an extortionate sum for a two-mile trip. She was reaching into her bag for it when she saw the ladder and sank back into the seat. 'I don't believe this, I can't go in.'

'Why not?'

'The ladder.'

'Sorry?'

'I'm superstitious. I can't walk on pavement cracks, I go out of my way to avoid black cats unless I'm sure they'll cross my path, I won't hold peacock feathers and I've made myself blind to single magpies. I always take Friday the thirteenth off work. I throw salt over my left shoulder and I never, ever walk under ladders.'

'Ah, now.' Tony's voice was gentle. 'This can be your first time to find walking under ladders is lucky. Did you ever think of that?'

'Did I heck. I'm about to take the biggest step of my life, and the first thing I do is walk under a ladder? I don't think so.' He saw that her agitation was growing. Her knuckles, pressed against her chin, were white. 'Oh God, you must think I'm a fool.'

'I don't. I have a few things I won't do myself. I'll go and ask him how long he'll be.'

'Would you? Would you really?'

He came back with the news that it was more than the workman's job was worth to get down off the ladder before dinner hour. He had five more signs to do after this one, and he should have had that one done before ten this morning. The fittings had been the wrong size.

'What time is dinner hour?' Her voice was hysterical.

'Half twelve.'

'But they'll give the office to someone else! I have to sign for it. Please, tell him I'll pay him anything to get him to move that ladder, just for two minutes.'

'No, I won't, because that would be unreasonable,' Tony said.

'Okay, I'll tell him myself. Can you wait here?'

'I won't.'

'I thought you were a nice taxi driver. I can't go in there with two bin-bags. I won't look professional.'

'I am a nice taxi driver, so I'll go in there for you, say I'm your assistant and hand over your cheque. I'll say you're busy on your mobile, so kindly put it to your ear, and then I'll get the agent to come out with the forms, since he'll need to witness you signing them. Will that do?'

'That'll more than do. You're an angel,' she smiled.

If I am, Tony thought, I'm a desperate one. Half an hour

later the agent went back inside with the signed contracts and Elizabeth had her keys. The meter was at €51.

'An omen,' she said, giddy with excitement. 'That's how old I am today.'

'Happy birthday, I hope you have a great one.' He felt drunk with all these facts coming at once. A sensation he hadn't felt in a long time.

'Listen, I know you probably have another job, but could you drive me to it, the new office? I just want to see it for myself, what I need to get to make it my own.'

He smiled. 'It would be my pleasure.'

'I'm good for the fares, you needn't worry. By the way, what's your name?'

'Tony Devereux.'

It sounded familiar, but she couldn't place it.

She sat in the sub-basement office, her bags taking up most of the floor space. There was a desk that wobbled, a chair that broke each time you leaned back against it and a filing cabinet with drawers that stuck. The colour on the walls was hospital-green bordering on morgue.

'What was I thinking of?'

She could hear a rodent scuffling in the yard outside. The only toilet in the building was three flights up. Next door was an indie record label, which increased the noise pollution to lethal proportions. A phone call to the environmental health officers would be in order, first thing Monday morning.

She loved it.

Already in her mind she was in the DIY shop, picking out paint, choosing a few pictures from her own supply at home. She came back up the stairs smiling. Tony was waiting.

'Do you know ...' Elizabeth stopped. 'Your face is familiar to me, now I come to think of it.' She never forgot a face, after the way she'd lived for the early years of Marilyn's life.

'I was thinking that too,' he said, smiling.

'Sorry, I didn't recognise you before. Where do I know you from?' she said, not as friendly.

'That's okay, you wouldn't unless you're good with the backs of people's heads. It might have been Phoebe who introduced us?' He stumbled a bit, aware of her reserve.

'Ah yes!' She was relieved to be able to place him. 'On Vico?'

'On Vico.'

'That wasn't today or yesterday. How is Phoebe?' she asked.

'She's doing well. Married, living out in Canada.' Five years sober. Five years since I met you face to face.

'I'm glad of that. She had a lot to offer. But you must have been disappointed,' Elizabeth said, relieved to know where she could place him from.

'How do you mean?' Tony was mystified.

'Well, weren't you and she . . .?'

'Now, she was a lot younger than me.' How could you think that?

'I only knew Phoebe through my daughter, Marilyn, and Marilyn only knew her through another friend,' Elizabeth explained. 'She was a bit wild.'

So you thought I was the kind of middle-aged man to take advantage of alcoholic women in their mid-twenties? Thanks, Tony thought.

'Sorry,' Elizabeth ventured, seeing she had upset him. 'I never considered it, we met for such a short time.'

'That's okay,' he said, thinking, I never stopped considering it. 'I should be flattered you thought so, really, shouldn't I?'

'What are we at?' she smiled.

'Sorry,' it was his turn to say, 'what d'you mean?'

'What's your meter at? I need to keep solvent before my venture starts.'

'Oh, you're near the eighty mark,' he said, looking through the window. He had no intention of taking money and had only kept it running so as not to frighten her.

'Right' – she swallowed – 'let's make it the even hundred and you can run me home. Can we stop at a cash point?'

They pulled in at a row of shops so she could use the ATM. He used the opportunity to run into a florist, leaving his purchase on the back seat. It was a dried arrangement in a basket, the only thing that was available there and then. 'For your birthday,' he said cheerfully, but he could see she wasn't even acknowledging their existence.

'Please, you shouldn't have.' In less than three hours this man knew so much about her. More than her own family. She got him to drop her at Theresa and Grace's.

'How much do I owe you?' she asked outside number 45.

'Nothing. Think of it as another omen, your first windfall on your first self-employed day,' he said, turning around. She could see his eyes were olive-green and the expression in them held something that made her uneasy.

'Please, no, you've been more than kind.'

It went back and forth, depressing and depleting both of them, and they settled on splitting the difference. He took fifty euros and silently accepted when she said she didn't really think it was a good idea to go out for a drink.

He also accepted, in pulling away from a house he knew wasn't hers, that he had lost his first and only chance. She ran down the path and banged on the door, leaving the arrangement on the backseat. Dried gypsophila, wheat sheaves and cornflowers.

Brigid was heading out for the shops to get a card for

Elizabeth's birthday. She saw Elizabeth get out of the taxi and saw the driver watch Elizabeth go up the path. She started towards him before he could drive away and held onto his open window. The look on his face registered with her, for a reason she couldn't understand.

'Are you for hire?' she snapped.

'No, sorry, I'm off duty.'

'All right, so, I saw you just dropped my daughter off, that's all.'

'Yes.' He coloured, unable to look at her.

'What's your game, mister? If you're up to any funny business I'll make sure you won't laugh any more.'

'There's nothing funny about my business,' Tony said, facing Brigid now. 'I got your daughter some flowers for her birthday and she took offence.'

'And how do you know her?' Brigid turned her head to one side.

'I've only met her twice.'

'And once was today?'

'Yes.'

'And you're buying her flowers?'

'Yes.'

Brigid looked in the backseat: cornflowers. She could never look at them without Marilyn's eyes, and John Joe's, the lost husband, the lost opportunity for the only thing that made life bearable – love.

'You bought those for her?'

'Yes.'

'Any reason?'

'Eh, they were nice.'

'And you thought she'd like them?'

'I just know I liked them, and I didn't have time to wait for a fresh bouquet . . .' He tailed off.

'What's your name, son?'

60

'Tony Devereux.'

'And which group are you working with?'

'City Cabs.'

Brigid had her pencil and miniature notebook and wrote them down. 'I know enough about you to have you sacked. Now you can run me down to the shops.'

Brigid never took lifts to the shops, let alone in taxis. This time she had two reasons for it. One was a need to interrogate further, the other was fatigue.

Grace was giving Elizabeth tea half an hour later when a knock came on the door.

'It must be a Jehovah's Witness, we seem to get a lot of them calling. They're fond of this road, for some reason.'

Elizabeth took a sip of tea, avoiding Grace's eye.

'I saw my daughter come in here while I was on the way to the shops.' Elizabeth wanted to bolt out the back at the sound of Brigid's voice. 'What's she at? She should be at work. And she's done up like a dog's dinner in that coat.' Brigid was already past Grace and into the kitchen.

'I took a day off. It's my birthday, and I did a bit of shopping instead of going to work,' Elizabeth began.

'Well, I'd have come with you if I'd known,' Brigid flustered. 'I'm finished since eight, as you well know.'

'I wanted to look at my kind of shops, Mother, and I've dinner to sort out. So I'm off to them again soon.'

'Oh, you have,' Brigid said. 'You've a right meal going on.' Tony had told Brigid about the office in an effort to prove he wasn't a stalker, and with no reason to think Brigid wouldn't know.

'What's that supposed to mean?' Elizabeth demanded.

'It'd be as well, Elizabeth, if you didn't hold cards close to your chest. Then we might get on more.'

'All this because I took a day off work?'

'It is her birthday,' Grace interjected. She thought people talked about things when they were ready to. It was no wonder, really, that Elizabeth remained so secretive about herself, despite being so open to others. Grace knew her like a daughter – with few specifics of her existence.

'Every day is this one's birthday,' Brigid said, sitting down. 'Now if I'm not interrupting, I'll have some of what's in that pot. Then I'll help you with the shopping, Elizabeth. It's a long time since we shopped together, isn't it?' Elizabeth rolled her eyes. 'Help, I said, not hinder.' Brigid's voice was surprisingly gentle. 'I just want a bit of your company is all. If it's not inconvenient?'

'Yes, of course,' Elizabeth said, her kindness speaking before she could.

7

Grace got ready to serve the Downes sisters, thinking of the previous day's visit, and this one. Brigid was still upstairs looking for a love to replace what she had never given to her daughter. Grace ached in sympathy. It was a route that held little promise for a woman like Elizabeth.

'Luncheon!' she called and got no answer, so she climbed the stairs. Theresa and Brigid pointed to the screen, neither able to speak:

I write on the behalf of my father, who you see addressing my wedding, about his son, and it is this wedding gives me courage to do this. My mother died seven years ago and she is the one my father would like to have grown old to die with. My father is a man who farms his land and keeps quiet about his thoughts. But he has given me a good life in education and in opportunity and I like to give him something. I give him my prayers each night and my thanks each day. I give him, in words, that he is the best father any could have.

And he needs a wife. He will not come to stay with me in Athens, and he will die in his home island of Skyros. My father is not an old man, though he is now sixty-five. He is young as his ponies. He will give you a home, but not a palace. My father, Nikolas, will live nowhere else. He will give the right woman love, but not trouble, as his son I know this. He values the silence of his world, he is a private man. For walking he will go many hours in the day, alone. While others sleep in the heavy afternoon he is watching the water, for the boat that brings his news. He has watched each day since his dream of five years. I think the boat brings his new wife. He thinks it will take him to his old one. But he is too young. So I must help, to end his waiting and make him happy again. Since I do not come to see him as often as I wish.

If you want to join him on his walks, as his wife once did, my mother, write to me, Kristos, telling me three secrets of your heart.

Can I tell her? Theresa asked with her eyes, and Brigid nodded. Theresa explained about the dream, with Brigid butting in to correct details, like the colour of the headscarf, the height of the waves, the location of the cottage and the knowledge that the man in the photograph, the groom, was the image of the woman in her dreams. The man beside him, Nikolas Faltaits, was his father.

'I don't want this to happen,' Brigid whispered.

'A lot of Greeks have those features,' Theresa suggested.

'I'm telling you, he's her spit. Whatever I'm to do, it's with them. This is not the sort of thing that happens to ordinary women like me.'

'There's nothing ordinary about you, Brigid. What you must do is act. You can write to Kristos,' Grace urged. 'And you can walk through the door his mother has been patient enough to show you for five years.'

Theresa pursed her lips. 'You're not the sort for flying. You'd be trying to take over from the pilot, in case he made a mistake.'

Brigid Monroe eyed her sister. 'I never flew because there was never good enough reason to before. You can write that I will be coming with three secrets of my heart, but I will do no such thing over an Internet. Those words belong face to face, where a person can receive them in a manner intended.'

'I'm coming with you so,' Theresa said quietly.

'What about Grace?'

'I'll stay here. The less people, the better,' Grace said, already logging on to a travel site to book flights, 'and I'll wait to hear of what I know will be a satisfactory outcome. This is a happiness you deserve, Brigid. Allow it.'

'Thank you for your help.' Brigid's eyes were filled and Grace pretended not to notice. 'But I can't go until after Christmas. I've the cleaning to get on with.' Nothing, not even death and love, got in the way of Brigid's cleaning schedule.

'The cleaning?' Theresa and Grace both asked. 'At a time like this?'

'If it's to be my last Christmas, I want it with my girls more than with my destiny,' Brigid whispered.

'You are sick again,' Grace said with a matter-of-fact manner Brigid was grateful for. 'There's no reason you won't get better again, a woman like you.'

'That's what I said,' Theresa said, hopeful for the first time since Brigid had told her the news.

'No reason but medical history and fate,' Brigid pointed out.

Grace booked two seats to Athens for 6 January, the first available date after Christmas.

Brigid didn't manage lunch, blustering that the chicken was too tough for human consumption. Grace took it in good stride, then left to write.

Brigid and Theresa sat in the kitchen and ate biscuits and drank their trademark tea, strong as they were, with four sugars. It had been a long, exhausting morning and it showed in Brigid's face.

'I'm telling you now, because you're the only one to have my wishes carried out. I don't want to be alive at all costs, hooked up to machines, tubes, electricity keeping me alive. If I can't do it myself, I don't want it done. It gives me no peace to think about that, but I can accept dying once I've done what I need to do for the two of them. And given Grace my proper apologies. I can see mistakes too clearly now.

'And if there's truth in her tea leaves, then I must be going to live on a bit, mustn't I?' She laughed, a little too long. 'I'd like to see how it all turns out.'

8

Even Esther the cleaner was intimidated by Marilyn's office in Larry Leahy Bookmakers. When everyone else went home Marilyn borrowed her Hoover and duster and gave it a going-over.

'Just make sure there's no one in the building,' Marilyn would say, checking the car park first. 'You know what glass ceilings are like, and in the betting world it's bulletproof.'

'I'm sure.' Esther handed over her equipment and sat on the stone suede couch with cream linen cushions. She drank freshly percolated coffee and ate biscuits for half an hour, watching a soap on the plasma television on which Marilyn was supposed to watch every horse-race known to man.

'I wish they did *EastEnders* in the cinema,' Esther said, falling back further into the sofa cushions.

Their routine saved Marilyn from heartache. She had impossible standards of hygiene and neatness in both her office and bedroom. Brigid used to sneak up with a duster, even running her finger behind the headboard, a place where only the fanatical clean, to find it sparkling.

Marilyn had decorated the office herself using the MD's grateful appreciation for showing the firm in a good light when she'd predicted the win of a talented outsider in a classics race.

She'd known from the figures that it was only a matter of time before this maiden, this horse who'd never won a race, actually won. His stats proved it – not just the finishing positions, but his times. He was never first, but every race he ran was faster because he was the pacemaker. He just ran free too much, went off too early, and seemed to lose his concentration. His trainer worked on that for a big race and had entered him as a supplementary entry for it five days beforehand, a sure sign he knew the horse was ready, and so did Marilyn's own computer programme, which calculated odds based on everything it was possible to know. Marilyn found out all she could from every available source with what anyone would mistake as a passion for her subject. And there was passion – for getting it right. If she went to bed with a vet report on dietary changes for thoroughbreds, it was for good reason. Going. Courses. Injuries. Illnesses. Riders. A quality jockey never has to choose a bad horse. Trainers' success rates are down to a formula, not speculation. The magic figures at the end of the columns represented the odds she suggested to her boss. They were frighteningly accurate considering Marilyn had never seen a racecourse or met a racehorse. He listened on most occasions.

This had been one of them. The little champion in the making was a late entry who won by a whisper, and Larry Leahy had the lowest odds on him. Where everyone else paid out, Leahy's showed horse sense and made a reputation for themselves. In an industry where all is speculation, where market dictated, Larry rarely got it wrong.

That horse lost few races after that. They called him Mari's Mount. Someone stuck a picture of her face imposed on the jockey's body at the photocopier.

Marilyn had no interest in watching a race at a track. She considered it to be against the interests of the company. Her colleagues were forever talking about it as if they would somehow, one day, be involved with a Danoli, a Seabiscuit, a Desert Orchid. All owned pieces of horses, an eighth of a leg or something, in syndicates. Marilyn received offers to do the same, but always said, 'No, thanks. It's not what I was paid for.'

Larry saw her ability to stand outside the circle as a valuable asset. Boardroom meetings saw Marilyn predicting as maths and form intended, the rest predicting as experts not only in numbers but in horses and market forces. Larry tended to decide on somewhere between the two.

'The truth is that's where the best position lies. That's why Larry Leahy's the most successful bookmaker in the country. He has the sniff and a respect for mathematics,' Marilyn told Esther as she Hoovered around her bunioned feet. Esther nodded. As a mother of seven she knew how to listen and to give eye contact while still not missing the telly. She saw her role in Marilyn's life as one of counsellor – say little, listen a lot, or at least appear to. Marilyn talked about her job non-stop from the moment she began to clean.

It seemed to Esther that the 'purr soul', as she called Marilyn, had nothing else to talk about. 'You'd think she'd wear high heels with all them lovely suits, not ould flatties, like meself,' she told her husband Ernie in one of her regular conversations about Marilyn. 'A lost soul, she is.'

'A lost soul! With her money, I'd lose me own soul,' Ernie grouched. 'Would you ever leave them sausages on for five minutes longer, so they're done like I like them?'

'If you're one who ignores maths you might as well throw a stick of dynamite into your local bank,' Marilyn was rabbiting, 'it makes that much financial sense. The big bookie always wins, because they've got people like me working for them, using a hard head against horse-lovers' desire to believe the best of horses. Backing fences is human nature, it'll go on till time's end. I expect you're wondering why I came to work here at all.'

'Yes, love,' Esther said, reaching for another biscuit and dragging her eyes off *EastEnders*.

'I was looking for three things. Can I list them? I find it works best if I annotate.'

'Exactly>' Esther wasn't looking any more, but then neither was Marilyn. She was standing on tiptoe, doing the top of the bookshelf, like she did every night.

'One: a way of adding excitement to my life. Two: a way of referring to my occupation that isn't "actuary". I loved the title in the newspaper advert: "Head of Risk Management". To subdivide my categories here, (a) it was what I had been doing all my life and (b) the word "risk" implied there might be some. And three: it was a way of meeting more men. I expect you know I've no boyfriend.'

Esther shrugged. 'Yes, love, but sure, not everyone needs one.' Someone in *EastEnders* was being unfaithful and Esther was watching it like it had never happened before.

'Oh, really? Great. I thought it was a topic of conversation with the guys here. I'm worried they'll think I'm gay – not that I've a problem with it – but I'm not, and it might decrease my chances of meeting someone decent, though that'll never happen in here. Their idea of good-looking is Jordan.'

'She's not bad,' Esther said, looking up. 'Ernie thinks she's lovely.'

'Esther,' Marilyn winced, 'too much information.' She'd met Mr Esther. He had a set of false teeth that looked as if they were made of china, yellow fingers, no hair, also recently retired.

'You're right. I said the same thing when he told me. I said, "I hope I'm more to you than a pair of breasts".' Esther lifted up one of her own carrier-bag-sized ones.

'Anyway,' Marilyn said, polishing the table furiously, 'to refer to them in the same numerical order. One: I very quickly realised that I had to be even more sensible in this job than any of the other firms I had worked in. Insurance firms tend to frown on unsafe bets. Bookmakers gamble. By definition this makes them foolish. Two: it got me round using the term "actuary", which is one up from pest controller and undertaker in the league table of off-putting jobs, but it's still ranked below politician, tax inspector and traffic warden. Three: I met lots more men. All of them gamblers. I left my laminate at home after the first week. It was going to be hopeless.'

'Your what, love?' Esther roused herself into the question. The credits were starting to roll and Esther needed her dusters back. Marilyn was doing the Venetian blind, one strip at a time. The therapy session wasn't over. Esther sighed and switched over to a Gold channel to watch a rerun, when Angie was in it and Den didn't look like a scarecrow.

'Larry's rich now, but he's been rich seven times and lost it six. His son, you know, Tommy, the one who cuts his nails at his desk and doesn't put the clippings in the bin? Yeah. He loathes me as much as Larry likes me. And before you think this is unresolved sexual tension, forget it. All I have in common with the man is that we're short and skinny. Tommy's got six kids to prove he has as much sperm as a man of average height. They're all going around on ponies in Kildare getting ready to be jockeys.'

'Me son-in-law said to say thank you for the last tickets, to Punchestown. He backed a few winners, on your advice,' Esther smiled.

'No worries. I couldn't bear to go myself. Larry says I should. "We might even find a nice man for you." I don't want to marry anyone in the business, they get up too early, work too hard and they rarely break even, just bones and their own hearts. Outside my working hours, which, as you can see, Esther, are considerable, I get on with my own life.' Marilyn was winding down now, ready to finish off with a quick polish of the door handle before driving Esther home. Esther had never driven and still she put her fingers over her eyes when Marilyn drove. But it was either accept the lift or wait for a 73B bus, which claimed to exist, though she'd rarely seen one.

Marilyn was about to polish the door handle when it turned and Larry walked into the office. He was wearing his navy crombie, which he would be buried in some day, with holes in the pockets from all the change he used to hold when he was a track bookie.

Esther was dropping Kimberley crumbs all over the soft pile and Marilyn was trying hard not to notice.

'Esther was a bit tired,' she managed to say. 'I decided to help her out this evening.'

'I used to wonder why you did a better job on her office than mine, Esther,' Larry laughed. 'Anyway, I just came back to give you the tickets to the Stephen's Day Leopardstown meeting.'

'Larry, we've been over this. I don't—'

'No, this time you do, Mari. My wife wants to meet you and after three years of working for me she's entitled to, is she not?'

Marilyn knew Tommy had been stirring it. She'd heard Geraldine Leahy was on pension and loved Daniel O'Donnell. Larry looked like he was married to such a woman. The fact she might be considered a rival was upsetting, particularly since she still had trouble on occasion getting served in pubs.

Larry pulled up his threadbare collar and smiled his kind-man-but-actually-a-business-beast smile. 'Now if you want me to keep quiet about your arrangement with Esther here, then I suggest I see you on Stephen's Day in time for the first race.' He left, and Marilyn was straight down on her knees picking up Kimberley bits.

'Could be worse, love,' Esther reassured. 'I hope he doesn't tell me super.'

'Could it? And don't worry about the super. She'd have me to deal with.'

Esther considered the super and Marilyn in the same room and decided it would be a duel to the death.

'That's my Christmas ruined,' Marilyn said on the way home in the car, Esther hanging onto the strap. 'Mind you, I don't have good ones anyway.'

'Now, love,' Esther said, 'if you have family at all you have a good Christmas. Think of those that don't.'

9

Christmas Day, Monroe-style. Tradition dictated the first frisson of tension surfaced at 10.30 a.m., when they went to Grace's brunch.

Marilyn helped serve, muttering as she spooned out the eggs, beautifully fluffy: 'Anyone for scrambled brain?'

She would watch Julie down the Buck's Fizz like it was water. Julie knew what time these annual events were at and turned up, assuming she was invited.

Brigid wouldn't even want to talk to Julie, who had to go to her own parents later on, and pissed was the only way she could stand it. They didn't agree with drinking, or Christmas. Mr Proper and Mrs Prim, Marilyn called them.

Brigid would be narky because Grace was a flawless, elegant, dignified, intelligent hostess. She prepared brunch because Brigid refused to relinquish her hold on Christmas dinner.

Laid out on the table would be fresh-baked croissants, baguettes, a cheese board, smoked bacon, cured hams, pastries, fruits, yoghurts and brown breads. Liqueurs were drunk with handmade biscuits and the most aromatic coffee and leaf tea for the traditionalists. It was beautiful if you could get past the goading.

'I wonder if anyone will have room for my offering?' Brigid frequently asked as she watched them all wolfing down food.

They skipped lunch and watched telly or went out for a walk in the afternoon to let hormones subside. But even as dinner was put on the table, you could be guaranteed a stock argument revolving around whether the gravy was meat-based or not. Brigid was the principal and only cook, allowing no help but for Marilyn doing the peas.

Six women would sit down at six to a traditional repast, peppered with loaded silences and conversation steering clear of politics, religion, family and Christmas telly. That left gardening and the weather. Then one year Elizabeth and Brigid came to blows over the garden, which only left the weather, so dinner went like this:

'It's very warm for this time of year, isn't it?'

'It's very cold for this time of year, isn't it?'

'I thought we'd have snow.'

'I knew we wouldn't have snow.'

Brigid would say grace while ignoring the woman named after the prayer. Julie, having arrived back from her parents, would slur her words and ask if she could have some of Brigid's famous plum pudding boiled in muslin. Grace genteelly reminded Brigid she didn't eat Christmas pudding and Elizabeth reminded her that she couldn't either, since Brigid made it with suet. Julie, Theresa and Marilyn ate double portions to compensate, feeling sick by the second bowl.

Brigid bristled.

Marilyn, always first to leave the table, went upstairs and took two Rennies. Elizabeth, always second, took nux vomica homeopathic solution. Brigid took two Panadol once Theresa and Grace went home to watch the Christmas opera on BBC2, which Theresa pretended to enjoy out of love for Grace. Marilyn watched it too on her portable and wished she had someone to pretend for like that. Brigid watched the video of the Christmas Mass. Julie got a cab home and tried to make it up her stairs.

25 December 2000 took a different form from the first

moments. Brigid was up before dawn to disembowel the turkey, something she wouldn't let the butcher do, saying, 'He's a man, they don't know how to clean out anything.' But the weakness was with her. She couldn't stand for long, let alone continue torturing the turkey. She had to rush to the bathroom to lean over the toilet bowl, and her gag reflex brought up tiny spots of blood. It was like her throat was closing over. Under her bed she kept packets of Complan for this and knew that would be all she could manage.

'Well, if the doctors couldn't find it before, they'll find it now, and they'll have to look for it after my trip.'

Each night now the dream came to Brigid, for longer periods, the woman more excited, insistent, eager. Brigid was terrified.

She had no choice but to head out of the house and knock on her sister's door. Grace answered. Theresa, a fitness fanatic and chain smoker, was already out for her early morning run.

'My dear,' she whispered, 'you look so pale.'

'Please,' Brigid said, pressing her palms together, 'I need help.'

'Then you have it.'

Brigid explained they had until Elizabeth and Marilyn woke up.

'If it's my last Christmas, I want it a good one. Don't be all nice to me, they'd never manage to swallow that. Much like me and food at the moment.'

Brigid helped as much as she could, which wasn't much. Grace was a calming presence.

'I suppose you knew before anything was said, with all your witchy ways?' she asked Grace.

'I suppose I suspected,' Grace smiled and spoke in just the right way.

'I may as well pick this moment, with none of them donkey-ears around, to apologise to you, Grace, from the bottom of a weary heart.'

'I won't be disingenuous and ask what for,' Grace whispered. 'A lot of it, Brigid, was hard to listen to.'

'As I realise. If I'd known how cruel I was I'd have been ashamed. At least you can have the pleasure now of knowing I'm beyond ashamed – I'm mortified.'

'A good Catholic word.'

'From a woman who hasn't been one. Please, Grace, forgive me.'

'I did that as I went along, Brigid.'

Grace left the house on the stroke of nine a.m. Brigid went back to bed again, closing her door quietly so only Persuasion heard, and went to her dream, which was with her now every time she closed her eyes.

Marilyn raised her head off the pillow at the stroke of nine. Her body was programmed to give her ninety-minute lie-ins on designated days. On her bedside locker were her gifts and a hairy old stocking her mother insisted on leaving in for her when she was asleep.

Marilyn had opened presents alone since she turned thirteen. For that birthday she got a pattern and wool, from Brigid. Marilyn's fingers needed occupying since she'd just given up competitive piano and now could only be per-suaded to practise once a week.

Elizabeth gave her an antique sari and a first edition of Dodie Smith's *I Capture the Castle*. Marilyn had burst into tears. She'd wanted a ticket to The Police concert, breasts and a boyfriend, but she still looked eight.

The gifts suited who she was but not who she wished to be. They didn't know about her longing not to be freakish, not to want to knit jumpers when everyone else around her in

77

school was ripping theirs. Marilyn was Val Doonican to everyone else's Adam Ant.

Knit one, purl one. It wasn't argued with when she announced she wanted to open presents on her own in the future. At fifteen she went through a phase where she would only give written reactions. That Christmas Brigid and Elizabeth stood outside her door before receiving instruction on a paper slip pushed under the door: 'Receipts please.'

'Well, at least she's showing some evidence of rebellion. It's like having Margaret Thatcher as a teenager sometimes, all responsibility and lectures,' Elizabeth said to Brigid.

That was the first year Marilyn bought a present for her father.

It was a madness she couldn't afford at the time. Marilyn saved what little she got from babysitting and cleaning for her college fund. She believed it would supply all the answers to why she couldn't ever behave badly. There she would have no previous history or association. There she would spring from her shell as Mari Monroe, indulge in hedonistic sex, drunken stirs, huge clusters of friends, raucous laughter and all-night parties in filthy bed-sits.

Julie, who'd gone straight to working in a boutique, helped Marilyn to dress like Andie in *Pretty in Pink*. A hint of punk, a lot of ribbon and a hundred per cent more make-up.

'Fishnets? Are you sure?'

'Yeah, de rigueur student wear. Even the fellas will be wearing them.'

College supplied other actuaries in the making, nerds in jumpers she wouldn't even class as bad, all of whom, like Marilyn, would go home to spotless bed-sits after a glass of orange. She fitted in and hated the fact.

'How can there be so many other people like me?' she'd

asked Julie, who'd managed to corrupt one or two future captains of industry in Marilyn's class.

'It's people like you make the world go round, it's people like me make it sparkle,' Julie had said, flashing her sequined knickers at Marilyn, who grimaced.

'Lose your virginity, it'll help,' Julie advised with all the carefree nature of one who still had beauty to squander. 'But not to the two I tried out of your class. It'll help if they know what their willies are actually for.'

Marilyn had found it hard to get anyone else to oblige and had to resort to copulation with one of them, long after college was over, at twenty-two.

'So,' he'd said after, 'is your gorgeous friend still around?'

'Not for the likes of that,' Marilyn said as she got dressed.

'You never told me, Julie!' Marilyn had torn into her later.

'I told you it would be crap with him.'

'But even if it was good, it's uncomfortable and always better for men.'

'Fact,' Julie nodded.

'So why bother?'

'It seems a great idea when you're pissed,' Julie said with early traces of pain that would grow with each year, until each encounter now had a desperation to it that Marilyn only knew from her first.

Marilyn opened the packages from Julie to find she'd received a Catwoman basque and a pink fluffy purse with a special condom pocket, condom supplied. In Julie's case, she was surprised it wasn't already used. She'd also given her a pair of hold-ups, which Marilyn appreciated about as much as she would do being held up in a bank, plus a gauze thong with feather boa bobbles. The message was loud and clear and changed little since their early twenties – a ride will make you a better person.

From Brigid she got a Post Office bond to go with the twenty-eight others, a pattern and wool and a book on cake-making.

Elizabeth had given her a book on Italian opera and its history, another antique sari to go with the sixteen others and an embroidered shawl to go with all the other embroidery at the bottom of the wardrobe.

From Theresa, she got a handmade jewellery box. The present of the year. From Grace she got a sensational clasp handbag with perfect stitching, a close runner-up.

Marilyn gave Julie a thousand euro locked into a long-term account, to force the idea of saving into her consciousness, and a silk and cotton mix ivory shift that cost the same as a doctor's average A&E shift, though no less life saving in terms of its beauty.

To Brigid she gave some special blended teas, all packed into Lyons boxes, otherwise she wouldn't drink them, though each year she said, 'Your Lyons tea tastes nicer than any I buy.' She also gave her a book of miracles involving Mary, a year's subscription to the *Catholic Herald* and a week of one-on-one tutorials with Trabolgan's Dan Draws, ballroom dancing instructor.

She gave Elizabeth a gardener's diary, an antique patchwork bed throw, an original watercolour by a dead up-and-coming artist with a note on how good an investment this kind of thing could be if she researched paintings instead of buying them because she liked them, and a cornflower tapestry cushion Marilyn had embroidered herself. Elizabeth's love of the flower came from her view that they were the colour of Marilyn's eyes. Marilyn knew, with advance embarrassment, that her mother would cry at the cushion.

To Theresa she gave a set of Snap-On tools, and to Grace a beautiful hand-knit cat-grey cashmere cardigan.

She gave a set of twenty-four-carat cufflinks with lapis lazuli inset to her father.

Her presents were saying all she could not.

Before going through Elizabeth's stocking, Marilyn opened her bedside locker with the key she wore around her neck. Elizabeth had one that locked too, and in it she kept clippings on Niall Tormey pasted into a scrapbook, so that when Marilyn finally met her father or knew who he was, she would have some record of him. She hated reminding herself.

From her locker Marilyn took out a lovingly wrapped package and placed it in the centre of her bed.

'Here you go, Dad.' She watched the door nervously, listening out for noises on the landing. None. He sat on the edge of the bed.

'Thank you so much, Princess,' he said. She knew it was naff, but every fatherless girl wants to be called that. 'They're well chosen, I'll just have to go out now and buy a shirt to wear with them. You can pick it.'

She heard Elizabeth stirring through the wall opposite her bed. Her room connected the other two, much like her life. She stuffed the cufflinks in the locker along with the other things, in case one day he decided to come and collect them, and her. Sometimes she gave them away to friends, or to charity. Most times she couldn't bear to. When she was low, she'd take them all out, her catalogue of desire for a father. She had to make sure the house was empty and laughed at herself, thinking, It's not as if I'm looking at porn!

When she went into shops she'd say, 'I'm looking for something for Dad. It has to be special, but not showy.'

'Yes,' one assistant had agreed with her, 'you know what older men are like for not wearing or using things.'

Once or twice they asked questions. Does he drive? Is he

into golf? She'd feel like they'd just shot her, so she learned to say, 'I prefer to keep his presents personal, not clichéd.'

Each year it got harder to find something for a man she wasn't even sure existed and who didn't know that she did. Each year she'd vow not to do it that year, but she couldn't get through Christmas without it.

Marilyn would have looked for him, if only for the option of a different surname, but Elizabeth claimed she couldn't even remember his first one. Something about that froze her. How could she be so careless in bringing a child into the world? She hit Elizabeth with this when she was younger. The rebellions were the wrong way round, with Marilyn chastising Elizabeth when she came home wild-eyed.

'For God's sake, Marilyn, I was having dinner with friends. Is that a crime?'

'Yes, when you're over forty and have a daughter waiting at home who doesn't have another parent to rely on.'

Now Marilyn could see forty coming for herself and wondered at how Elizabeth had stood such precocious sanctimony.

She opened her stocking: homemade fudge, a little ring with an aquamarine stone and some filigree earrings. She liked the fudge and would have liked to like the others. She decided to wear the jewellery to Sunday dinners for Elizabeth's benefit.

There were also two tickets for a concert and two tickets for a ballet not due until the summer, along with a note: *You don't have to take me. Bring a beau.* Elizabeth was a *Gone with the Wind* fan. Half in jest but really wholly earnest, she said it was the title fit for her life. *No doubt you'll have one after Grace's prediction. Happy '01 darling, happy life.*

Not an unusual message from someone as feeling as Elizabeth, but it got an unusual reaction from Marilyn – a single tear.

Elizabeth tapped on the wall, Marilyn's cue to get up and come into her bed, their Christmas ritual. Marilyn loved Elizabeth's room, feeling as relaxed in it as she wasn't with her. At least the walls didn't try to see into the soul you weren't sure you had. Before she got in beside her, Marilyn looked at the books piled high on her desk by the window.

'D'you have to read all those before the exams?'

'Yes, I do, and no, I haven't.'

Marilyn warmed her cold feet on Elizabeth's warm legs. Elizabeth, being a mother, didn't complain. Marilyn allowed herself to be cuddled in a way she wouldn't stand for on any other day of the year. They dozed together, thinking of Grace's perfect coffee to come.

That morning, for some reason, her mother sang 'John O' Dreams' into Marilyn's hair, which she used to do when Marilyn was a child. At the first note Marilyn felt herself relax in a way that made her tense again, but the power of memory was drawing her back, to what they were, even before 51 Verbena Avenue.

'I remember my own father,' Elizabeth whispered, 'singing it to me.'

'And I remember you singing it to me, in the place with the green peeling paint.'

'You remember that?'

'Yes, a bit.'

'What do you remember about it?' Elizabeth's voice was sharp.

'I remember you giving out to two people with no clothes on moving about on the mattress across the floor.'

'That's why we came home.' Elizabeth's voice was soft.

'Thanks for sticking it out here,' Marilyn whispered.

'You've nothing to thank me for. We were far better off here.'

'You as well?' Marilyn enquired.

'Yes.'

'What about your dad, what else do you remember?' Marilyn was emboldened. Elizabeth was rarely this open. This was a window, a cornflower window. 'You never mention him. You must've been afraid I'd tell. I know I had a habit of ratting to Brigid when I was younger.'

'Has anything changed?' Elizabeth raised an eyebrow. 'I can remember almost nothing. That song, and then there's a beach. He's holding me over waves, high above them, then just as they crest, he's dipping me into them. It's what I've always imagined sinking into those frothy white clouds you see in summer would be like. It's ice-cold, spicy, and the water sparkles in the sun. I don't think I knew anything more thrilling.'

'Didn't he leave on your third birthday?'

'Yes.' Then Elizabeth said what Marilyn never expected to hear: 'I have a memory from that too. He was carrying a small case, and I saw him going. But I never told your grandmother. I was afraid she'd stop my cake from coming.'

'How can you have known? You were only three!'

'I was the three-year-old child of a drunk. You become much more aware of things than you should. And his eyes, the same colour as yours. That's all I remember, I'm afraid.'

'Yeah, well, that's more than I have, isn't it?'

'It is,' Elizabeth answered. 'I wish you could have known your father.'

'That's mutual.'

The doorbell went. Marilyn ignored it, waiting for more information, but Elizabeth was glad of the excuse to get away. She hadn't meant to say anything. Honesty didn't get many chances in the house.

Only Julie rang the doorbell, everyone else had a key. Brigid wouldn't sanction it in her case.

'Sorry,' she said. She had the glazed look of a night with Prince Charmless. 'Shower's broken at the flat. Can I?'

Elizabeth stood aside to let her wash away the grime of the one-night stand.

She was making coffee in the kitchen when Marilyn came in. 'Where's Brigid?'

'Don't know, but everything's done. Turkey's in the oven, ham's cooked, studded with the cloves, in the fridge. Spuds and veggies peeled, everything.' Elizabeth's voice suggested that she wished she had the skills to be so prepared in advance, for all eventualities. 'What did you think of the presents?' she asked with her back turned.

'Lovely. Will we have a bit of fudge now?'

She turned and smiled. Something chased that smile. Marilyn had forgotten to say thank you, to even mention the gifts.

Will the balance ever be right between us? Elizabeth thought as she sipped her industrial-strength coffee.

Will I have brown or white toast before Grace's? I prefer white and always make myself eat brown. Today I'm going to have a slice of both. Marilyn broke out of routine.

They went round to Theresa and Grace's for more gift-opening and everyone thanked Marilyn profusely for theirs. The nine months' planning that had gone into them paid off. It was the last Christmas where Marilyn would be so ruthlessly prepared, and it diverged from tradition by being almost tension-free. Not once did Brigid ask for sliced pan or 'proper meat' or 'a bit of cheddar cheese, please, for a change'. Grace and Brigid even sat beside each other, though in silence.

'You're not eating much,' Elizabeth observed.

'Brigid was helping in the kitchen and nibbled a lot in there, with me. I'm not that hungry myself,' Grace said in a quiet voice that somehow everyone listened to.

'Grace, you should have more, you're fat as an ant,' Brigid said, keeping up an antagonistic appearance. 'Now, if everyone's finished, I'll start the clearing up.'

'I'll help,' Grace joined her.

Elizabeth raised her eyebrows to Theresa. 'When did the war end there?'

'Call it an armistice.'

But Elizabeth still made her way to the kitchen with two plates as an excuse. As she went in the door, she saw Grace busy while Brigid sat on a stool, taking tiny sips from a glass.

'Eggnog,' Brigid said, holding up the glass.

'Eggnog?' Elizabeth repeated. She knew the smell of the sugary powder. She threw her serviette in the bin and saw the Complan packet. 'Enjoy. I have to use the loo.'

In Grace and Theresa's toilet there were palms in pots. Elizabeth ran her fingers along the fronds and let her heart sink. She had managed Brigid's illness last time, taking care of all tasks. When it was over, and Brigid recovered, they went back to living as they always had. But there were things that Elizabeth would never forget, and the smell of Complan was one of them.

It's Christmas, she doesn't want me to know, she reasoned with her silent reflection. What am I going to do? I've the new business, I've exams, I can't manage like I did the last time. The guilt of those thoughts, the shock of realisation, made her cold. She ran her hands under the hot tap, just to warm them.

Things began clicking into place – Brigid angling to spend time with her on her birthday. Asking her twice in one afternoon if she was happy.

'I think I'd use the word "content", with my lot,' Elizabeth had told her, holding her at arm's length, as always.

'All the more reason to make this work, give her something to be proud of.' She raised her eyes again to the mirror and realised that this time she was speaking aloud. 'And myself.'

The whisper in her head was there for the rest of a long

day. She'll never beat it again. What are you going to do without her?

'When we get to your house, Brigid, let me do the running round,' Grace urged.

'No, Elizabeth will know, look how close that was.'

'Elizabeth can't stand to touch meat, she'll be happy to let me help you, especially if I make gravy with vegetarian stock,' Grace coaxed. Brigid gagged on the last drops of her drink. If Elizabeth hated the smell of Complan, Brigid hated it more.

'It'll have to be you, then,' Brigid conceded. 'But I have to give the appearance of doing it, you see? To keep them unwise to it.'

'Yes. Now, where is your throat spray? It'll numb it off for you.'

'The painkillers are doing that,' Brigid sighed, 'for now.'

'They'd rather know, Brigid.'

'I'd rather they didn't.'

Christmas dinner, a similar dream. Even Julie was capable of staying on, rather than being poured into a taxi.

'Julie and me are going up to my room,' Marilyn said like she was still twelve.

'Come on,' Julie sighed. 'You must like the Catwoman basque? Gorgeous, isn't it?'

'If you're a Page Three, yes.'

'Ah, now.'

'Ah what? You're holding a silk and cotton shift that makes you look like a painting. I'm holding PVC slapper underwear.'

'I'm just trying to lighten you up a bit. Have a bit of a laugh with your name instead of carrying it around like a bomb. And I'm not sure about this – it's . . .' She hesitated, fingering the fabric.

'Tasteful?'

'The sort of thing you'd look great in.'

'I'm ten inches shorter than you and I've got a brown bob. If I wore it I'd look like a nun at bedtime. You look like a goddess.'

'Why don't you go blonde? It would suit you,' Julie said, flushed with the pleasure she always got when people praised her appearance.

'Nature made me a colour that male field mice find irresistible. Brigid says highlighted hair goes grey quicker and that it'll be "the end of me",' Marilyn said, repeating the phrase Brigid always used about Julie, that and 'you're no Julie Andrews'.

'I still think it would be fabulous,' Julie insisted.

'You think? By this stage, judging by what you have to do to keep it up, I'd have spent four full weeks being streaked, pulled, foiled, capped and fed bad coffee. According to statistics—'

'Are you ever without them?' Julie interrupted.

'—zero point zero zero one per cent of the population is naturally blonde. One quarter of the world population fakes it. That revenue could wipe out the developing world debt. And on a personal basis – let me work it out – quarterly hairdos over a sixteen-year period at current rates of currency . . . so far, that's . . .' Marilyn paused to scribble on a notepad. 'Four thousand euro, rounded down for argument's sake, spent on bleaching – hardly a sound investment.'

'I wouldn't say that. It's given me a lot of sex.'

'It hasn't given you a husband.'

'Marilyn, you can't hide from the fact it would suit you.'

'To be insecure? Marilyn Monroe wouldn't let anyone else with blonde hair on the same film set. She was thirty-five when she died. Wouldn't she have been better off as nut-brown Norma Jean Baker?'

'No. Blonde made her rich, fabulous and desirable. She might have lived longer, okay, but she'd have had a desperate life.'

'There's nothing not desperate about being a Hollywood star. Of that period, especially. Not much has changed. The blonde is always seen as the dirty one. As evidenced by you.'

She'd only been joking. Julie would normally have laughed this off, but she stood up. 'I want you to be safe, Julie, that's all. Secure,' Marilyn blurted.

'Safe, yes. Look what it's done for you. Security.'

Marilyn was suddenly very tired. 'Are you coming with me tomorrow, to the races?'

'Naturally, I've the outfit laid out and all. Good night,' Julie said, leaving the shift on the bed. Marilyn shoved it in the locker on top of the cufflinks.

Who's the more pathetic one? she asked herself. The one who buys presents for someone she's never met, or the one with some sort of dream?

She couldn't sleep for the answers that came to the question, so she went downstairs for hot chocolate. Brigid was in her housecoat and rollers sipping Complan. Like Elizabeth, Marilyn instantly made the connection.

'I thought you couldn't stand that stuff since you got sick.'

'Ah, it's years since then, I want to lose the Christmas bulges.'

'Brigid,' Marilyn scolded, 'you're skinny as anything, and it's Christmas Day. You're supposed to wait until January.'

'Don't you "Brigid" me, you better be after keeping out of trouble with that Julie one. I hope you and her aren't going to end up like Theresa and Grace. No man would have those two.'

'They don't want one, Granny,' Marilyn said, emphasising the name she rarely called her. 'A few years ago no man was good enough for me to go out with.'

'Don't you "Granny" me, either. That was before you got on in years. You're no spring chicken and you'll have to get settled up soon. Me and your mother won't be around forever. Some mother she is, not getting you fixed up.'

'Arranged marriages are a Muslim tradition, Granny. You wouldn't like that.'

'There's nothing wrong with the Muslims. At least they wear plenty of clothes, unlike your friend.' Brigid stood.

'What's wrong?' Marilyn said immediately. 'Have you been to the doctor?'

'I've no need of one, my last check-up was all clear. That's only a few weeks ago. Nothing but bones and old age and too much work on me.'

Marilyn, still upset about Julie, let it go.

10

From the outside, the hospitality suites at Leopardstown race-course, where the powerful meet to socialise, looked like their old school, a place Marilyn and Julie hated. The people heading upstairs were dressed in wintry designer clothes.

Julie tried to ignore this. Underneath her charity-shop coat, which she was going to dump in the car, she was in a slip dress, like the ones she'd seen on TV in Best-Dressed Lady competitions at Ascot and Galway. It hadn't occurred to her that these were spring and summer affairs. On Stephen's Day Leopardstown held a meet for everyone to blow away the Christmas blues, often in the presence of a north-easterly wind.

Still, at least I'll stand out, Julie said to herself. She was over her hurt at Marilyn's comments and happy to be prospecting. 'You never know, he could be just around the corner,' she said aloud.

Marilyn rolled her eyes. She'd brought Julie for moral support, but should have realised that her support was never moral. 'They could all be bastards,' she warned.

'At least in there they're not poor ones.' Julie grinned and shrugged off her coat as Marilyn pulled into a car park space.

'Marilyn, would you like me to do it?' Julie suggested after the first five attempts.

'No. I'd like you to be quiet and lay off the champagne when we're up there.'

Marilyn was tense enough to snap, what with having this in front of her and having left Elizabeth behind in a stew at home because they weren't going on their customary Stephen's Day walk followed by hot toddies in Dalkey.

'I thought you said you'd never go to one of those things. We always have this day,' Elizabeth had said.

'We can do it tomorrow. Larry's wife says she wants to meet me. I have no choice.'

She didn't get an answer. Elizabeth's silent treatments hurt more than Brigid's. Brigid's implied 'after all I've done for you', whereas Elizabeth's implied 'after all I've done for you, and more'. The velvet-backed notebooks that were an extension of Elizabeth – she was never without one – were to write intentions in for the year to come. The trouble was that Elizabeth had more ideas and imagination, whereas Marilyn got stuck after the first one: 'Move out.' She'd had the same notebook for several years.

Julie parked in two manoeuvres, having slid across to the driver's seat while Marilyn hopped out. Marilyn watched with envy, then dismay as Julie got out, wearing a posh department store's make-up counter and a dress Marilyn wouldn't have worn even in August. Marilyn was wearing a padded parka, blue polo-neck sweater, jeans and Ecco boots. But she said nothing, remembering the Catwoman incident.

Outside, with the punters, Julie stood out like a sore thumb, in this case caused by frostbite. Two flights of stairs up, in a corporate suite, at least she was warm. As was Larry's greeting to them both, especially when he introduced his wife, Geraldine. Julie made off straight for the drinks trolley with him, leaving Marilyn with Geraldine.

Geraldine's first glance was guarded, but her second was as welcoming as her husband's. She and Marilyn had figured each other out within two seconds. Second one revealed to Geraldine a woman who looked like a teenager, but of the pimply variety, not the naughty type. Second two revealed to

Marilyn a cosy kind of woman who could have been her granny instead of the hard case at home. They tucked into the tea and biscuits, ignoring the fact they were at the races, treating the corporate suite like a café.

'My life has all been Larry,' Geraldine, leaning in to her, whispered without a trace of resentment. 'I admire you young ones, with all the opportunities that you take to do your own bit. He thinks a lot of you.'

'I think the same of him. He's grumpy, but he's honest.'

'Would you believe now, Marilyn,' Geraldine said, her eyes creased in a way that said she'd never been under a knife or had any intentions of turning Stepford, 'he said the same of you. He can't rely on—' she started, but Tommy appeared at her elbow.

'I see you met my mam. I told her all about you, Marilyn.'

Marilyn knew Geraldine had been going to say that they found Tommy unreliable, a gambler – a bad thing in a bookie. Too much horse and not enough sense. In the same moment she didn't want the responsibility of a promotion she could see was on the cards. The actuary at heart wanted to run away from this approval, rivalry and decision-making. She was a right-hand woman who didn't know what her left was doing. The guests had thronged out for the first race.

Geraldine watched Marilyn's face as Tommy moved on. 'You don't like him.'

'No. I'm sorry, I know he's your son.'

'Families. It's the season for them,' she sighed. 'Though most of my apples turned out good, there's one or two now, Mari, keep me up at night.'

Marilyn's mouth worked while the rest of her listened, horrified. 'Don't worry, all of mine do. I have the sort of family that ends up in films, only worse, because at least in films they have male characters.' She gave her the rundown because she couldn't stop herself and finished off by pointing at Julie, whose knickers were visible through the film of material she imagined was clothing her. 'At least you don't watch the horses either,' Marilyn sighed.

'Oh, I watch them all right, and what they do to people,' Geraldine said wryly. 'I don't know, something tells me your mother's not as bewildered or your granny as sick as you might think. If she's had cancer before, she'd know to tell you before she needs treatment. It's too serious a thing to keep to yourself. Even if the tea leaves say husbands are on their way.'

'Next you'll be telling me my great-aunt isn't a lesbian,' Marilyn smiled. 'I've spent three years at Larry's trying to hide all this about myself.'

Geraldine laughed. Her mind was more progressive than her hairdo. 'Let me reveal something now. My husband needs to retire a bit. Not entirely, I'm not fool enough to expect that. You're the one to help him do that. You'll keep Tommy measured. And by the shouts I'd say the race has finished and we're out of time. We'll talk during the next one.'

She could see Julie wrapped round a short-arse banker, cheering in her overeager way, while he cheered her breasts. It was miserable and grasping. Marilyn felt a wave of depression that she didn't belong in this world as much as she'd never belonged in any of the ones she'd tried to fit into, including and especially the one she was born into.

Julie was the first back in, flushed, heading straight for Marilyn. It appeared the little weasel was more than even she could handle. He was stuck to her shoulder and had his hand clamped to her waist. Marilyn stood up to contain what she was sure was turning into a situation. In her head she was already giving Julie the lecture in the car on the way home. That's when she saw the knife, the one that had been sitting beside the cheese board selection.

The wife, the one who'd been sent home, had it pressed into his back. She'd ordered them in from the balcony just as the race was finishing, to avoid being noticed. Not a single person had.

Julie was whispering. 'You told me she was your sister.'

The crowd hadn't begun to filter in, but as luck would have it a photographer whose job was to snap for social diaries was inside loading up film. Larry and Tommy came after him with an associate, a big man who Marilyn didn't notice since she wasn't taking her eyes off the situation.

'Larry, shut the balcony doors and lock them before anyone else gets in here.' She spoke in a way that made him do it without knowing why. He couldn't see the knife. Someone trying to get in saw what was happening just as Larry moved. There was shouting outside and people backed away from the window. Geraldine, still seated, was as calm as when she'd been chatting to Marilyn. 'You'd best pull the blind as well, Larry,' she said.

At that exact moment the photographer snapped, and the click caused the wife to jab the knife harder into the husband's suit. He gave a small, pathetic sound and tried to take his hand away from Julie's waist.

'Leave that exactly where it is,' the wife ordered, 'that's my evidence. Someone call the police here.'

'I think the police won't read as much into that as what you're doing,' Marilyn said.

'Do something,' Tommy hissed at her, 'she's your friend.'

'Tommy,' Geraldine said, standing up. Marilyn could see she was as tall as Larry was small – an odd couple. They'd never have got any points on The Scale. 'He's yours. I've warned you before about him.'

As if to illustrate the point, the banker was urging his wife over his shoulder, 'It was her, she came on to me! Said to send you home!'

That's when Marilyn sprang into action, wrenching Julie away from the banker's arm. If the wife stabbed anyone she was going to stab him. The wife gave a little scream and jabbed again and the husband screamed louder. His suit was torn and he was bleeding.

She was wailing now. The police would surely be outside in a few moments. Marilyn could hear people in the balcony shouting instructions at the crowd. With the photographer in the room, Larry would be all over the papers, and Julie. The wife was saying, 'You know what he did the day that was in it, yesterday, for his children? Walked out at eleven and came back at four. He didn't even bother to shower the smell off. Four children he has and he barely stayed for Santa.'

Julie was hunched over, weeping. Marilyn could see the wife's shoulders tight round her neck, her ribs poking through her expensive blouse, paid for with a life that made her feel cheap.

'Look,' Marilyn whispered to the wife, 'you knife him, he wins.'

'What?' the wife asked.

'He gets to prosecute you for assault. That leaves your kids without a mother or father. They'll give him the kids.'

'He wouldn't want them, he doesn't want them or me. It'd suit him to see me jailed. He knows my family would take care of the children.'

'Exactly. See it for what it is. This woman, she's my friend, I'll get her to testify for you in divorce proceedings, or whatever action you decide on. This is not the right action. Trust me.'

Julie was shaking. Marilyn could see the wife's eyes begin to focus, grasping what she'd done. The police announced themselves at the locked door. She put the knife down and started weeping herself. Geraldine put her in the seat beside her and spoke to her like a child. Larry opened the door for the police. The husband was about to burst out the whole story to them when Larry got in first.

'Nothing untoward, was there, Frank? Just a domestic.' He clapped a hand over the surface wound and gripped the banker's side harder than his wife had.

'We heard there was a knife,' one of the Guards said. These were officers sent to help out on track days, no senior among them.

'No, no knife or anything like that, just a tiff, sorted now, officers. Someone let them in from the balcony in a minute, and get a crate of good stuff up to warm them. Free bets all round, too, and that's including you two when you're off duty. Come straight up here.'

Julie and Marilyn had a surname for men like Frank Whelan – Snake. Julie had charmed more than one. The police left. Larry spoke quietly to Frank now, with Tommy at his side. 'Think of it, Frank, a man with your job and reputation, splattered over the papers? No promotion to headquarters after that sort of thing.' He turned to the woman.

'Eileen,' she whispered. 'My name's Eileen.'

'Eileen,' Marilyn said, standing beside Larry, 'it was all very funny, wasn't it?'

'It was.' Her voice said she was stronger than Frank Snake would ever be.

A man put a coat on Julie's shoulders, as she was shivering. Marilyn didn't see him, concentrating instead on Eileen. He couldn't but admire Marilyn's actions. He wanted to say so. He wanted to say more. But she was still managing the situation.

'I'm going to take you home now,' she said to her, 'before anyone else tries to talk to you.' Marilyn looked directly at the photographer, who raised an eyebrow back.

'Well, Mari, you'll go to extremes to get out of a race meeting,' Larry smiled darkly.

'Isn't she just right?' Geraldine whispered.

Tommy was escorting Frank out.

'Mari, what about me?' Julie trembled as she said it.

'What about you, Julie?' Marilyn was colder than she intended to be. 'This woman needs more looking after than you.'

In the corridor Marilyn heard the people pouring back into the room and Larry, in his booming voice, announce, 'Free champagne, brandy, whiskey, wine, just shout the order,' followed by a cheer.

Larry paid the photographer a few thousand for his film and silence. He told his son that he'd better sell a horse to pay him back and advised him to pick his friends more carefully in the future. Then he and Geraldine drove home and talked about how right Mari Monroe was for the new position.

'You couldn't have asked for a better interview,' Larry said.

'She'll make the new thing happen,' Geraldine agreed.

'I'm not sure what I'm going to do now,' Eileen said, addressing her own thoughts more than Marilyn.

'Where would you like me to drop you?' Marilyn asked her, driving extra carefully. The last thing she needed was one of her customary prangs. I should be good at driving, she chastised herself, it's so practical.

'I don't think I can go home,' Eileen said, holding on to the seat-belt. Marilyn could see she was trying to stop her hands from shaking, as her voice was. 'He might be there. My sister has the children.'

'Okay. Tell me where that is and I'll get you there.' Marilyn tried to sound reassuring instead of desperate that Eileen wouldn't ever decide to get out of the car. She hated strangers as passengers. They were too judgmental when she ran into lampposts.

'Please,' she whispered, 'I can't face them all just yet. I need to recover.'

What place better than number 51?

Elizabeth was there, she called out as soon as the key went in the lock.

'I stayed behind. I thought we'll go together on New Year's Eve, maybe? I'll get over my antipathy to it,' she said, stopping when she saw Eileen.

'This is Eileen. She's had a bit of a shock and she needs to calm down before she goes home. Can we give her tea?' Why do I always ask, like I still need permission? Marilyn wondered.

Elizabeth was already on her feet. Marilyn looked at her moving about, tending to needs. Another stray to be minded.

Eileen told them everything over a two-hour period about life with Frank, and there was a lot to tell. Not once did she mention Julie's involvement, which Marilyn was grateful for since Brigid came in in the middle of it all.

'You need to get yourself some advice,' Marilyn advised.

'Where can I go?' Eileen looked at her as if she might know.

'To the best solicitor money can buy, and make sure he pays for it.'

'I don't even have my own bank account. My husband's well connected. He has friends all over who have friends all over. He'll hide it all before I get the chance to try and claim it.'

'Solicitors can act quickly in situations like this,' Elizabeth spoke softly.

'If you can pay them. I can't. I know nothing about the law and you can be damn sure he does. I've looked after his house and his children, he's looked after everything else. He'll leave us stranded.'

'I know someone who might be able to help you, who might do a win-win deal,' Elizabeth assured her, as if she really did, but she wasn't prepared to tell her in front of Brigid and Marilyn.

'Don't get that glass ball out, now, Elizabeth, the woman needs real help, qualified,' Brigid snapped.

'Please, Mother. I've worked in the legal profession for three decades and if I don't know someone who can assist her, there would be few who do. Eileen, leave your numbers with me. I'll contact you.'

Marilyn drove Eileen to her sister's house, ignoring her miffed feelings that her mother had taken over the rescue operation as best she could.

'She's a good person, your mother, capable.'

'You're the second person to say that to me today.'

'Your friend, tell her no hard feelings. She isn't to know what he's like.'

'That's more than she deserves. She should have learned by now about men like him.'

'Why?' Eileen looked at Marilyn and thought how beautiful and unusual her eye colour was, but how unnoticed. There was no shine to them. 'I spent thirty years with one. Let me tell you now, Marilyn, it's not a lack of intelligence that picks men that bad, it's lack of belief you can get any better. She's . . .' Eileen paused. '. . .wasted on the likes of Frank when she could do so much more for herself. And what about you, do you have a boyfriend?'

'No,' Marilyn laughed.

'Well, you should. Let this failure give you some advice. If he's not kind, he's not right. If he's kind, give him every chance.'

Marilyn never forgot her words.

As she drove back home she discussed the situation with her father, visualising him in the front seat where Eileen had just been.

100

'You did well, Marilyn, saved the day.'

'Not that I got any thanks for it, she stole the show.'

'If you're talking about your mother taking over, then you have to realise it's her area, not yours. You don't know the first thing about divorce.'

'I would do, if you'd ever married my mother.'

'You're being unfair.'

'I know, I'm always unfair where she's concerned. I can't help it.'

'Have you asked yourself why? And slow down.'

'Stop telling me how to drive, you're a figment of my imagination. That's why I'm unfair. I should have known you.'

'You will, Marilyn, someday, and what's to guarantee you'll like what you meet?'

'Now you're scaring me,' she whispered, pulling in off the road. 'You're not real, I made you up.'

'The men are on their way – who's to say I won't be one of them?'

'But even my mother doesn't know who you are!'

'In your heart, do you really think your mother is the kind of woman to forget the man she conceived a child with?'

Marilyn tried hard to will the question away, but in the end the answer came, unwanted.

No.

11

Tony Devereux's decision to love Elizabeth was based on one chance meeting for five minutes, a meeting that had left Elizabeth's head almost as soon as she walked away from him.

'Hearing the call-out over the radio for her today, I thought, this was it, the destined moment.' He laughed without happiness in telling the young men, Colin and Mick, about her. He considered them to be his foster-sons. Through his work as a sponsor he had heard of two friends being released at the same time from prison who needed a home. They couldn't go back to their old lives and needed each other's support as well as a roof over their heads. So he gave them three months rent-free and they found work on the sites. When they could afford to move on, they never left.

The lads had come in at tea-time to find him slumped in a kitchen chair. 'Tony, you look like you haven't been to bed at all,' Colin said, flicking the kettle switch and reaching for the coffee jar.

'I haven't,' he'd said, then found himself telling them. For five years this had been his secret. Now he'd shared it with three people inside a day, one of them being Brigid. 'The mother of the bride,' he finished, shaking his head. 'She didn't want anything to do with me.'

'We always knew you were a looper,' Mick said, shaking his own head in response to the story.

'Leave him alone. After all he's done for us, could you not think of something better to say than that?' Colin snapped. 'You could always call round and see the ma again, now your head's straight. You didn't really fill her in about yourself, did you? And what you did for Phoebe that time?'

'The problem with the ma is she's a bag, am I right there, Tony?' Mick asked.

'She's not the most approachable of people,' Tony said. 'And if I had told her exactly what I was doing with Phoebe, it's breaking anonymity. We don't do it, do we? Ever.'

'You can tell her about the work you do, outside taxiing. That's saint stuff, and all ladies like her are dead religious. Come on, Tony! It'll never be as bad as you think, and the daughter will never be as good,' Colin said, trying to give Tony perspective.

'She might never be what I imagine. But I'm certain she's meant. Truth, as the great philosophers say, is higher than experience. She's just the one my soul decided on. And before you say anything, I know connections work on different levels. On a practical level there isn't a reason in the world why a woman like her would pick a man like me. But all souls look alike, and mine recognises hers as an equal.'

'Her ma thinks you're a stalker and she thinks you're weird. I'd say you have a pretty unequal chance there,' Mick frowned.

'He's right,' Colin had to admit. 'You have the advantage of having tried now, but any more than that, considering the reaction you got, might be foolish.'

'No. The taxi call-out was the call to arms. There's adversity to be overcome in everything worth having. I'll have another go, once this shame has worn off.'

'You'd be better off letting your soul know it isn't going to work,' Colin sighed. He loved Tony Devereux. The words 'decent', 'odd' and 'gentle' were invented for him. If he were six feet tall and handsome he'd have been any woman's dream. Why did God put the best people in such ordinary bodies and terrible haircuts?

'Well, lads, we'll have a good Christmas anyway, won't we?' Tony said, trying to rise above it.

Three weeks later and he still hadn't managed to get her out of his head. He spent the entire time controlling his anger and self-doubt at how he'd let her mother extract information out of him, and how he'd failed to use his opportunity as he should have.

He got through Christmas Day only by knowing that tomorrow he would set it all right. He was going to walk up to her and simply declare his impression that she was the only woman for him.

He even let the boys look after his hair, though he was far from comfortable with the results. 'I don't feel myself,' he said. 'Jelly's not my style.'

'Good, because yourself didn't do a good job the last time, did he?' Mick observed. 'And it's gel in your hair, not jelly. You're not a puddin'.'

Stephen's Day, five years previously, was the first time he had seen Elizabeth. It was a Sunday and he'd got through his second Christmas sober by the skin of his teeth. He'd driven to the Vico Road viewpoint out over the spread of water that some compared to the Bay of Naples for beauty and breadth. She had been sitting on a bench, pulling out a notebook. Her hair fell over her face as she wrote – she had to keep pulling it back behind her ear – and she bit her lip as she concentrated. He had been lost to that movement, knowing with a surety his life had always lacked that he wished to sit beside her and begin a conversation that would lead to knowing each other for the rest of their lives. It wasn't a woman like her I wanted, it was her, he thought. He'd driven to the viewpoint again the following Sunday. She was there. From then on he'd taken the taxi plates off. He lived for the sightings, drank in the last seconds of her receding with the loss you feel when you're on the last pages of a loved book. He'd get out of the car and sit on the bench where she'd just been and talk to her in his imagination about her week. Never in a million years would he have considered her to be a legal secretary. He would have guessed a crafts person, a holistic practitioner, something artistic.

Phoebe, whom he was sponsoring in AA, phoned him just as he was about to head off one Sunday.

'I'm just going out, but I'll meet you in two hours,' he said.

'By that time, Tony, I'll have been drinking.' He knew she wasn't bluffing. 'Where were you going?'

'Sunday walk, to the Vico.'

'I'll come too. At least you'll get your fresh air while I burden you.'

She was sitting on Elizabeth's bench when he arrived. He wanted to tell her it was someone else's. They sat, looking at the view, and she did her talking. He tried not to turn his head, but he could see Elizabeth's trademark velvet, hair and gait as soon as she came into view, and he played Lot's wife.

'Hello,' Phoebe said.

'Sorry' – he turned back to her – 'you were saying?'

'Hello – to someone I know.' Phoebe was waving, and Elizabeth came over.

'Phoebe! I haven't seen you for years! Are you well?'

'I'm okay.' Phoebe knew her. It was the beginning. 'This is Tony, he's a good friend of mine.'

'Hello, Tony, good to meet you. Phoebe, do you still see Marilyn?' Elizabeth was actually coming to sit down, beside her.

'No. I haven't seen Julie either since about six months ago, when I got sober. She's still drinking like a fish. I thought you'd know that.'

'Marilyn doesn't tell me much. Have daughters one day and see how much they tell you.' It was meant as a joke, but it didn't sound like one.

'Yeah, I didn't tell me own parents anything. I tell Tony more.'

'Do you? Well' – she looked at them and formed the impression that she was interrupting lovers – 'aren't you lucky to have a listener in your life?' Elizabeth herself ached for the lack of one. 'I'll see you again. Good luck.' She rose to go, and he waited for his own mouth to say something, but it couldn't come up with anything better than goodbye.

And then Phoebe was telling him about a boyfriend whom she'd treated badly in drink and still loved but who'd emigrated to Canada. Tony was persuading her to follow her dream as his own walked away. 'Go for a fortnight, look him up, see if he's ready to forgive. You'd have the advantage of having tried,' he said, thinking, An advantage I don't have.

'How do you know her?' he finally had to ask.

'Elizabeth? She's my friend's mother. She was always really interesting-looking, but Marilyn hated her, totally embarrassed about her.'

'Why?'

'Well, the way she looks. A bit unusual.'

'A bit wonderful.'

'I see you've got a crush. Well, she doesn't have a boy-friend, I can tell you that much.'

'How do you know that?'

'She never had one. They all live in a co-dependent pile in the one house. Mother, daughter, granddaughter.'

Tony smiled. Co-dependency was a term Phoebe had only just learned the meaning of and she brandished it around like a weapon to show how well she was, how much she'd moved on.

'Marilyn was always moaning about not having a da.

Come to think of it, Marilyn was always moaning. Their second name's Monroe, and you should see her, she looks like your average accountant. Except she turned out to be a way-above-average one. The name thing gave Mari balance.'

'How d'you mean?'

'She's got two chips, one for each shoulder.'

Tony laughed out loud at that. 'And Elizabeth?'

'She's chip-free. In fact, she was gorgeous in her day.'

'She's still having it,' Tony said in a low voice.

'I tell you what, let me fix you up with her, if I can!'

'Phoebe,' Tony insisted, 'we'll stick to you. You need fixing up right now.'

He was too kind, always too kind. He fixed Phoebe up so well she took off to Canada, after her boyfriend, and married him.

Tony went back to watching Elizabeth. He did try to speak to her once, but it went pear-shaped when she walked past him, preoccupied. He knew he hadn't made a sufficient impression.

Stephen's Day was the day Elizabeth took stock, Tony knew after five years' observance. Her daughter shared it with her, but she wasn't as given to the ritual. Even if it was raining Elizabeth still wrote, under a bright green poncho.

On Stephen's Day 2000 the lads waved him off. 'If you pull this off, Tony, we'll give you the extra cracker left over from yesterday, all to yourself,' Mick yelled.

He smiled. They were in their early twenties and took love as for granted as they did time. Despite the fact they'd lost some of them. Prison took young people with habits off the street and made them even less able for independence, for life.

She didn't come. He waited until nightfall, for fear that something awful had happened to her. He got home at six and immediately scanned through the paper for road traffic accidents. By midnight he was pacing.

'Come on, Tony, she'll be there next week, same as usual,' Colin urged.

'Maybe she went out with another fella,' Mick suggested. 'What're you looking at me like that for? I'm only facing facts.'

'That's not fact, that's supposition. She's always there Stephen's Day,' Tony barked at him and left the room.

'No wonder they call it Boxing Day in England. After Christmas you want to beat the shite out of your relatives. Did you see the way he looked at me? I thought he was going to let fly. I don't even know what "supposition" means,' Mick reeled. Tony never raised his voice.

'It means supposing.'

'Well, I'm not supposing as much as he is, am I?'

Three days later he still hadn't gone out to work, unusual for a single taxi driver in Christmas week.

'Armageddon's here,' Colin whispered to Mick. 'Tony's not shaving.' He was known for his obsessive attention to personal grooming.

'I don't know what "Armageddon" means, either. Everyone's cleverer than me in this house,' Mick said, shovelling another lump of cold turkey into his mouth. Tony normally cooked for them, even their meat, which he didn't eat himself. There was nothing else in the fridge.

'It means the end of the world. We'll have to do something. The drink's not far behind.'

'I know.' Mick was chewing with his mouth open, which made it impossible for Colin to look at him. 'How many houses are there over in that estate?' Tony's house was only two miles away from Verbena Avenue.

'Hundreds.'

'That's better than thousands. Get your coat on.'

'What?'

'We're goin' door-to-door selling, like when we nicked stuff.'

'Ah, Mick, I'm not sure.'

'Are you sure you want to see him take to the gargle?'

'No.'

'Then we have to find this one and make her go out with him.'

'How do we even know what she looks like?'

'I never thought of that. He says she looks like a painter.'

'No, not a painter, a subject,' Colin corrected, but kindly. Colin had more education in his background, but as little love as Mick had been shown. They'd been brother junkies and now they were brother survivors, both only just starting to live the life they'd lost. 'We could check out that picture in the hall.'

'The nudey woman one?'

'That's not nudey, that's art.'

'It is nudey, she's no clothes on. I have eyes.'

Colin ran into the hall. 'Botticelli. Venus.'

'Okay' – Mick passed him a coffee – 'let's get out before Prince Charming gets up.' Tony hadn't surfaced before two for the past few days. He was sticking to his night-owl schedule, except he hadn't even sat in the taxi.

'Next month's bills will have to be met by us if this keeps up. He's missing out on his bumper week of the year,' Colin said as they walked down the road. 'Why doesn't either of us drive? We could do the shifts for him, on our week off from the sites.'

'You may remember we were done for vehicle theft? It's a bit difficult to get a public vehicle licence. Now get knocking.'

It took them fifty houses to get their story straight, and it was still suspicious over two hundred houses later when they knocked at 45 Verbena Avenue. Grace answered. 'Hello, young man,' she smiled at Colin. 'You're looking for?'

'Elizabeth Monroe, me dad used to know her. He drives a taxi and bumped into her a few weeks ago. He's found out they're related.'

'So,' Grace enquired, 'where is your dad?'

'He's, eh, gone home for a while. We're helping him do house-to-house.'

'Fine, go and get him.' Colin stalled. 'Well, what are you waiting for if it's that urgent he speak to her?'

'Sorry, it's just my, eh, brother, is here with me on this road, and we've done over two hundred houses and found no joy. So I must be a bit shocked, really. Would it be all right if I spoke to you first?'

'I think so,' Grace smiled. 'You called at the right time, no one's about.'

Even as Colin was being shown to Grace's kitchen he felt pressure. First of all he hadn't been able to spot Mick before he went inside. What if this old one had nothing to do with Elizabeth Monroe? He was going to be waylaid by an old woman with a posh accent. She probably had a butler to do the killing for her.

'Son, I'm not going to harm you. If anything the risk is the other way round,' Grace said in a level tone.

'You haven't phoned the police or anything, have you? Before you answered the door? I'm not a burglar or anything.' Any more.

'No, I promise you that. Tell me, was your father the man who dropped Elizabeth to this house a few weeks ago?'

'Yes.' Colin didn't have to lie. This meant Mick would be at the right house by now, a few doors down, making a hames of it with all his considerable social skills. 'I think, if you don't mind, we should get on down to the one she really lives at.' He rose.

'We will, once you answer a few questions.' Grace motioned for him to sit.

'What're you selling?' Marilyn barked at Mick.

'Nothing. Is your ma in?'

'Excuse me?'

'Your ma,' Mick said, but thought to himself as he eyed her, Though I'd say you were hatched from an egg.

'Will no do you?' Marilyn got ready to close the door.

'Afraid not. You see, me dad used to know her. He drives a taxi and bumped into her a few weeks ago. He's found out they're related . . .' Mick gave the spiel, wishing he'd worn his court suit instead of his tracksuit.

As he spoke he watched the woman's expression change from hostile to doubtful to interested, and then she was gripped.

'You'd better give me your name,' she said. It was hard to mistake the excitement.

'Mick. Me dad is Tony, Tony Devereux.'

Marilyn walked up the stairs and stared at the cornflower window. Shell-suit is probably my brother, she thought. My second name is probably Devereux.

Elizabeth tried to get to grips with a passage of text that kept swimming before her eyes. She was immersed in the detail necessary to take on the case Eileen Whelan had presented her with, already aware it was too much, especially now that Brigid was ill again. Elizabeth had been watching her like a hawk to see how much food she was really eating. So far she'd found at least seven dinners dumped in the bin.

Each time Elizabeth tried to get around to the subject, asking how her last check-up went, Brigid smiled brightly and said, 'Grand, the all-clear as usual, that weakness isn't mine any more.'

It was amazing how well she was hiding it. Her eyes were shining lately and her manner was pleasant to everyone, even Elizabeth and Grace. Part of Elizabeth didn't want to challenge this equilibrium by bringing up an awful subject directly.

'There's a young man down at the door who said his dad dropped you off in a taxi,' Marilyn explained as Elizabeth's heart sank. 'And he thinks you're related.'

'Marilyn, tell him to go away. Please.'

'No, I won't. He's my half-brother, isn't he?'

'Marilyn, for crying out loud, he's nothing to do with you or me, he's chancing his arm,' Elizabeth said, snapping her book shut.

'How do you know?' Brigid appeared on the landing at Marilyn's raised voice. 'You said you never knew him. Now there's a man downstairs who says his dad is related to you. Unless Brigid had any illegitimate kids, then you're lying.'

'No. He is.' Elizabeth stood up.

Colin was finishing up describing Tony Devereux in minute detail to Grace, including how he'd first met Elizabeth.

'My dear,' Grace smiled, 'he sounds perfect.'

'The problem is he doesn't look it. Tony's a bit square, well, actually, a lot.'

'It's sad to see the beautiful in unremarkable bodies, but the soul shapes the face, Colin.'

'That's close enough to what Tony said, too.' Colin had the sense he was involved in something being directed far outside of him. This old lady seemed comfortable with that.

'The question is, will Elizabeth realise it? Let's go and see her now.' Grace led him out of the house.

Elizabeth came to the door, but Mick wasn't at it. He was in the kitchen, where Brigid was making him a cup of tea. Elizabeth went cold.

'I'm sorry, Elizabeth, the fella was perishing, I took him in for some tea. He's not a Jehovah anyway, or a Mormon.'

'With teeth like mine?' Mick grinned. Nothing Ultrabrite there.

Elizabeth didn't look at Mick.

'Listen. There's better than you've ignored me,' Mick said. 'All's I can see is there's a lad in a right state two miles away from here because he has feelings for you.'

'I don't know anything about him, he's not my responsibility. He helped me out for a day and he got the complete wrong impression.' Elizabeth was now staring at Mick, her eyes blazing.

'You know, you do look like his picture, the Venus one. I'd have known it was you I was looking for. And Colin. Would someone mind going outside to see if there's another lad on the street?'

Marilyn went immediately.

'Would it do any good if I said I didn't want to be looked for?' Elizabeth was rubbing her forehead. It felt like there was a clamp on it.

'No, missus, it wouldn't. He's known as God in AA because of all the young ones he's helped. He took me and Colin in when we got out of prison – that's hardly a reference for us. Colin's not me brother, he's me friend. Sorry about lying. But I'm not lying when I say Phoebe wouldn't be married and living in Canada without him.'

Colin and Grace were at the gate when Marilyn got to it. Marilyn's eyes were shining. There were two men in her house! She could handle being this one's sister. He looked less like he'd fallen off the back of a truck.

'They're inside.' She gestured to Colin to go ahead, then pulled Grace back.

'These are my brothers, aren't they? My dad's going to be here, soon, isn't he?'

'No, Marilyn.' Grace put a hand on her arm. 'These men aren't related to you. They live with a man who has loved your mother for a number of years, but he's afraid to approach her. He's a known figure in AA, helps others in it, and they're all concerned he's going to fall off the bus.'

'The wagon, Grace,' Marilyn said. She could feel the disappointment settling on her.

'Marilyn, your turn is coming. What's needed now is to persuade your mother that this is hers.'

'It's always about her, Grace.'

'If that were true, then your mother would have left this place long ago, and you would have had Brigid bringing you up. It's always been about you, from the moment you were born,' Grace said sternly. 'Now come inside and help. It's needed.'

'It'll never be my turn,' Marilyn said as she went up the path. But then, she was conveniently ignoring Julie's visit of two days ago, and what she'd been trying to do then.

12

On Stephen's Day Julie watched Marilyn leave the race course with Eileen, not even saying goodbye to her.

'How am I going to get home?' The entire room was looking at her. If it hadn't been for the jacket over her shoulders she would have felt naked.

'I'll give you a lift,' said the man who'd put it there, 'get you away from here. Larry – I'm running the poor girl home, is that all right? We'll talk again.'

'Thanks, Sean.' Larry sounded more grateful than Julie could stand. They drove in silence. At her building she tried to hop out, but her legs gave way from under her.

'Come on,' he said, 'we'll get you a big pot of tea and a bit of a sandwich. You can't have eaten anything for a year to wear a rig-out like that.'

She tried to refuse, but her body felt like it had been run over.

Inside she sat on her bed while he poked around in her kitchenette and came up with tea and sandwiches. She thought she'd throw up at the first bite and then she couldn't stop. The tea had sugar in it – she hadn't drunk tea like that since she was six. Her parents gave her tea to keep her quiet, when all she wanted was someone to listen to her. Marilyn didn't. No man ever had, no matter how loudly she dressed. Sean listened.

'I'm always making a show of myself, I can't seem to help it. I don't know why she puts up with me, why anyone does.' His jacket was still around her shoulders. 'I'm sorry, I don't know you from Adam and I'm telling you all my troubles. I never do this,' she said, knowing he didn't believe her.

Frank Snake had promised her champagne, a chance to get to know each other. She had got that, without the benefit of champagne. It wouldn't help to say she genuinely hadn't thought the woman was his wife. Here was a man with a kind voice and a nice car too, a four-wheel drive. He'd have been a better bet than Frank Snake. She stood up.

'Where are you going?' he asked her.

'To get the whiskey I keep for special occasions such as this.' She gave him a worn smile and produced a bottle and two glasses.

'Ah no, I think I'll be heading.'

'Listen, you've seen where I live, you saw what happened today. I've no pride left, and no friends, most likely. I just want some company.'

'All right,' he said, 'I'll just go down and put some money in the meter.'

'No,' she said firmly, 'you'll run off. I'll do it, give me your keys.'

He winced because he knew his heart was too soft, but there was no telling what this girl would do to herself if he left.

By eight o'clock Sean was glad he'd stayed. Underneath all the desperation, she was great. And she was gorgeous. Julie Purcell was looking at him and thinking he looked a bit grizzly-bearish, but he was lovely.

'It's a giant pity I can't fall for the likes of you before I get touched up by the likes of Frank. Could you ever tell me why that is?'

'I suppose we – well, me – we're not as big of a risk as the lads with the money,' he shrugged.

'You have a great car, you have horses, you were in posh circles today.' Her brain was affected with the whiskey, but she was still working hard on the calculations. Marilyn would have been proud of her. Was there any way she could rescue this?

'I was there for my work, but my work isn't money work. It's to do with training horses and I'm afraid I don't have the big winning kind. Larry Leahy asked me along because my father was a great race-goer and he knew Larry when he was working the tracks.'

'So you've no money at all, then?'

'Afraid not. What I have I put into the yard, and that's not enough to stop me having debts an elephant would be smaller than.'

'Oh well, I have to not fancy you, then, if that's okay. I'm looking for someone rich. You can see why,' she said, gesturing around her. 'To get me out of this.'

'No harm done.' He thought she was joking by the smile on her face. 'You'll find plenty of rich men happy to have a woman like you.'

'Really?' Her hand went up to pat her matted hair.

'Of course, you're beautiful.'

Julie sighed. The compliment and the whiskey rush gave her a warmth that had been missing all day 'Would you like some more sandwich spread? It's all I've left. You'll have to have it without bread.'

'I tell you what – Julie, isn't it? Will we go down to the pub and get a proper dinner?'

'No, you've no money and I've no money.'

'Ah, I didn't say I'd no money on me, just not the millions you're talking about, and I've always enough for a roast dinner. Will you be my guest?'

She couldn't touch the leather chicken, cardboard stuffing, bullet potatoes and overcooked vegetables – another pound lost in the great skinny marathon. Over several pints for him and more whiskey for her, he pronounced her 'grand'.

'Don't call me that when you've just called an inedible meal the same thing.' She was in jeans and a jumper, had no make-up on and was laughing. Underneath she had surprise on for him, of the Catwoman kind.

'Julie, I have much lower standards than yours. I should be home and in bed.'

'And with any luck you'll be in mine,' she grinned.

'Oh, I couldn't do that.'

'Why couldn't you? What's wrong with me?'

'Nothing,' he said. Before she'd got too drunk to care she'd noticed that he had that unusual combination of black hair and green eyes. Had his mammy been up to no good with a foreigner, she'd asked, leaning in to him.

'No, she was with my father all her life, from sixteen. They went abroad for the first time just before they died. Will that do?'

'Your mum and dad's both dead?' The grammar was slipping and so was the urge. But he was fitting something, she wasn't sure what.

'Yes.'

'Wish mine were.'

'Don't wish that, Julie.'

'You don't know them . . .'

'Sean.' He kept telling her and she kept forgetting.

'Sean, when was the last time you spent the night with a woman?'

'I have to be honest and say it's been a good few years. I don't get away from the yard much and when I do I don't seem to have the right tone for the women. They like them smart.'

'Then let me say this – it would be an honour for me to break the fast for you. You're a lot smarter than anything I've shagged lately.'

'Ah, come on, Julie, you should learn to think more of

yourself. But I'll take the couch. I won't be able to drive home now anyways.'

'I don't have a couch.' Her eyes were full of tears. He could see that the truth of what she was still wounded her.

'Sorry, Julie, you're pissed and I'm old-fashioned about taking advantage.' He hated making anyone cry, much less a woman. 'I'll go on the floor if you have a blanket.'

They wobbled home, drank a coffee and fell into bed intending to sleep, and because she was a woman and he was a man, they did more than that.

'Sorry about that,' he slurred afterwards. 'I didn't mean for that to happen.'

'Forget me being a damsel. I gave that up after the first dragon. It was very nice,' Julie sighed.

'My mother used to say that when I brought home art from school, and I turned out to be no painter.'

The next morning he surprised her by still being there. It made her awkward, but glad she had someone to share the hangover with. And the sense of desolation.

'How the hell did you manage to get up, after all we drank?'

'I'm used to getting up, for the yard, around the five o'clock mark. I had a lie-in until seven today. I got rashers and sausages in, and juice. I'll put a raw egg in it, for the stomach and the head.'

'Do that and I'll die.'

'Dry toast, then.'

'Sean . . .' she started, glad he was dressed, wishing she were, trying to think what to say.

'Look.' He turned around, shyer than she remembered for a man who'd told her a lot about himself. And knew a lot about her. 'I'm not here to put you under pressure. And any million-aires I know I'll put your way. I didn't want to go off without saying thank you for "breaking the fast" for me and giving you a bit of breakfast. It looks like you've gone without it as long as I've gone without a woman.'

They ate two platefuls of food and she confessed that if he weren't there she might have been in the toilet bringing it all up again, especially if it was an audition day.

'Well, Julie, I have a suspicion you need a good therapist. You see no good in yourself. They say therapy is good for that.'

'I know, but you just don't know what the world is like for women who have only their looks, Sean. It's hard keeping them, especially now that I'm thirty,' she said, shaving off two years like she did her legs – habitually, daily. 'That's why I need a rich lad to pay for the personal trainer.'

'As a man of forty I'd love to see thirty again. Well, you're welcome down to my stables any time, and I'll run you around the track with the rest of the mares, they're all as mad as you are.'

The sense of humour Julie seemed to have lost recently returned, and she laughed. 'I feel like I've known you all my life, like a brother, like my friend Marilyn.'

'Now there's some woman. And some friend. For the size of her, she's brave as a beast.' He excused himself to go wash himself and use her toilet.

'Will you sing to yourself, because you live in a small place, and I'm shy about this kind of thing.'

'Only if you do.'

He hummed a Nick Drake song. Marilyn loved Nick Drake. It sounded like he was brushing his teeth with her brush – she'd have to get a new one. The man had bachelor's manners. Then he went on to Nina Simone.

Marilyn had played Nina Simone on the piano, once upon a time. She loved her music. A sick feeling arrived in the pit of Julie's stomach that had nothing to do with alcohol.

A man made for her best friend and she'd just spent the night with him. Julie was searching drawers when he came out.

'I hope it's not a gun you're after.'

'No, but if you don't mind I'll use you for target practice, except I can't find the thing. Never mind, never mind, sit down. And I'll remember the key ones, if I think hard enough. Do you believe in God?' she asked him and he looked at the door before saying yes. 'Good. You get five for that, I think. Have you got a pen?'

'What if I were to tell you that I knew the woman of your dreams?'

'Julie,' Sean said carefully, in the tone of one who didn't want to open any more wounds. He even picked up her hand and turned it over.

'Not me. I mean someone else, someone so fussy I never believed you existed, but you do. And she has to meet you, but you have to promise me, faithfully, that you'll never tell her how we met.'

'I think you're a small bit mad.'

'Right. And you're not really, are you? You're safe, so is she. Being with you might make her less the way she is.'

'You're selling her very well. So far I've got rigid in mind.'

'Yeah, well, you're right and wrong. She's not rigid and frigid, but she's great at pretending to be. All you have to do is sing what you sang.'

'Nick Drake? I like him all right.'

'And the other one.'

'Nina Simone? Beautiful pianist, she is.'

'She plays piano! She likes the simple things in life. You're simple.'

'Thanks for what I think, if I wasn't so simple, is an insulting compliment.'

'She'd like the name Sean too. What's your second name? And stop fishing for your shoes. I've hidden them.'

'I think I need my mother here. It's a small pity she's dead.'

'Answer a few simple questions and you're free to go. It's all I ask.'

'My last name's Monroe.'

'Fuck off.'

'It is, why would I lie? Is there something wrong with it?'

'Can you change it?'

'Only if I want to, and I'm partial to it. All of my family has it in common.'

'Then get onto it, it's the only blot on your future happy horizon.'

'What's she got against Monroe?'

'You're not related two generations back to a John Joe Monroe, formerly of Sligo?'

'No, we're Wexford Monroes, have been for centuries. What's wrong with being one? Is it the planter ancestry? Are you a raving republican?'

'She just doesn't like it.'

'What's her name?'

'Marilyn,' she said.

When he heard the name he didn't have to think twice. But not for the usual reasons. Sean Monroe had no picture of Marilyn Monroe in his head – he had a picture of the woman Larry Leahy called Mari Monroe.

'She did a great thing yesterday, she's a fine woman. I'd have been delighted to meet her.' He nodded as if to agree with himself. Suddenly he remembered the force of feeling that had gone through him when he watched Marilyn tackle Eileen Whelan. 'But there's the not inconsiderable matter that I have shared sexual relations with her best friend.'

That's when Julie almost decided not to go through with

it. In another second she remembered that this was a debt-ridden man living down the country with muck and shite for best friends. Marilyn would love sorting him out. Julie would drive him to further ruin with her insecurities.

'Is there any better way, Sean? I know a lot more about you than I would about others I could have set her up with. I know you'll be good for her, and she doesn't need anyone rich. She needs kind, and interesting, and . . . good!' Julie was motoring now, watching his face for acceptance and getting it. 'So you'll agree to this? But I'll warn you now, her second name is Monroe too. I'm telling you so that when you see her you don't make the mistake of saying something.'

'About what? I don't have any cousins named Marilyn, so we're not related. There's a Mary, though.' Sean looked at her with sea-green eyes that had a brilliance to them not seen in ordinary men. Julie wished she was good enough for him, but she'd have to be a different person. She'd have to be Marilyn.

'Are you serious? You don't make the connection instantly?'

'With who?'

'With the most celebrated sex symbol of our time?'

'Oh, the actress one. I'm not much into films. No time to watch them. Too tired by the evening, or off racing.'

Julie was high and sad at the same time. If only her soulmate was round the corner and Marilyn was setting her up. The chances of that were slim, since Marilyn never took chances. Still, it was a brilliant way to get back into Mari's good books. But part of her was standing in front of spinsterhood and regretful this wasn't about to happen to her.

'You're up next week, for horse sales? Good, I'll be organised by then.'

'Julie, aren't you being a bit hasty?'

'No. She needs a boyfriend. You could be gone by next week, now you're oiled again.'

'I'm sorry?' Sean asked, looking mystified.

'You really aren't a film fan, are you?' Julie smiled as she spoke. 'Dorothy oiled the Tin Man in *The Wizard of Oz*. Then they went off in search of his heart.'

'Oh.' Sean was now smiling. 'That's right. I saw it years ago. I could do with finding mine again. It's been missing a while now.'

'I thought you said you had no girlfriends for a long time.'

'No, it's not been the same since I lost my parents. They weren't perfect but they were the best any child could hope for.'

'I remember you telling me about them last night, sorry for what I said about mine.' Julie reddened. 'I was drunk. It must be awful to lose them both at once.'

'It was the worst thing I ever went through. Whatever happens to me in the future, it could never be as bad as that. I went to identify them. The sisters couldn't do it.' Sean put his hand up, in the way of quiet men who have no wish to say any more, but then a thought passed over his kind, broad face and he looked at Julie in a manner that made her wish she had what he needed. But she was already letting go of the fact she hadn't. And what he said next fully convinced her of her growing understanding that Marilyn Monroe was born for this man. 'Can I tell you, Julie? A small bit about my mother? It's something I never told another soul.'

'Of course you can, Sean, it's the least I can do after all you did for me yesterday.'

'I'd do it for anyone, Julie, and I'd do it twice over for a woman as nice as you. Since you're a small bit mad you'd have liked my mother, she was never one for the polite people. It was only the open ones she liked to be around. The neighbours for miles all have stories of things she had said to them that put their noses out of joint. But then they always had stories of her kindnesses. She was outspoken and everything she said was the truth, which I'm fond of myself, Julie. When I saw your friend help you yesterday I saw a true friend. She put herself in danger to help you.'

As soon as he said this, Julie's eyes welled up and she nodded. 'I used to do the same for her in school. She had a terrible time, being so small. It wore me out the amount of looking after she needed. When we got older she did the same for me. I'm the basket case now and she's my handle.'

'It would be fair to say, Julie, that your friend Marilyn made an impression on me. All the time the dispute was going on I knew myself and Larry Leahy could lift her out of it at any time, so I knew that there was no real danger . . . Anyway, I got this sense of déjà vu, they call it, of my mother and something she said to me, after a busty one with a big attitude gave me the run-around, down home.

'She was a good-looking woman, no more than yourself, but she had ideas about herself and wanted me to fit them. I came home from seeing her, bullish, and my mother was at the table, waiting for me. I was in my thirties then but she still waited up. I sat down to the cup of tea she made me and I couldn't say a word, I was that angry. Then it came out, and a few tears with it. My mother was fond of tears. She said men crying them made them stronger men, not weaker.

'Now she was an outspoken woman, as I said, fond of talk. But she listened to every word I said and didn't say, and there was a big long silence after it. I finished my tea and got up to go to bed, but she pulled me back down in the seat. "Now Sean," she said, "I'll say this only once. The right woman will strike you and when she does her impression won't leave you. You'll find her marked in your thoughts, and the mark won't rub out."

'Two weeks after I had that talk with her, my parents

were dead. Every word of that conversation stayed with me. It was her last advice to me and she gave me a lot more over the years, both my parents did, that I'd never have taken as for granted if I knew I was to lose them like that.'

Sean wasn't speaking to Julie any more, but talking to the grey sky visible from her bed-sit window.

'It would be fair to say that Marilyn made an impression on me. I'm rusty in the concerns of love, Julie. But that's what I'm after. It's that I want. A life shared with a woman is a blessed one. I saw how it made my father. Men build houses and women make homes of them ... Sorry for going on.'

In the following silence Julie put herself in Marilyn's place and knew beyond doubt that she would fall in love with every word this man said.

13

The Monroes were still listening to Colin and Mick on the subject of Tony Devereux and his work in the community.

'He sounds like an archangel,' Elizabeth sighed, 'and I'm flattered – no, I'm disconcerted – by the fact he chose an idea of me to take a fancy to.'

'It wasn't taking a fancy, he loves you. He says all souls look the same and that his chose yours as his equal,' Colin quoted Tony. 'He knows it's not practical as much as you do. You're obviously way better looking, but if you could just give him another opportunity to be a bit more normal with you. You didn't see him at his best. His does arty things. He reads, loves pictures – paintings, I mean.'

'He likes Botticelli,' Grace chipped in.

'He does?' Elizabeth loved Botticelli.

'He has a ' Mick was kicked under the table '— painting, thinks it's like you.'

'Venus,' Grace added.

'That's a nude!' Elizabeth flared. 'I don't want someone I don't even know thinking of me as one.'

You see? Mick glared triumphantly across the table at Colin.

'Now, Elizabeth, let's not be prudish. He sees the facial similarity,' Grace intervened, 'the hair, the ethereal sensibility that has always been yours.'

'He's kind,' Mick put in his bid. 'He won't even kill slugs in the garden.'

'He gardens?'

The two lads had to shake their heads.

'I did see how kind he was,' Elizabeth pointed out. 'I still wasn't interested.'

'But he didn't tell you about himself, all his work he's done. You'd do no better than him. He's decent, a hero even.' Colin believed in what he was saying.

'If he's kind you have to give him every chance,' Marilyn said, quoting Eileen. Elizabeth turned to her as soon as she spoke.

'You think I should?' she asked.

'I think you should,' Marilyn echoed.

'And so do I,' Brigid added. 'There's nothing I'd love more than to see you settled with someone.' She didn't mention she already knew Tony, and her face told the lads not to mention it. Any knowledge of motherly intervention would ruin the possibility.

Elizabeth looked at her mother, now, knowing where this wish came from, wishing she didn't.

'Okay. I agree to meet him, with one condition.'

Mick and Colin rose out of their seats, cheered and patted each other's back.

'My daughter and mother meet him first, to interview him.'

'Ah no!'

'Ah yes. If they're as sure after a face-to-face talk with him as they are now, then I'd be happy, interested even, to see him.'

'Good, so,' Brigid agreed. 'In fact, I've a few others to see on your behalf, Elizabeth.'

'I'm sorry?'

Grace was shaking her head violently, but Brigid was used to ignoring Grace. 'I had arranged another few gentlemen on the computer for you with Grace and, well, we were going to see them first. I've had it in mind for a long time that you need to settle down.'

Grace waited for the explosion, as did Marilyn, and they were surprised when it didn't happen.

'Did you now, Mother? It's nice to know you're taking care of me, still, and I'm over a half-century old. People would be delighted for such concern shown for them.'

'Now, Elizabeth, if you're trying to be smart, I'm only trying to help.'

'I'm not trying to be smart, but I am trying to say this is intrusive, and a big problem with us is intrusion, isn't it, Mother?'

'Yes, you could say it and I couldn't deny it. But for every mistake I made I stopped myself making ten. Not just with you, with everything.'

Elizabeth looked at Brigid. 'I know the feeling, it's one I've often had. I can't believe you do.'

'I'm happy to interview the candidate. I have all the right questions to put to him,' Marilyn smiled.

'Can I just point out that if Tony has to stand at the back of some queue, as his managers we won't be happy.' Mick pointed a finger.

'No, that won't be the case. The subjects we found on the Internet were very bland. But we've arranged to meet them, and it's only courtesy to follow up,' Grace explained. 'We come from a generation that practises good manners. Now, all this talk about fate's making me hungry.' Grace stood. 'Brigid, would you mind if I made something small to eat for ourselves and your guests?'

Marilyn and Elizabeth now waited for an explosion, but there was only assent from Brigid.

Everyone sat down to Welsh rarebit. Elizabeth and Marilyn were happy to see Brigid enjoying hers, and enjoying herself. The details were worked out, numbers exchanged. At midnight Colin and Mick got up to leave.

*

In her bed that night, Brigid had trouble getting her eyes to close from all her anticipation, both for herself, next week, and for her daughter. She took the photo out of the drawer and kissed it.

'Night, Joe, night, little girl. Here's to happiness, for us all.'

As soon as she closed her eyes again, the woman was waiting. 'I'm not even asleep yet,' she said aloud.

Dreams were merging with waking to form a new reality.

'What're you two up to?' A sleep-drugged Tony was standing in front of them, freshly shaven. Once he'd woken up, he'd quoted the Serenity Prayer, as he did first thing each day on wakening, repeating the line that meant the most to him: 'Accepting hardship as the pathway to peace.' As soon as he'd said it today, he knew he had to get up and on with it. 'I'm just going out to do a few hours' work.'

Both of them were smiling at him.

The Library Bar, Central Hotel, 30 December. He was meeting a panel to decide on whether he was suitable for the job of taking out Elizabeth Monroe.

'That's tomorrow,' he said to them, like tomorrow was a spaceship.

'That's eight shopping hours to get you fixed up to look like something other than a first-generation Trekkie,' Mick suggested and Colin nodded.

'Sorry, I have to go as myself, or I won't be myself. You've done a great thing for me, more than anyone has ever done my whole life.' He went out taxiing, to think.

'He's a brave little bollix, isn't he?' Mick said to Colin.

14

Marilyn was at her desk on 27 December, eating yet another turkey sandwich, when Larry walked in.

'What are you doing in work?'

'It's not an official holiday,' Marilyn said defensively.

'Don't worry, I knew you'd be here. I also knew no one else would, all hung over from yesterday. You did a great job yesterday.'

'Larry, I'm hung over myself from fright. My friend was half the reason it happened.'

'She wasn't to know, though she's on the cheap side. But Frank Whelan's a lot cheaper. I found the photographer a bit dear. I had to give him five grand, out of the tills.'

'I'll pay half of that, since it's my friend who instigated it.' Marilyn felt greasy in letting the slur on Julie slide.

'Thanks for offering, but Tommy has the bill to foot there. His friend was the one with the wife and knife, and he certainly made no such offer. Geraldine and I were talking, and she thinks this is right, to tell you what I've been thinking along the lines of ... we want you to—'

Reception buzzed. 'Someone' was looking for Marilyn. The tone told her it could only be Julie. Larry left her to it.

Julie was in reception staring out at the car park, her Mini broken down in the centre of it.

'Don't give out, look at the way yours is parked.' Marilyn's car was taking up the habitual two spaces.

'This isn't the place for an apology,' Marilyn said.

'Good, I haven't come to give one. I have a peace offering, though.'

'I'll call the AA for you.' Marilyn was irritated that, as usual, Julie had a problem she had to fix, embarrassed that she looked like a Page Three girl and mortified that this was happening at work.

'I'm not a member.'

'I joined for you the same time as I did myself. They'll sort you out. Come up to my office for a coffee while we're waiting, Ms Purcell.'

'You're ashamed of me,' Julie stated. Marilyn didn't answer. 'Don't worry, I am of myself. I'm tired of this, Mari, always feeling like you're better than me. But listen,' she said, changing tracks, 'I've found Mr One Hundred – actually, he scores higher than that.'

'Julie...' Marilyn was wary.

'I mean it this time. He's just the one for you. He's even into horses.'

'Ideal, as I don't even like them. You'd do well to apply the same principle to men.'

'I would, would I?' Julie followed Marilyn into her office. 'Well, Sean thinks you'd be even better if you went to a few race meets. He's a trainer.'

'I give five per cent for animal lovers. Trainers live with them instead of women.'

'He's not married, no kids.' Julie ignored her. 'He's got a crinkly smile and a dint in his nose and kinky hair, and that's the only thing about him that's kinky.'

'How would you know? No more crumbs from your table, we tried it once. Remember how I lost my virginity? And what he said to me after?'

'This isn't crumbs,' Julie said, thinking, More like last night's dinner. 'He's lovely and considerate in all ways, and that usually means bed.'

'Where'd you meet?'

'He was the one who took me home yesterday.'

'Oh yeah?'

'Don't be like that, he's the perfect gentleman. Far too good for me.'

'Julie.' Marilyn sat at her desk, needing the distance. Julie followed her around it, oblivious, as normal, to the need for boundaries.

'How much did it cost you to get the photographs?'

'It didn't cost me anything.'

'Oh, good!'

'It cost my boss five thousand.'

'Oh God. I was going to offer to pay it back.'

'Were you now? By selling your car? By the way, your breakdown truck is here.'

'Please, Marilyn, I'm a fuck-up, but I'm not the kind who takes married men off their wives.'

'You are, you do it in front of them. She was in our house for two hours yesterday, crying. Her name is Eileen Whelan.'

'Can you give me her number? I'd like to phone her and apologise.'

'Don't worry, she already has yours. For the court case.'

'Look, you're right in all you say, but I didn't realise and I just want to make things better. Please, Mari, let me introduce you to this man. I don't care if you don't have anything to do with me, you'll want something to do with him.'

'I don't want to discuss this here any more, okay?' Marilyn could see there was no way she was going to get Julie out of the office. 'Come round to the house tonight.'

That evening, in her room, Marilyn used the opportunity to have a proper go at her. 'I can't believe you! I have to work with all those people. You have no idea of how to behave.'

'And you have no idea how to listen, Marilyn. I've said sorry, I've offered to call Eileen Whelan. You get taken in, you do foolish things.'

'I don't.'

'Really? Then what did I see when you gave me the Christmas present I left behind? A present with a "To Dad" label. In your handwriting.'

'Thanks for humiliating me further.'

'I'd never have mentioned it but for the fact you've done it to me most of our adult lives.'

'What do you mean?'

'You slag me and you make me feel more like a slag, more than I already am. I'm riddled with mistakes, but at least I make them. I just wanted you to try this lovely man. This is a date, not a proposal I'm offering you.'

'Why are you doing this, Julie? You want to keep in with the horse set?'

'If you think for one minute it was self-interest that motivated this, then you think wrong.' Julie stood up. 'It was for you. He likes Nick Drake and that Nina Simone song you love, "In the Morning".'

'It's a Bee Gees song covered by Nina, and it doesn't mean anything.'

'Well, he sang the Nina version, and I can see I'm wasting my time. Let's give the calculator something to work out, will we? Let's ask it to compute the chances of love at first sight in a cruel, bastard world. Then give me the odds, Mari. Because I'm going to bet all I have, half nothing, that's what will happen when you meet him. If ever.'

Brigid caught up with Julie in the hallway. She opened the front door, then slammed it and said, 'Now, she'll think you're gone. Come upstairs with me to my room, young lady. I want to hear more about this man.'

'How did you hear?'

'I couldn't fail to!' Marilyn's music was already turned way up. Julie dried her eyes.

'Why don't you want him for yourself?' Brigid asked when they were in her room.

Julie looked at Brigid, her eyes showing all the times she'd let herself down. 'Because he's not a big enough shite for me. I go for third degree when I get burned. His mother told him to hold out for a woman who made a burning impression. He saw Marilyn at Leopardstown, sorting my mess out. I'm setting her up with the best man. But don't worry, Brigid, he's not for me. I'm keeping my heart for the worst one.'

'So did I,' Brigid surprised herself by saying. 'You'll get it right one day. Just wear a top that covers you up, is all. And get him over here on Friday, for dinner.'

Marilyn couldn't sleep. She got up and went online, to compute the odds of Julie's challenge. The world population clock, for that moment, read 6,505,715,000. She watched the lives being added at the rate of two a second.

When she looked at the death statistics it was easy to work out that for every second that passes four people are born and two die. So whatever the chances were of love at first sight, they increased with every passing second.

Naturally Julie's chances were more significant than her own. So if Julie was so emphatic about this man, then it might be wise to trust her, given her vast experience in the field.

The thought brought a smile to her face and relaxed her enough to think sleep, too, was now a possibility.

She climbed back into bed. 'It's not your mind that's the trouble, though, is it? It's your heart. You don't believe in love at first sight. Even though the figures are telling you there's an ever-increasing chance of it,' she whispered to herself. Her father's voice came out of the night:

'Now you have it. You can't use figures to hide from life. The calculations caught up with you in the end.'

'Yeah.' Marilyn giggled. 'And the woman who told me to work it out never passed a maths exam in her life.'

She fell asleep, enveloped in a feeling she didn't instantly recognise: hope.

15

Greyness, cold and penury pressed in on Elizabeth before the month of January had even arrived, but her situation was better than Eileen Whelan's. Frank the banker knew how to freeze accounts. She and the children had never left her sister's house. Frank had gone straight home to lock them out, then had the locks changed. She was making hourly phone calls for funds to feed them and to try and get their clothes out of the house.

'It's why I didn't divorce him years ago, Elizabeth. I knew it'd get ugly. He used to clock the miles on my BMW. I had to tell him exactly where I was going.'

'Treating you with the same suspicion he deserved. The difficulty is proving his infidelities,' Elizabeth sighed. The sigh was enough to warm the office. She'd been embarrassed leading Eileen into it, saying, 'Sorry, Eileen. Remember, at any stage if you want a proper solicitor I'll hold nothing against you.'

Eileen had looked around, the hesitation in her face obvious. She was a middle-aged woman on the slide, approaching another middle-aged, as yet unqualified woman with no previous credentials to hammer out a deal with those who did them every day. Her features set. Elizabeth noticed and said, 'Come on, you can be honest here if nowhere else.'

'I don't have the money to pay for anyone, not even you.'

'I told you, this is win, gain. But didn't you think of this before you threatened him with a knife?'

'I hadn't planned to. He sent me home and I went, as usual. I got in the car and saw the little black mile-counter. I found myself careering back up the stairs, and to be honest I don't remember much after that. I suppose all the lip-biting built up.'

Even as she was speaking Elizabeth was thinking she ought to send her home. But she knew she wouldn't. At the very least this case gave her an opportunity to expand her knowledge. Her lecturers praised her grasp of the subject and her humility in dealing with it. As had Dickey's clients.

'Maybe they should all wait until their forties to take the profession up,' her tutor had remarked.

'Common sense doesn't exist in law,' Elizabeth had smiled.

Her tutor smiled back and wished he wasn't married. There had been a time when Elizabeth had wished that too.

'Have you anything, anything at all that might help us?' Elizabeth asked Eileen. 'Any evidence of affairs?'

'Well, I did try.' Eileen handed over an envelope with seven or eight papers inside it. 'He was the sort to go through his own pockets before I did. He kept his wallet and his briefcase to himself. I only ever got to look in them when he'd had a few drinks, and even then he wasn't the kind to fall down. Too much to hide to be caught.'

'Can I open this?'

'It's why I gave it to you.'

Elizabeth took out two receipts for flowers. 'He could have given those to anybody.'

A hotel bill.

'This is in his name only. A double suite, but his name only. It proves nothing.'

A jeweller's receipt.

'He could have bought these earrings for his mother.'

A personal bank statement featuring six lodgements, all cash, amounting to eight or nine thousand pounds only in total.

'If they're backhanders, they're not high enough amounts to be considered backhanded enough.'

Two lodgement slips signed by a woman, which caused Elizabeth to look straight at Eileen.

'I knew you'd find those interesting. They're not to be used in the court. She's a friend of mine, a good friend. I saw other documents too, but I didn't get a chance to copy them. I took a big risk taking those. And I'll never do anything with them, but they might lead somewhere else, you never know.'

The amounts on the lodgement slips were for ten thousand and nineteen thousand pounds, a lot of money in the late seventies.

And the signatures on the slips were those of Frank on one and Judith Tormey on another – Niall Tormey's wife of thirty-seven years.

'They'd normally be with us at the races, but they're never around for the Leopardstown meeting. If she'd been there he'd never have sent me home. Judith knows how to handle Frank. But then, she's got enough power for him to have to respect her.'

Elizabeth wondered how Eileen could fail to notice her flushing but then realised she was probably used to ignoring menopausal symptoms in women their age, out of politeness. Elizabeth wasn't menopausal. She was petrified.

'When did you get these?'

'Over ten years ago. From his briefcase. There were statements, there was company letterhead, attached to these. I took only what I'd get away with.'

'These documents are twenty-five years old. He carried them in his locked briefcase for that many years? If he's hung on to them for so long,' Elizabeth managed to say, 'there are reasons. Can you remember what the name of the company was?'

'Magpie Holdings – you don't forget a name like that.

And there were lots of other slips. But again, I don't want Judith in this. She's been good to me. And I can't help liking her husband, though he's one of Frank's cronies. He'd never treat a woman like Frank treats me. He has charm.'

Yes, Elizabeth thought, he has that.

'Perhaps we can bargain with these,' Elizabeth said, admiring her own coolness, 'with that kind of signature. Tomorrow's New Year's Eve. Make some resolutions about enjoying your next year.'

'So long as we try to do it the legit way first,' Eileen was keen to point out.

'Any way we'll do it will be legit. Your husband is the one who has to worry on that score.'

As soon as Eileen had gone, Elizabeth put her head on the desk.

This is too close for comfort. I should send her on to someone else. I can't afford to go near this.

A part of her already knew she was going to do it, and that it would lead to him. This was what she wanted. Not only for herself, but for Marilyn. The want in her daughter's eyes when she'd thought Colin and Mick might be brothers and Tony might be her father was unmistakeable.

'I don't see why we have to meet them when we're going to go with Tony Devereux.' Theresa took a drag on her Sweet Afton. She had iron lungs, having smoked them since she was twelve. Everything about Theresa was strong.

'Because those three gentlemen wrote to us and they deserve the courtesy of response.' Brigid was curt. 'And why I didn't bring Grace instead of you I'll never know. You're here to run them if they get out of hand, you hear?'

'I'm a lesbian – why do you always equate that with bouncer duty?'

'And what about me? Why am I here if you brought

Aunty Theresa?' Marilyn asked. 'Don't you trust my judgement?'

'Well, love, you haven't had many in the way of boy-friends, have you?'

'I think she's had more than me.' Theresa shook her head.

Marilyn went to the loo at five minutes to six.

'Theresa, with my condition you'd have the sense to put that thing out,' Brigid snapped.

'Sorry.' Theresa reached for the ashtray. 'I wasn't thinking. You've been more yourself the past few days, so I almost forgot.'

At the stroke of six, Marilyn walked back in, as did Bachelor Number One. His hair was snow-white and he carried a walking-stick. The judges looked down at their notes: Fifty-seven, own business, enjoy hill-walking.

'He looks like he had trouble getting up the steps,' Marilyn observed.

'Too old for me, let alone my daughter,' Brigid hissed.

Theresa was already on her feet and steering him to the other side of the bar, where she bought him a tea, then sent him home twenty minutes later. 'He was eighty, but he's been told by his great-granddaughter that he passes for years younger.'

'That's not years, that's decades.' Marilyn shook her head.

'Yeah, he used to climb Croagh Patrick every year till he was seventy-nine and had his first stroke. He likes to meet "nice women for a chat". He's lonely since his wife died. I could've talked to him all night.'

'And he's a liar,' Brigid snapped. 'A time-waster, like Elizabeth's father.'

'Never mind now. The next one might be better, and he's due shortly,' Marilyn said to calm things down.

He arrived five minutes early and scanned the room with narrowed, practised eyes before heading for the bar and ordering a pint and whiskey chaser. Five minutes later he ordered the same and knocked back the second whiskey. Poetic nature, quiet living, respectful of the fairer sex and looking for a happy ever after. Own house and car.

'Alcoholic, owes his shirt – seeks soft women to keep him afloat with a few lines of poetry and the promise of love. That man is going nowhere near my niece,' Theresa reworded.

'Imagine if Elizabeth was here on her own to meet them? With her bleeding heart she'd take them all home. We may as well go. He's ten minutes late.' Brigid stood.

Tony rushed in then and apologised for getting caught in traffic. He was nervous, but he had no difficulty meeting Brigid's eye, like he had the last time. There was something in him she hadn't noticed the other day, when he was reeling. Substance.

'Don't worry, my mother's always late,' Marilyn said, cocking her head to one side. Even though they'd said he would be, he looked too ordinary to be true to the description Colin and Mick had given. 'I'm Marilyn. This is my grandmother, Brigid, and my great-aunt, Theresa. I understand you know an old friend of mine, Phoebe.'

'I do, a good person she is. I'd like to get you all a drink, for coming out for my benefit,' he said. His best feature had to be his olive-green eyes that gave the impression he had all the time you needed.

'Isn't it us supposed to buy you one?' Theresa asked. 'Since we're doing the questions?'

'That's not the right way round. I'm old-fashioned.'

'One up already,' Theresa whispered.

Tony Devereux put one Tio Pepe, one glass of Heineken and one soda and lime in front of the right people without having to ask.

'Well, let's get down to business,' Brigid set off. 'Marilyn has a few questions laid out for us. They're all about you. We don't want to answer any questions about Elizabeth. Is this clear?' Tony nodded. 'First and foremost, you believe you're in love with her, from what we're told. Can we ask why?'

'I can't explain it, I just know it.'

'But surely you must have some idea?'

'I have plenty. Certainly she's my perfect woman, to behold. From the way she spoke to Phoebe, and the other day in the cab, and just watching her over the years, I could tell all I need to know.'

'Which is?' Marilyn asked.

'Well, my sense of her, if that's what you mean, is she's a woman given to impulse and ideals. She's got an obvious artistic side and I think she'd have a consuming interest in the esoteric, but there's something else, something withheld, like there's a part of her life she doesn't even want to acknowledge. And she's been hurt in love, as I have, you can tell by the way she won't linger if a lone male tries to engage her. Like me.

'In the company of other women, and men she trusts, she's warm, open. She'd rather age than hide it. She loves her garden, I know that by the way she looks at plants, reaches out to them as much as if they're the friends that she sometimes meets at the Vico. She has few close ones because her conversations embarrass a lot of people, she can't linger on the small talk. If you ask her how she feels she has a genuine answer. She cries easily but that can be confused with being overemotional. Elizabeth can tell strangers intimate details of her life, yet hide the most inconsequential things from you, her loved ones. It marks her as being a bit underconfident in who she is. Her bearing is confident, but she isn't, her practice shows otherwise. Her habit of apologising before she even starts a sentence, for instance.

'What else? Well, she can't bear to tie up her hair or wear anything restrictive. Animals like her. I can't understand why she doesn't have a dog. A dog would suit her, but I think cats are drawn to her because she's reserved. She has their grace but not in her walk, it's clumsy because she doesn't know how to stop looking at things. Most of her pursuits are solitary – I know she studied and I found it hard to believe when she told me it was law. She's superstitious, has a good voice, but wouldn't like to sing out in company. She has a powerful ear and desire for music. She'd like to draw, so she appreciates painting all the more. She understands human nature and sees more in it than it sees in her.

'Marilyn, well, everything in her life is about you. Once she's decided on loving you, you can't be unloved, so her child would be loved to hell, heaven and back. You can shut her down with dismissal all too easily. She's the kind to notice every nuance and remember too many of them, even the ones that weren't there at all. Brigid, she's afraid of you.

'She's the kind to give her heart once and I hope it wasn't to Marilyn's father, or I'll have even less of the little chance I know I've got. She's got ideas about love that might not match this world's reality. If she chose early, and badly, she'd be happy to be on her own. Her head has all the company she needs.

'I'll press on if I'm not boring you. You see, she's my favourite subject, and being able to describe what I know of her, to her family, is a great privilege. Can I go on?'

They nodded.

'She has a way with words, and could even write if she put her mind to it. But her mind is on something else, almost all the time, and the way she moves tells me she's pre-occupied with it. Wherever Elizabeth is, she is rarely with us in the way others would be. But when you ask her to listen, you'll find her ears are yours. And I learned tonight, she's a bad timekeeper. I'd love to know if she likes to dance, but you're not going to tell me, and I don't blame you. I told you too much, Mrs Monroe, when you confronted me. She's not the kind to betray confidences like I did that day. I only did it, I must say, because I would have imagined you'd know what she was up to.'

Marilyn and Theresa glanced at each other. They clearly didn't know about that first meeting either, but Brigid ignored them.

'How can you know this?' Brigid whispered. Marilyn and Theresa could feel breath coming back into their lungs.

'Observation, Mrs Monroe. I know, I can't not, because I imagine her.'

'She might be very different,' Theresa broke in, but her instinct told her that he knew her like none of her family did.

'That's right, she's a story to you,' Brigid added.

'That's what my lads say, Colin and Mick, but now they believe in my instinct as much as I do. They see my conviction and I know my conviction.'

'Everything you said was right!' Marilyn burst out.

'That'll do, Marilyn! We have to behave professionally about this. And you wonder why I brought Theresa with me?' Brigid cautioned. 'Well, Mr Devereux, we have more questions, and a one-sentence answer will do. So if we could just get on, I'm sure we'll all be happier.'

'Well, you'll be, Brigid.' Marilyn was terse. Here was a genuine prospect and her grandmother was scuppering it with trademark rudeness. Tony smiled to her that this was okay. He drove taxis, he knew how to handle the bullish.

'Can we stick to The Scale?' Brigid ordered. 'You see the first question?'

The question of appearance. It was Tony's worst category, but Marilyn still gave him the full amount because he was so presentable and appeared so safe. Brigid wrote eight – he was a bit small for her liking. John Joe had been small, and look where it had got them.

Ability to speak about himself in a manner that doesn't send you to sleep: five per cent. Full marks from Marilyn. Two from Brigid – they'd only known him five minutes, after all. His devotion might prove boring after ten, and terrifying to Elizabeth.

Ability to ask about you: twenty-five per cent. Full marks again from Marilyn – if he knew so much about Elizabeth, he would get to know anyone. He scored thirteen per cent from Brigid. Never give all the marks, same as you should never give all the heart – it could all be a very convincing act.

Solvency: thirty per cent. Both gave fifteen. His mortgage was almost paid, but he was still paying off his taxi-plate loan, which was why he worked nights.

Ownership of an animal: five per cent. He got full points for wishing he had a cat. Persuasion would react well to this decision.

Mother affiliation: five per cent. Mother was dead, a drinker. Theresa wasn't surprised to see Brigid give him full marks.

Granny affiliation: five per cent. Devoted to her. When she was alive, she saved him from his alcoholic mother. Full points from Marilyn and Brigid.

Belief in Supreme Being. 'There definitely has to be something. The Catholic God? I hope it isn't, he near beat me to death in school. I believe, in what I'm not sure.' Full points from Marilyn, but none from Brigid, who put her fingers on her miraculous medal. There was only one God, most definitely Catholic.

Interest in alternative lifestyle: 'I see a homeopath and I practise Tai Chi. I find since I took them up I'm fitter than when I was pumped full of doctor drugs.' Ten per cent plus from Marilyn. The Scale rules were hers to break. Minus ten from Brigid, who decided to stick with Marilyn's instructions.

Psychoanalysed: five per cent. 'Yes, I went to see a marriage counsellor with my wife, but I still didn't earn enough money, so she left and I went to see the counsellor on my own for six months or so. I wouldn't rule out going to one again, since it helped, but I'm of a mind you can sort yourself out if you try hard enough. The Vico view is my therapy. And interest in others.' Full points.

Overanalysed: minus ten per cent. Brigid still took off six for him going at all. By this stage Marilyn was wondering if she could still officially be adopted at thirty-two.

The ability to buy a present without needing a dictionary of hints: seven point five per cent. 'I'm not great at present buying,' he confessed, 'unless she likes paintings. I love watercolours, I even buy them when I can, for taste, not for investment. What use are they if they're worth twice as much in a few years but I don't like them enough to have them on my walls?' It was like listening to Elizabeth.

Devotion to the woman in his life, coupled with awareness of himself: six per cent at current rates. 'There was a time when I gave too much to be considered interesting, and I won't do it again.' Full points. Brigid even managed a half smile. She could see a day when she would share the Yeats poem with him, advise him on how to manage Elizabeth.

Bad jumpers – three per cent out of two point five. Tony got more than the maximum points for wearing a Pringle special.

'Right, that's it.' Brigid snapped her notebook.

'I think we should deviate a bit.' Marilyn spoke up. 'I think we should ask Tony if he has any other detail he wants to add.'

'There is,' he said quickly. Then more slowly he added: 'I drank for seven years and I'm sober seven years. I wish I hadn't and I'm glad I did at the same time because I wouldn't be who I am now.'

At that Tony excused himself to go to the gents', leaving behind him a slightly startled but admiring interview panel. They added up the scores: Brigid had awarded him 90.5, while Marilyn had given him 118.5.

'My main worry is his drinking.' Brigid spoke first. Marilyn kept an eye out for him.

'He's in recovery. The nearest John Joe got to that was vodka for his breakfast to get rid of the shakes,' Theresa pointed out.

'Once an alcoholic, always one. I'm just trying to be cautious here.'

'Don't be.' Marilyn's face was flushed. 'Be excited. He's right for her, we all know it. You don't need numbers to know this man adds up. In fact even if he scored zero I'd know he's right for my mother. Numbers can't tell you everything.'

'Marilyn's right, and you're right.' Theresa smiled at her niece and said, 'He's great, and he's an alcoholic, which we knew before he came here, which is why they say one day at a time. He's done seven years of one days. You have to look at the numbers, Brigid. He's a high scorer, even with you.'

'That's out of one twenty-five, not one hundred, and that's only two-thirds of the way there as far as I'm concerned.' Brigid would have gone on, but Tony was back.

'Hope that wasn't too hard on you, Tony.' Marilyn spoke first, determined to give him a good impression of them.

'I'm glad for the opportunity. They didn't grill me like that when I tried for the Guards and I still didn't get in.'

'Just as well,' Theresa grinned, 'Elizabeth would hate you if you were one.'

'In fact, if she has any sense,' Brigid spoke slowly, 'she'll get to know you. We'll pass on your details and we'll recommend she meet you.'

Tony didn't feel drained any more. 'One chance is all I need.'

'Well' – Brigid surveyed him over her reading glasses,– 'you didn't make much of the first one.'

'Okay,' he conceded, 'one more, that I've had time to prepare for.'

'Take it easy. She's really bad at picking up the phone,' Marilyn advised. 'In fact, she has a mortal fear of them. Calls them guillotines for cutting the voice off from the rest of the body.'

He smiled, putting this snippet into his store of information, and asked if anyone needed to be run home. He was on duty now.

'No, I drove in,' Marilyn smiled.

'Can I say one other thing?' Tony asked.

'If you must.' Brigid wanted to get home and rest. She wanted to be near her own dreaming now, having listened to his.

'You told me she liked cornflowers, Brigid, and I can see why. They're the colour of Marilyn's eyes.'

'You did it!' he said aloud to his eyes in the rear-view mirror.

He took out his mobile to distract himself and saw seven missed calls on it, all from home.

'Well, you bollix? We were waiting over two hours!' Mick said after the first ring.

16

The house, number 51, looked like any other, but the idea of eating dinner with a bunch of strangers, all women, gave Sean Monroe heartburn.

'Don't worry' – Julie was reading him – 'once you've won them over you're on for a roast dinner, and I know how much you like those.'

She smiled and Sean hoped someday some man would see the value in her. He would have done himself, but he needed less trouble, not more.

'It's nice of her to invite me to her house.'

'Nice is not the exact word I'd use,' Julie smiled.

'So she doesn't know I'm even here? I don't think I can go through with this, Julie.'

'Remember what your mother said, Sean.'

'She didn't mention any names when she said that, Julie.'

'But you had a feeling, didn't you? About Marilyn? If we hadn't slept together you'd be less worried and more willing to write it off as nothing ventured nothing gained.'

'That's true enough, it's like I already have something to hide.'

'You don't. If you want the awful and absolute truth I've slept with more men than I've had dinners.'

'Well, you don't eat many of those.'

'True, but there's rarely a week goes by that I don't end up in the sack with someone. You were nothing special, it meant nothing, Sean. She'd almost expect of me to have tried you out first.'

'You're not making me want to stay any more than I did five minutes ago, Julie!' Sean pointed out.

'Listen, I don't have to. You have that feeling in the pit of your belly. You said it yourself. Don't deprive me of my chance to prove to my friend that I can do something good for her. And for God's sake don't deprive yourself of the chance to find the woman you will marry.'

'That's putting it a bit strong, now.'

'No it isn't, otherwise you wouldn't be here. And there's a woman who lives in that house,' Julie said as she pointed emphatically to 51, 'who needs you to make her understand that fate is not something that happens over summers in church grounds. The truth is she's as desperate to meet you as you are to meet her. Only she doesn't know it as well as you do.'

'Okay, okay.' Sean put his hands up. 'You have me persuaded.' But inside himself he knew it wasn't Julie doing the talking, it was his mother. In the past week she had rarely left his dreams. It was as if she was still alive, she was that real to him. He was about to take a big chance on a hunch.

Sean got out of the car with his new friend and chaperone, and walked towards 51, to find out what answer awaited him.

Brigid was stirring the two gravies – one veggie, one meat. Elizabeth knew the world had shifted on its axis, or else Brigid was after something. 'Elizabeth, I need your help.'

Brigid looked up. The black rims underneath her eyes made Elizabeth speak before she thought. 'You not sleeping again?'

'Bit of stomach trouble, all the rich food over the season. A man is coming along for us to meet. He might be a nice boyfriend for Marilyn.'

Elizabeth put down the spoons she was setting on the table.

'To go with the one you keep asking me to ring?'

'I didn't ask, you promised you would, there's a difference.'

'I will, when I get time. I'm busy at the moment. Where did you meet this man? Are you trying to get us all out of the house?'

'No. I didn't meet him, Julie did. Now hold on, Elizabeth, I know I'm down on the girl, but her intentions seem good. If Marilyn could see beyond her own nose, and that's a long way for her, we could be looking at a husband and children.'

'She doesn't want those, she's always telling me—' Elizabeth began.

'You know as well as I do she's afraid no one will want her. She hasn't been lucky with men and she hasn't had much example from us, has she now? We have to face that and other facts.'

'And what are they?' Elizabeth's eyes narrowed.

'She's looking for a father instead of a boyfriend. She's too old to be someone's daughter and we have to help her see that, before she's too old to be someone's mother.' Brigid sounded war-weary.

'You think we're responsible?'

'Yes, I'm afraid I do. Me more so than you. Will you try, for her if not me? Just to see? And remember to ring Tony Devereux, you'd never get as nice a man.'

'That's what Marilyn keeps saying.' Elizabeth began to realise Marilyn was wanting more than Elizabeth's happiness. She was seeking a father figure, a way of understanding men that fathers are supposed to give to daughters.

'I heard Julie saying this man's good with broken animals,' Brigid said, her voice so quiet it was hard to hear, 'which means he'll be good around here.'

Elizabeth knew that the only thing that made her mother's voice quiet and reed-like was the cancer. She found herself saying, 'It'll be nice to have a man at the table. After dinner I'll phone Tony too.'

Sean was in his jeans and his worst jumper, worn on Julie's advice. It made him look like a granddad golfer, with all the diamonds on the front. The first thing he said on coming through the front door was, 'That's a lovely smell of dinner.'

'Could I get you a cup of tea or something, Sean?' Brigid busied herself while Elizabeth began to talk to him at a set kitchen table. He never set a table – he ate like the horses, on the hoof and practically out of a bucket. Elizabeth could read people as well as he could read horses, he saw.

'Marilyn's due back soon.'

'And your ordeal will be over, or just beginning,' Julie laughed shrilly, more nervous than he was. He has his mother and father's good intentions behind him. Keep an eye on me now, Mam and Dad, I need you for this hunch I'm going on.

Elizabeth said she didn't like what happened to horses in the name of entertainment. He surprised her by saying, 'What you don't realise, Mrs—'

'I'm not. Elizabeth will do.' They all ignored Brigid's 'huh'.

'Elizabeth, what you don't realise is that the horses love it. If they're brought to it right, they'll do nothing else. They're born for it. It's like you doing exactly what you want with your own life – it's the best feeling in the world. But maybe we should talk about your daughter, since that seems to be why we're both here.'

'Oh, my daughter can wait. What I want to talk about, Mr . . .?'

'Sean will do.'

'What we want to talk about, Sean, are your concerns.'

Brigid smiled as she stirred the pot. Elizabeth was using her own words, in the same manner – businesslike, cautious. It was good one of them was up to the inquisition. Brigid felt more tired by the minute. But interest kept her on her feet, moving about.

'Tell us all about those concerns, as much or as little as you want to. For starters, how did you get into racing?' Elizabeth carried on.

'I was always in it, in a small way. A farmer, with one or two horses. Now I'm a horse trainer with one or two head of cattle as an interest. I sell them in tough months.' Best not to say how tough, he thought. 'My parents died on me at the same time, in a crash, and I saw then that life was for living,' he admitted. 'I mortgaged to get the stables up and running, and started with two bangers of horses. I made them so they could go a bit better. That got me my reputation. I've been working at it ever since.

'It's from early in the morning until late at night. The modern worker wants a thirty-six-hour week and I could do that in a day and a half, which might not recommend me to your Marilyn.'

'My daughter,' Elizabeth smiled, 'works as hard. This is Sunday, remember. That's where she's been all day.'

Julie could see they were warm to him, and it made her proud. At the cooker, Brigid thanked St Jude, patron saint of lost causes, whom she prayed to every night for help with her mission to find husbands.

'Why are you doing it, if it's so hard and for so little return?' Elizabeth asked.

'You have to love it and if you don't you'll leave it well behind. There's so many ups and downs in it. I had one horse, won his first race. On his third race he broke his leg and had to be destroyed on the course. The owners don't feel the same pain for it, they only see the horse now and again.

154

The insurance covers them. Me, now, I see them every day and the reason they come to me is the owners have got no good out of them and want to cut their losses, so they don't care for the animal anyway. I haven't managed to turn every so-called bad horse to good. But I'll get some good. A time-consuming business it is, Elizabeth, Brigid. Which is why Julie is fixing me up with your daughter, since I haven't the time for myself.'

Elizabeth, Brigid and Julie found themselves involved.

'One of the reasons I don't watch racing, or enjoy my daughter being part of it, is the way they whip those horses to the finish. It's brutal,' Elizabeth admitted.

'You mean you have others?' Brigid enquired. 'What are they?'

'They're not relevant to this conversation.' Elizabeth's tone told them all to leave it there. 'We're here to quiz Sean, not me.'

'That's fine, and to answer you, nine times out of ten they're only showing the horses the look of it. It's the noise of the whip does the trick. I'm a simple man, Julie tells me' – his eyes joking – 'who'll try anything else anyone suggests first. Anyone works for me is the same. By the way, Elizabeth, not to get too technical on you and you new to the sport, but whips are felted now so there's no horse marred. And no one wants to see a horse marred. You'll find the game has gone so expensive that the owners and trainers won't stand for a bad jockey, a brute. But in the case of my latest horse, well, she's had everyone, looking to make money out of her quick, pushing her on too early.

'She's a small little chance, called Delaney, I only paid two thousand for her. The work in her's costing far more. Six months and I've only got her calmed. I've ponied her up with my best old lad, Noble. My father used to race him in his day, and that was nearly twenty years ago. By name and nature he's noble.'

The sound of a key in the door made everyone remember why Sean was there. Marilyn's footsteps were on the stairs.

'She never comes into the kitchen straight, Sean,' Brigid said, 'she has to change, then she'll be down. She'll be a few minutes and then she's to do her peas. When you've tasted Marilyn's peas you'll be keen on her, I can tell you.'

'Would this be a good time to admit I smoke?' Sean asked. 'I'd go out the back if that's all right, for a calming puff. I'm suddenly very nervous.' Julie followed him out to the patio for company, thinking a puff herself might suppress her appetite, and nerves.

As a woman who couldn't cook, Marilyn had one exception – marrowfats, soaked for a day and night, cooked for exactly forty seven minutes, then smothered in butter and black pepper, with a drizzle of an ingredient she never revealed. They were the reason her mother hadn't gone vegan. It wasn't until they were being drained and stirred with the mystery addition that Elizabeth said, 'Marilyn, we've someone coming to dinner.'

'Great, who is it?' From Elizabeth's voice, she was sure it was Tony.

'Julie, and the man she met who she thinks—'

'Call him and cancel.' Marilyn was so angry she wanted to hurl the peas, and so hungry she didn't. She never cut off her nose to spite her face; that would be too female. But she ran from the room, into the hallway.

'Marilyn, he's a lovely man called Sean, who works with horses.' Brigid followed her.

'Not you as well! I rely on you for reason around here, Brigid. You must be sick again the way you're carrying on trying to marry us off. What're you doing drinking Complan and playing Cilla Black?'

'Marilyn, for a sick person I've never felt better in my life.'

'Really? Because I think you need a doctor! In the past

month you've turned into her.' She pointed behind Brigid, at Elizabeth.

'If I have,' Brigid smiled, 'thank you for saying so.'

'It wasn't meant to be a compliment. And can I remind you that Grace doesn't read tea leaves as a religion, they're for entertainment value! The only man I want in my life is my father. I don't want a smelly horseman with insufficient social skills to conduct his own dating affairs. I want a dad to tell me about men, before I end up with one.'

'Please, Marilyn.' Elizabeth took a step forward.

'No, stay where you are, and turn off the waterworks. Your tears always stop arguments. Julie made a show of me, and I could have lost my job and this man is involved in a business I want nothing to do with after working hours. Also I don't want the hassle of a man, I've so much going—'

'So much going on? You go nowhere but to your evening class, you do nothing but work,' Elizabeth pointed out.

'It might seem that way to you, but I have interests.'

'But you're not interesting, Marilyn, you're stuck in a warp of safe, confined activities. Your life is slipping away.'

'I'm safe because you were never that, Elizabeth. I work hard and do well because you never did, you wasted your opportunities, and I won't do that.'

'You have no idea what you're talking about.'

'I'm talking about someone who can't get it together, someone who hides in her mother's house from the world and then tells me that I do the same. I'm led by example.'

'Marilyn. You don't know the half of it.'

'Well, that's because I don't want to. I'm not the type to get pregnant and call it fate. I'd call that lack of contraception. I'm not the type to use crystal balls and cults and fucking tea leaves to determine who I am. I deal in realities, Elizabeth, because you don't and never have and will continue to—'

That's when Brigid spoke out. 'Don't speak to your mother like that. Is that the way we brought you up, to insult her for all her efforts? And there's no use blaming her for what she was if you're not going to get on with life yourself. That's a kettle calling a pot blackened in my book, and that's—'

'Do you mind, Mother?' Elizabeth interrupted. 'Do you mind letting me alone to discipline my child?'

'"Child"! Listen to both of you,' Marilyn railed. 'It's what you treat me as! It would make a well woman sick, living with this pressure. I'm telling you now, you can expect me to move out at the earliest opportunity. I've had just about as much as I can stand.'

Julie left Sean outside when she heard the voices in the hallway. She sat at the table, her head bowed, thinking, I'll show her, I'll have him. Even if I have to get up at five with him every day I'll have him, and show her what she's missed.

Sean knocked on the patio doors, looking to get back in. Julie had locked him out until the dispute died down. She couldn't look at him.

'I'm going to my room,' Marilyn announced.

'You can't,' Brigid intervened. 'It's rude and I took the liberty of taking all the keys out of the locks.'

'Then I'll go outside.'

'He's outside, with Julie, having a cigarette.'

'A smoker! That gets nothing on my scale. Doesn't anyone know anything about what I want?'

Marilyn couldn't get to the front door either, since her mother and grandmother were standing in the way. She had no choice but to run out past Sean Monroe with a pot of peas in her hand and lock herself in the shed. It was sub-zero outside. She attempted to eat her marrowfats, but the hunger had gone out of her. She settled for the warmth of the pot.

★

There was a knock on the shed door.

'I won't come out until he's gone.'

'He's outside,' a male voice said. Marilyn thought it had a smile in it. 'He just wants to say goodbye before he heads off, and to apologise for turning up on your doorstep.'

'I'm so sorry they did this to you, and me. They're mad. Very nice to have met you.'

'We haven't, but nice to have talked to you through a door anyway, Marilyn.' He said her name as if it belonged to her, not a tortured cinema icon. 'I may see you at the races, your boss Larry knows me.'

'I don't go to them.' The last time he saw her she'd been charming a knife out of a woman's hand. That would make anyone look magnetic. Now she was hiding in a shed from her family, and from seeing his face set into polite rejection. She would never be the kind of woman men wanted, unless they needed financial advice or a mother ship. 'I'm at the other end of it, the betting end,' she called out so he would hear her, in case he was gone.

'I bet you, Marilyn, if you open the door you'll be under no pressure. I wanted to meet you, Julie and your family had little to do to persuade me.' He spoke softly, with the truth that had been his mother's trademark. 'I wanted to see the woman who could talk another woman out of knifing a bad husband. That was something to see, I can tell you. It impressed me very much. It would be very nice to set eyes on you.'

Her thoughts ran amok – No, it wouldn't, you'll hate me when you see me. No man's ever liked me enough to stay. I'm dull. I'm chaste. I'm plain. I'm opening the door. Driving her on was the hope born out of calculation. How possible is love at first sight? Julie had insisted it would happen for Marilyn, with Sean.

His voice weighed lightly on her, no demand in it; already he offered her protection. He saw her humiliation in having best friend, mother and grandmother do this.

There was a bear waiting outside. From the moment she set eyes on him, she knew fate was tired of not being able to get through to her. She had been in the same room as him twice and not looked twice, once at the racecourse, once in her own kitchen. The third time, in the shed, was plain lucky.

'So, Marilyn...' He stepped inside the shed. 'What do you do?' An awkward question from a man who treated everyone the same way.

'I'm an actuary. I deal in risk management for Larry. You don't have to be an actuary, but it helps.'

'Well done on taking one of your own. Is that plant pot set to collapse if I sit on it?'

'No,' she assured him, then apologised when it went from under him. She'd been sitting on them for years, but then, she was about half his size. She was already thinking that they would look ridiculous together. She was already working out ways not to care. You were right, Julie. He's here. I'm not ready for him. I don't look my best. But he's here. I'm not letting him out of my first sight. In her mind the world population count moved up two digits. She took a breath, held it, released it. Her search among the billions, employing tactics like The Scale, was over. With a surety she had only ever found in figures, she knew this was what she wanted, in a way she had never wanted anything before. But for her father. Well, I can't have him, so this is just as good. Better, because I actually chose him. I choose him.

'Sorry, sorry.'

'It seems that's a word you're fond of, Marilyn. Why are you apologising when it's me barging in on you?' He crouched down, but even then was looking down at her, never taking his eyes away from her face. She kept hers on the door. 'They told me I had to try to get you to come back in. You'd stay out here all night to prove a point, they said.'

'That's not true.'

'I don't know whether it is or not, yet.' She loved the way he said 'yet'. 'And I'm at fault here, for going along with them, on account of wanting to meet you.'

'It's not your fault, it's them, they're always at it.'

'Bringing men home for you?'

'No, no, this is the first time they've done that,' she rushed. 'They all want me to be different from what I am. I'm much the same as I'm ever going to be.'

'Well, there's not a thing wrong, from what I can see. But I'm not one to judge by appearances.' Seven per cent up already.

'Do you mind,' he asked, 'if I have some of your peas? I'm really hungry.'

'They're still hot.' She offered them. 'But I've only the one spoon.'

'The one spoon will do.'

They stayed in the shed a while, or what seemed it. The others said later it was a full hour. She hadn't had her watch on, otherwise she might have checked. Then they left the cocoon, as he called it, 'to get a bit of meat, to go with the lovely peas. Will that do you?'

They were all at the patio doors, but shot off to their places like kids who've seen the teacher.

'We'll pretend we didn't see that.' He had tree-bark skin, lined, rough and grained. She wanted to reach up and touch it. Love at first sight. For fools. Which is why it works. He was holding the pea pot and looking a bit unsure.

'We're going in, are we?' She was hanging back more than he was. 'It won't be that bad. We'll tell them that we like the look of each other but we need more time. Will that do?'

It wouldn't. It felt like he'd lashed her across the face.

'I'm not a horse. I don't need to be broken in. If you're the one needs the time, then you say it,' Marilyn said.

'You're right. You're like, what, a little fairy. And I'm not good with words for women, so I may as well say it like I would to a horse. I like horses very much. I love them, in actual fact. It'd be fair to say that if you feel half what I feel having had time in your company, without knives or friends or family's intervention, you'd be loath to go in. But they all got us to here and we should give them some time. There's a good roast on in there and I've only one corner of my stomach filled.'

'I can only do peas,' she warned him.

'I can do an egg, toast, a pot of tea. We won't starve, so.'

They were all starving waiting on dinner and couldn't even pretend to have a conversation. Sean looked as ill at ease now as he'd looked comfortable with Marilyn in the shed and she realised already that it was easy for them to be alone, no matter how unusual the circumstances.

'Everyone,' Marilyn said, looking at Julie, whose lipstick had teeth-marks in it, 'this is Sean.'

'We know that.'

In a kitchen that hadn't seen a man at the table for almost fifty years, he seemed to have always been there. Grace had come for dinner with Theresa. She gave Marilyn a single nod and looked at her cup on the sideboard.

After dinner, the talk turned to music. 'Julie tells me you play piano?' Sean smiled as he said it. He could barely stop himself from smiling all through the meal. For him it was a confirmed case of love at second sight. Whatever this slip of a woman wanted, he would find a way of getting it for her. His mother was right, it was this simple, once it was the right woman.

'Yes.' Marilyn looked straight at him, her glasses exchanged for contacts. The colour of her eyes took his breath away. 'But not just now if that's all right with you.'

'And you like Nina? Isn't she the best?' He spoke to her as if there was no one else in the room.

'Yes, to my ears anyway. She trained at Juilliard but they wouldn't let her be a concert pianist.' Marilyn spoke with an enthusiasm the others had rarely heard. 'I have some club recordings, from Paris, they're rare. Would you like to hear them?'

'I would love to.' Sean smiled as he answered.

'They're up in my room?' She said it as a question because she didn't want the others to think she was being rude in spiriting him away. But right now all she could think of was being alone with him. The only place she could think of where that could happen was her bedroom, her sanctuary. She ignored the looks on their faces: he has won you over, they said.

'Why don't we go out ourselves, Julie?' Elizabeth's tone said they would be celebrating.

'Welcome to my world. Sorry.' She kicked herself for saying that word again. 'It's bland. I never know what to put on the walls.' She put on Nina.

He sat on the edge of Marilyn's bed, as she imagined her father did, and seemed to fill the whole room with living colour.

'Tell me about yourself, it's been mostly about me during dinner.'

It was gone midnight when she stopped. She held nothing back, but for imaginary fathers. He wasn't ready for the hallucinations just yet. She told him about her piano, fear of the future, sliding scale, secretive mother, warlord granny, amazing aunt and mysterious wife, incapable best friend who had done what she could never do – take a chance on a stranger. She gave him warts and all. She needed him to know her, because she was sure Sean would disappear because of the dream-like way in which he'd arrived. He stayed on watching and listening and picking up her hand now and again.

'Well,' he whispered, 'that's the kind of answer I wanted. I want to hear more, but I have to go.'

'Can I come too?' she asked, thinking to herself, If you're going to change, you may as well do it overnight, or on the same one. You may as well drive off into it, if he wants you.

'I don't know, Marilyn, my house is rough and ready.'

'Isn't any man's?'

'I suppose.'

Grace and Theresa had waited after everyone was gone.

'Well, sister, you've made great progress. Off on the rest of your mission tomorrow, to find the last half. If you can have three halves,' Theresa smiled. 'Are you ready?'

'All ready.'

'What are you going to tell them?' Grace asked.

'Nothing. I'm leaving a note is all I'm doing. It would be a sad thing if we can't do what we like, at our age. Now I'm up to bed, you let yourselves out.'

Both felt for her. Not that they'd say it, not that she'd let them. Soft. Brigid heard the door close as Grace and Theresa went out. She heard them talk to each other in low voices as they walked down the path in a tone of intimacy, a warmth and privilege to it that was the prerogative of lifelong lovers.

All of a sudden she felt alone, with pain and death coming for her. She reached into the locker, for the smiling family in the picture offered her the comfort they always did.

'I just sent my little granddaughter off with a stranger,

after happiness. I hope it comes easy to her for the rest of her life.'

The lady came to sit on the edge of the bed.

'Now don't be expecting too much of me tomorrow, I'm only human, not like you,' Brigid whispered as she drifted off to sleep in safe company.

In the pub Julie cried with Elizabeth, said she didn't know why she was.

'You did such a good thing for her. Even Brigid had to admit it. It was brusque, but it was a thank-you.' Elizabeth was watching her. 'I'm wondering about why you were so unselfish with such a lovely man. If he came into my company first, I'd have been tempted to keep him.'

'You weren't a witness to the circumstances. He took me home after the Eileen Whelan incident.' Elizabeth allowed Julie to be honest. Brigid and Marilyn seemed to want her to be dishonest, just like everyone else. 'Even if I could have had him, I'd be no good for him, he deserves better than me.'

'Well, I wouldn't say that. But I do believe in the fact that if you do something wonderful, you get something wonderful in return. Life is kind as well as cruel, Julie.'

By the time Elizabeth got home it was after midnight. Too late to ring Tony. She wasn't pleased to see her mother had left the number, in bold digits, by the phone. A note underneath read, 'No excuses. He works nights.'

She tried the mobile number and was relieved when it was powered off. She chose not to leave a message.

Over in Loughlin's Wood, Mick and Colin came in from their NA meeting.

'Yes, lads, it's housework,' Tony said, washing the kitchen floor.

'Did she ring?' Mick asked. Colin had given up on it, but Mick held himself responsible for the resurrection of Tony's hopes.

'No.' Tony leaned back on his knees. 'But she will. Check my mobile.'

Mick picked it up. 'It's out of juice, Tony, just like you for not having powered it at a time like this.'

'She'll call, I know it,' Tony was saying weeks later, when Mick and Colin no longer brought the subject up.

17

On Saturday 6 January, the Feast of the Epiphany, Brigid caught six a.m. Mass and came home to pull her packed suitcase out from under the bed. She left a note on the table:

Gone to Trabolgan for a few days with Aunty Theresa. Please refer to fridge for meal order. Make sure Marilyn gets her meat.

Theresa arrived, with Grace, just after eight, when Elizabeth had gone to work. She had taken to working Saturdays, so she could study also during the week.

'What are you doing here, Grace?' Brigid didn't want anyone but Theresa on this trip.

'Just to wish you bon voyage. I have a present for you, you ingrate.'

'It's no holiday and I don't need anything!' Brigid's nerves were on edge.

Grace pressed a package into her hands. 'Open it when you get there. And remember – you don't travel on the day of Epiphany for nothing.'

The flight attendant knew Brigid Monroe was a first-time flyer and was over-solicitous towards her.

'If that one keeps this up until Greece, then I'll have to get out that door and take my chances swimming,' Brigid snapped.

'She's only helping, Brigid.' Theresa put her paper down. She hadn't read past the first line of any article. 'Take the flecking pills sitting in your hand,' Theresa said, using her sister's own manufactured swear word.

'Those pills are for emergencies.'

'What would you define as an emergency?' Theresa stopped, realising Brigid Monroe was keeping the plane out of the water with rosaries and willpower and her customary ill-tempered reaction to anything that might be considered as assistance. It was going to be a long five hours.

'Will it be hot in Greece?' Brigid smoothed her duck-egg-blue skirt. It was the suit she had married John Joe in. She had chosen it for its single-breasted lapels and simple lines, knowing there would be very few times she could afford anything as good. It had fitted every year and almost every occasion of her life since, to the point where it was even fashionable again, after half a century.

'You needn't worry, it'll be cold and grey, just as you like it.' Theresa's prediction proved true. Athens was ten degrees and poured upon with all the rain God could spare from Ireland. Kristos was carrying a sign, with one word: Monroe. He smiled on seeing them, not needing to be told.

'Ladies, Athens and the Faltaits family welcome you. Please come with me, the car is waiting. My wife is there. Today is our big Christmas and we invite you to the house, for the dinner of Elena.'

'Are we not forgetting something?' Brigid asked.

He stopped trying to take the trolley from Theresa. 'I am sorry.' He inclined his head.

'I have three secrets to tell you, of my heart. My first husband had all of my heart and broke it. My family is all that matters to me, that's second. Last and most important, my greatest fear is love. Love for a man, and without consideration, I won't overcome it. I'm not as scared of dying as I am of love.' She twisted her lips together. 'This is why I'm here.'

Kristos took her hand. 'My father is the most willing to help of all men. He is also afraid, having lost my mother. You will be happy to know each other, Mrs Monroe.'

18

The farmyard was at the end of a long laneway that looked like the Celts had made it and no one had bothered to maintain it since.

'House' would not be the word she would have used to describe his living arrangements – 'hazardous', 'hovel-like', 'basic' and 'filthy' came to mind. She'd seen cleaner public toilets.

There were darts, golf tees, nuts and bolts in every drawer and debris on every surface. Enamel mugs and cracked plates were scattered everywhere. A pile of *Racing Posts* had mice nibbles. The sofa was grubby and the kitchen table was covered in what looked like horse feed and handwritten training programmes. The fireplace was a saving grace. She noticed he cleaned it out well, since that was the man's job in any traditional house, but anything that was traditionally a woman's was out. The stereo, radio and television were the only things that gave it away as belonging in this century.

Sean watched Marilyn try not to be horrified. He could see her lips curling in and the tendons on her neck standing out. He could hear his mother giving out stink to him for not being less of a slob. He knew his sisters, all house-proud, would be down on him like a ton of bricks too. It was his own fault for never letting them help him out, as they asked to. But then it was also the fault of the five women in his family for never letting him lift a finger for himself.

What do you expect if you ironed my socks for me? I

haven't a clue and this is the result. The woman who made the impression on me now has the worst impression of me.

Well, you'd better get on with apologising to her, he heard his mother saying, as if she was in the room.

'I'm sorry for the state of the place. Will you have tea?'

'Don't worry.' Marilyn smiled at him and he could see it was a brave smile. He was grateful for it. 'I've seen far worse,' she lied.

'You don't see it when you're here on your own. I'm busy with the outside, you see. Will you have tea?' And almost as if to back him up, a loud noise came from the stable. 'I'll have to go out.'

Given that the place was years old, most likely haunted and that there was nowhere to actually sit down, Marilyn decided on going with him. One of the reasons she didn't like horses was that they were so big, but so, she reasoned, was he. The stables were arranged into three blocks. They went straight to the building that was smallest and furthest away from the house.

'Delaney,' Sean sighed, 'will I ever be done with you?' He turned to Marilyn. 'It's my isolation unit, where I keep the latest addition with the oldest hand. The old boy is Noble, and the new filly is Delaney. She's been here six months and we've felt every day of it. Noble's on extra food, he's doing so much work.'

He was pulling back a bolt to reveal what sounded like a screaming banshee, with a cudgel in its hand for company. She was the Marilyn version of a racehorse, a bit small for the job.

'I know, she's only just more than a pony, fourteen and three-quarter hands. I'd say there was go in the mother, an ex-racer, then a school horse, would you believe? You'd want to see this one jump. She's half kangaroo,' Sean whispered. At that point she proved it, rearing up against the stable wall.

The horse on the other side, as big as she was small, was backed away into a corner, the whites of his eyes showing, ears flat back, nostrils flared.

The cement stable floor was cleaner than both Brigid's brasses and Sean's kitchen table. Hay was piled high and fresh. It was clear he devoted all his energies to where the animals lived and not where he did. She'd have to rectify this. She buried herself behind the door, and wasn't asked to come in.

'Delaney,' Sean said. Her head wheeled round. If she had been a dragon, fire would have come out of her mouth, but instead she grunted and her tail clamped between her legs. 'It's because you heard the cars, isn't it?'

Noble, the big bay, was whinnying, sticking his head out of his box, trying to get at Sean. But Sean was focused on Delaney.

'You're priceless, you are, you know he'll only let you have it when he sees you.' Delaney tossed her head at this, as if she were agreeing. Marilyn could see her stable walls were covered with sponge foam, but her kicking at it had loosened it in parts. A padded cell.

'He's only next door,' Sean coaxed.

Delaney was having none of it. Her tail rose high and her neck arched. All her muscles seemed to stand out at once, and she began a dance, picking her hooves off the ground and stamping, throwing her head from side to side. Sean looked at Marilyn, then back at her.

'Okay, just for tonight.' He spoke softly and evenly. The bolt went back. She let out a high whinny and darted at the door.

'No, that's not the way. Slowly, or not at all.' Sean's tone was enough to calm her and then he opened Noble's stable door. If Marilyn had been Noble, she would have bolted, but instead he nickered, a low, soft sound from a horse's belly that tells you he sees you as a friend. Delaney turned into his stall, not an edge of ground wasted, not a moment lost.

'Now then, the pair of you.' Sean bolted up. Delaney shuddered and leaned into Noble, who closed his eyes with the patience of a tired saint, having first nipped her as admonishment.

'You see the way she got in there? That's the magic of her.' Sean walked but made no attempt to touch Marilyn, addressing the night more than her. 'She's fast and knows exactly where to put herself, but she's the divil to get to work. I've had her in with Noble since she got here. Out in the field at first, it was still the fine weather. He chased her round three days solid, teaching her manners. She's bright, but her spirit's got in the way with all the mishandling. She won't even sleep without him. We pad out her stall, but you can see what she did to that. She heard the cars tonight and knew she could kick up.'

'You should have stayed with her, stuck it out, I wouldn't have minded.'

'But I would have, Marilyn. And if I can't give you time tonight, when I only know you, it doesn't give us much of a chance, now does it? This is going to be hard,' he said, not feeling the need to hide.

'Hard times are better than lonely ones,' she told him.

Sean made tea and Marilyn tried to ignore the limescale floating in the top of her mug. In her holdall she had her travel-size bottle of Domestos, two changes of knickers, six of socks, two of shoes, jeans, fleece, waterproof, laptop and mobile satellite unit should she need to contact work, a first-aid kit, a portable CD player and some CDs, toothbrush, razor, and Immac. But she had left her floss behind, for the first time in her adult life.

She didn't have wellies and in the middle of winter in a

farmyard it was like going out naked. She was trying to ignore her wet, mucky trainers, trying to find a way of showing an interest in what he was doing and wishing she had listened to work colleagues more closely.

'Will you have to break the horse? Isn't that what they call it?'

He looked at her, and she could see he was saddened. 'That horse is long broken. It's fixing I have to do now.'

'I'm sorry, I know I should know. But I haven't the first idea about them, other than they're four times the size of me and I'm scared of them.'

'Fear of them is good, they can kill you. Respect of them is better. When you've spent time around them, when you're easier with them, it'll be that you feel.' She loved the implication.

'How did you decide on her?'

'Horse trading' – Sean smiled into his cup – 'is a law unto itself. There's more risk in it than betting. You try to buy a horse with the best legs you can possibly get. They have to be pretty well made. The mind of them, that might be worked on, but you don't try and buy a skinny-malinky horse with little legs.'

'A bit like me?'

'Nothing like you, Marilyn. For a small woman, you're very well made. But it's not a romantic way of putting things, is it?'

He was an anorak on horses as much as she was on figures. After a few back-and-forths, a silence grew and then they were unfamiliar with each other, and for a split second she was scared.

'Marilyn.' He said the name as he would always say it, like he would never shorten it. 'Do you want to go to bed now? There's a couch for me, in the room beyond.'

'I thought you might stay in the same bed as me?' She felt

herself redden in saying it. He remembered Julie. He hadn't known then, he told himself. 'I don't want to stay in it without you. To be honest, I'm a bit scared. I'm not a country girl.'

The sheets were appalling. He showed her a spare set, which were worse.

'I'm sorry, I'm no use at this kind of thing.'

'Well, I am. I have a blanket in my car, so if you don't mind we'll use that instead of the duvet.'

She could have died happy in the cold bunker bedroom that night with Teflon cobwebs. Beforehand she had to listen to horse pillow talk – he talked to ease her until she wished he would stop. She didn't know how to put her mouth on his, so instead she listened to how when horses are at full gallop there's only one leg on the ground at a time. 'That's why when you buy you have to pay most attention to the legs and what's in their eyes. The horse and I will work out most other things in between.

'Will we go slow?' he asked then. 'Isn't it best to get to know each other?'

She knew he was right, and settled for the warmth of him.

He lay awake for a short while, feeling the warmth of her, a drug to his lonely skin. At the corners of his happiness a guilt chewed, for not being entirely honest about how he had come to pursue Marilyn. Then, in sleep, she turned and pressed into him, and he knew he would be satisfied to live with that dishonesty for as long as he could feel her do that. She was too vulnerable, he could see it as well as others couldn't, he saw too her feelings for him were as new and strong as his were for her. To tell her would be to crush a flower. There was no reason but the alleviation of his own conscience.

Are you protecting her or your own interest in her? he asked himself. He found the answer was both.

*

174

He came into the kitchen from the yard. She was putting on the kettle, having first descaled it.

'I lit the range,' he smiled. 'It might be too dirty for the kettle now.'

'Did Julie tell you to wear that?' She pulled the rib of his jumper, amazed to find she was grinning at six in the morning. The tiredness at the back of that grin was about to be dealt with by coffee.

'No, I'm afraid all my jumpers are as bad.'

'Well, you can forget whatever else she said, because I'm not using those rules any more. I've got new ones.' That got her a kiss. A kiss from a bear was a big sensation. Sean looked into her eyes for a long time.

'I've a cheek bringing you here, and getting you up at this hour.'

'I invited myself, and you didn't get me up.' She wasn't going to lie in that squalor on her own.

Sean winced at the coffee she'd handed him before making a porter-strength tea. Their first difference, left unchanged in meeting each other. Everything else became different. He told her about his parents. The crash had happened five minutes' drive from this house, which had once been theirs.

'At least I had both of mine for a long time. When did your father die?'

'He didn't. He might have, I don't know. I never knew him.'

'I'm sorry.'

'So am I.'

'Well, you've a good enough mother for two. She's got a knack of making you feel comfortable without forcing comfort on you. And intelligent, you both have a good helping of that.'

It was like he was talking about someone she didn't know. Just as when Tony had talked about her. She wondered if

175

Elizabeth had called him and knew well she wouldn't have. Elizabeth moved slower than time. And she thought of Brigid. Marilyn didn't want to think about her being sick, she didn't want anything to encroach on this time. She asked, 'How did Delaney get her name?'

'The owner was Delaney. Her registered name's Lady Delicia, but Delaney stuck because of the song.'

'Which song?'

'You know, the old Irish one.' He sang it gently, but she could hear the baritone was more than good:

> *Delaney had a donkey*
> *Everyone admired*
> *Permanently lazy*
> *And permanently tired.*

'Poor horse, to be known for that.'

'That reputation made her a small chance. I only paid two thousand for her. The work in her is costing far more. Six months and she's still stuck to Noble. He was a good runner in his day and his day was long ago. And I think it'll be all right, but there's a long way to go before it is, and no way of getting there quick.' He was leaning forward now. If she hadn't been there he'd be talking in the same manner to the wall, it was so much on his mind. 'She's not bred to be the horse that she is. Her father was a flat stallion, broke through the fence to get at the mare. She'll get going, though, and after she gets going the people will take her to heart.'

He sounded like he needed convincing of this himself. She couldn't help, so she stood up to make him some toast, which she burned, not knowing how to do it on the range. He took over with the next batch, still talking. 'She's four going on five. If something goes wrong we'd have her for breeding. She's a chestnut, with that star right in the centre of her forehead. My gut tells me she's that, but my head says I'm a loser. Maybe she hasn't the breeding on paper, but still, she was bred pretty good and the parts of her ancestry papers where you get good horses you get a real good one. If she catches up, she's the horse that will do everything right. She'll learn real quick if I could get her going.'

'And if not? If she doesn't learn?'

'Well, the fella with me when I was buying her told me it's not a horse whisperer she needs, but a silencer on the end of a gun. It won't happen, Marilyn,' he said, putting his hand on hers. 'That's a little horse with a lot going for her. It's probably the same as people going to buy clothes. In the back of your mind you know what you want but if someone told you to tell them exactly what it was, you just can't come out with it. Until you see it. I saw it.

'A good horse is an intelligent one. People don't give them the credit that they deserve. A good horse has an awful lot of brains. They know when they're doing right and wrong. I have some nice horses, but I have none like her. She has two of the three things you need – determination and ability. We just have to give her the third – the will to win.

'Most days she's on her own doing the work, but now and then we persuade one or two of the others to go with her. When we're out at the gallop – the place I work the horses,' he said, seeing he had to explain to her, 'she'll never give up at any time. If they go off early she'll wear them out and they'll fall away. If they hang back she'll speed them up to get it the way she wants it. But as soon as I take Noble away she wants Noble. And I can't even get her into the horsebox, let alone to a racetrack. So there's still more work than I've time for.' He rubbed his hands across his eyes and she could see he was tired, even before his day began properly.

'How did she get so bad, Sean?'

'They left her with her mother long after she was a

weanling. Then they saw she had a spark, speed, and they took her away too quick and she hasn't been right since. She's just looking for her mother is all she's doing. She associates anything bad happening to her, like being over-raced and worked to the bone, with being taken away from a mammy. From the day I put her with Noble, she adopted him as her new mammy. So I'm stuck with knowing what to do. It's slow or it's not at all with this one. I'd better go and do it, or I'll never go out.'

'I'll come with you.'

'Once you stay well back.'

He didn't need to advise her twice. She had planned to start cleaning, but there'd be a whole three days for that. Marilyn Monroe was going to have a long weekend. On Monday, she was going to phone at nine to say she wouldn't be in and they wouldn't question it, given she'd worked the holidays when she shouldn't have. It would go around the whole building that the robot had phoned in sick. Some wise individual would leave a tin of Castrol GTX on her desk, with a 'get well soon' card.

As they left the kitchen to go out in the yard, she saw his post on the table, most of it unopened, all of it bills.

'Your second name isn't Monroe, is it?'

Sean nodded. 'I hope it doesn't cause you too much heartache?'

'If there is,' she smiled, 'there's not much I can do about it now.'

19

Kristos had wanted them to stay over in Athens, and so had Theresa, but Brigid had insisted.

'We're not here for a holiday. I have business to attend to.'

'How far is it to the island?' Theresa wanted to know. They'd been travelling since morning and Brigid was far from well.

'Three hours by car, two by ferry, no more, perhaps less. Elena has cooked, so we must eat, then catch the evening sail.' Elena clapped her hands when Kristos translated. 'She is happy to go, we always go to our home island for the feast day.'

'You should have told us.' Brigid shook her head. 'We'd have come another day.'

'This was the day God sent you.' Kristos pressed his thumb into the table like it was a calendar. 'We will come back again in the evening of tomorrow, with or without you. But one day in Skyros, for us, is worth one month in Athens.'

Elena spoke no English, but her welcome needed no words. Brigid recognised that the food she served them was plain and honest without being fancy. Once she put the herbed lamb in her mouth, she knew it was the finest she'd ever tasted. 'This would convert my Elizabeth to proper eating.'

'She can see you like,' Kristos smiled. Elena spoke rapidly to him, pulling at his sleeve. 'Elena finds it strange that women would come from so far away, the advertisement was in Greek, for Greeks. We never expect this.'

'Has anyone else replied?' Brigid was worried into asking.

'No one who I would wish for my father. Many women looking for land and an old man to take it from.'

The ferry was bobbing up and down like a cork in the high wind. At least the rain had stopped and the sunshine was brilliant, though without warmth. Brigid held onto the rail and looked at the horizon for the entire journey, at Theresa's advice, to avoid seasickness.

'Well, sister, you wanted big waves, you got them,' Theresa said beside her.

Brigid watched for a sign of land. This could have waited until morning, but she couldn't. Fear was rising. In the flat in Athens she had deliberately avoided looking at photographs. If Kristos's dead mother was the woman with the headscarf, she would have been too afraid to carry on. Nikolas had no advance warning of their arrival, not having a telephone.

'It might be that he would even want us to leave again, immediately,' Brigid wondered aloud. Kristos insisted he would show them hospitality.

In last night's dream the woman in the headscarf had been as nervous and expectant as she was, rubbing her hands together, pulling her palms along the sides of her face.

'If it's not as you intended,' Brigid had told her in her dream, 'then something else that was meant to happen will happen instead. Now quit peppering, you're making me even more nervous.' Her nightly visitor had seemed reassured with this.

January, a long way still to come out of winter. The whole island was celebrating the Epiphany. But Nikolas Faltaits was alone, cutting back his vines in preparation for spring. From his patio he could see the ferry arriving, as it did twice each day, once in the morning and once in the evening. It was a mile out from the harbour of Achilli at Skyros when he put down the ball of twine and picked up his hat. He got into his truck, knowing the value of feelings over reason, knowing this was the sailing his wife told him about in his dreams.

She was coming down the gangplank behind Kristos. She had dove-grey hair and a high forehead and wore a blue too cold for her pale skin. Nikolas knew that when they got back to his farmhouse, he must make her rest, since she was suffering. Before he even met her he knew he was going to lose her. He had done this before, he knew how it should be done. This did not make him any less afraid. He consoled himself with the thought that one day he would have two women to meet in paradise.

As the boat docked Theresa saw a small pottery shop to one side, a balconied hotel where they were due to stay, literally a stone's throw from the landing station, two canopied restaurants and a provisions shop. A road wound up the hill and whitewashed houses dotted the terraced farming land of pencil-thin cypress trees and clusters of olive groves. At the top of this road, at the very brow of the hill, Kristos pointed to the Faltaits farmland.

All the buildings at the harbour were whitewashed. The doors were either plain wood studded with copper fastenings or painted turquoise, some finely carved with geometric designs, indicating that the days of Byzantine weren't dead in Skyros. It remembered everything.

Brigid could see nothing. He was here, waiting. She knew even before his son shouted out.

He stood apart from the main throng of greeters, mostly there to pick up relatives. They were the only non-Skyrians on board. His son ran forward and embraced him, which the father accepted warmly, but his eyes were on Brigid. Elena was pressing a package of lamb into his hand, but he was urging her to hold it for him until they got to the house.

181

Kristos began to explain to his father in Greek, but Nikolas held a hand up. He knew the woman for who she was and why she was there. There was no need for the door of Brigid's dreams – it had opened the moment she'd landed.

'My father says you will not stay in the hotel, he keeps the house clean, but not beautiful as when my mother lived there. For this he apologises. And for not preparing Christmas feast, as all other houses on the island do. He is alone, he would not come to us in Athens, he hides from festivity, since Nyphi's death. Nyphi, my mother.'

He was tall and used height to his advantage. His features were all proud and definite, none hiding behind another. His eyes were almost black, his skin paler than his son's. His hair curled still, even in greyness. The people moved around him in a way that implied they deferred to him.

'My father is like the ancient king Lycomedes, of milk skin,' Kristos smiled. 'Here they say he is his ghost. He apologises for not having English.'

'There's no need.' Brigid held out her hand and he shook it. They led the group off the pier, side by side.

She felt it inappropriate to be wearing the suit she had married her husband in. Here, she could see, was a man who would have made her life, and her, quite different. It was a shame it was coming so close to the end. It was a blessing it was coming at all.

Nikolas took them through the double-door front entrance. Theresa saw the tears in Kristos's eyes. 'He has not used them since my mother was carried for burial,' Kristos said.

Inside Nikolas took four steel pots with decorated ceramic handles out of the cupboard and put them on the stove. He had an earthen jar with a cork lid and heaped out coffee. Theresa sighed with pleasure. She swung both ways where coffee and tea were concerned.

'I'm sorry, Nikolas, I can't drink that,' Brigid said, through Kristos.

He nodded and reached in for another jar. Into it he put some herbs, repeating the same word over and over.

'Mountain tea,' Kristos interpreted, 'and honey he is putting in it, for you.'

She put it to her lips. It was a degree warmer than tepid and smelled of the summers she'd never had the chance to enjoy. The lump in her throat seemed to dissolve for a few moments and she took her first unhindered breath in what seemed like months. It was all she could do not to lie down and sleep.

Nikolas took her hand and led her through the door she had seen in her dream, except now she had no fear of it. She was in the main bedroom. She was here to rest.

'What's he doing with my sister?' Theresa half stood.

'The room he has not slept in since my mother died.' Kristos couldn't speak any more. He had his own memories to deal with, and went outside to be with them.

Nikolas watched, from the chair where he had slept, as soundly as her. For the first time in seven years he had not dreamt about the boat. Instead, Nyphi had been busy getting things ready for the new arrival, showing him where everything was, before putting on her headscarf as she closed the door, blowing him a kiss, knowing he now had the strength to let her leave.

'When this woman is sick you can look after her. When she dies you can mourn her. Not in the way you have mourned me, Nikolas; you will go back to being in the world, being a man who can go outside, see people, sit in the homes of others. You are too big a man for such a small existence, and she will show you this,' Nyphi said to him with her eyes.

His wife had been a terrible one to win, since she'd had no idea of her own strength and had been afraid of his. She had been very young, twenty-three, when he had been in his late thirties. She was the only woman he had met he could consider marrying. When she had died before him he had refused to let her pass in the same way that he had refused to give up on pursuing her as a bride.

The woman lying in this bed now, where Nyphi had died, knew all of her strength and used it. It had contributed to this great illness she was suffering from. He could see the disappointment that came from loving the wrong man.

Now, he was determined, she would not know that disappointment and she would give him the strength he needed to let go of a strong love.

Brigid recognised where she was and fell back into her pillow, having nodded to him. It was his cue to leave.

The sun found Nikolas's patio, which was sheltered and overlooked the sea.

'In summer' – Kristos was sitting with Theresa – 'there is jasmine, bougainvillea, flowers everywhere. We have sometimes grown orchids. My father loves his garden. The soil is stony, limed, you say, but he can make things grow. In summer the poppies take over, many wildflowers, whole meadows he keeps, just for the flowers. He knows what they have, to make things better in you, sicknesses. When I make enough money I will leave Athens and come here to do what he does. The teacher at the school retires, and we will come here, for this job.'

Theresa could hear Elena in the kitchen. She'd already been to the neighbours for bread and baklava, honey and yoghurt. The bakery and dairy had been closed for the holidays. They had been lucky to catch the ferry yesterday.

Nikolas would have been perfect for Elizabeth, Theresa thought. What was Brigid doing taking him over, especially when she was so convinced she had little future left? Would she not have been better giving all this to her daughter?

It was exactly what Brigid Monroe was thinking as she looked out her bedroom window, the window that had given Nyphi many hours of pleasure. The ferry was leaving the harbour. When she'd arrived last night it had been cold, but Nikolas knew how to shelter. Now, she was witnessing a hint of summer. She knew that Elizabeth would find this place a paradise. Why was she taking the opportunity for herself, as if she had no choice?

It was the look of him, the way he held his hand out – I know you.

But the truth of the matter was that she was a seventy year old woman with cancer. No tomorrow was certain. She put her hand to her throat automatically. It was like she had never felt the weakness. Maybe the doctors were right, nothing felt strange. If anything she felt hungry.

An old mind plays tricks, she thought as she started to get dressed. Outside she could hear the others talking, eating a breakfast she was looking forward to. Nikolas was banging about in the sitting room and the small lean-to kitchen that had been built onto the house. He was a DIY man, then. John Joe knew nothing about nails, but he was familiar with crucifying. She shook the bitter thought off and took the photograph out of her bag. Last night had been the first in years she hadn't kissed it. That nightly ritual was the place where she left her vulnerability and now it was unavoidable, everywhere, falling in late love with a man who met her off the boat.

She opened the bedroom door to find Nikolas, full of purpose in emptying out all the cupboards and putting things on display, mostly on the conical-shaped hearth on the wooden plugs she'd noticed last night.

'*Skamnia, skamnia!*' He gestured to her to sit on one of the carved stools he took out of the corner shelf.

'This stool' – Kristos came into the room followed by Theresa and Elena – 'is a *skamnia.*'

185

'I gathered that,' Brigid said in a gentle voice, a gentleness that would come to be her daughter's most defining quality. She surprised herself. It was like listening to the seventeen-year-old girl who had fallen in love with John Joe Monroe. Kristos and Theresa came to sit beside her. Nikolas put a wooden box on her lap and gestured for her to open it.

Inside there were small hand-carved seals and spoons and thread spinners. Nikolas pointed to his own hands, as having made them. On the shelves in the hearth Nikolas was placing vases, plates, bowls, glassware.

'This area is called the *aloni*, and the fireplace is the *fgou*,' Kristos advised. 'It is the most important part of the Skyrian house. All have beauty and use. Many hundreds of years old. The glass is Venetian, the ceramics, some are Byzantine. A Skyrian house is a museum. You are seeing something unique in Greece. Our wealth, our culture and history, is all in this place. We are the leaders of what you would call folk art, always the artists have come here. And some never leave. The poet Rupert Brooke is buried here, they say Homer lies here. Homer's hero – Achilles – he sails for Troy from this harbour. Theseus, the great hero, he was a Skyrian. Neoptolemos, son of Achilles, winner of the Trojan war – also Skyrian. We are famous in Greece.'

His father was gesturing impatiently at him to explain the embroidered cloths he placed on the table, sewn with fine orange thread.

'It's all wonderful,' Theresa breathed.

Brigid whispered so Kristos wouldn't hear, 'These are the things she showed me.'

Nikolas went to the kitchen and came back with plates. Kristos's talk ran to keep up with him. 'The plates my father has now are from Rhodes, the dishes come from Kastri.' He was breaking with the excitement of seeing all the things that had been part of his childhood and those of his ancestors. 'Life!' he cried. 'Life is coming to the Faltaits.'

Nikolas was talking now, gesturing to the outside: 'Nikolas!' Then, pointing to the artefacts inside, 'Nyphi, Nyphi.'

'He says my mother did this, and his mother before her, brought these things to here. He says his precious things are outside. For a Skyrian woman the house is her place, she makes it beautiful, spends the family money on all you can see, as—' He couldn't find the word.

'Inheritance.' Brigid found it for him. She thought of what she was leaving Elizabeth and Marilyn: a bought council house and a few thousand euro, saved over a lifetime. Nothing as personal as this. There wasn't even jewellery. Anything for herself had been a luxury she couldn't afford. She'd been too caught up in the everyday to see what was important. Music, Marilyn's music. Elizabeth's garden. A man she didn't know a day was showing her what she hadn't seen in a lifetime. She wanted to go to her room and cry. The room that had been Nyphi's.

Nikolas gestured to what he had put on display, then threw open the bedroom door and pointed to the bed, the view from the house and finally, his arm making a wide circle, indicated everything. He put a hand to his breast and his eyes on Brigid.

Kristos interpreted when he got down on his knees in front of her, speaking as he would to a lamb, lifting her hands.

'He says my mother knows you are the right woman to replace her, and she has told him to take the treasures out, to make the house for a woman again.'

'Grace said this would happen, Brigid,' Theresa said.

'If you mention those flecking tea leaves now!' Brigid stood, but she was smiling as she said it. Everyone in the room now understood – they'd had a part.

It was up to Brigid and Nikolas now. Brigid's first act was

to go to her room and put on Grace's present – a turquoise two-piece in chiffon, to replace the duck-egg blue. Nikolas smiled and inclined his head when she came back to the room. Theresa cheered, Kristos and Elena smiled. Brigid inclined her head, once.

By the end of lunchtime, Kristos was saying he had to go back to Athens that evening.

'I'm going with them,' Theresa said, putting a hand on Brigid's arm. 'I'll be back Sunday, to get you. If you're coming.'

The weakness wasn't mentioned when everyone left to go to the harbour. Brigid and Nikolas drove back up the hill in his old truck, which had no dashboard and a cushion where the seat had collapsed. She had a house to get on with. Nyphi's cloth house-gloves were a perfect match for her hand.

She cleaned all the artefacts with warm water and nothing else, they in need of it after so long in storage, and he cooked more lamb, made potatoes, green beans, a mixture of lentils and split peas.

'It could be a dinner back home, Nikolas, only tastier, even the yellow stuff – I've seen my Elizabeth eat that.'

He showed her the calendar, indicated Lent, shook his head at the lamb.

'No meat for Lent? That's a throwback. I'll do the same this year, then, in Ireland. It looks like I'll be eating my daughter's food. A first, I can tell you.'

Brigid knew it wasn't what was wanted, staying. She had to go home for others. Her mission wasn't completed. By the time she died she wanted Elizabeth and Marilyn to have their heart's desire too.

They had seven days to enjoy together, one for each of her decades.

20

Marilyn followed Sean as he led Delaney and Noble up through two fields to the two-furlong circular gallop, made of specially coated woodchip. Beside it was a steep hill, of five furlongs. The grass gallop.

'She used to buck and kick all the way. I had to lead her in the end, keep long reins either side of her. Her old saddle was right over a bad part of her back, so she gave hell about that. A bonesetter got her right, then we had to get this saddle specially made, only a light thing it is and it's raised over the vertebrae giving the trouble. Saddles are like gloves, they have to fit the horse. But Delaney got used to them hurting her and that's why we don't ride her to the gallop, she gets all up about it.'

'So what's different when she gets there?'

'The gallop, Marilyn. She's a racer all right.'

'But you say she hated racing.'

'No, she just used herself up before she even got to the start line. And she lost her nerve. Now she gums to get going. Her times are all first class, even with me on her back. I make her look like the donkey in the song, I'm that big on her, but she won't have anyone else.'

Marilyn was holding the stopwatch, the horses' turnout blankets for after the workout and a bag of carrots, which she hid on strict instruction. On a signal she went ahead to open the gate. Delaney started dancing, then paused for a moment, turning to look at Marilyn, before trotting through.

Once Sean got to the railing she stood stock-still and waited for Sean to mount her. It did look ridiculous. He glanced over at Marilyn, shrugging: *What can I do?* Then he slapped Noble's rump and off he cantered, a pacemaker, for one circuit. As soon as Delaney and Sean overtook him, he peeled off and stood under a tree, head down, munching.

For twenty minutes Sean reined Delaney in, something she wasn't happy about. Marilyn suddenly knew what 'champing at the bit' meant. She fought the restraint the entire time. Then Sean leaned into her and rose out of the saddle. She took off like her feet were feathers. They lapped four times before heading up the big hill. Up until that point Delaney hadn't lost pace, and Marilyn saw that she lost the title in the uphill effort. The ground wasn't frozen, but it was hard and the sound of her hooves, a steady rhythm as each leg hit separately, echoed in the still morning air, her grunts of effort magnified.

If she had taken off like Pegasus at the brow of the hill and started floating through the cloud cover, Marilyn wouldn't have been surprised. Her ears were flat back, her nostrils flared and her breath charged out of them, the steam clouds like speech, intent, fire.

She was the most extraordinary sight Marilyn had ever seen. She couldn't understand how she could have ignored the beauty of a horse in full flight for so long. All Delaney's edginess and madness slipped away and she became poetry. Sean pulled her up only when her head dropped. Her withers twitched – she was satisfied. They eased off to canter, then finally walked. At that moment Sean clicked for Noble, who fell in beside them. After a few laps walking Sean jumped off and rubbed her down, praising her all the time. 'Good girl, good girl.'

Then he let her go off with Noble.

Sean came over the gate, vaulting it like a boy. She smiled at this action, knowing there was a bit of him showing off to her.

'Look at her, a thin white line at the top of each hoof. That's known as a coronet, a little princess, she is. And she knows it – look at her head, held to one side, well done, girl, a good girl you are. Hand us the turnout blanket, Marilyn.' He leapt over the gate again to put it on.

'The straps stop it from getting twisted when the horse rolls about, and watch this one, she's like a lamb at play in the paddock, it's like she's done no work at all. She has great stamina,' Sean said as he went across to open the gate to a larger field on the other side of the gallop.

Delaney careered around, bucking and kicking, then got down and rolled, as Sean had predicted.

'For a princess she likes to be mucky! This is her time, just to be a horse,' Sean said as he reached Marilyn's side. Almost as if Delaney heard him she reared and whinnied. Noble took it into his head to chase after her.

'That's all the exercise the lad needs, she keeps him busy. She's back in her own stall tonight. I've a lump hammer and I'm going to knock through a bit of the wall so she can put her head in to him. He's given me six months' effort to get her this right, and now we need to break her away from him.'

'What if she won't?'

'She will.'

'How can you tell that?'

'The thing that will take her away is the racetrack. When she's up at the gallop, it's not like it's work for her. That's why I hold on to her, let her have her head only when she's peppering. The keener she is to do it, the less she'll be hanging on to him. You can see why I love the work, though, can't you? It's not like work at all.'

He was smiling like it was Christmas, and in fact it still was. The Feast of the Epiphany used to be known as Little Christmas. Brigid had always said she preferred it to the big one.

They stood with their arms around each other, watching the horses, sharing the quiet. A good hour passed that way. They spoke one or two words, if that. Then it was time to lead them back. All he had to do was hold up the carrot bag and they came careering over. Marilyn was nervous – she barely knew where the brakes were on her Saab.

'I think I'll have cornflakes, so, or I could go and get rashers for us?' He looked jubilant. Delaney came through the gate after Noble. 'Can you trust me yet?'

She had to nod, because she did. But she knew what was coming.

'Then take my hand. Just look into my eyes and take my hand when I ask. I put the lead rope on Noble and she follows like a foal.' Sean spoke as she walked beside him. 'When you think of what Delaney's been through in bad hands, to trust us even as far as this' – she loved the way he said 'us' – 'it's an honour really. What a horse will give if it's not hurt. Now, your hand, please.'

Behind her a mad horse was loose, behaving like a tame one.

He's here, she told herself, and held onto that.

They were at the breakfast table when his two helpers, cousins who looked more like twins, arrived, laughing and calling about the fancy car outside and what kind of fancy woman would own that? When they saw Marilyn they reddened. So did she. They were both called Mike. Sean just asked if they would like tea.

'We saw them stabled, eating like it's going out of fashion,' one of them said.

'She's done her work, then?' the other of the Mikes asked.

'She has.'

'Any improvement on her?' It sounded like a daily question, and they smiled, slightly, to hear him say yes.

'Good times?'

'Good. Marilyn did the timing for me.' She flushed again. They nodded, but not in her direction. 'And she likes the look of Delaney on the go. Even with me in the saddle, she's going well.' The other two were slight, small men. Sean, it was obvious, was not the person to be riding out a future racehorse.

They all got up and went about their business. Marilyn began to clean, playing scales in the dust, before wiping them away forever.

Sean came in at one o'clock to find the kitchen sparkling. 'Where's the newspapers that were on the table?'

She smiled. 'In the bin.'

'I'll have to go get them out, so. There's a mart on Friday, I need the details of it, a cow or two to go. What about the fixings, for the old stables? There's a door I need to get at, after lunch. I only left them fixings there until I was sure I wouldn't lose them.'

'Are you saying,' she whispered, 'that everything I've done is wrong?'

'No, no, it's just . . . different, is all.'

'Clean is different? A thank you would have been nice.' It looked like her long weekend was going to be very short, after all.

She went out into the yard. The Mikes were busy. She wondered what she was doing here, a fish out of the bowl, until his hand came to her shoulder.

'Thank you for restoring the kitchen to a thing I recognise to be a kitchen. Thank you for taking the chance and coming down here, to what I know is not your kind of place. Thank you for your eyes, Marilyn, a blue I've never seen before, and for your touch, a woman's touch, which I need. And I'm sorry, heartily, for all my rudeness. You'll only find me grateful to you in future.'

*

If he was no cook then she was worse, but she could make sandwiches and she'd done a plate of doorsteps with white turnover loaf and sheets of cold cut ham, mustard and mayonnaise.

'You're priceless, I couldn't pay enough for you,' he beamed and went out with the plate to the Mikes, who were too shy to come in.

'The boys say I can have the afternoon, they'll look after things. They haven't given over slagging me. What would you like to do?'

The sheets were washed and tumbled dry. He was surprised to find his bedroom as he'd never seen it, clean and tidy with things in their proper place, Marilyn included.

They talked and came close in their loving to deciding that they'd waited enough, but then something in him, which she took to be the gentleman, held back, waiting a little more.

Later, she spent the evening with him, helping him get the horses bedded down for the night. She handed him things and forked hay into feeders and poured water. She couldn't go near any of the horses. When they came to Delaney's stall, she was stabled on her own, with a head in Noble's.

'It's done the trick,' Sean grinned, 'you've brought luck with you. And given me a few new ideas, for things.'

Delaney put her head back over her own door at his voice.

'She wants a pet,' Sean whispered to Marilyn. Delaney reached around and buried her nose in his breastbone. 'That's the sign that the horse gives their trust. And we earned it, didn't we, Noble?' All the time Sean spoke he was rubbing her head rhythmically, speaking in the same fashion – hypnotising.

They went to bed and got up to the same kind of day as

usual. For others it was a Sunday. Sean, who never had a day off, had to work harder on Sundays because the Mikes didn't come in. Marilyn helped him as much as she could outside and killed herself to get the inside looking more like how the late Mrs Monroe had kept it.

By Monday she ached so much with all the physical effort she was putting in that she felt justified in phoning in sick. As the receptionist put her straight through to Larry, she thought she overheard someone shout in the distance: 'Monroe is human! Call the papers!'

Despite feeling she had never worked so hard in her life, by nightfall Marilyn didn't want to go home. The thought was unbearable. She still had the fridge to clean out.

At the tea table Sean's face wasn't as clear as it had been. It was hard for him to look at her, and she felt her stomach leaden, the pain of what would happen if his feelings changed. Men and love was a foreign country, and she had no passport to it. But she was going to have this and what came with it, even if it ended up like Brigid's, a whole life lived in memorial of a brief marriage.

Finally Sean broke the silence.

'How can I ask you to match up with me in this, Marilyn? I go racing every night of the summer. Some weeks I only have enough for the petrol there and back and I eat a pan of sandwiches I make myself. If I go to the West to race I'm gone from early and I might not be back until three in the morning, and I still have to be up at dawn the next morning. The owner wants me racing as much as they can to make money. If you come here for your weekends you won't have any time to yourself, for anything else.'

'This is my decision to make, Sean. Let's get to know each other first.'

She was surprised at how mature she sounded, when all

she visualised was dragging him to some country church and slapping a ring and vows on him so she wouldn't lose him. Love requires strength, and she found it. His uncertainty gave her the push she needed to get out the door. If they were to continue they would need everything she had earned and more. They both had to do some thinking.

As she was getting into the car, he pulled her back.

'Friday,' Sean whispered, 'won't be long in coming.'

'I'll get off early, I'll get down as quick as I can.'

'It won't be quick enough for me. A minute after you've gone is when I want to see you, if the truth be told. But we're going to have to get used to this, aren't we? For the first while, anyway, till we see how things turn out.'

Elizabeth came out of the sitting room as soon as Marilyn's key went in the lock. She'd been hoping for a quiet entrance and a bolt to her own room, just to be with her thoughts and go over each detail.

'Julie's phoned a few times this evening, said she didn't want to disturb you on the mobile. Will I make a hot drink?'

'Okay, please. I should've phoned her,' she said, the thought only just occurring to her. She hadn't thought of Julie once all weekend, the friend who'd found him. She could see longing in Elizabeth's face. She asked impatiently, 'Did you ring Tony Devereux?'

'Sorry, I know I promised, but I couldn't face it. I've got a lot on my mind.' Elizabeth looked like she hadn't slept.

'I won't stay up late, I've got a lot to do.' Nothing in Marilyn's head was to do with work. They wandered into the kitchen. 'And don't treat Tony like a penance. You could feel this, with him.'

'I think what you found is rare,' Elizabeth said, making camomile tea for them, from her own dried flowers, as Nikolas was making for her mother.

196

Elizabeth sipped from her porcelain butterflies cup, not speaking, giving Marilyn time.

'Where's Granny?'

'Trabolgan, with Aunty Theresa, on a whim.'

'A whim? She never has those. And I thought it wasn't open yet.'

'It must be. She needed a break, she looked tired this holiday.' Elizabeth was reaching for words. 'I had the house to myself all day. It was very strange, but I worked the garden and did all the jobs I don't normally get a chance to do, when everyone's around.'

'Didn't you go to Trabolgan?'

'I wasn't asked.'

'She must have decided to use the Dan Draws instruction voucher, couldn't wait. Maybe she fancies him.'

'Maybe.' They both smiled at the idea of Brigid fancying anyone.

'What about you, Marilyn?'

'Grace was right. Where I was concerned, anyway. And maybe Granny's going for Dan and then it's just you.'

Marilyn could see Elizabeth needed a few details of joy to get on with the business of building her life without the presence of her daughter.

'He lives in a lovely place,' she began, 'but it's a bit like the cabin in *Calamity Jane*, it needs a woman's touch. I could run up a few chintz curtains . . .' She was laughing at herself, him, their ridiculous situation. She had said she couldn't stay up late, having so much sleep to catch up on, but she was still talking at three in the morning. They agreed to put a stop to it. Elizabeth stood, crossed to the other side of the table and embraced her.

'It's too soon to tell,' Marilyn said, the actuary in her rearing its head.

'It's not at all too soon. He's right for you, that's all there is.'

★

At work the following morning Marilyn ordered a jungle of flowers and had them sent to Abrakebabra, where nothing magical is made. Julie had to order a taxi to get them home. She left work immediately, telling them they were sent by a big producer who wanted her for a part in his next movie – as if their arrival wasn't dramatic enough – and came straight to Marilyn's office where she was received with the kind of welcome the last visit had lacked.

They went out. Marilyn didn't make it back until ten past two.

'He's so right, I was so right, he's so right,' Julie kept saying.

It was hard for Marilyn to answer. 'Thank you for finding him.'

'My pleasure, Mari, my absolute pleasure. May you live happy for the rest of your lives.' And may he never tell you, because I never will, she thought.

When Marilyn got home from work she could hear Grace in the kitchen talking to Elizabeth. She assumed she'd called round to hear the news too.

'Details coming up, prepare to be lovesick!' she said. Sean had phoned her three times that day already. Then she saw that neither Grace nor Elizabeth was smiling, and there was a letter on the table, which Elizabeth was folding.

The letter was from Brigid's specialist. As soon as Elizabeth saw the hospital logo on the front of it, she had ripped it open and read that Brigid had missed an appointment. It was advising Brigid to phone and make another immediately; the specialist had some test results she wanted to discuss with her.

Elizabeth had phoned Trabolgan. Trabolgan didn't open

until the last week of April. Elizabeth phoned Grace, who came straight around.

'Okay,' – she got straight to the point – 'where have my mother and aunt gone?'

'Greece.'

'Why? Quickly, please, Grace, before Marilyn gets home.'

As she was saying it Marilyn arrived in, bursting into the kitchen. This was a new departure from a routine that usually saw her race up to her bedroom to change.

'What's that?'

'A letter from Dickey, telling me I'm made redundant,' Elizabeth said like it didn't matter.

'What are you going to do? You've been there since I was small.'

'Get another job. In fact, I already have one. I saw this coming, didn't I, Grace?' Elizabeth looked at her.

'Don't worry,' Marilyn cut across them, 'I'm not so much of a Nazi that I'd give out to you for what's not your fault. I'm just concerned, that's all.' There were tears in Elizabeth's eyes. 'Look, if you're this upset about it we'll sue him,' she urged.

'Sue a solicitor?' Elizabeth smiled. 'A bad idea and a long process. No, I'm putting it behind me, Mari. In fact I'm doing something you might term as risky. I'm going out on my own. Eileen Whelan is going to be my first client, and you brought her right to my doorstep.' Elizabeth managed a smile.

'That's great! That's brilliant!' Marilyn enthused. 'That's almost unbelievable!'

'Not really.' Grace smoothed over the faux pas with faultless expertise. 'Your mother hasn't studied for seven years at night for nothing.'

'Oh, no, I didn't mean that it's unbelievable you're doing it, Elizabeth. I just mean it's unbelievable how well things are going, for us all. You'll be great at it, Mum, you'll be first class. I'll do your accounts. Anything!'

'Thanks, Mari.' Elizabeth was touched to hear this, wondered why she hadn't just told her daughter straight off and then remembered: she had expected her to express concern more than congratulations. It seemed the judgemental streak might be working its way out of her. 'Right now it's a single entry, for a single client. But there'll be more.'

'There will,' Grace and Marilyn said in unison. Elizabeth couldn't take any more approbation, along with what she'd read in the letter. It was too much for her to get used to.

'Now, Grace, you came over to hear about the lovebirds, so would you excuse me? I need a few moments in the garden.'

'What's up with her, Grace?' Marilyn asked after Elizabeth had left. 'Please tell me.'

'Change, darling. She's changing her job, her daughter is changing – it's hard when you've given over your life to things and they leave. Nothing you can do about it, though. She's happy for you. Now fill me in before I burst with curiosity,' she said, leading her to the table and away from the patio doors.

21

Nikolas gave Brigid mountain tea and more herb blends and for the seven days she didn't take a single pill. Each morning and evening they went to feed his ponies. They'd been his main mode of transport on Skyros in his younger years and now were friends. They reached only to his waist. For the first day she had hung behind him, then got a grip of herself. Come on now, don't be soft, she told herself, they're little bigger than dogs.

By the third day they raced up to her as well, so she learned to get on with liking them. It wasn't hard.

Each afternoon she and Nikolas walked the island or spent time in his fields preparing for the new growing season. He let her walk side by side with him, but not work. But he was understanding that she wasn't one for sitting down, no matter how sick. No one came to his house and he didn't go anywhere, but it would be hard to find a more popular man. Everyone on the road greeted him and spoke to him before shaking her hand, then went back to speaking to both of them as if she understood what they were saying. She smiled as if she did.

Brigid knew she had to go home to her responsibilities and he understood that she might never be back, so the night before the ferry came he took her down the coast in his truck. They walked over a bridge and the river below was banked up with turtles on either side. She could smell the sea and over the brow of the hill, she saw the headland, with a ruined windmill and a little chapel hewn into a rock face. Beside it were giant boulders, at tide level, where an artist had carved sculptures. They were surrounded by history, intention and erosion – like life.

In the little chapel, a Greek Orthodox man declared his love for a Roman Catholic woman and gave her a bronze and silver ring with semi-precious stones for her finger, rich in thought, artistry and history, being two hundred years old. She took off John Joe's ring, the only jewellery she had to pass on, and threw it in the sea, not wanting to pass on the luck that came with it.

Brigid Monroe was now a bigamist, never having divorced, not believing in it. She was married now, to a man she loved, in front of God and the stars.

That evening, their last alone together, he pulled out the last remaining item that had been put away on Nyphi's death. For Brigid Monroe he played his bouzouki, music full of the sea. On this same instrument he had sung and played his wife out of the world, at her request.

Then he picked up his clay pipe and puffed, holding her hand. She said what she had said each evening to him: 'You're a throwback, all right. I remember my granddad, God rest him and keep him, doing that.'

On this night she couldn't bring herself to say it, knowing it was the last pipe she would see filled and lit. It was strange not to wish to return to everyone she'd devoted her life to.

'It's just the novelty, isn't it, Nikolas?'

He looked at her.

'*Melancholia.*'

'Yes, it's the same word in English. The last time my heart broke more slowly, I must confess. My love.' She looked around, for fear someone would hear her being so soft, realising she was alarmed to be hearing it herself.

'A picture, Nikolas? Of Nyphi? Icon?' She spoke in a quiet hour which saw him almost asleep, in his chair, beside her bed. Nikolas went to a drawer to take out the photograph that would normally sit in the bedroom. Her last action on her last night in his home was to kiss a picture, as she always did at home. But it wasn't of John Joe and the past she lost. This time it was of Nyphi, her friend from dreams, who had given Brigid hers.

When the ferry came she and Nikolas were already at the harbour and neither of them had much call for demonstration. They had done their embracing in private, like all people of their generation. To do so in public would be insincere. Before she boarded, she could see Theresa waiting for her, knowing not to intrude on this. She shook his hand in the same way as she had when she'd arrived, but her eyes said she loved him. They used their great strength in their goodbye.

He didn't let go of her with his eyes until the last possible moment and she didn't stop looking at the harbour until it was no longer there.

If she ever saw him again, she wouldn't be able to leave a second time.

On the ferry she threw her duck-egg-blue suit into the same sea that was now the home of John Joe's ring. The lump in her throat was back before landing on the mainland.

Theresa only spoke as they boarded the plane. She knew Brigid had no call for idle conversation. 'I have to tell you, I called home. Elizabeth is beside herself, she knows. Grace called in to her, she found her with the letter from the specialist for the next appointment. She said she rang Trabolgan and found it's not even open. You were never a good liar.'

'To think of all the years I spent going to Trabolgan when there were lovely places like this I could have been visiting,' Brigid sighed.

'Brigid,' Theresa's tone warned her, 'there are things to be faced soon.'

'I know, I know. I wanted them both at home to have time, without me being a damper on their lives. I held them back enough.'

'You held them together as well.'

'And punished them for it, Theresa. I don't want Marilyn told.'

'Oh, for God's sake, Marilyn is a grown woman!'

'Who's feeling like I'm feeling right now, Theresa, and I don't want anything spoiling that. And there won't be one far behind for Elizabeth, I'm certain of that.'

'How do you mean? She hasn't even rung Tony, so Grace says.'

'There was a look in his eyes, Theresa, that I knew nothing about before Nikolas. I saw it the first day when he was parked outside your house, watching her go into it. Women have the right to see it in men who love them. John Joe never loved me enough to look like that. Whoever Elizabeth loved, whoever Marilyn's father was, it was the same for her. She'd never seen that look until she met Tony Devereux, and it's scared the living daylights out her.'

'Brigid, she lived in hippie communes, a kibbutz. Marilyn's father was a one-night stand.'

'Tell me, Theresa, do you know Elizabeth at all?'

'I do, as well as you do.'

'Then you'll know that even at eighteen she was one of those who live on romance, and romantics don't make children without depth or knowledge of the father.'

'But she's always said—'

'I know what she's always said. Consider her nature. Even then it was deep – foolish, but deep.'

'We all make impulsive mistakes with lifelong consequences, Brigid. I think you're reading too much into—'

'I am not. I know her in a way I wish sometimes I didn't. She's my own daughter and she always made me uncomfortable. Brush her with a feather and you'd scratch her, in her young days.'

'Not any more,' Theresa said.

'No, she learned secrecy all too well, for all her bleeding heart. She hides her Christmas cards, that girl of mine. Whatever happened still has her prisoner, or she'd have told Marilyn who her father is. I'm certain she knows, always have been. And she'll ring that taxi driver, or I will.'

The pilot announced descent and the 'fasten seat-belt' sign went on.

'There, I didn't feel a bit of that,' Brigid grinned. Theresa had never seen her grin in over seventy years.

22

Elizabeth was waiting at the airport with Grace.

'Let me thank Grace, before you go on at me, for a beautiful outfit,' Brigid said immediately while Elizabeth noticed how well she looked, how strong her voice was again, 'and for more kindness than I deserve. And before you begin, Elizabeth, I'm sorry.'

'Not here. I've got more to say to you, but not here.'

'You look a picture in it, Brigid, it's the blue for you,' Grace smiled. 'The other was far too cold.'

'You'll be glad to hear she got married in it,' Theresa whispered as she steered her wife away. 'Will we travel home alone?'

'I know you're angry with me for not telling you,' Brigid began as soon as they got home. 'I didn't want you to have any unnecessary worry. After the last weakness, I know what it takes out of everyone. Did you tell Marilyn? I'd like it if she didn't know.'

'I've known for weeks, Mother, so you can save the subterfuge. I've kept it to myself because I knew you wanted to. Then, on Tuesday, I get the letter from the new specialist. You missed your appointment. How could you be so irresponsible after all those people did for you the last time?' Brigid didn't answer.

'Then I find out you've gone off to Greece! Couldn't you at least have allowed me to enjoy that with you? After all those miserable flecking, to use your own word, weeks spent in a wet Irish holiday camp that I gave to you?'

'It was thoughtless of me,' Brigid conceded. 'But I had something of my own to do. I needed Theresa for that.'

'What would have happened to you if you'd come over weak, to use another of your phrases? Do you think an island hospital could have done anything?'

'Elizabeth, please, where is Marilyn now?'

'Where she'll be every weekend now – Wexford. She's not back until late tonight. She's also taking Monday off, if you can believe it.'

'Oh good, it's all it should be,' Brigid said and folded her hands.

'You're sick, Mother, and you're not to go off gallivanting again like that without permission,' Elizabeth warned.

'Whose would that be, now?' Brigid was smiling. 'The doctors' or yours?'

Elizabeth looked at her with wide eyes and an open mouth, only just having spotted the new ring, a bronze and silver band studded with amethyst and turquoise, decorated with spirals. It could have been any of the ones in Elizabeth's jewellery box.

'I hope he's as good as the father you picked for me.'

'The past is what it is, Elizabeth.' Brigid's tone hardened, the grey of Ireland settling in on her. 'I can do nothing to change it now, but I hope to make amends and see to it that you and Marilyn are happier than I was.'

'You never allowed yourself to be,' Elizabeth snapped.

'Granted, and you're the same in that. Have you phoned that nice man?'

'No. And let me point out a few things – it wasn't me who made my daughter an actuary. She'd have been a pianist if I'd had my way. And hers too. I didn't drive my daughter away so she ended up alone in a delivery room screaming for the mother she never had.'

'For the love of God, Elizabeth, please don't say that,'

Brigid whispered. 'I would have been there if you could have called, and I'd have held your hand and looked after you all through it. Even before it. The thought of you keeps me awake nights. From the day you left the house I never got a night's sleep with worrying and looking for you. Don't think I didn't scour the place. It wasn't me who drove you onto the kibbutz.'

'I wasn't on any kibbutz. You can't have looked that hard, I was living in Rathmines.'

'Well' – Brigid sat back – 'I'll talk to you about it again, Elizabeth.'

'The only thing I want to talk about is your forthcoming appointment with the oncology unit on Thursday. You have to be in at eight a.m. and have fasted since midnight.'

'I can't, I have work, they'll have to change that.'

'No, Mother, I already changed that. Until you have a clean bill of health you aren't going back to work. And I'm off work too, to take you to the hospital. From now on I go with you on every visit. No questions, no moaning, no messing.'

'Elizabeth, I'll do everything you ask of me. If you phone the man in question.'

Marilyn arrived home on Monday night close to midnight to witness Brigid Monroe drinking filter coffee out of her chipped china cup, wearing turquoise chiffon. It had been washed and dried every night and she'd worn nothing else since Saturday.

'Oh, it's a lovely lift it gives altogether. Thank you, Elizabeth. If all these years I'd known it could taste like this, I'd have been drinking buckets.'

'Where's the ring from?' Marilyn put her bag down. She was thrilled to see her grandmother looking so well. Christmas must have been a false alarm.

'It's one I wanted so I threw the other off a cliff. Now, tell me about you.'

'Grand.'

'And Sean?'

'Grand.'

She sat back and sighed, satisfied with that. Brigid and Marilyn often spoke in such Morse code.

'Good. I've news myself,' Brigid began.

Elizabeth sat at the table with them, not raising her butterflies mug to her lips, while Marilyn sat down and Brigid told her about Nikolas.

'I met a grand man myself, and I married him. It's in the eyes of God, not anyone else's business. He's all anyone could want.' Her silver hair was swept back instead of set in rigid curls.

'At Trabolgan?' Marilyn asked, sipping what was strong enough to knock her over. When Brigid decided to drink coffee, she went for it. Her pupils were wide, her skin flushed.

'No, at the last minute we went to Greece, for a change.'

Marilyn's mouth opened. It was like living in another reality watching Brigid's lightly tanned skin, polished nails, unlined face. Everything about her was different, looser. She even had eyeliner on. She had always said that Cleopatra wore it and it was therefore heathen.

'It was sunny every day, but enough of that. I want to hear more about you and the horse man. How's the little one he was telling us all about?'

'Delaney? Nuts. But talented nuts,' Marilyn said before interrupting herself. 'Sorry, Brigid, just to return to the subject of your first trip abroad and your second marriage?'

'Yes, Nikolas is also very good with horses,' Brigid smiled in turn. 'You can trust a man who's good with animals.'

'Granny, am I dreaming?'

'No, love, but don't make so much of it. It's just life moving about, like it does. And do you know, Marilyn, Nikolas, my new husband, has ponies. Isn't that a coincidence now? I wonder if that was in our cups when Grace looked at them.'

'Brigid, are you sure you're all right?'

'All right?' she snapped and Marilyn saw the tiredness behind the bright-eyed flush. She knew illness was the only thing that could cause a seismic shift like this in a stone-hard woman. 'Why shouldn't I be all right?'

'Sorry, you're right. It's all just a bit out of character.' Marilyn backed away.

'And what if it is? Isn't it time I started living? Shouldn't I have done it years ago?' Elizabeth and Marilyn nodded at this. 'Let me tell you now, while I can, for I'm not gone on this kind of soft talk. I never let myself go. If I learned too late it's a lesson you can learn from me. Chase happiness, and leave security behind if it doesn't give it to you. There's nothing secure in chains.'

At midnight the house phone and Marilyn's mobile rang simultaneously. Brigid went to the hall and they heard the unmistakeable sound of a bouzouki on the other end of the line.

Sean said, 'Will I phone you back? You're not saying anything.'

'My granny went to Greece, met a Greek, married him, sort of, and he's on the phone playing music to her. He's singing now, we can hear him even as far as the kitchen.'

'I'll let you go and learn more tomorrow,' he said just as Brigid hung up.

'Now, you turn that thing off, it's bad for you anyway, gives you cancer.' Brigid pointed at the mobile. 'And sit down. We've still got your mother to sort out.'

'Mother,' Elizabeth sighed, 'please. Don't mention Tony again.'

Marilyn spoke. 'Two-thirds of this family is in love. We want the same to happen to the other third. And Grace says it will – you always listen to Grace, it's you she read the leaves for, not us.'

Elizabeth shook her head. 'The world doesn't work like that.'

'It does, we know it does now,' Marilyn insisted. 'The men are coming to the Monroe house! There must be a planetary alignment somewhere that got Brigid and me out of our boxes. For God's sake, don't get into the one we just climbed out of. We've always been too realistic, haven't we, Brigid?'

'Don't "Brigid" me, I'm still your granny, even if I am a bigamist.'

'Marilyn, please.' Elizabeth raised a hand. 'I spend my days working with women who've been disappointed in love, who come to me because the man who was supposed to protect them wants to take all they've built together in the name of love for himself. He usually has a younger prospect and is usually in complete denial of his own mortality and responsibilities as a parent. That's how love turns out. Just as it did for Eileen Whelan.'

'Did Elizabeth tell you she's gone out on her own as a family law consultant?' Marilyn asked Brigid.

'She didn't. Tony did. The first day I met him he said she had rented a new office. Before you hold that against him, Elizabeth, he did expect your own mother to know about your new venture.'

'Yes,' Marilyn backed Brigid up. 'You're in law, not crime. Why didn't you tell both of us?'

'I thought it would be too much trouble, you'd both give me more grief than I needed. You'd both think it was a bad idea.'

'No we wouldn't!' Marilyn exclaimed. 'We'd have helped.'

'By assuming I was incapable and trying to set it up for

me, Mari? By cleaning the place and getting rid of papers you class as rubbish and I see as evidence, Mother? Let's be honest now, all of us, about what you think of me. "Flaky", that's the word you use to describe me to your pals, Marilyn, isn't it? It never suited you to think I might be something other than tofu and Tarot cards. You might have treated me with more respect. I think I earned it anyway, regardless. Now that you've discovered the magic that's in the world, you're behaving like a born-again. You have to respect magic, not expect it to happen to everyone. Please don't keep on at me, I don't want the pressure. I have enough to deal with in setting up this business, single-handed, and sitting my exams. I hate to ruin your unsullied opinion of me as an airhead.'

Into the silence that followed, Brigid made a request. 'Marilyn, you know that piece of music your mother loves?' Brigid asked.

Marilyn knew – 'Sospiro', by Liszt. 'Would you ever go out into that hall and play it for us?'

Elizabeth pinched the bridge of her nose, determined not to cry and also realising she now needed stronger glasses, as her mother had done at exactly her age. She was getting older, she was getting to be Brigid, and soon Brigid wouldn't be here. So it had to be said, the single truth that had kept things as they were for so long.

'You drove magic out of this house, and out of Marilyn. And I let you.'

Brigid stood behind her, stroking her hair as if it was acrylic, unaccustomed to such displays. Aching for all she had not done. 'I need a chance. Will you give it to me?'

Marilyn played the last notes and then the rich silence fell that follows beautiful music. 'I'll play the piano every day for you, if you'll meet Tony Devereux,' she said as she walked back into the kitchen.

★

Tony turned to Mick and Colin. 'That was her. Sunday next. Dinner.'

'Well, she took her time,' Mick sighed with relief. 'I was nearly about to go round there again.'

'Are you sure about this, Tony? She took weeks to ring you,' Colin said.

'I'm sure that it's the right thing to do. It's the only thing.'

23

Theresa shook Tony's hand in a way that stopped circulation.

'Great to see you again, the results are on. The others are in the kitchen. Elizabeth's out for her walk' – as if he didn't know, but he didn't dare go today – 'and her daughter's on the way back up from Wexford with her chap.'

The door opened to reveal a pencil-thin, elegant creature with a perfect smile and a swathe of grey hair twisted into a chignon.

'This is Grace,' Theresa introduced.

'What will you drink, Tony? We have chilled beer and wine. There's anything you'd like, I'm just helping Brigid with dinner.'

'Soda water.'

'That's chilled as well.'

'Wouldn't you know it?' Brigid shouted from the kitchen, 'She thinks of everything. It's a wonder she's not God. Tell him I'll come and see him in a minute. For now he's to say nothing till he's been told what to say.'

'You'd better get in here before she gets on to you.' Theresa pulled him into an armchair. Grace came through with his water with ice and lemon and a linen napkin she'd found in Brigid's sideboard.

'Wedding present,' Brigid had told her.

'You never used them.'

'I was keeping them up for good occasions,' Brigid laughed at herself. 'I suppose they were never good enough. This man coming to see Elizabeth is enough of one. Take them out, and the tablecloth I never use either, and the silver canteen. What was I ever waiting for, Grace? Can you tell me?'

Grace looked at her. 'Someone to get married.'

'This is the first time I've ever watched the results with anyone in this house.' Theresa's smile was the kind that could comfort the dying. Her great heart was obvious, and Tony could sense that she was his ally. 'Newcastle against Man United, still playing, scoreless, though I expect you knew that.' Tony had revealed to Theresa that he was a Newcastle fan.

'To be honest, I haven't been able to focus on anything today.'

Theresa studied him. 'You have it bad, Tony.'

'I do.'

Then Newcastle scored in the ninety-first minute. In the ninety-second the final whistle went. They cheered.

'Who knows, Theresa, maybe it's the day of the underdog?'

'It could well be. Just raise your game, Tony, and don't take no for an answer. That's all the advice I have.'

The doorbell rang and Theresa went to it. There was another male voice.

'Sorry, it's just begun to lash or I'd have waited for Marilyn. She's still behind me. After giving out to her about running red lights, she's proving my point by taking half an hour at each one.'

'Come on in and meet Tony. His knees are knocking, but his team won.'

'That's a plus,' Sean Monroe agreed as he walked into the room and bent to get under the doorframe. Tony couldn't remember ever seeing a bigger man.

'Sean Monroe, pleased to meet you.' He took Tony's hand and squeezed more life out of it than Theresa had just done. 'Marilyn says you're here to get to know her mother? I was in the same position a few weeks ago with the daughter. They're a great family for fixing each other up. I was as nervous about it as you are now, and it went grand for me.' His smile lessened on hearing a car pull up on the kerb outside and a screech of brakes.

'Excuse me, Tony.' He ran outside and came back with Marilyn.

'Tony! It's great to see you again!' Her enthusiasm was heartening, though she clearly wasn't sharing it with Sean at this particular moment.

'Thank you, Marilyn, for persuading your mother this was a good idea.' Tony decided not to mention that he had made the connection between her first and last names. It struck him as strange that Elizabeth would do such a thing.

'She still doesn't think it is.' Marilyn felt she had to be honest. 'But the rest of us feel it's the best idea.'

'Tony,' Sean stepped in, 'my advice is that you might think about getting two seats in the shed.'

At that comment Marilyn laughed with all the lightness of being Tony thought she had seemed to lack. She perched on the arm of the sofa beside Sean with a restless quality that, given time, would merge with his restfulness. For now she was contentious with him and the contention said, I'm afraid you won't stay. But as far as Tony could see, everything about Sean Monroe said he would.

A key turned in the door. As soon as it did, everyone went quiet.

'Mari, did you know that you passed me? Did you not hear me screaming like a fishwife? I'm soaked to the skin,' Elizabeth called.

Marilyn shot off the chair and out into the hallway. 'Sorry, I had trouble getting away from lights all the way up from Wexford.'

216

'Newcastle won. Tony supports them,' Theresa called out with forced jollity.

There was a hissing sound in the hallway.

'I'll be down when I've changed. I'm going to my room.'

He had anticipated reluctance and he got it. Sean clapped Tony on the back. 'That's lucky. I had to go outside to the shed, you only have to sit outside on the landing. In this weather that's a blessing.'

'He's right, Tony,' Theresa said, 'go up. She needs to see you on your own, not with an audience around. It's the last on the right.'

He stopped at the sight of the cornflower window and had no doubt Elizabeth had been the one to have it installed.

'Could you hand me in a towel? The bathroom's across the hall.' Her hand came out to collect it and she didn't shut the door again. He saw a corner of her room and knew her to be exactly as he imagined.

'I suppose,' she said, leaning over her dressing table, most of her out of sight, 'this is what you call a half-blind date. It's what I am, I'm afraid, but I'm too vain to be seen in these yet.' She picked up a pair of glasses with a turquoise-blue frame and peered around the door at him for a second before disappearing again. 'Human eyesight begins to deteriorate at exactly forty-seven and three-quarters. For me it's a quicker process. Mind you, I do want to stress this is not a date.'

'I know that, and I also know you've agreed to it against your own wishes. So thank you. And the fact that you need glasses, well, I'm glad you have one flaw,' he said before he could stop himself.

'Oh, I have far more than one.' She stood in front of him and gave him a smile. She had no make-up on, her hair was in a turban and she was wearing glasses, letting him see her as she was, in harsh overhead light. He watched her and she

217

put her head to one side. 'We're not in the first flush of youth.'

'Thank God we're not, would you want to go back?' he asked, and she smiled in shaking her head.

'If I could have the face and body I had then with the knowledge I have now . . .'

After a minute's silence, he searched for something to say. 'That window, it's stunning.'

'Do you think?' He could hear her pleasure, as well as see it.

'I do.'

'I had a friend of mine make it. I love cornflowers, they're the same colour as my daughter's eyes.'

'I realised that.'

She moved behind the door now and looking into the mirror she could see her surprise that he had already made the connection.

She came out in bare feet and a long navy velour dress with river pearls beaded around the neckline. She made even the plainest of dresses beautiful with her additions. Her hair was out of the towel he'd handed to her. He wanted to dry it, comb it out. 'I'm starving, and I'm sure you are too. My mother's a good, solid cook,' she said on their way down the stairs. 'And she likes a man who likes his meat.'

'I'm sorry to hear that, because I'm vegetarian.'

Elizabeth's smile broadened.

On a Sunday night in late January, the Monroes sat at a dinner table and watched two men eat extra portions. It felt like Christmas dinner without the loss. The only one missing was Julie.

Elizabeth talked to Tony about art, gardening and herself, the light of the candles on her face. She leaned into their conversation, enquiring, contributing with knowledge.

She had the social surety of Grace, which Brigid and Marilyn lacked. With her friends Elizabeth was a bright, vivacious conversationalist. Tony's regard for her interests and ideas made her so in his company. 'I think there's a thin film between worlds, don't you?' . . . 'I understand that a child was born in Nepal who spoke seven languages from the minute he learned to speak. Doesn't it make reincarnation a distinct possibility?' . . . 'There's an exhibition of Caravaggio in London, I'd like to see it, for the way he uses light . . .'

After dinner, during coffee, Marilyn, who'd been quiet for the meal, absorbed in just listening to Elizabeth, went to the piano and played softly – Miles Davis, 'Concierto de Aranjuez' – as if she often did so after dinner each night.

She took a short break at eight-thirty and reached out for the phone before it even rang. Nikolas Faltaits was as punctual as Marilyn was, making his customary call from the phone box at the village *platia* in Skyros. '*Kalispera*, Nikolas!' Marilyn greeted.

'*Kalispera*, Mareelen,' he shouted in the way people who aren't used to telephones do. 'Brigid?'

She took the phone. '*Kalispera*, darling.'

'Darling?' Grace whispered. 'In earshot of everyone? Has this world gone mad?'

'Yes,' Elizabeth smiled, 'at long last.'

'Do I hear another musical instrument?' Tony asked Elizabeth, who was pouring him another coffee.

'That's right. It's Nikolas, my mother's new husband.'

'It sounds like a bouzouki.'

'That's right, he's in Greece.'

'For how long?'

'Forever, he's Greek.'

'We can't persuade him that we can hear him just as well as if we're sitting beside him. He plays at full pelt every night, for ten minutes, then Brigid phones him back and they talk. They're just about to wind up now. I'll go back out and play. Are you coming with me, Sean?' Marilyn smiled.

'What do they say to each other?' Tony asked Elizabeth.

'Language isn't a barrier. She talks, he talks. The look on her face when she comes off the phone tells me she's been understood.'

'The lads told me I looked like that, after you phoned.'

Elizabeth shifted, bringing the subject with her. 'Tell me about yourself.'

He told her about his drinking and devoting his life to helping those in the same situation.

'It's what I consider to be my work. The taxi gives me the money and the flexibility to do it.' It made him more than he seemed, she thought, to have such a story at the back of him. But she could feel no attraction, which made her sad, but thankfully not awkward with him. She could tell he preferred the truth to anything else. Immediately, she thought of Niall, as she always thought of him in these situations. His looks, his charm, all tied up in the way he could tell lies as if they were truth. Had he had Tony's decency he might have got what he wanted.

'Do you like going abroad?' Elizabeth smiled.

'I haven't gone as much as I should, or will do, once my taxi-plate loan is cleared. Then I'm visiting every place I can before I die. That's the plan, anyway.'

Brigid hung up, having whispered ridiculous things for a woman her age into the phone.

'You know,' she said in a way that told them all her energy was restored after looking tired and silent at dinner, 'I think we'll have to get that plastic runner off the Axminster carpet.

What's the use in a lovely carpet like that if we can't walk on it?'

Elizabeth came into the hallway to share a silent cheer with Marilyn. Halfway there. No one clapped at each interlude between Marilyn's piano pieces. Elizabeth, sitting beside Tony and Grace, appreciated him picking up on it.

Part of him was intimidated, the rest pessimistic about his chances. She was so much more than he was. Now, at least, he had the satisfaction of her company. He watched the clock, willing the minutes to move slower.

'It's a haven, this house,' he said and caught the cloud in Elizabeth's eyes, though Brigid was delighted in a way that kept her commandments, without showing it.

Sean was nursing a brandy, sitting on the bottom step of the stairs, listening to the music. Theresa and Brigid went into the easy chairs by the fireside. 'This place has never been as happy, Brigid, and I was a girl in it,' Theresa said.

'Was it this easy all along, Theresa? If only,' Brigid said.

'No if-onlys.'

At midnight Marilyn played Miles Davis again, 'Round Midnight', a cue for everyone to disperse.

When Tony, Theresa and Grace had gone, Elizabeth said, 'Tony Devereux is one of life's good listeners.'

'You did more than well, Tony,' Theresa said as they walked out on the path and Grace nodded. 'The thing now is whether she'll let go of hardship.'

Sean and Marilyn hovered, not sure of the sleeping arrangements. He had to be up in four hours and wasn't looking forward to a sofa, but there was no way a man of his size could sneak anywhere in the house.

'Don't be looking at each other like that. I'm not saying I agree with it, but that doesn't mean it doesn't happen,' Brigid snapped over her shoulder as she walked up the stairs. 'Last one up turn off the lights. And no flushing in the middle of the night, remember, flushing wakes me up.' Elizabeth, Sean and Marilyn Monroe all smiled.

Sean and Marilyn made love with quiet, with streetlight. 'Do you realise you're the first man to spend the night here in half a century?'

Tony Devereux was lying on his bed, listening to the same rain Elizabeth was listening to, thinking if he didn't wake up tomorrow that would be a good thing. He could be no happier.

Brigid kissed the memory of Nikolas, having no photograph. She ran a finger over the old one, wishing the gone man well, and sighed with a longing for the new man to be here, beside her, sharing the hollow in her lumpy old bed. Sharing next week and the ordeal to be faced.

Julie had to sit down again on the bed. It was five in the afternoon. She hadn't managed to get dressed and was due at the Monroes, for dinner. There were four missed calls on her mobile and three voice messages. She listened, hoping for an answer to supply the question going round in her head.

One was from Abrakebabra telling her she was sacked. Big news. She hadn't turned up for work in a week. One from her mother. 'Julie, your father's got the chiropodist. Last-minute cancellation.' Which chiropodist worked Sunday? 'Can you leave lunch until next time? Bring that special jam you found that he likes, he's run out. See you then, as usual.'

The last message was from Marilyn.

'I hope you're coming over. That man I told you about, Tony, is having dinner with us. Hands off, though, he's for Ma. Can you believe it? You'll be next, Julie! I know Grace didn't say so, but it's what you deserve.'

I got exactly what I deserved, Julie thought as she looked out her bed-sit window. The sky was cold, grey, as she was. She sent a text: 'Can't come. Work. Audition tomorrow. Love to all.'

Six seconds later one bounced back.

'Good luck. Happiness.' Not a very Marilyn message.

Julie didn't need to take the test. The evidence was there in the toilet bowl each time she tried to eat anything un-mashed.

At seven p.m. she was still lying in bed trying to decide which was worse, the sickness or the depression. It was the one thing she prided herself on doing well. Now she might be chief bridesmaid with the groom's child.

'What are you going to do about this?' she turned on her pillow and asked the mirror. It answered back, 'The only thing I can.'

Marilyn and Julie met on Friday for lunch to celebrate their good fortune. Julie wasn't capable of eating anything, but then, Marilyn didn't find that unusual. Marilyn stayed a size eight in the midst of profiteroles; Julie gained weight at the sight of them. One did things well, the other badly. Marilyn had talent, slimness, industry, opportunity and now the love of a good man. Julie's beauty, at one stage in their lives, had been worth more than anything. But beautiful women aren't supposed to screw up like this, Julie thought.

'You've got dark circles under your eyes,' Marilyn chastised.

'It's excitement. And so have you.'

'Correct, for the same reason. I wake up thinking about him and go to bed dreaming about him. This is it, thanks to you. What about you?'

'Me too. I haven't been able to sleep for thinking about it.'

'I don't understand, why did they come over here to audition for *Cats*?'

'It's been in London for so long everyone's been in it.'

'I see. Well, when's your first show?'

'Monday, three weeks.'

'When are you going?'

'As soon as I can pack.'

'Will they give you money for the move?'

'No, but I'll get by.'

'You?'

'Yes, me.'

'You'll have to pay for a deposit, plane fare, hotel while you're looking for a place to live. It'll cost a fortune. They should be subbing you.'

'I'm in the chorus, Marilyn, not the top cat.'

'I suppose, but if they came over here they should at least be willing to move you over there, properly.'

'Will you stop running it down? If my big break's not big enough for you, then—'

'You're right, sorry, it's fantastic. I'll fly over for the first show. Sean mightn't make it, but I'll be in the front row. Maybe Elizabeth and Brigid will come too now that Brigid's turned into a jetsetter in her eighth decade.'

'Yeah' – Julie tried to work up some enthusiasm – 'who'd have thought Mother Brigid would turn Shirley Valentine? I'd love to see the old weapon. I'll let you know when it is.'

'You already said, Monday three weeks.'

'That's what they anticipate. I might need more rehearsals.'

'Now who's running herself down?'

'Look, I'm just being realistic here.'

'Okay, okay, Julie, no need to bite my head off. You're a bit edgy with this.'

'Sorry, it's nerves.'

'That's all right, I'm nervous myself at the moment. My boss keeps trying to block book my diary so he can promote me.'

'I'll have to get threatened with a knife more often,' Julie smiled. 'You'll be made managing director next time.'

'Funny,. Marilyn winced. 'I had to tell him last week that I'm seeing Sean just to get him off my back. He knows him well.'

'Obviously,' Julie sighed.

'He's stopped hassling me now, probably waiting to see how serious it is with me and him before he makes a move. I hated having to tell him. Anyway, what about you? I hope this makes your parents a bit more involved in your life,' Marilyn reached for something to say.

'Them? I didn't bother telling them. I've fallen out with them for good this time.'

'You say that every other time.'

'Well, now I mean it.'

Julie had gone round, unannounced. It took them five minutes to answer the doorbell.

'Oh,' her mother said like she couldn't place her. 'Today?'

'No, I just called round on the spur of the moment. Can I come in?' To the house I was born and raised in? Can I get through the door you've left half-closed? she thought.

'It's a bit unexpected, Julie. Your father's indisposed, could you come back later?'

'You know what? I don't have to come back at all.'

She didn't turn around when her mother called her name.

'Did I ever tell you they christened me Juliet?'

'Yes' – Marilyn sat back – 'you did.'

'I didn't know. Until I went to get my passport, that time. Wouldn't it have been lovely to be Juliet?'

'No – in our school, no. Trust me, as I'm named after another female icon.'

'But I was a fair Juliet once, wasn't I, Mari?'

'You still are.' Marilyn's tone was businesslike, as it always was when she was providing reassurances. 'So, will I see you before you head off?'

'Course.'

Julie and Marilyn left the restaurant and walked in separate directions. Marilyn was unsure why she felt such an ache, so much so that she couldn't get into her Saab but turned around to go back in the direction she'd come from. Julie was long gone. Marilyn found herself crying, for no reason. Then she found there was one. Her best friend was moving to England. Their goodbye had been muted, tense and restrained. That wasn't what their friendship was like. She dialled Sean.

Later that evening there was a knock at the bed-sit door. Sean was outside, with flowers.

'I heard you were going, and I had to thank you in person, for everything.'

'You drove up here for that?' Julie wrapped her dressing gown around her. He was embarrassed to see her in it, she could tell.

'I was up anyway, she's done the car again. I had to collect her.' Sean raised his eyes, conspiratorial.

'You daft bugger.' Why didn't I try to hang on to you for myself? 'Will you come up?'

'I won't, the woman is waiting for me. I'm not late for her, but I wouldn't like to be. I just wanted to give you something, to have my own words with you. I'm a bit guilty about how it all came about.'

'That was no fault of yours, you tried to fight me off. I'm the persistent kind.' And foolish with it – there's a combination, she thought.

'You're the best kind of woman, Julie. I had to thank you in person, for all you've done.'

'You've said that twice now.'

'And I'll go on saying it.'

'At the top table?' Julie smiled.

'Don't know about that,' Sean surprised her not passing it off as a joke. He was too sincere for frivolity. She wished she had been guilty of more sincerity. Still, she noticed, he didn't appear as easy-going as he once had. A bit of Marilyn's edge had found its way into him, and he didn't appear to be happier for it. But he was certainly more purposeful. 'I'm a lot to take on and she's got a lot to lose, going with the likes of me. I'm a bit set in my ways and have a hard life ahead of me.'

'I know her, Sean, this is it for her. Don't lose this chance. God knows the rest of us are dying trying to get ours,' she said as she closed the door.

'Pregnant slag – should be ideal casting material for *EastEnders*.' She tried to joke with herself, but there was no joking through this.

On Monday afternoon a good-luck card came with a sterling draft for two thousand pounds inside. Trust Marilyn to supply her gift in the correct currency.

To my best friend, with my love. Can't do this in person, too embarrassing. May you have all the luck you deserve. See you soon.

She had to leave tomorrow, or she'd never go.

On Tuesday she took a flight over to the UK with Marilyn's money to abort Sean's child. At the hotel she saw the concierge put his eyes back in. He gave her the best room. Not so long ago he'd have got to share it. Now she sat on the bed by herself and said aloud, 'Too complicated for EastEnders, this is pure Hollywood.'

24

Elizabeth began talking before the specialist even opened the file.

'I've only just been made aware of my mother's condition. I want to know how you found it and what you're doing to treat it.'

The consultant, Nuala Brady, took off her glasses. 'First of all, good morning to you both, and let me ask, Brigid, how are you?'

Brigid's hand went to her throat. 'Never better. My voice went a bit during the Christmas, and my appetite. But I've been eating solids again, and gone on a holiday. I'm sorry I missed the tests last week, but I got plenty of sun.'

The consultant smiled. 'I'm glad you did, but you also need to tell us if you're not coming in so we can give your slot to someone else. And we would also like to know immediately if there are any changes in your condition.'

'I was afraid you wouldn't let me go on my holiday, or would advise me against it.'

'We can't stop you from doing anything you want to do, but you're right, we would have suggested you didn't go, but from what I can see, I'm glad you did. The last bloods found discrepancy.'

'I've been drinking a lot of mountain tea,' Brigid broke in. 'I think it's helped with the loss of appetite. I don't feel as much tightness any more, or much of the lumpy sense in me throat.'

'That's good. Now if I can just fill Elizabeth in on what's happened up to now. We've found it difficult to locate the primary cause of Brigid's pain. It's not showing up on the CT scans and X-rays. But she feels there are lumps in her throat, which—'

'The mountain tea,' Brigid tried again. 'The lumps seem to feel smaller after it.'

'Mother, will you let me find out what's going on here?' Elizabeth asked impatiently.

'I'd have thought you'd be interested in the tea, you like natural things.'

'I want facts right now, and I want them from the doctor, not you.'

'Well' – Nuala pressed her fingers together – 'the short answer is that we're doing nothing until we're sure of what we need to do.'

'Sure of what exactly?'

'We can't find much right now without opening Brigid up in several places, all of which could prove wrong and none right. We're having to investigate using gentler methods.'

'But before, she had a growth in the base of her throat, and you took that out straight away!' Elizabeth exclaimed. 'Surely it's dangerous not to be treating her in the same way?'

'It was one lump and the diagnosis was straightforward. This could be cell cancer, a slower-growing type. The round of tests she's in for today should prove more helpful.'

'But not conclusive?'

'Cancer is a protean illness. It can change shape and form – metastasise. We have to be sure of what we're doing if we want to treat Brigid successfully.'

It had been five years since Brigid had first been diag-nosed with cancer of the oesophagus – and she had been lucky to survive. They both remembered the odds quoted to them. Most die within a year. One in five survives for five years. It had been five since Brigid was last operated on and they'd practically forgotten the retired specialist's prognosis.

She had been so well.

'If you're ill you've done something to be,' Brigid had informed everyone last time. She told them, and herself, that she was going to get better. 'Never smoked a day in me life, that's why. It's only the smokers die of it, you know.' No one was about to dissuade her. If it made her better, her own manufactured facts would be fine.

This time there was no manufacturing. Sore throat, dreadful tiredness, weakened vocal cords, loss of appetite, weight loss and a choking sensation that left her unable to speak. But then, after Greece, she felt so well.

Nuala Brady began softly, because she had seen that Brigid had begun to hope for a reprieve, or even recovery, and she couldn't give her that.

'Some of the tests indicate abnormality, some not at all. The bloods are confusing. But they're no longer clear, as they were in November.'

'Could it be that she's masquerading the symptoms, producing them out of a psychological need?' Elizabeth ventured, though she knew where it would get her.

'What are you saying? That I'm making this up?'

'She's not, Elizabeth,' Nuala Brady intervened. She needed her office in five minutes, and she needed Brigid to be calm for her next news, which was that she needed her to stay in that night and prepare for some exploratory procedures that required a general anaesthetic. 'That's why I've arranged for you to stay here and instructed you to fast.'

Fasting was easy at the moment. Brigid's appetite had receded again since coming home. 'I'm not staying in any hospital bed, the last time I didn't get a wink of sleep. All those coughing oul' ones, moaning about the place. That's not me, I'm not sick enough yet.'

'Again, it's your decision, but you need to co-operate while we find the cause. And to determine that I now need to

do another endoscopic ultrasound, a gastrointestinal exam-
ination and a laryngoscopy to rule out things as much as to
explore them further.'

Brigid rolled her eyes. 'I've had more cameras down me
than dinners. But if it keeps me alive, I'll do it.'

'Remember, you've beaten this before,' Nuala said at the
same time as Elizabeth. And no one beats it twice, all three of
them thought then.

Elizabeth went home to pack a bag for Brigid, then went
straight off to work, because Brigid ordered her to.

'You've got your own business now, and I've got mine. I
don't need fussers. It would worry me more if you weren't at
work. I have company enough here.'

Brigid settled into her private room, something she never
agreed with or to until she got sick the first time. Everyone
was so kind, like they had taken a course in it. It comforted
her. She thanked God that Marilyn had forced her to take
out medical insurance and began a letter to Nikolas, via
Kristos.

*To think a few days ago I was sitting on your patio and we
were watching the sea together. I hope to do it again, and you
know you're always welcome at my home, though I know you
don't like travel any more than I did, and to be honest,
Nikolas, it's lovely where you live, and where I live just
doesn't have the same charm. I've kept things in a square all
my life and the house proves it. Though Elizabeth has added
her touches. She got on the telephone to Kristos, she said, to
tell him. I'll be in touch, on the telephone, when I'm out of the
hospital. The doctor says there may be nothing wrong. All this
time worrying about the future, and now I don't have much
of one left.*

Nyphi was there.

'I didn't think I'd see you again.'

Nyphi stood by her bedside.

'You went through this yourself, Nikolas and Kristos told me. I can't thank you enough for passing them on to me. He's as good as you are, to me.'

Nyphi looked at her hand.

'I know, the ring, it's funny having it, when you were buried wearing the one he gave you.'

Nyphi shook her head and put her hand to her lips.

'It's not the way women of our age talk, I know. But I may not be able to for much longer.'

They found three small lumps no bigger than safety-pin heads. It was in the very early stages. There was more hope once it hadn't spread. Brigid was almost cheerful when she got the news.

'Good, now we get on with getting rid of it.'

It was decided that she was to go for treatment the following Monday. Five days to wait. They prescribed a special low-protein, dairy-free diet for her to try to build up some energy for the forthcoming onslaught. Elizabeth followed it to the letter, rounding up her healing friends and removing all tea leaves and dairy products from the house. Brigid tried to get the rest of them to intercede.

'She's not eating anything unless it's on the sheet and she's not going anywhere that isn't good for her. Mass is allowed,' Elizabeth conceded. Elizabeth spent all the time Marilyn wasn't in her room on the Internet, looking for new developments and information on Brigid's condition. She refused to go to work even though Brigid begged her to and Theresa and Grace offered to mind her. It was decided to keep it from Marilyn for another week so she could enjoy her weekend in Wexford. Then they phoned her, asking her to come a bit early on the Sunday. She was sitting at the table with them by eight o'clock. They didn't have to say anything.

'It's back, isn't it?'

'How did you know?' Brigid asked. Elizabeth rested her hand on Marilyn's shoulder.

'Complan at Christmas.'

'Ah, you and your mother have too clever of a nose. I'll have to change me brand.'

'You're going in tomorrow? Do you think you could have left it any later to tell me?'

'It was my decision, Marilyn,' Brigid insisted. 'I want you enjoying life.'

'You're my grandmother.'

'And I want to see that smile on your face each Sunday. Then you can help me with the bedpan every Monday! That'll be nice for you!'

'How can you be so cheerful about this?'

'Because I have a wonderful family and a man at the back of me. Mine's an open world.'

'She's right, Marilyn,' Elizabeth intervened.

'And before you go anywhere, I want you to do the same and get on with life. Grace has the job of day nurse, you two have your work to do.'

'Now—' Elizabeth started.

'Now nothing, you went through all the minding of me the last time, and this time you have to mind yourself, Elizabeth. That business is your life now. And you both know that I like to go through these things with the minimum of fuss. You'll do me no good with attention. It only upsets me.'

'Oh, I forgot!' Elizabeth suddenly exclaimed. 'Tony Devereux! I never cancelled the drink with him. Since we got the news, I've been brain-dead.' Elizabeth put a hand to her face.

'There's no need to cancel that drink,' Brigid snapped. 'The same applies to men as working – the more you do, the better.'

'Mother! You'll only just be out of hospital. They might not even let you out.'

'I know Tony's not spectacular, but please give him a chance to know you, and when you know him, you might be more of a mind to love him.'

'It's not fair, when you're the way you are, to put this pressure on me.'

'The pressure's on us all, Ma.' Marilyn rarely used the word and only when she had something important to say. 'It's finding people to share it with that counts.'

25

'For God's sake, you were doing this five years ago. It's Monroe, not Munro,' Elizabeth tore into the receptionist.

Brigid had to put a hand on Elizabeth's shoulder. The stone-faced receptionist handed over the file, which had all her records and which she would carry now, from room to room, for any uniformed professional to pick up and peruse like it was a telephone book instead of an account of one woman's walk towards death.

'Sorry, Mother,' Elizabeth said quietly. 'It's just all so familiar.'

Brigid nodded. They went to the waiting room, which still had the same innocuous décor and landscape prints on the wall.

'Nikolas called last night, when you'd gone to bed,' she whispered to Elizabeth, because there were others waiting. 'He did his usual singing.' They both smiled. It was a full-throated, life-giving sound, if out of tune. Soon Brigid's voice would become thin again, and tinny, like listening to an old transistor. 'He put the phone handle out to the wind. I could hear it rustling through the trees, and then he played some music that sounded just the same. Then he sang, cats screeching as usual, but lovely.'

'I know, I heard it from my room. Kristos wrote to me on his behalf, for you to read when you got here.' Elizabeth pulled a card out of her handbag.

'You read it to me.'

'It's long.' Elizabeth could hear the trolley coming down the corridor.

236

'Then give me the gist.'

'He wanted you to know that he and Elena and Nikolas made a pilgrimage to a place on Skyros for you, known for healing the sick. It's the remains of an old temple, with a small church built on it. They camped outside and lit a fire. Then they paid someone to keep it burning for seven days. So tonight there's a fire lit somewhere on the Mediterranean, just for you.'

Brigid took up her daughter's hand and squeezed until it was white. 'Go home now, love. Get out for that drink, or I'll get cross.'

Then the nurse came, wheeling in the drip, and it all began again.

Tony chose the pub because of the privacy it offered. 'Before you bolt and before I say anything that makes you, let me get you a drink.'

She wanted white wine. He went to the bar and offered the barman a drink for himself if he opened a fresh bottle. The barman looked across at Elizabeth and smiled at Tony.

'Good luck there, mate,' he said as he poured Tony another orange juice.

She was dressed in crushed velvet with piles of auburn curls. 'A little help from Clairol,' she admitted when he complimented it. He took in the soft lines around her eyes, the full lips that she pulled in as she listened, a glimpse of her pearl teeth and the tilt of her head. To have her sit in front of him was like having a favourite painting come alive. The chance to watch her seemed wrong, like he wasn't worthy, and he struggled to contain the feeling. She sipped her wine and they watched the fire. He took a deep breath.

'Marilyn plays the piano beautifully.'

A veil fell across her eyes. Most wouldn't have noticed, but he was aware of each tiny gesture. 'No doubt about that,' she answered. 'There never was from the day her fingers touched the keys.'

'She didn't go further with it, then?'

'Well, I had a hard job getting anyone to notice it, including her. It just wasn't meant to be,' she said without bitterness, but this was practised.

He left it alone and looked for something else, since she wasn't talking. He could see she wasn't rude; if anything she was afraid to start a conversation for fear of not appearing to be a listener.

'Sometimes havens can be traps,' she said suddenly into the silence that had grown. 'When you were at our house, you said that it was a haven.'

'I meant that anyone could be comfortable there. And I'll never forget the cornflower window.' He shifted. This was no informal get-together, it was a business meeting. He caught sight of himself in the mirror behind them. This is what lack of confidence looks like, he thought – sloped shoulders in an out-of-season jacket. I'm no good at this.

'No man has been happy there, Tony, for as long as I've lived and long before that,' she said, quietly and gently. He could ignore it, chat on, charm her back, but his reflection told him he wouldn't. A man can respect the wishes of others too much. 'Tony, I didn't instigate this, and right now I'm not ready for it. There's a lot going on.'

'Could you be clearer, please?' He managed a smile.

'Look, to use the cliché, it's not you, it's me. Love, for women my age, is a rare thing. I've discovered my life is better without it.'

'Elizabeth, I couldn't agree more. I'm divorced. I gave my wife everything and still she wanted more than that. I paid her maintenance when she was living with a millionaire. And when he kicked her out she came looking for what I had built up in the years without her. It almost sent me back on the drink, that pressure.'

'I'm sorry, I didn't know you'd been married.'

'Does it make a difference?'

'Yes, it does, because you'll understand when I tell you that I loved someone. I gave up everything for him except my child. I gave up the truth. So I can't lie to you when I say that there's nothing inside me right now, even less than there is normally. My mother's very ill, Tony, she could be dying. I have to be honest and I have to ask something of you which I have no right to.'

He lifted his head.

'I have to ask you to help my mother. She has cancer and a lot of her time is spent worrying about me. Would you consider seeing me the odd time? I could confront her with the truth, but right now I can't. I know this is awful. I know I'm asking a truthful man to lie. But I don't know any other way.'

'Of course you can ask it of me,' he nodded.

'And you know that there's no possibility . . .' She couldn't finish and he could see she was close to crying.

'Just call me when you need me.'

'Thank you, Tony.'

'Don't mention it. I'd do the same for anyone.'

'Would you like to stay for another drink?'

'To be honest, Elizabeth, no. I hope you understand.'

'Of course. I'll walk home, if you don't mind.' She should have felt relief, but there was a weight of pain in her chest. Life is always the wrong way around – one person wanting, the other rejecting.

In Loughlin's Wood they made him tea and gave him sympathy, but they didn't agree when he said that he was going to keep up an appearance.

'Tony, will you not give yourself a break? She's broken

your heart. I know her mother's sick, but it's none of your concern.' Colin put it to him straight.

'Life's a bitch, and so is she for asking you.' Mick looked like he wanted to make another house call.

'Don't ever call her that again,' Tony warned.

'Or what?' Mick said. 'Don't be fucking yourself up, for fuck all, for fuck's sake.'

'I get the message,' Tony said. 'I know you're concerned. I thank you for it, but I have a mind of my own, lads, and it's made up.'

Tony went to bed at the same time as the day-shift world did. He just couldn't join them in sleep, and after long hours spent thinking he got down to a single choice – tomorrow morning he could buy either a bottle of whiskey or a packet of cornflower seeds.

'Well?' Brigid called from her room as soon as Elizabeth came through the door. 'Did you give him any kind of chance at all?'

Elizabeth went up to her. Brigid had reacted so well to treatment that they'd let her home the same day.

'We'll see each other, occasionally. I want to move slowly. I'm too caught up in other things. Please don't criticise me, I'm feeling bad enough as it is.'

Marilyn appeared on the landing in time to catch what Elizabeth had said. Elizabeth went to bed, not wanting another three-way debate.

'Well?' Marilyn asked as she came into Brigid's room and closed the door.

'Well, she's doing it for my sake, and no other. But as long as she's doing it, there's a bit of hope.'

26

The weeks turned to February. Valentine's Day saw two cards on the mantelpiece.

Elizabeth was outside waiting for Marilyn to give her a lift. Things had changed in that regard. Marilyn cared less for work, Elizabeth more. Her studies were piling up, her finances dwindling. Dealing with Frank Whelan's solicitor was like dealing with Godot – he never turned up, he didn't answer calls and saw no need to write letters. Had Elizabeth been qualified, she knew, it would be a different story.

He simply didn't take her seriously, and if Eileen had to wait until June, when Elizabeth did qualify, she would go under, living on handouts from relatives, asking Elizabeth to write letters to utility companies to keep things connected. Frank had had them all turned off before she finally got back into her own house, which he had to let her into.

Frank Whelan appeared that morning. Elizabeth put the key in the door and out of nowhere he stood beside her. He was small. If Eileen's accounts were anything to go by, this was the smallest man in the world.

'Mr Whelan, I do not discuss my clients on the front step of my office,' Elizabeth said, thinking of the handful she'd had so far. 'And I do not intend to jeopardise my reputation by consorting with my client's husband.'

'Let me in. It's in her interest.'

'If you wish to make an appointment, to discuss your wife and nothing further, here's my card.' She closed the door in his face.

As she walked into the office, the phone rang. It was his mobile. She jotted down the number quickly – he'd changed it so Eileen couldn't contact him.

'How much is it going to cost, this appointment?'

Elizabeth paused. 'Five hundred euros.'

'You've some neck.'

'I'm afraid a cheque won't do.'

'I don't have that cash on me.'

'Then take an appointment in fifteen minutes' time, Mr Whelan.'

He put the money on the desk. 'Look at this office. I've got a bigger toilet in my house.'

'"Your" house, Mr Whelan?'

'I want to come to an arrangement on that.'

'An arrangement? What would you be suggesting?'

'You can make enough to get out of this bunker and a foot on the ladder. Maybe even get your exams. I talked to your former employer, he says you were very capable, but he had a fair few stories . . .'

'That's none of my concern. And if you wish to make a formal complaint about me, you can do so through—'

'Now, your daughter, she's your concern. Fine daughter you raised, she's a dab hand at making a woman see sense. I hope you're of the same disposition. It'll be worth fifty thousand to you, no questions. I'll give Eileen something, of course, but she's not having half. Sure, she did nothing for it. Not like you, a woman with your own business,' he said as he looked around the office.

'Mr Whelan, your wife bore and raised four children. She's living off her sister's charity. Your house is valued at over two million, by three separate agents.'

'I'll give her money once she sees sense. If she married

anyone else she'd have had the kids, but not the cash I made.'
Frank was righteous.

Elizabeth nodded. 'I can see what you mean.'

'If you can, then we're getting on.'

Frank did all the talking, Elizabeth did all the listening, nodding where appropriate.

At the end of an hour, he leaned back in his chair. 'Your daughter didn't lick the smarts off the ground. When this is all sorted out, maybe you and me can have dinner?'

Elizabeth nodded again. He grinned. Then she spoke, and he stopped smiling.

'I'm happy that you've given me the five hundred euros in answer to my first letter,' she said as she opened a file, 'of 7 January, which requested that sum for a week's shopping and petrol expenses, plus clothing, school transport and extracurricular activities for two of your children. Now you only owe us another four thousand. I'll pass this on to your wife.'

'You were nodding to all of this.'

'I nod frequently when I understand something.'

'Nod to this, then. I never forget a face. I got the hang of you all right. You're nothing like you were then. Dublin's a small place, Elizabeth. There's a lot could come out if I let it. You have the bitter look about you. As does your daughter.'

'I think we're entering the realms of the ridiculous here. Consider one name, Mr Whelan – Magpie. Then I'll ask you to leave.'

'He'd never tell you anything,' Frank said, leaning across the desk.

'I have no idea what you're talking about, but I do know of Magpie Holdings, and I have records. You'd better see your way to what that means.'

'Where'd you get them? You must've stolen them.'

'My source, Mr Whelan, is my client. I'm representing her.'

'Eileen had no access to them either. There's nothing missing from my paperwork.'

'I have a photocopy in this envelope, which you can take with you if you wish. It's one of several my client is aware of.'

He opened the envelope and read it.

'This is a lodgement slip, it says nothing, proves nothing. It's not even in my name.'

'The others that my client is aware of are bank statements, Mr Whelan. From the same period. And I've been to the Companies Registration Office. Their records unfortunately don't show when companies dissolved, as this one has. Funny how it ceased to exist just when Ireland was becoming more prosperous.'

Frank Whelan left without ceremony.

She was trembling. Niall had taken them to a flat sometimes – it must have been Frank's. But Niall had gone to great pains to ensure she was never seen by anyone he was associated with, let alone in conversation with them. She'd never imagined she'd have to use Eileen's trump as her own defence. It left her floundering, sure she'd broken any number of codes of conduct.

She pulled herself together. By the time Eileen Whelan came down the stairs Elizabeth Monroe was calm, handed over the five hundred euros and advised her client. 'I think we'll be hearing from his solicitor.'

'What did it?' Eileen wanted to know.

'The name Magpie was enough.'

'I thought the company had ceased to exist. You showed him what I gave you?'

'I showed him and I told him we were aware of the bank statements.'

'But I don't have any of those.'

'I made sure not to say we had possession of them, merely that we were aware of their existence.'

*

On his mobile, Frank called a number. 'I found someone you used to know, very well. Do you remember you used to spend time at my place?'

'Don't talk like this over the phone,' Niall Tormey snapped. 'Come over to my office.'

'Not until I've seen my solicitor. I've got things to take care of first.'

Frank made another call. 'I have some information that could prove useful to you.'

'How useful?' a female voice asked.

'I'll come and see you.'

'I'd rather you didn't.'

'Ah now, I've got good news for you.'

'How good?' She was still undecided.

'The best.' He waited in silence.

'There was a time when your information was free.'

'This is free, if you'll have nothing more to do with Eileen. You won't want to when I tell you. She knows we liked bird-watching. Magpies. She wasn't as dozy as she made out.' Frank was afraid now of how much Eileen might have on him. He didn't want anything shared with anyone, not even the Tormeys.

'I suppose,' Judith agreed immediately, like giving up a thirty-year-old friendship was easy. 'I only knew her through you. But I wouldn't say she was dozy, Frank, I'd say she was frightened.'

As soon as he hung up, Judith Tormey picked up the phone again.

'Eileen? Are you free to talk? You just left the solicitor's? Yes. Sorry I haven't been in touch, Niall told me you and Frank were splitting up. I'm feeling a bit the same way myself. Will you come over for lunch? Soon?'

Frank Whelan's solicitor, long known to him, was remarking that for a mean man he could be very stupid.

'You're paying her off like she has information on you, Frank. You should be sharing that information with me.'

'As if. I'm telling you – give her the house, and another few bob. Sign before they get time to think.'

Frank paid his solicitor enough for them to send over an approved letter by courier that same day. Elizabeth replied within twenty-four hours – the offer wasn't enough. Through the land registry, Elizabeth had tracked down at least one property Frank had owned through Magpie, a property bought for a song and sold when the area was rezoned for business development just before the company closed down.

'How did you get onto that?' Eileen asked when Elizabeth told her what she'd found.

'I thought about what I would do if I was using inside-track information on financial and business development. I'd play Monopoly – speculate, buy houses. But I'd never build hotels if I was concerned about becoming known.'

In light of this, Frank's solicitor thought it more than appropriate to agree to the demand to sign over the house entirely to Eileen and the children, along with a one-off payment of one hundred thousand euros to cover her expenses while she sold it and moved to a smaller property.

'I could get you more,' Elizabeth said, looking into Eileen's eyes.

'No.' Eileen was quiet, too quiet for someone victorious. 'The house will look after me and then set up all the kids after that. It's enough.'

'I'll grant you, it saves you huge sums in court battles, and his solicitor is a great battler.'

As Eileen was leaving, she asked Elizabeth a question. 'How much did he offer you, exactly?'

'No money would have been worth it.'

'You've earned more in recommendations, let me assure you. I have plenty of friends in my position.'

'Your husband was a betting man, Eileen. Don't feel the need to bet on me. This was a lucky break. Be careful who you recommend me to. And please always let me know first.'

'Yes,' Eileen said, surprised at the Elizabeth's firmness of tone, 'naturally.'

Still Eileen's friend came into the office the following week, unannounced.

'Eileen told me she wanted to call you, but I persuaded her not to. You know how public my position is.' The first thing Judith did was pick up a business card off Elizabeth's desk. 'Elizabeth Monroe. You look like someone I know, but I can't place exactly. I'm good with faces, never forget one.'

'I'm not,' Elizabeth forced herself to lie. 'I can't remember yours. Though I do, of course, know your husband.'

Doesn't everyone? And they'll know him more before I'm done with him. Judith thought before she began to speak. 'I see Eileen got the house, and the kids sorted. If you can do the same for me, you'll be doing well, but my husband is ten times the operator Frank is. They knew each other too long to be good for each other. Like Eileen, I don't want an Old Boy near this.'

'Mrs Tormey, I can't manage your case. You need serious help, and you can afford it.'

'Why? Because of who he is? Isn't that more reason? I have proof that he even had a child behind my back. I can ruin him with all I have. You should be jumping like a Jack Russell to snap it out of my hands!'

Elizabeth looked at Judith Tormey. She knew the claim was true. She knew Niall had never made a move professionally without his wife's approval.

'I want you to start immediately. I want the settlement

done and dusted so that I can come out with it all by spring of next year. That's not a long time, only nine months. You can make a child in that.'

'Why nine months?' Elizabeth forced herself to ask.

'Election year.'

'I see. Do you know where the child is?'

'No, but I have a copy of a private investigator's report, right here. I paid the man twice to give me the same information he supplied Niall with. He's kept the report all these years, in his safe. I kept mine too, in mine.'

'So you have separate safes?'

'For valuables. If we were ever broken into, he doesn't know the combination of mine and I don't know his. Politics is about striking when least expected.'

'Life,' Elizabeth said, placing both palms together as if in prayer, 'is about that.'

Judith Tormey smiled. 'Do you know he does that with his hands, when he's concentrating?'

Elizabeth kept hers glued together.

'Are you sure that I don't know you from somewhere? What was your name before you married?'

'I didn't change it.' Elizabeth watched her. Judith stared back.

'Well done indeed. You give up a lot when you give up a name. Will I show the report to you? I'm afraid I can't leave it until we've discussed terms and you've signed something.'

'No, thank you. Ruining public reputations isn't my bag. And at this time I have a very sick relative who needs me, so my focus isn't entirely on the office.'

Judith Tormey stood up. 'Thank you for not wasting my time, Mrs Monroe. Or is it Ms? The modern way? Good afternoon.'

Elizabeth closed the office at three to get home to Brigid,

whose illness could no longer be hidden. It was the beginning of Lent. When she was eating at all, Brigid was eating Elizabeth's vegetarian cooking.

'Nikolas doesn't touch the meat for the six weeks, so neither will I.'

What was Brigid's saying? Christmas is significant, but Easter is decisive. Elizabeth would have to tell Marilyn about her father, well before Easter.

As Judith Tormey approached Elizabeth's office, she wondered what her husband's ex-mistress would look like now. She knew Niall – he was the type to have a mistress, and some were no danger. Elizabeth had been anything but confident. She'd been an arm clinger – Niall had liked that. From the minute they'd watched her speaking at a public debate at which he'd been judge, her ability had been obvious, if not her self-belief. Judith had known this would be his next one.

If Niall could see her now Judith suspected that he would still find her attractive, but it gave her a certain pleasure that he would also be shocked to see the fifty-something face of a once-raving beauty, since he hadn't been around to see her age slowly over the thirty-three years since Elizabeth had disappeared. Elizabeth had taken the child that Niall had promised to Judith. Judith had never forgiven him for it, or her for that matter. No wonder it helped Judith to see what time had done to her rival.

Then a thought struck her. I look older than her. And another thought. I am older.

The reality of who Judith Tormey was hit her. She was a doyenne just about to lose her job as her freefalling politician husband threw away the last vestiges of his career by trying to oust his own leader. A leader she had cultured as an ally with carefully constructed dinner parties and 'chance' meetings at charity functions where he had done a lot of talking and she had listened, as if devoted. Of course Niall had far more intellect and would have been a greater presence in such a position. But he had played cards wrong at vital times. The longer they had served together, he officially, she unofficially, the less inclined Niall had seemed to listen to her.

If the rot in their marriage was to be examined it would have begun at the time of Elizabeth Monroe's disappearance with the child. Judith had always been prepared to put up with mistresses, once she held on to the status of being married to the master. When he had promised to bring home a child, for them to bring up as their own, she had known where that child was coming from. He had never said, and hadn't needed to.

She had everything ready for a June arrival, as she had been advised by Niall.

Then July had arrived, and she had asked, with her customary patience and diplomacy, where the baby was.

'There is none coming,' he went white in the face as he spoke.

'What?' She couldn't not lose her composure. They had prepared carefully for this, as they did all their arrangements. They had even discussed names. 'But we have it all organised, upstairs, a nursery.'

'We'll have to get unorganised.'

'Niall, please.' She couldn't hide the sense of loss, the shock that this was not going to happen. 'I need this child.'

'You need this child?' He looked at her with a contempt he had always managed to withhold in his dealings with her, but she knew was there. He had never loved her. But she had once loved him. It had been brutal to realise it was not reciprocated, that she was a career consideration as much as all the other arrangements. She had one affair, as a retaliation, with disastrous consequences. Then she had come to terms with who she was, just as she was doing now over thirty years later. But she couldn't come to terms with not getting the baby to bring up, for herself. She knew better than to argue there and then.

It wasn't mentioned for a week, then she gave him a drink when he got home from the work that was his life, and brought it up again.

'I know we can't have that baby. But couldn't we adopt? It's clear I'm not going to have a child, from the tests. We could have any number of children, if we adopted.'

'I don't want anyone's child, Judith, I want my own.' He whispered it. They never had mentioned anything so directly, before or since.

'But that isn't possible.' She saw his honesty as her opportunity to persuade him, she was already practised in this art, having been groomed for it in a political family where men made careers and women assisted.

'It will be, if I can find her.'

'Niall, if she's not prepared to give the baby to you, you can't take it.'

He looked up from his drink then, asked, with a coldness she felt still in her spine, 'What makes you think that?'

'Don't be such a fool, Niall! You have power, but it's not absolute. You can't take something that's not yours.'

'*She* is not a *something*. She is mine. And before you get on your moral high horse, and talk to me about infidelity, will I tell you what the surgeon said to me after your operation to sort yourself out? He said that you had been operated on before, he said the scarring was man-made. Don't go giving me arguments about me trying to find the child I made, when it's obvious you got rid of one, along with any chance we had for a family of our own.'

*

The daughter. It was information she could impart to create the impression that she trusted her. Elizabeth's reaction showed she no longer lacked confidence. But then, Elizabeth knew that Judith was a magpie, and Judith knew that little sparrow Eileen had given her that information. If only women could stick together; instead all three of them had betrayed one another.

'Do you know he does that with his hands, when he's concentrating?' she'd said. Elizabeth hadn't budged. Judith was filled with admiration for her.

She'd left the office and come up the steps with a smile. Frank's information had dovetailed nicely with Eileen's. Now it was just a matter of tracking down a birth certificate, and business was done.

Judith had told Elizabeth she wanted the settlement to be finished by the next election. She had thought Elizabeth would still resent the man who had ruined her life, as Judith now did.

She thought wrong.

27

Elizabeth shut up the office for the week while she tried to figure out what to do. On the Saturday, she had Leon Marks, a well-known shamanic healer, come to the house for Brigid. Brigid was enjoying the eclectic procession of medicine folk that arrived on a regular basis to the house.

'He'd know about mountain tea,' she advised Elizabeth, who was busy on the computer looking for cures, miracle or orthodox, for an answer that wasn't there.

Leon was the best in his tradition. He'd come from the West of Ireland, where he lived an almost heremitic existence. He held Brigid's gaze and said, 'I'm going to put on some drumming on the portable stereo, and I'm going to light this bundle of herbs. It's called smudging.'

'All me life I've cleared up smudges!' Brigid joked as she settled into the pillows. Leon grinned as he wafted smoke about with a long white feather, humming.

'I'd like to put some sacred feathers in your hair.'

'Oh, I'm happy to go along with the lot,' Brigid grinned. 'The smell of the herbs reminds me of Greece.' She chatted while he prepared the ceremony.

Fifteen minutes later, she felt her spirits were lifted. That morning the fear had settled on her, as it usually did on waking, but now, maybe due to the distraction of the whole thing, she felt energised.

'I'm enjoying this, and the bit of music. I hope it's not pagan, though.'

Leon shook his head and smiled. 'It's the kind of pagan

God loves.' He carried on with the sage and rosemary bundle, which was seriously smoking now.

'Elizabeth, have you taken the battery out of the alarm?' Brigid cried just as it went off.

Elizabeth scrambled to stop the alarm, and when she finally managed to stop the high-pitched squeal she heard laughter from upstairs. Brigid and Leon were sitting on the bed.

'Mother, can I point out that Leon is the country's best healer in this tradition and I'm paying for his petrol, his B&B and the fee for coming here, and you're laughing. Can you not just take this seriously?' Elizabeth couldn't believe she was saying this, but her mother's good humour in the face of death, and her own inability to cope with what was coming up, made everything unbearable.

'It's okay, Elizabeth. Laughing is a serious matter.' Leon said it gently, but it could never have been gentle enough for a chastened Elizabeth, who left the room and went straight to her own to cry herself out. Leon left an hour later. Brigid showed him out, since Elizabeth didn't reappear, and he insisted that she be left alone.

'I'm sorry, Leon, she has no manners.'

'I think she has beautiful manners, and is beautiful.'

'Well' – Brigid's eyes lit with further opportunity – 'she's going a-begging if you're that interested?'

'She'll never have to beg, Brigid, and I'm gay,' the tall man smiled.

'Another one! You should call in six doors up and meet my sister, there's a lot of you about these days.'

'More than ever,' Leon smiled, 'since the world became a more honest place.'

'Well, I'll tell you now, if you don't tell my sister. The world is a better place for you. I don't know who wrote in the Bible it was wrong, it certainly wasn't God. The gay people have all the fine qualities.'

Leon took it for what it was – an apology she still couldn't make to her own sister.

'Leon,' she said, surprised to find her eyes moist and embarrassed, 'you remind me of my husband, the Greek one I was telling you about. We're not officially married, but the spirits know all about it. You'll be like him in a few years' time, honest, tall and that. He's coming over to see me.'

'When?'

'I don't know exactly. His former wife, she's in spirit now, turned up to tell me last night.'

'How wonderful.'

'It will be. He'll make Elizabeth go back to work – she has her own business and wouldn't go near it this past week. Now, son, how much do I owe you? It should be me paying for it, it's enough that Elizabeth set it up.'

'Nothing, you have paid me. This service is a gift to you as it was to me.'

As soon as Leon left, Elizabeth came out of her room, her eyes puffy. 'Sorry, I fell asleep. I have the cheque here for him, where's he gone?'

'Home, without a penny. You'll have to send it to him when it's all over.'

'What do you mean?' Elizabeth said, watching her mother, who was looking at the cornflower window on the sun-filled landing.

'When I die.'

'Don't say that.'

'I'm not intending to go without trying to stay, but I'm ready to go on to the next place. If I get some more time out of God, then I'll use every minute. So either way, Elizabeth, I'm happy. You'll have to forgive me for not being miserable. Help me by doing the thing that worries me most – looking after yourself.'

'I am looking after myself, I'm just qualifying. I've just set up my own firm.'

'You're alone. Marilyn has the perfect lad for herself now; you can't hide behind your daughter any more.'

'It wasn't that I hid behind her, it was that I had to hide her. And I'll tell you why.'

They went down to the kitchen, where Brigid drank hot water with lemon and Elizabeth had an industrial-strength coffee. She wasn't the ill one, but it was like Brigid's illness had taken her over, and she realised it was because here, after fifty-two years, was a chance to know her mother. There was too much to clear up, so she began with the biggest secret of all.

'Do you know the politician Niall Tormey?'

Rathmines, 1968

Elizabeth opened the door to her bed-sit and found Niall Tormey in the doorway. She was coming up to nine months pregnant and he was full of concern.

'You look worn out. Do you have the spare key? Just in case anything happens in the next few days, so I could get in. I'm sorry I didn't get here before now, there hasn't been a moment,' he apologised.

'Sorry, I don't know where the spare is. My brain's jelly. I'll get one cut for you.'

She hadn't seen anyone in over a week. She never saw anyone now but him. The conception had been an accident – hers. But he hadn't abandoned her. If anything, he had become more solicitous. Ten years her senior, a man in his prime, he had all the resources to keep her and he had used them.

'You should've let me move you somewhere decent.' He seemed to have trouble even wanting to sit down. His well-cut casuals were at glaring odds with the shabby surroundings, dirty since she had no energy to clean.

'I don't want to be too much trouble. You're giving me enough as it is.'

'And I could give you more.' He leaned forward in the chair he had finally chosen.

'Niall' – she could barely say it – 'could you please hold me? I know it's not like that for us any more.'

'Not right now.'

'Please, I don't want to lie about this.'

His embrace was awkward and brief and left her feeling more lost than when she'd humiliated herself by asking for it. 'There's something we need to talk about – your future. It needs to be secured, things need to be fixed for you. I want to make sure that happens.'

It was like he was the father she didn't have, like he was her saviour. She was relieved that he could see what was needed. She and the baby couldn't stay here, they would need somewhere proper. They would need him.

He offered her three thousand pounds, enough at the time to buy a house and car outright and start a new existence. He offered her the chance to get into a course of study and 'put all this behind you'. Then he offered her a house and a car as well as the money. 'You'll be set up for life.'

The price was the child. It was the only thing in his life he couldn't fix. His wife was unable to conceive. Elizabeth had thought they didn't have children because they didn't sleep together. She'd met Judith at the same function at the same time as she'd met Niall, and it was an impression she had formed that he had never disputed. Now she knew it wasn't true.

There had been a debate organised for young members of both parties to argue the toss on local issues at local level.

He was one of the judges and she was one of the speakers. He made a point of coming to her at the end and saying how much he admired her.

Judith was right behind him. She was elegant, attractive in a thin-lipped way and cold. She was used to watching her husband's charm and knew where it ended up. He took Elizabeth's address and said he would be in touch with her, with a possible work offer. She told him she would turn it down, on principle. But she wouldn't turn him down. And she thought that she could handle herself – at seventeen she thought she could handle a twenty-seven-year-old rising star politician. When she left home she'd lied about her age and told everyone she was three years older. Later she would realise she was a child when it came to life, one who had been sheltered by her mother to the point of not being able to deal with it.

She felt so sophisticated selling fine clothes in the day-time at a department store and making love to a powerful man in the evening, at least, whatever evenings he could make it. It was all so French. When she got caught it was all so Irish. In the beginning he could make it most evenings, in the middle his visits were twice weekly and by the end just once a week, to check on her progress.

The dull pain under her breastbone would come back to her in dreams. It began the moment the offer was made. He saw her silence as a bargaining strategy. 'Six thousand, and all the rest too. Last offer,' he said.

He didn't understand that she was imagining looking at her child in newspapers, raised as his. The despair she felt told her she still loved him and it sickened her.

'What would you tell Judith?'

'I wouldn't have to. She'd be grateful. And she'd be a good mother. The best,' he said as if he had ordered her to be.

For a snatch of a second she thought she might just take

him up on it. She didn't want the child. She wanted to go back to working in Switzer's and having men look at her, having fun, a future. She was a nineteen-year-old unqualified mess with no means of supporting their child without his help. Now she realised she might not even have that help once the baby was born.

'Of course, it can't be my name on the birth certificate,' Niall was explaining as if she'd already said yes. 'But I'll adopt as soon as possible. It will want for nothing.'

'Except its mother,' she said, as if she wasn't saying it all.

'Now don't be like that. You know you're not capable . . .'

'Capable of what?' She didn't ask it like a question.

'Looking after it.'

'I take it I still have a choice here?'

'Yes, naturally.'

'Then my choice is thank you, but no.'

He stood up immediately. She saw that he was angry and wasn't going to show it. She had always known what the arrangement was. She had never expected to love him so much that she was willing to accept anything. Except for this.

She almost went home to Brigid that night, but too much had gone on there and she had the certain sense she wouldn't be accepted. There was no way she could arrange a marriage before the child came, as was the custom. That had happened to her mother, married in May. Elizabeth had been called an early Christmas present, but in reality she was right on time, a full-term baby.

Niall left and she marvelled that he had waited until so near the end, when she was most afraid, before revealing his intentions, and had involved his wife. She knew he must have told Judith before making such an offer to her. They were a business, and a successful one at that. She waited until she heard the front door close before opening the cutlery drawer, taking out the spare key and putting it in the bin, wrapping it in tissue paper first.

Five days later, when she was screaming for her mother, the midwife said, 'Your mother can't help you now, but I can. Now push. You can do this.'

Alone.

Still, she was sure that when he saw their daughter he would be like her, unable to do anything that didn't involve protecting her. He came to the bed-sit and saw Marilyn, though she told him she still hadn't thought of a name.

'She looks like an Ursula,' he said as she held her shell-pink, tiny hand. 'My mother was Ursula.'

Elizabeth felt herself lighten at that.

'Are you sure you won't reconsider?' he said immediately after.

'No. More so than ever, no.'

'No child of mine is growing up in a place like this.'

He wasn't angry, but rather spoke like he was sorry for her. This frightened her more, as if the decision would be taken out of her hands.

'Do you have a spare key yet?'

'No.'

'Then let me have yours and I'll have one cut.'

'No.'

He knocked the next time, and when she opened the door – she had promised herself she wouldn't – he put his foot in the door. The doctor was behind him. They left because she threatened to scream the place down for assistance.

Once she had persuaded him to go, she knew he would have her sectioned, an easy thing to do with an unmarried mother. She tried to leave errands until the end of the day, believing if she left the flat in broad daylight she would be caught. One night, just after dusk, she was walking up the road and saw two cars outside the old Georgian house that her flat was in.

With the money she had left from what he had given her, she disappeared in the clothes she stood up in, with Marilyn, leaving everything she owned at the flat.

Elizabeth knew never to trust her feelings for a man, or his for her. Each time a man came near her, she found herself loosening that attachment as soon as she became close to him, and finally severing it. And all the time she watched Niall's progress and wondered what her life would have been like if Marilyn hadn't come along when she did.

'I'd have wasted more years,' she answered her own question. 'And she was what he was supposed to give me.'

It was an answer, but it failed to acknowledge all her feelings.

If it hadn't been for the communes, she never would have survived. At first she was horrified at the prospect of living there, but then, in the welcome they offered, she realised her mother's social attitudes were embedded in her like pieces of shrapnel. Brigid's verdict on hippies was that they were all 'layabouts'. Some were, some weren't. Her daughter grew up without a father, but she had five of them in the first three years as Elizabeth went from lover to lover. Drugs killed communal life before the establishment did. The places got dirtier and seedier and one morning, when she woke up on a single mattress on the floor with her daughter curled into her and saw a couple having sex across the room, she went home.

Brigid shook her head slowly from side to side.

'Well.' Elizabeth felt like she wanted to lie down on the

bed and sleep. 'What a disgrace I am, for depriving my daughter of a father. Letting her grow up in conditions like that. She remembers still, you know, the reason why we came home.'

'I don't think that. I think you knew the man and you acted on what you knew.'

Elizabeth's eyes filled with tears. 'But when Marilyn got older, when he couldn't take her from me any more, I should have done something then. She's always wanted to find him.'

'I think Marilyn has always wanted to find the idea of him. She's always had a strong enough mind, she could have coped with knowing this earlier.'

'Do you think I don't know that? He didn't reply to my letter.'

'But he'd have had no option if she had turned up in person.'

'You're right.'

'Now is better than not at all. I can help you with how she reacts, and there's no doubt she'll react badly.'

'When would she not have done? I know this'll be the end of her and me.'

'Not if I have anything to do with it.'

'I didn't have the strength to stand up to you,' Elizabeth whispered, looking into Brigid's eyes, 'or him. I just ran away from both of you.'

'Well, you have it now.'

'I know.' Elizabeth looked out at the garden. She hadn't had the same time to look after it since the business began and Brigid got ill. 'I'm going out into the garden. When she comes home tomorrow night, I'll tell her.'

It was almost midnight when Marilyn walked through the door, but they were waiting for her.

'What are you two doing up? Look at the state of me. We

had a fight. I'm with his horses, morning, noon and night,' she said in a way that told them she was loving it. 'Well, not exactly with them. But Sean says I'm getting better. They're still huge but not as terrifying. I've even begun to like the smell!'

They were smiling at her, but they didn't encourage more conversation.

'Marilyn, his horses are his livelihood. And he's right,' Brigid smiled. 'Don't fight with him on my account.'

'OK.' Marilyn sat down. 'Is this about Brigid?'

Elizabeth looked at her. Should I tell her? her eyes asked. Brigid nodded her head.

Elizabeth told the truth, simply, directly, not attempting to protect herself with excuses. For Marilyn there wasn't one. The truth took one hour of explanation, during which Marilyn was silent.

'So that's it?' she finally said.

'Yes.' Elizabeth waited for what she knew was coming.

28

'Funny.' It was like she hadn't breathed for the hour. 'I'd never have expected someone like him to be my father. What would he see in someone like you?'

'Now, Marilyn,' Brigid stepped in.

'No,' Marilyn protested as she rubbed her palm across the back of an aching neck. But she couldn't feel the tiredness any more, she couldn't feel anything. She heard her voice and her voice sounded reasonable, like she was in a meeting at work, dealing with a particularly big problem in her usual matter-of-fact way, keeping emotion out in order to solve it more efficiently. 'No, it's just that you have so little in common with him. I mean he was one of the most powerful men in the country until recently. He was finance. That's more important than Taoiseach. It's obvious, isn't it? Where I get the numbers from now. And I would have got a lot more, wouldn't I?

'I mean, I'd have been someone, wouldn't I? I wouldn't be living here with Mammy and Granny, in my thirties, grateful to have my first proper boyfriend.'

'Marilyn, you didn't just have a head for figures, you had a gift with music too,' Brigid said, because it seemed Elizabeth was beyond words. Having parted with her secret she didn't own it any more, she didn't own anything. She had spent all her energy in giving the long explanation of what happened, leaving out the part where Niall had tried to have her committed. She glossed over this saying they had both wanted sole custody. How could she tell her that? What kind of shock would that be on top of what she had just learned? The fear of losing her daughter paralysed her.

'Yes, yes, that's true as well, good point.' Marilyn raised her finger as if she was taking all the comments down. As if there was pen and paper in front of her. 'I'd probably have had the chance to play without the pressure of realising it pays buttons. I'd have had enough money to do just what the hell I liked with my life.'

'Elizabeth! Say something! Defend yourself!' Brigid got out of her seat.

'I've nothing to defend, she's right.'

'That's not true, you'd have done anything to help Marilyn. Anything!' She addressed Marilyn. 'I saw the state your mother came home in, young lady. She lost her youth in trying to hang on to you, and if I'd been a better parent she'd have hung on to it and gone on to do her studies before she was in her forties. Your mother gave up what she had in the way of prospects to live with me, overbearing though I was, to bring you up properly. She'd have walked over hot coals to get you anything you wanted!'

'Really?' Marilyn's face crumpled and her tears fell, tears of disbelief, of hurt. The meeting was no longer a business matter, it was a matter of lost identity and opportunity. The father for whom she bought presents, the man who sustained her in dark moments, was nothing like the one whom she saw regularly in the media. He was a shark, a smiling one, but a shark all the same. 'Then why didn't she tell me about my father?'

'I tried. I contacted him when you were eighteen. He never answered my letter and I made sure it ended up in his hands and no others. I have a scrapbook, I kept it for you, with all the personal articles I found over the years. The other stuff is in the public domain.' Elizabeth found her voice again, but it tailed off when she saw Marilyn's expression. It was one she'd seen on the faces of many clients over the years, who had just had severe shocks. Marilyn was getting ready for rage.

'A scrapbook?' Her voice was still level. 'A scrapbook in place of my parent. If he wanted nothing to do with me it was because it was too late. At eighteen I was grown up. He probably thought we were after his money.'

'No. It was his reputation he was worried about,' Elizabeth snapped, 'he was always more worried about that. But he liked money as well.'

'A bon viveur? I could have done with a bit of that.' Marilyn laughed harshly. 'I still don't understand why you didn't tell me. Even if he wanted nothing to do with me by the time you got round to it.'

'I didn't want your life spoiled by the fact he didn't want you. It happens all the time, Marilyn, I see it in my work,' Elizabeth stressed.

'Your work. You were a lot more suited to it than I realised.' Marilyn shook her head as she spoke, the bitterness rising. 'You had a lifetime's experience of separating kids from their natural parents.'

'Right, that's it. If you need to hear all of it, I'll give it to you, Marilyn.' Elizabeth fought back. 'My work is about protecting people who were in my position. Powerless, frightened people with no way of defending themselves. I have the experience for it all right. I had to go on the run, not just because he wanted sole custody. He was willing to do anything for that, Marilyn, including hurt me.'

'So, he was a bastard, that's great. It's nice to know all my instinct for the greater good comes from you.'

'I didn't say that.' Elizabeth's voice trailed off. She knew from experience any attempt at rational discussion was over. From now on the arrows would fly and they would be in her direction. It was as she deserved. She could see Brigid had given up too. It was time to let Marilyn rant.

'No, you couldn't, could you? Only a bitch could keep her child from knowing her father this long. Even if you'd just told me who he was! I could have made sense of so many more things! If you had any idea of the amount of questions I've had . . .' Marilyn was weeping now.

'She has an idea, she had plenty to ask her own father,' Brigid reminded Marilyn, gently.

Marilyn stood.

'There is a world of difference between a raving alcoholic and a man who could have run the country.'

'He tried to have me committed.' Elizabeth let this out in a bewildered attempt to pull some ground back.

'I wish he'd succeeded.'

'He would have taken you from me,' Elizabeth called to her before Marilyn walked out the door.

'And where would that have left me? Better off than being brought up by you.'

She couldn't remember how long she walked in the rain without a coat, thinking, The former Minister for both Finance and Sport is my father. A politician she never had any time for, a man of less than average height. Not kind, not a bear, not someone like Sean. She found herself, exhausted, sitting on a bench in a bus stop.

'Does he even think about me?' she asked out loud, then thought, What will I do with all his presents? What do you give the man who has everything, except children? The things I bought are all wrong. I'll give them to Sean. If I'd gone to more meets, I'd have met him. I bet Sean's even met him.

And where was Sean now? Marilyn raged in her head. Training a mad horse in Wexford. Where am I? The left-wing illegitimate daughter of a conservative politician and a lunatic woman who avoids cracks in pavements and collects omens in jars, only she can never remember what they were omens for.

'I'm nothing that I thought I was. I'm an undersized, unfortunately named woman from a working-class background with a big brain and a successful career and a culchie boyfriend!' she shouted at the sky, but it didn't stop raining on her to listen. 'I might even have been a politician – look at all the work I did for the opposition! Now there's a story: "Father and Daughter on Opposite Sides of the Dail". I could've gone to a posh school instead of the local cutthroat comprehensive. I could've been Marilyn Tormey, pianist daughter of Niall Tormey, who attended his daughter's first concert hall recital and is pictured here with her at the National Concert Hall. But I couldn't afford to be, could I? Too much risk. Nothing ventured, nothing gained.'

'You took a risk with Sean,' the father of her imagination said. 'You opened the shed door.'

'You don't exist!' she yelled in her head. 'You're nothing like him!'

Her tongue was dry and swollen from all the crying. She even hated Sean right now for being the big lump he was, with no drive other than to look after horses like they were his wives.

She hated herself for reacting in such an ugly way, for being so ugly all of her life. He might not be nice or a bear, but her father could have made her feel beautiful. A father like him would have protected her.

A quiet voice inside her contradicted her: You've seen him on television, smiling one minute, throwing daggers the next. She took the decision to protect you. She gave her life to that decision, living with a mother she couldn't stand.

'I don't care!' Marilyn screamed at the voice. 'I want my father's name.'

Some drunk lads went by and started making comments. She

268

screamed at them, 'Fuck off and back again, you dickheads.' And they did. No one wants anything to do with mad people. She had spent all her life trying to be sane, sticking to every rule that was ever written about propriety. And where had it got her? Fatherless in a bus shelter at three in the morning, with a best friend who wasn't answering text messages or calls, a betraying mother and a granny who backed her up in the betrayal.

Where was Sean? Why wasn't he there? Why was he working eighteen-hour days in a loss-making venture? Why was she in love with a loser? Because, despite the job and the elephant-sized brain, she was one too.

At 3.30, having dozed off in the bus shelter, Marilyn snapped awake. A car – a Saab – pulled up. Sean was suddenly beside her.

'Marilyn,' he cried, sheltering the rain from her without suggesting they get into the car. 'My own broke down on the way up,' he whispered. 'I had to hitch the rest of the way. Or I'd have been here sooner.' She looked up at him as if she'd never seen him before.

'How did you know?'

'Brigid phoned, Elizabeth's in too much of a state. She's out looking for you on foot. Tony's driving around as well. He's got every spare taxi doing the same. We'd best go looking for your mother now.'

'No. I hope she drowns or gets run over.' She could see in his eyes that he couldn't understand cruelty, whatever the reason. The men coming to the Monroes were all doormats. They'd have to be, to put up with their crap. She could see now why Elizabeth had no problem passing over a taxi driver. She'd been a mistress of one of the most powerful men in the country.

'I don't want to go home.'

'Then you don't have to.'

They drove to Wexford, and he put her into a reasonably clean bed with a cup of hot milk. Then he gave her his arms, and that drove away the hard edges of pain for a while.

Tony found Elizabeth at the same bus stop an hour later.

'It's all right, you can get in. Sean found her.'

'I know, I saw them leave. I just wanted to sit where she'd been.' Elizabeth was soaked. 'I found her ages ago, but I didn't want to drive her off again. I just sat behind that hedge over there, watching her cry. I caused this, Tony. I made this. A bunch of drunk men walked by her and she screamed at them. How could I have put her in this awful place?'

'We'd better go back to your house. Your mother is ringing the controller every five minutes. Sean's taken Marilyn to Wexford.'

'Only to be expected, isn't it?' Her face crumpled. 'Did my mother tell you?'

'She only said that Marilyn found out some details about her father, and I told her not to tell me any more.'

'You're a good person not to want to know.'

Tony didn't say that Brigid had told him anyway. Brigid had asked him, almost desperately, to look out for Elizabeth for the next few weeks. Her hands, as well as her voice, had been shaking in asking him. Tony had already agreed to drop her to the hospital the next day for her treatment.

'I'm never going to see her again, Tony.' Her hair was plastered to her head and her shoulders ached from the damp seeping through them. She had Marilyn's coat in her hands but hadn't put one on herself.

'You will. When the storm dies down, she'll see reason. Come on, get in the car.' He drove fast – she was soaking – but he wished he could go at cortege speed.

'Do you see reason in a woman taking away her own

child's history? You want to know me? Well, here's my big secret. Marilyn's father is Niall Tormey, ex-Sports Minister, kicked out to there from Finance. Now he's not even on the front bench.'

'I know. I read the papers.'

'His wife came to see me the other day, for legal advice. She's going to divorce him and intends to use Marilyn as part of her smear campaign.'

'Does she know you're her mother?'

'Yes,' Elizabeth said quietly. 'She knew it before she even came into the room.' She looked around the car. 'You know, I've talked more about myself inside this cab than I've ever done in my own house.'

'It must be the driver.' Tony smiled at her. 'Now get inside, get dried off and get sleep.'

As she got out of the car, she said, 'I have to wake up to this tomorrow.'

29

February. Nikolas Faltaits was watching all the signs of spring's arrival with the glad heart of anyone who is close to plants. From his patio he could see the ferry arriving, as it did twice each day, once in the morning and once in the evening, into the harbour of Achilli at Skyros. From here Achilles sailed to the Trojan War and the fulfilment of prophecy.

Nikolas picked up his hat. From his house he took a jar of home-grown olives, and pickled courgettes to place in another jar, and put dried dill and tarragon into paper bags. Everything fitted into a small holdall with one change of clothes and his bouzouki. He got into his truck, drove to the harbour and left on the next sailing.

In Athens he went to his son's house. Elena phoned Kristos at work and he came home. After a short conversation, it was agreed. For the first time in his life he bought a plane ticket, from Athens to Dublin. Kristos drove him to the airport.

'I should have gone before,' Nikolas said to no one.

Kristos suddenly remembered something.

'You don't have a passport.'

At the passport office they said it would be two weeks before it would be issued.

'I don't have that,' Nikolas said to his son, rather than to the official. 'I will have to drive my truck to Ireland.'

'You'll still need your passport,' the official advised. 'Passports don't just apply to the sky traveller.'

'Your truck is thirty-five years old,' Kristos reminded him. 'We'll go in my car, I can come with you.'

The official, a Greek who knew the value of stories and the love that wrote them, stamped the forms. Nikolas Faltaits had his passport within five hours. He could catch the next flight. Kristos called the Monroe house and Elizabeth answered. Marilyn had been gone two days. Nikolas would be there by the next afternoon.

The pain was there again for Marilyn, in the morning, hunting her down. Sean had gone out to the horses. It was already well after nine. She got up with the intention of cleaning and found that she couldn't. She put on her wellies, which she had found in a children's shoe shop – she was only a size two. They were sensational candy-striped turquoise and usually sat beside Sean's well-worn black size twelves like a poem about happiness.

She usually went into the yard with a wheelbarrow and mucked out the stalls, once there wasn't a horse in sight. Today she didn't have the energy. She made a coffee and took it outside, where she could hear the horses at the gallop with Sean and the two Mikes, who still didn't say boo to her. She contemplated calling Julie, but her mobile was permanently switched off.

Without knowing why, Marilyn found herself at Delaney's stable door. She was worked first and by now was having her breakfast, bothering Noble for his. When the stable bolt went back she raised her head and her whole body tensed at the approach. Horses are flight animals, and Delaney took it to tearaway proportions.

'I'm not going to bother you.' Marilyn spoke without looking at the horse directly, which Sean had advised her to do. Give the horse time, bend your head and turn to the side and they'll fall in with you. 'I just want to sit down here.' She pulled up a camping stool that sat in the corner for the long nights Sean had put into Delaney when she first came. 'Until life gets easier.'

Marilyn sipped her coffee, Delaney munched her hay and Noble tried to ignore both the neurotics taking up space in his life. Then Marilyn started crying again, as softly as possible. She knew it was going to take much longer to cry that way – she needed great heaving sobs. She stood up to go. That's when Delaney stuck her head over the stable door. The only person she had ever done that for was Sean.

Marilyn looked over her shoulder and Delaney immediately snapped her head back in. Something made Marilyn sit on the stool again, and start seriously crying. Delaney knew what this was about.

By the end of it Delaney still had her head over the half-door, ears twitching. Marilyn didn't look at her or attempt to move.

'I just can't go back. Would you be able to?' she asked the horse. 'And I can't stay here either. I have to get to work. I'm supposed to be in work now. I never get in after half past eight. And it's ten, and I'm not there. They'll think I've died. And home, they don't know where I am, not that they deserve to. Do you think I should I ring the Dáil, Delaney, and ask to be put through to my father? What did your dad do? Mine's a high-ranking politician with no clue as to my current existence. He only saw me once. Anyway, I'll just phone in sick, if that's all right by you. I'll do it on my mobile. Oh no, I haven't got it, or any clothes. Or money. I'll go to the house.'

When Marilyn came back Delaney still had her head over the box, waiting to hear the outcome, as Marilyn thought she might be. Marilyn pulled the stool a bit closer, but Delaney tossed her head at that, so she put it back exactly where it had been.

'Sean had already phoned work, so no doubt he phoned the house too. I talked to Larry and asked for all the holidays I haven't bothered taking, from today. That's six weeks, Delaney. I'd had a fantasy someday to go around the world or something, but it looks like I'll be spending them in Wexford, if your owner will have me.' Noble was asleep by now, but Delaney was listening intently. 'Larry wasn't happy. My granny's got cancer, I should be up in Dublin helping, but instead I'm down here. I don't even want to go back to see her. How selfish is that? She thinks my mother was right to keep it from me. Backed her up. Okay, I know she didn't say that, but . . .'

Sean came in at dinnertime to find sandwiches and tea ready.

'Can I stay?' Marilyn asked. 'Six weeks.'

'You can stay six years. Sixty.' He reached out for her. 'If I had more to offer, I'd say the rest of your life.'

'Is that an offer?' The look on her face was so wide open, so fearful, it made Sean afraid for her.

All the vulnerability was at the surface now, and she had no fight in her. It's a lot to happen to a little woman, go easy on her, but tell the truth. She's had enough of lies, and you're no better for the one you told her at the beginning. He answered her softly.

'It will be, but not yet. It'll be an offer when I have something to offer.'

'Sorry.' She reddened in saying it. 'I shouldn't be so presumptuous, after only a few weeks.'

'Yes, you should, you know how I feel about you. Will it do you to know I never intend not to be there for you, Marilyn?' He remembered his father telling him that was what a good marriage was all about. 'Besides, my sisters have taken to you. They know I've a good one, I wouldn't be allowed lose you.'

'They've taken to me?' She was so grateful for the feedback it made him feel sorry for her. 'Good.' Her eyes filled with tears. 'It looks like I'll need replacement family and friends soon. I tried to get in touch with Julie today, on your phone, to say what had happened. I haven't heard a word from her since she got her big break. Typical. I hand over two thousand pounds and she skives off without a backward glance.'

'I think you know that Julie would prefer your position to the one she's in.' Sean pushed back Marilyn's hair and slid off her glasses, so she could get at her eyes to mop them.

'What makes you say that?' Marilyn leaned back in his arms, to look right into his face. He felt like he'd been punched in it.

'I mean she's one of the loneliest women I ever came across.'

'Yes . . .' Marilyn's voice trailed off. 'I know she is. I should have been more sympathetic, I'm always giving out to her about something. I probably won't get another chance now she's dumped me.'

'Hey, hey, what's this?' Sean pulled her into his arms, pressed her against him. 'Julie loves the bones of you. Didn't she put us together?'

'I know.' Marilyn sobbed. 'I just feel like I'm losing everyone, like there's nothing to love in me. I try my best but I put people off with my manner. I don't make jokes or sing songs or catch people's eye.'

'You caught mine, Marilyn, and you held it.' Sean spoke into her eyes, the shine visible now in tears. The colour took his breath away. 'You're down on yourself. You're in the quicksand and all you have to do now is hold on to my hand. I'll pull you out of it.'

After years of either fending for herself, or fighting to get out from the protective clutches of mother and grandmother, she felt the relief of being able to relax into his love and care. It weighed so little on her, it felt so easy to be loved with Sean Monroe. She remembered a Quaker phrase she had read. To worship lightly is to love.

She felt all of his worship and no demands with it. In that moment she promised herself she would give back to him as he gave to her now, for as long as she could. For as long as she was able.

'Delaney and I were talking.' She spoke into his body. 'Well, she did a lot of listening. Is it okay if I don't clean up the house today?'

'It's all right any day, Marilyn.'

'Since you don't like me doing it anyway, since you can never find anything afterwards.'

'Not at all,' he lied. 'You're here to get over your shock.'

She spent the next six weeks talking to Sean, and to the horse. Marilyn never touched her; Delaney would never allow it. But they sat side by side and her head would almost touch Marilyn's, so that Marilyn could feel her breath.

People kept phoning from Leahy's to ask where things were. Brigid and Elizabeth phoned every day until Sean advised them not to. Sean kept trying to get Marilyn to speak to her mother.

'They say Nikolas has arrived, for a little visit,' Sean told her.

'He can use my room.'

'They say he doesn't need it, he's in with Brigid.' Marilyn raised her head at that. 'She says they're married. Will you talk to them?'

'Just ask how her treatment is going,' Marilyn instructed Sean.

'Tell her it couldn't be better, I'm not nearly as sick as I was the last time,' Brigid told Sean the next time he rang. 'We just want her to know that we're here for her if she needs us.' Brigid was lying, and Elizabeth was hovering in the background.

'She already knows. She just needs to be left alone,' Sean whispered, but Marilyn still heard and nodded her confirmation.

In later weeks Brigid didn't call as often. Marilyn, absorbed, didn't see this as any more than respecting her wishes. She got Sean to check on how the treatment was going, and the same word came back. Fine.

It was just as well that Sean had less to worry about in the yard. Delaney started to improve. Marilyn didn't do anything except clean (well), cook (badly) and talk to her. Sean said it was the talking that did it. Marilyn went to the horse's stable for therapy and in doing so took the focus off Noble, who always used her visits as a chance to rest. One morning, Delaney allowed one of the Mikes to ride her instead of Sean. With so much less weight in her saddle, she barely touched the ground.

The third round of chemotherapy robbed Brigid of wellness.

'Of course, this is yet another thing Marilyn hasn't been informed of,' Elizabeth said as she held her mother's hand where the drip was being fed.

'She's a lot to get used to, knowing that gobshite is her father. And as for you,' Brigid said, shaking her head, 'you'd think you'd have learned from the father you had about rogues.'

'He wasn't then what he is now.' Elizabeth watched the rest of the bag feed into her mother's vein. She wished she could take the sickness on herself. Brigid saw the thought and smiled.

'I've had more life than you and I want you to enjoy the

life you've got. Now cheer up, there's a good girl. Third time lucky.' Nuala Brady had told them this was the treatment where people got sick, if they were going to.

Three days later, Brigid signed herself out of hospital, saying she felt more dead than alive in it. 'If this is going to kill me, it's going to do it at home.'

At the same time, Nikolas Faltaits was being guided through arrivals at Dublin Airport by one of the cabin crew who'd looked after him on the flight. He held on to his small satchel and bouzouki. She ushered him through passport control quickly, knowing their tendency to take bewildered foreign men with no English into small anterooms.

'Thank you for the concert, Nikolas,' she smiled. 'We all enjoyed it. Even the captain after he got over his shock.' Nikolas had played on the plane, against regulations, but the other passengers had protested when the crew had tried to stop him.

Theresa was waiting for him and they shook hands formally. On his way from the airport Nikolas kept shaking his head, pointing to the development and the motorists and pedestrians making their way through it.

'*Melancholia*,' he whispered.

Theresa smiled. 'It's the same word in English. We can't all live exactly as we wish to, Nikolas.'

By the time they pulled into Verbena Avenue, Nikolas was in the back of the van examining all Theresa's tools. '*Exochos!*'

'I'm glad you like them. We're here.' He folded himself up neatly, as if he wasn't the tall man he was, and climbed into the passenger seat again. Looking at the house he shook his head sadly, looked at Theresa and put his hands around his neck. '*Thanatos*.'

Grace came to the doorbell. Theresa wanted to check how

Brigid was, afraid the emotion of seeing him might be too much. When Brigid could talk, she talked of little else but him.

'She's asleep on the sun lounger by the patio doors. Nothing to eat or drink today. The district nurse put in a drip for fluids,' Grace said.

He followed them through the hallway, having wiped his feet carefully before stepping on the recently exposed Axminster. She was wide awake and smiling. He went onto his knees and took her hand. '*I syzygos.*'

'That means wife,' Theresa whispered.

'I know.' Grace took her hand. They left them.

Elizabeth came home from work late. Eileen Whelan had called in to ask why she had refused Judith Tormey's business.

'If it's principle you're turning it down on, you're foolish. I thought you'd be over the moon at the chance to make a name with a client like her.'

'But she knew you were using her signature on Magpie lodgements to get a good settlement out of Frank,' Elizabeth said.

'Oh, we have more history than that. She knew I'd never use it in a public way. I told her as much when we met at lunch. We don't speak about things directly, Judith and I, but we have our way of talking to each other, and being entirely understood.'

'Did she want to know about Frank?' Elizabeth found herself asking, out of curiosity.

'No, she knows all there is to know about him.' The way Eileen said it made Elizabeth wonder what was at the back of it. But it wasn't her place to ask. 'But she wanted to know all about you, the woman who beat one of Dublin's best solicitors into a brilliant settlement. I thought she saw an opportunity for herself. I know she hasn't been happy with Niall for years. And I thought you would have seen the same.'

'It was just too big a job for me, Eileen.' Elizabeth had to remind herself that Eileen had lived with Frank and had ignored his practices for the sake of their children, not because she was unprincipled herself. But sometimes, when she talked about ignoring Judith's business involvement with Frank at some stage, Elizabeth had trouble liking her as much as she did.

'How do you know her, Elizabeth?' Eileen looked at her.

'I'm sorry?'

'How do you know Judith? How does she know you?'

'I'm sorry, Eileen, I can't say anything except that it has nothing to do with you and Frank. Please don't ask me again.'

'So you do know her. That's something she'd never have told me. I'd never have allowed her to call on you unannounced if I thought it wouldn't be for your benefit. I was genuinely trying to help. I told her that I know Magpie isn't the kind of association she wants everyone knowing about, but Elizabeth is a principled solicitor, well, almost!'

Almost is right, Elizabeth thought. You don't know what I used to get Frank out of my office.

'And I've had a bellyful of people lying to me. I came to you for answers because I know you're trustworthy,' Eileen finished.

'And you wouldn't say the same of Judith?' Elizabeth asked.

'I would not. I phoned her a few times in the past few weeks, to see how she got on with you. She never answered. When I finally got her, it was like she never needed your number for anything. She says she and Niall are sorting it out.'

'Maybe they have to.' Elizabeth was relieved to hear the Tormeys weren't getting a divorce. In the three weeks since she'd met Judith Tormey, she'd let time slip by without having contacted Niall, as she knew she had to. Every time she tried to pick up the phone, she failed to. Behind that failure was the knowledge that she didn't want to deal with seeing him, to witness him register her age in the way Judith had. At least now she didn't have to fear exposure for herself or Marilyn. Now she just wanted to go home, to meet Nikolas. 'I have to go, Eileen.'

'I hear from Judith that your mother isn't well.'

'That's right,' Elizabeth said, bringing down a curtain between them.

As Eileen left, she said one more thing: 'I want you to know, even if you're not telling me everything, I'm always going to be grateful to you.'

At the bus stop there were groups and couples just heading out for the night to the cinema or restaurants; it was still too early for the pub. Too late for her. Tony's cab pulled in, and she couldn't help smiling.

'Your chariot awaits.'

'Tony, how do you know exactly when I leave work? Every evening?'

'Well, one or other of the lads passing by radios in to tell me. They know you've got a sick mother and that I want to drop you home. It's part of taxi life. One of the drivers has a kid coming off heroin. Her ex-boyfriend's a dealer, still around, so any time he's seen in their area, we all have the description of him and we radio in. Things like that. Most of us have worked together a good few years.'

'Please, Tony, there's no need for this.'

'There's nothing in it, Elizabeth. You're having a rough time, I want to help and this is a small way I can. Besides, if the lads in work didn't tell me, Brigid would. She got Theresa to phone me' – Brigid could no longer speak properly – 'to say you had a visitor coming.'

On the drive home she thought about telling him that the threat of exposure was over, but she wanted a night off, after twenty-one of them, from thinking about Niall and Judith and all that went with them.

'Will you come in?' The answer each evening was no. 'Don't you want to meet Nikolas?'

'I think it's more important you do, without a stranger in the house.'

'Tony, you're not a stranger, you're a good friend, to myself and my family. We can't thank you enough.'

As he pulled away, another radio announcement went out for him. 'Tony, your man is in the Gresham Hotel, came in one of ours. No official bus. Do you want to hover outside? He might need lifting home.'

Nikolas was in her garden, examining her plants in the moonlight, Persuasion roping herself around his ankles. He stroked her absent-mindedly, concentrating on what Elizabeth had put into the garden, nodding at everything.

'Is it okay if I meet him outside?' she asked Brigid. 'Will I turn on the lights out there?'

Brigid shook her head.

He looked up as soon as the door opened and pointed at the groups of tulips and daffodils providing the first spring colour, against a whitewashed wall, in a raised bed at the end of the garden.

'*Eikona!*' He pointed to them. '*Eikona!*' He pointed to her.

He was everything she'd imagined him to be. The scant memories she had of her own father came back to her, and she saw that this man had none of that fear.

'Icon,' she whispered to herself, 'a picture, I think that's what he's saying.'

He embraced Elizabeth and touched her hair, like it was silk. He kept repeating a word – '*Poissi.*'

'Must mean beautiful,' Brigid wrote.

Later Grace would inform them that it was poetry. 'Do you remember the Sappho course?' She smiled at Theresa, who had slept through most of it.

For now Grace and Theresa had made themselves scarce, leaving a salad made with Nikolas's olives, focaccia, some chilled white wine and an apple pie. Also a note: 'Anything you need.' Brigid watched them eat and gestured impatiently each time they stopped.

'Nikolas,' Elizabeth said, 'when it comes to eating your dinner, you get away with nothing here.'

He nodded. He had no idea of what was said, but every idea of what was going on.

It was a silent meal full of peace. Afterwards Elizabeth turned on the lights again that lit up the garden and powered the water feature. Nikolas exclaimed at the sight: '*Orofos!*' And for the first time since she'd paid the electrician an arm and a leg for it, she found it justified to someone other than herself.

'Marilyn has to meet Nikolas. I'll go away for the night so she can come.'

'Time enough,' Brigid wrote. She was asleep in her lounger within five minutes. Nikolas picked her up in his arms and carried her up to their room. For the first time in fifty years, Brigid Monroe would share her bed.

Elizabeth began to clean up and was surprised to see Nikolas back in the room again. He was a big man but he moved like a cat. He sat at the table again, fingers folded into one another, elbows out to the side, watching her. She felt no discomfort. He had a plain look in his eyes.

'Tea?' He nodded. 'Or coffee?' He nodded again.

She made coffee, but when she went to pour it into a mug he stood and stopped her. He picked up Brigid's chipped china cup, unwashed, out of the sink and held it to his lips. Elizabeth started to weep at the sight. He put down the cup, sat down in the chair and, smiling, put his hand over hers. Her tears were a good thing. The more she cried away from Brigid, the less likely she would be to cry in front of her.

Around midnight, Tony had a politician in the back of the taxi, groaning about his need to get back to Leinster House. There were road works, even at this hour, working on the new over-ground train line that had turned the city into a car park.

'A late call, is it?' Tony enquired.

'Yes.' He didn't want to say any more.

'Can I point out one thing, as an unobtrusive driver of a public licensed vehicle?'

'The first I've met, but go on,' the politician sighed. This was why he never rode in a taxi unless there was no other method of transport. The days of having his own chauffeur were gone. He couldn't be seen to have a private one, because then he wouldn't be a man of the people, which was his calling card come elections.

'Was it not your government that planned this infra-structure? These road works?' All men are equal in traffic jams. He would never have this chance again.

'It was, just don't tell the press that.' The passenger had the resigned tone of someone about to resign. 'And you'll know the last ministry I had was minor and wasn't related to this pile-up.'

'Oh, I wouldn't call it minor, sport is the only thing people in this country care about these days. You're more important in that department than you were in Finance.'

The politician smiled without smiling, said nothing.

'Sometimes, when I sit in this traffic, even at this hour, for this long, to earn my living, I wonder who's responsible.'

'I'll tell you two things, if you ever want my job,' the senior politician said, looking out at an Ireland he'd once helped to run before falling out with the current Taoiseach. 'Don't think and don't, for God's sake, say. You'll win from that. Otherwise you'll be driving this the rest of your life.'

'I don't mind. I'd rather do this than do what you do,' Tony said.

'You might think we're all a shower,' the politician said, 'but you know, I've done more good in office than bad, that's the truth.'

'I'm glad you see it that way,' Tony smiled into the rear-view mirror, 'because it's hard to get into or out of bed otherwise.'

'Okay,' the politician, bored by this Joe Soap, said. 'What makes your day? What makes you get out of bed?'

'If you really want to know, and even if you don't, I'm going to tell you. A woman.'

'You mean you've found the thing we're all supposed to be looking for?'

'I think by your tone you suppose it doesn't exist.'

'Oh, I didn't say that. I just know what you're talking about doesn't make the real world go round.'

'Without it nothing gets done. And the prospect of it is the best feeling on Earth. The search for love matters more than position.'

'Ah, but then you turn into companions.'

'Without companionship you can't enjoy any kind of position.'

'You have me there, I can't disagree.' The politician leaned on the passenger seat headrest, a person at last, which is what Tony was good at bringing out, and a curious one at that. 'Who is she, then? Tell me about her.'

'Her name's Elizabeth. She has the look of Botticelli's paintings around her, a purity she has. Even after everything that's happened to her. She put her own life second to her child's. But now that she's got the chance to live again, it doesn't look likely that she'll get to enjoy it.'

'What's wrong with her?' The politician looked concerned.

'People are what's wrong with her. People who don't know her want to harm her, so all of us that do know her have to help her.'

The politician wrote down the driver's serial number. When they arrived at Leinster House, the politician got out quickly. 'A lovely name, Elizabeth. Keep the change, and give my regards to her.'

Niall Tormey went straight to his office to clear away the relevant paperwork, in preparation.

30

'I didn't come here for counselling.' Julie was sitting in a room with a woman who looked like benevolence itself – round, homely, kind. 'I came here to get sorted.'

'Since we started talking, you haven't used the word "abortion".'

'At the front desk, on the phone, even in the consultation room everyone called it a procedure.' Julie arched an eyebrow and reached into her handbag for a cigarette, before remembering she couldn't even smoke, it made her sick. 'I'm picking up on that.'

'Sorry, but some of our clients are very traumatised.'

'I know,' Julie conceded. 'I'm not that delighted myself.'

'That's why we need to know, for your sake, your reasons for wanting this.'

'I think those reasons are private.'

'Fine. I should point out that this is a confidential session. What you tell me here I don't reveal even to other staff, but it's my job to assess your ability to handle – the procedure.' The counsellor smiled at her own training. 'It's not nothing. Women afterwards can feel a variety of different emotions.'

'What are they?' Julie put her hand to the nape of her neck. This was what she hadn't wanted to consider.

'Well' – the counsellor spread her hands – 'it depends on the individual. Relief, loss, emptiness, elation, a sense that they now have another chance.'

'I'm likely to feel all of those,' Julie shrugged. 'I'm not with the father and I'm never likely to be. I have no means to support this child.'

'I'm sensing that's not all.'

'The rest of it is none of your business.'

'As much as I would like to say that's the case, I'm afraid it isn't. Please trust me when I say this is for your benefit. It's part of what you're paying for.'

'Which is a lot.'

'I know. We're one of the better clinics, we provide aftercare and I'm part of that. I counsel you, if you wish, for a number of sessions afterwards.'

Julie then told her: 'Look, I got threatened with a knife by a woman whose husband wanted to get into my knickers, and had to leave straight afterwards. My best friend rescued me. She was pissed off because I tend to get into trouble, and also the incident happened to occur in front of all the big brass in her company. So she let someone else see me home while she looked after the woman. That someone was a man. Naturally, being me, I shagged him, before I realised he was the absolute match for my best friend. So, through my intervention, they got together. Next thing I discover I am pregnant by this man. He's a lovely man, she's a lovely woman, they have a lovely life set out in front of them. I don't want to jeopardise their happiness. I don't want this baby. I don't have parents that give a toss. I don't have any job, and any money that I have I am spending on this. Will that do you? For your files?'

The counsellor listened, then said, 'Given that you have no support system over here, and none of your family can know, I think it might be beneficial if you take the after-sessions. We hold them at a different building, to prevent the obvious associations.'

'So I'm doing the right thing?' Julie was suddenly nervous.

'I can't answer that question, but I can say that you appear to have made a responsible decision in the right frame of mind.'

★

'Lying in bed in a hospital gown – it's a funny thing when you're not even sick,' Julie said to the daytime television host chatting to a couple holding hands on his cosy couch. If she could crawl into a daytime television programme she would, and live there for the rest of her life. Julie was one of the people who couldn't understand why Truman Burbank, the character played by Jim Carrey in *The Truman Show*, had struggled so hard to get out. A perfect world had been designed for him; she'd have stayed in the bubble.

One of the things she'd told the counsellor the day before was that she never wanted children. She'd given the example of her own childhood as a reason why.

'That can change if you meet the right person, find yourself in the right situation,' the counsellor had said.

Fat chance. The operation was scheduled for 11.15 a.m. There was a knock on the door and a nurse, a quiet woman, came in. Everyone in this clinic was quiet, kind.

'Julie, we'll be taking you down shortly. The porter's on his way up.'

'Why do you have to wheel me?' Julie asked. 'I'm not sick.'

'It's procedure. Afterwards you won't be conscious. We need the trolley down there for you, so we may as well wheel you. And you've been fasting, don't forget.' The nurse had no idea how used to fasting Julie was. 'Are you ready?'

The porter was at the doorway and the nurse leaned down to release the brake.

Back in her hotel room, five hundred pounds poorer, still pregnant. The clinic had charged her the full fee, quietly, kindly. She still didn't know why the answer to 'Are you ready?' was no. But she was going to use those after-sessions to find out.

*

The counsellor sat opposite her.

'My mother has always looked after my father's every need, and ignored mine. My name's Juliet on my birth certificate. I didn't find out until I was over twenty. No one told me. I want to know what it feels like to love someone and have them love you back, because you're related. If I give up on this child, it'll be like how my mother gave up on me. And I never, ever wanted to be like her.'

'Your child isn't your child yet.'

'Well, I don't know how in the hell I'll cope, or why I'm doing this, but it will be. I appear to be making an irresponsible decision in the wrong frame of mind.'

The counsellor smiled. Julie smiled back.

She signed on at the local DSS, near the hotel. They put her in a high-rise in South London, after housing her in a B&B for the homeless for three months.

'Not quite the penthouse I had in mind,' she said as she shut the front door.

'You were lucky,' her neighbour Magenta, who had three children with three fathers, all absent without leave, advised. 'People'd have ten kids to get in here.' They gave her forty-five pounds a week, which she survived on. She cleaned a wine bar on the King's Road for cash. The owners said that once the baby came, they'd give her work behind the bar. After all, she was a good-looking girl.

'Made a bit of a mess of things, obviously,' the landlady said to the landlord.

Over the intercom the voice of Niall Tormey asked Elizabeth if his visit was convenient. She had only just arrived in before him.

'It has to be,' Elizabeth said. 'Come in.'

Waiting for him to enter, she couldn't help thinking what a mistake it had been to go out on her own. One single act, such repercussion.

The door opened. The latte she had on her desk was going to grow cold. The memory of him came from inside her body, a reaction rather than a thought process.

'Can I sit down?' He didn't look around him; all his attention focused on her. This was what he did. People were flattered to have a powerful man's entire concentration.

'You can. I'm afraid I've nothing for you to drink.'

He smiled. 'What's that you have?'

She pushed the latte across the desk. 'Have it if you want.'

'You read the papers this morning?' He didn't touch the coffee.

'I heard the news. If you don't want to go, your party seems to want you gone.'

'It's speculation because I walked out of the Gresham last night.'

'What are you doing here, Niall?'

'To see what I can do to keep you out of this. Judith may react badly.'

'She doesn't know?'

'No. I don't want you hurt by what doesn't involve you.'

'Oh, come on, Niall. I'm aware of what you have to lose if a mistress and child come out at the same time as your resignation.'

'I haven't resigned.'

'You will.' There was an empty space in her where feeling should be. She had watched him for over thirty years, never been able to get away from him. Almost every week there had been a picture or a mention of him in the news. Even in the conversations of friends she had heard his name mentioned. The temptation to contact him had pushed away the possibility of anyone else. She was aware now that this was the same emotion she had felt when her father shushed her as he walked out the door. Only Niall had just walked through it. The days when she was young and beautiful had been pearl days and she had given a whole string of them to him, keeping nothing back for herself. But Marilyn. By looking at her, he knew all she was thinking.

'What's she like?' he asked, voicing what he'd wondered each day.

'A lot like you.'

'Too much?'

'Yes. She's determined, brilliant and focused.'

'What's her name?'

'Marilyn.'

'Please, tell me you're joking.'

'I'm not.' She hung her head. 'The midwife who helped me was Marilyn.'

'And you were a Monroe? No wonder we couldn't find you.'

'Who's "we", Niall? On second thought, don't tell me. We need, at all costs, to keep her out of this.' Elizabeth looked at him.

'Does she know about me?'

'Yes. But not until recently. Judith came here.'

'I know, which is why I'm here. I've been hearing a lot about you, from a lot of different people, after over thirty years of nothing.'

'No, you heard from me when she was eighteen, which you chose to ignore. Niall' – and this is where she compromised, for Marilyn – 'I know Judith's been associated with at least one venture.'

'You need to tell me what it is before I can do anything.' He sat up in the seat opposite her.

'Magpie Holdings.'

He stood up.

'That's not a name you should say to everyone, and it's not a name you should worry about. I'm here to tell you that I'm going to sort out the Judith problem. I was told it was still a concern of yours.'

'It was, until I heard you were a cosy couple again.'

'Judith and I, cosy. Ha.' He threw back his head. 'I've got to think about some things, do a few others. But when I'm done, when I've fixed it up, could we please meet again?' He looked at her like he'd forgotten all the other business. 'I want to explain.'

'There's nothing to explain, Niall, we both know what happened.'

'All I can say is that I wanted to be a father as much as you wanted to be a mother.'

'I didn't want to be a mother at all, until she was born. I was caught.'

'So was I.'

'Nonsense, you know perfectly well you could have looked after us both in a decent way and I'd never have said anything to anyone.'

'Ah now, Judith knew about you! How could I keep a secret like that hidden for so many years?'

'The same way I did. I kept it a secret until just a few weeks ago, from everyone, including her.'

'How did she react, hearing I was her father?'

'She wasn't overjoyed. I had to tell her what you tried to do to me to get her. I had no choice. I haven't heard from her since. I presume she hasn't contacted you either?'

He shook his head.

He looked at her and she could see that he was in pain in the way his body reached back in the seat, as if to avoid her, and for that she was glad, because it meant realisation had landed. He couldn't hide behind his excuses any more, he couldn't justify things to himself, because he couldn't justify them to her.

'If you think I don't feel guilt, you're wrong. I live with regret every day of my life.'

'Regret is fashionable among failures. You failed her, and you failed yourself. If you ever see her, you'll see she's worth more than any trophy position. She's an amazement, her brain is the size of Ireland and her ability to take on tough situations and make them happen—'

'I know, just like me,' he interrupted, wanting this to stop.

'No, Niall.' She looked as if she was sorry for him, something he could never stand. 'Just like me.'

In looking at her, Niall didn't see the lost youth. He saw what Tony saw, a manner and dignity that added ceremony to who she was. A graceful woman with an independent mind. She'd grown into that the hard way, and he knew he was a good part of the hardship.

'I'm not going to run away from this.' He rose. 'Anything you throw at me I'll take as what I deserve, but I'm not turning away from it. I want to see you.'

'Maybe,' was all she could manage. 'Don't think too long about what you're going to do for Marilyn. If you're going to switch ships you need to think very quickly. Now if you don't mind, I have work to do.'

He left to get on with his other business. That night the party switch would become official. They were to announce it at a gala dinner.

He made a phone call to Judith. 'Judy—'

'Don't "Judy" me. It's a done deal, bar the official stamping. This is suicide. If I'm not worth consulting on this, you could at least have forewarned me. I may not be your wife in anything but name, but I run your campaign in this constituency.'

'They're switching me to another.' His voice was as cold as

hers. 'And you'll be doing exactly the same job. We have to move house is all.'

'Move house? You're never here! My father was in this party and his father before him. I don't want to work for that shower.'

'They finished me, Judith.'

'Because you tried to resurrect a leadership contest with a crowd of thugs for supporters. Do you blame them? If I wasn't married to you, I'd finish you.'

'I'll get a senior office. A chance for us both. You know how popular I am in the polls.' There was no denying it, he had a charm the country loved – the punter's politician. He had the touch of the common man, but was easy too with the ruling classes, having long been one of them.

'If it was a chance for us both, why couldn't I be told? Let me answer that for you. You don't even trust yourself.' Judith put down the phone.

All afternoon she waited for the phone to ring with lifelong friends and associates from the party asking for more information. When it didn't, she knew it was over for her too.

'That's the last time you do this to me, Niall. Whatever else happens, I do to you.' That evening she watched it on the news and left her lounge – vast for a family and a park for a woman living on her own. Judith phoned the bookmakers, to speak to the child who should have been hers. Larry himself took the call.

'This is Judith Tormey, Niall's wife. I'm looking for Mari Monroe. She helped my friend Eileen Whelan recently. I want to thank her in person.'

'She's down the country with her chap. She's got a few weeks off,' Larry explained, and gave her a Wexford number. 'Congratulations to your better half in the new set-up. I hope he gets Sport again. We could do with him relaxing the betting laws, needle-sharp they are.'

'I'll get him to look into it,' she said, out of habit.

★

The following day Niall called Frank Whelan and arranged to meet him for a celebratory drink. The news was front-page. People kept coming up to shake his hands, others ignored him.

'Like old times, this is, Niall.'

'Indeed, Frank. Everyone thought I was finished.'

'They don't know you.'

'Did you know that Judith saw Elizabeth Monroe?' Niall asked suddenly.

'I had no idea.' Frank looked as if he hadn't. 'Why would she do that? It'd be like making herself known, giving her advance warning.'

'How does Elizabeth know about Magpie?'

'I didn't know she did.'

'Oh, but you do, Frank. That's how Eileen and her got the house and cash out of you.'

'If Elizabeth told you . . .' Frank didn't finish the sentence.

'She didn't. Eileen told me.'

'What? What would Eileen be doing talking to you?' Frank was trying to work it out.

'She's trying to protect her new best friend from threat. Eileen is loyal, Frank, as she was to you, once.'

'Sorry. It didn't seem relevant. That magpie information's as damaging to Judith as it is to us.'

'It is. This conversation is for your benefit as much as mine. Wipe the account. Copies getting into the wrong hands would be a mistake at this point.'

'We were only doing what everyone else was doing. Using information in the same way everyone else was.'

'No need to justify things to me, Frank. Save that for the tribunal. We're dinosaurs, forced into retirement, not clever enough to be corrupt now. Techniques have improved beyond our recognition.'

'Says the man going to be made a senior minister when they get in next. It's different for you, you still have a career to hold on to, I'm sidelined after the racecourse day, it's the biggest secret in Dublin.' Frank didn't reveal it was Niall's own daughter who had helped him to keep it.

'I'll help you as I've always helped, now I've moved on.' Niall patted Frank's shoulder. 'I'll help you now and say, phone Judith, tell her to check my safe. She knows the combination. There's something in it will interest both you and her.'

Frank stayed seated. He had no choice, he told himself. Niall was the man with the power. He phoned Judith Tormey.

In the safe were Magpie accounts, labelled, dated, telling a story with Judith and Frank Whelan as main protagonists, a two-million-pound story of investment during his period as Minister for Finance. The name on the account was Judith Morgan, her maiden name, but the date revealed she was married. Judith, of course, had been acting in his interest, in projects, companies, developments that had all gone on to do good things.

Niall Tormey had no real interest in this paperwork, having copied it years ago. What he wanted Judith to see were the two photocopied documents: a copy of a patient list and a receipt, both dated 1965.

'He knows about London.'

'No one knows, how could he know?'

'He knows, that's all I can say.'

'What are we going to do?'

Judith listened to Frank's question and was disgusted that she had ever had anything to do with this man. She pictured Niall, back in his office, the look on his face she had always been on the right side of, up till now.

'What about the Magpie documents?' Frank asked. 'Do you still want me to erase them?'

'Did he tell you to?'

'Yes.'

'Then don't. It will prove that we were trying to hide something, and he already knows what else we were hiding.'

Judith sat down in her empty living room and realised, for the first time in her life, there was nothing to manage. There had always been something to manage.

In 1965 she had had too much to manage. An affair with Frank, which was so short-lived it barely happened at all, had led to an unwanted pregnancy. Looking back she couldn't imagine how she had let it happen. She and Niall had only been married a few years. She knew now that he did not love her in the way she loved him, never would, and she was hurting. She decided to play him at his own game.

Her big mistake was having sex with Frank Whelan in the first place, but close to that was letting him take care of the contraception. Lazy men always leave things until the last minute.

When she found out she was pregnant, at a time when Niall wasn't even sleeping with her, she knew there was only one thing to do. She made the arrangements and Frank paid for them. He accompanied her because he was as afraid of Niall finding out as she was. The clinic was official, but the operation itself was illegal. It was described as an appendectomy. But she still had her appendix. Frank had receipts. He told her that if he ever had to, he'd tell Niall. He would deny it was his, say he had been helping an old friend out of a mess.

'I help him in other ways.' She could see Frank relished having this power over her. 'I have a flat he uses. I have enough dirt on both of you to take up farming.' She didn't react because she still felt like she hadn't arrived back in her body. From then on her periods were irregular and painful.

When Niall finally suggested children to her, a few years later, it was obvious he wanted them as much as she, and it united them for a time. Then it became clear, after tests and an exploratory operation, that they never would. The surgeon on this occasion was brilliant at his job and a good friend of Niall's. He told Niall the full facts and Niall, presumably, told him not to mention it to her.

It was round about then that Elizabeth had conceived her child. When Niall told Judith they would after all have their own baby it had been the answer to a prayer. But the baby never came, and something inside her died. She built a life around being a brilliant political wife. Frank married Eileen shortly after this. She was barely out of her teens. Judith took her under her wing a bit, knowing what kind of life was in store for her, but also so that she could keep an eye on Frank.

Frank had always profited by the friendship with the Tormeys, so he'd never used the information against Judith. Now, three decades later, when it was too late to hurt anyone but her, it had been dredged up again.

'He must have told him, given him the receipts for spite, because I met Eileen for lunch,' she whispered into the emptiness. 'Niall had no documents up to now. Or maybe he had them all along.'

She was wrong, the proof had fallen into hands that knew, ultimately, what to do with it.

So Judith Tormey was left with a decision to make. Comply or be left entirely alone. The gala dinner, at which Niall would be announced as a new member of the opposition for the next election, would start in half an hour. Judith knew she could get him on his mobile.

She picked up the phone. 'I've been thinking, about your kind offer. I'd be happy to be your campaign manager.'

'I'm delighted, Judith. We make a great team. And we

won't be dragging the past into this new future of ours, now will we?'

'That was your priority, wasn't it? Not Elizabeth and Marilyn at all.'

'It was all my priority, Judith. I've never liked anyone who tells tales.'

Niall phoned Elizabeth from his office. 'That's fixed.'

'How?'

'So it works, that's all you need to know.' The way he said it dragged her back to a bed-sit in Rathmines. 'Elizabeth?'

'Yes?'

'I'd like to talk to you.'

'Do we have anything to say?'

'You know as well as I do that the answer to that is yes.'

Tony was outside the office when Elizabeth finished.

'Would you mind if I walked home today? I need to clear my head.'

He knew as well as she did that it was about what the papers had said that morning.

Before he went to dinner Niall phoned Eileen Whelan at home. 'Thanks for that, Eileen, it saved me a lot of digging around.'

'I didn't do it for you. I did it for Elizabeth and her daughter.'

'I realise that.' Niall sounded sincere. 'And I can only thank you for saving us all from what would have been a no-win situation.'

Eileen had two more pieces of paper she had held back from her solicitor, unless she'd absolutely had to.

'Well, Elizabeth, you'd never have gone off with someone else and had something to get rid of, now would you?' Niall said to himself. He felt no recrimination towards Judith and Frank, despite the fact he'd found out what they'd done for certain only a few weeks ago. Eileen had handed over her information and told him to do what he needed to with it to protect Elizabeth. Funny how he, the person who had persecuted her the most, was called on now to assist her. Funny how he didn't feel anger towards Judith and Frank, but then, he knew them, and himself, for what they were.

'We're the kind to have no friends, only alliances,' he said as he poured himself a whiskey, drank deeply from the glass, pressed the buzzer and sent his secretary home. Over the intercom she said, 'Congratulations again, Mr Tormey.'

'Yes. Thanks.'

He felt no sense of celebration that he had won a new political lease of life, knowing he had done it to save himself from humiliation. He could handle failure badly, but shame not at all. His whole life had been dedicated to avoiding it. But this most recent shame had brought a gift to him – in being demoted, he was removed from himself, from his previous power, and he saw what he had done to achieve it.

They had thought he would retire, had even suggested it, so he planned one last surprise. Now he had to see it through, when he had never had less desire for it.

'A lacklustre politician is an unemployed one,' he reminded himself, but it seemed he wasn't listening. His imagination carried him back to the times of a young woman, a young love, prospects, when all things had seemed possible. And he knew she had been faithful to him. For thirty-two years she could have exposed him, and she had never done so. Had she hated him, had she sought revenge, she could have done it a long time ago.

'Even if you had realised it when you got her letter, but

no, not you.' He winced at the bite of the liquid on the back of his throat. 'You're a slow learner, and you over sixty.'

It came down to this. If it was a night for celebrating he had no one to share it with.

31

Weeks after Julie had left, having failed to get through to her mobile, Marilyn rang the theatre where *Cats* was playing. Afterwards, she put the phone down and tried the police, to report a missing person.

'You'd best get her next of kin to come in and make a report,' they told her.

Marilyn phoned Julie's mother.

'We haven't heard from her in weeks. Her father's out of the jam she brings. She called round and we weren't expecting her. I couldn't let her in, her father's a bit funny at present.'

'You didn't let her into her own house?' Marilyn asked.

'Now, Marilyn, she hasn't lived here in years. She never contributed.'

'She was a child.'

'I know, but that boy, bringing him into her room. Her father doesn't take kindly to that kind of – anyway, I have to go, he's looking for some tea.'

'Mrs Purcell, Julie has gone missing.'

'Oh, yes, we know. We set three places for lunch for five Sundays and cooked for three of them. We know exactly how much we both eat. It's a waste of the rest. You'd think she'd let us know. You were always the responsible one.'

'Mrs Purcell, with all due respect, you never gave Julie the chance to be responsible.'

'I don't think it's your place to say so, Marilyn, even if it was the case, which it isn't,' she flustered on the other end of the line.

'My own mother bought Julie's first tampons and bra. You've never looked after her, and this is the result. She's running away again, from her own failures. Now, if you want to put things right I suggest you file a police report and let's find out where she is.'

'I'll have to get him to do that. I don't know if he's up to it at present, he's having turns. She'll turn up, she always does.'

'She's not a lost dog!'

A brusque male voice took possession of the phone. 'I don't see what this has got to do with us! She's a grown adult.'

Marilyn came off the phone in tears. 'They won't do anything. Her mother's too weak to stand up to him.'

'I'll phone your mother. She'll know what to do,' Sean suggested. Marilyn didn't object.

Elizabeth got Tony to drop her over to Julie's house. After half an hour, they left with the signatures on forms they had collected from the police station.

'There's something wrong with him,' Tony said.

'Yes, that's why Julie is the way she is.'

'No, I mean there's something wrong. He's got a funny look, like he's on medication.'

'To be honest, Tony, I don't care what those people are up to. The way they were with Julie was heartbreaking.' Elizabeth picked a current photo, from Christmas, and gave the form to the police.

Sean took the call from Elizabeth, and told Marilyn that it was all in hand.

'Why has she gone, without telling me?' Marilyn asked him.

'If she doesn't want to be found, you won't find her, and when she wants you, she'll let you know.'

'I suppose you're right.'

He held Marilyn's hand across the kitchen table she disinfected daily. There was also a basin of disinfectant at the door now, for wellies. 'Don't give out,' she'd said, 'you should know after foot-and-mouth that you can't be too careful about these things.'

The two Mikes had taken to eating their lunch in their van.

But he couldn't deny that the house was beginning to look less like a shed, even if still had a Spartan look. They ate the takeout meals she brought from a Wexford deli. Expensive, delicious, love food. She couldn't help it; the fact she had someone to care for sent her nurturing instinct into overdrive. If she had criticised Brigid and Elizabeth for this, she now understood. She was worse.

'You don't have to do all this,' Sean said frequently.

It hurt her that it irritated him to see the place so clean. What man wouldn't want a fifties housewife who had turn-of-the-century success in the workplace? Then she realised that that was the problem – for every penny she made, Sean made nothing. He lived hand to mouth on borrowed time and with the calm of a man practised at ignoring it.

She offered to do his books. 'Think of it as rent,' she said.

'No, that's too much. I'll muddle along with them.'

The bank statements were falling out of drawers and the unopened bills, all red, were gut-wrenching to witness and not be able to do anything about. Marilyn began to realise Sean's biggest flaw was his pride, as large as his honesty.

Honest people can tell lies. When they have to. For a terrible moment he wondered if Julie had got pregnant. But she'd assured him that she was on the Pill. 'It's the one thing I never mess with,' she'd said.

'I just don't understand it, she tells me everything. It's because I've been ignoring her since I met you,' Marilyn kept on to him.

'Marilyn, she introduced us.'

'I know, but she'd love this for herself.'

'I don't think so. I think she wants a lot better than me for herself.'

'Well' – Marilyn looked at him – 'I don't think that's possible.'

The police knocked on Julie's door one night with a social worker from the Missing Persons Bureau.

'We found you through checking the list of recently signed claimants. We're here to tell you your parents are looking for you.'

'My parents? Not anyone else?' Julie asked.

'This form is for next of kin. But we've also had a call from a friend.'

'Can you tell them that I'm well, and I don't want any contact?'

'Is this because of the pregnancy, Ms Purcell?' the social worker asked quietly. 'If it is, we're sure you'll find that they'll support you. In our experience, most families do.'

'Please, don't tell them.'

'We have to respect your wishes, but a phone call now and then would make your parents' lives a lot easier. We have experience of how parents worry.'

'I don't understand,' Marilyn badgered Sean. 'She fixes us up together, then fecks off. Did she want you for herself?'

'I can tell you the answer to that is no.' Sean wasn't smiling. He was preoccupied with Delaney to the point of distraction. Marilyn knew it was because of his finances. She could solve so many problems, if only he let her. Marilyn was sure that, when Delaney won her first race, Sean would ask her to marry him. So she followed every inch of progress.

Sean was so worked up about Delaney and her progress that Marilyn decided to put on the Catwoman basque Julie had given her at Christmas, to go with her new fuller figure. No work pressures, lots of free time and five meals a day meant that for the first time in her life she had cleavage. She came down the stairs to serve dinner in it.

'What's wrong?'

'Nothing. You look . . . funny.' He stood gazing at the floor.

'It's okay, the Mikes have gone. Sean! It's for a laugh.'

'I'm sorry, Marilyn. I don't find it funny.'

He stopped himself from going after her when she ran out of the room. How could he tell her – when it had all gone so far – that he'd had sex with her best friend wearing the same rig-out? What he wished now was that he'd been honest from the start. He followed her upstairs to begin apologising. Whatever confidence being with him had given Marilyn, he'd just taken some away.

Marilyn let the weeks pass until the six of them were almost up. Then Niall Tormey became front-page news. She forgot about Julie.

'I think you should ring him,' Sean stressed. 'You can't make progress until you do.'

'He'll be too busy now.' She'd gone out to buy all the newspapers and watched every television and news bulletin, for news, for pictures. His wife looked like a weapon, but she smiled by his side, as all the good ones in politics do.

Even the housework lapsed as her obsession grew. When he left the papers, Marilyn felt bereft, like she'd lost him again.

'Marilyn, you have to do it sometime, it may as well be now,' Sean pleaded. 'And phone Larry. Your six weeks are up.'

'So you want to get rid of me, do you?' Each day she knew she was getting harder to live with as the pressure mounted inside her.

'No, I don't, but your boss needs to know what you're at, and so do you.' Sean was firm. 'Brigid isn't well, she needs you to go and see her too. You can't keep hiding.'

'You keep telling me that Brigid's fine, and as for hiding, why not? Julie's doing it.'

'Julie's not the point. Your life is the one you need to sort out.'

Larry wasn't overjoyed to hear she wasn't ready to come back just yet. 'We've got things we need to discuss, Mari,' he said.

'I know, I know. I'll be a few more days sorting things out here.'

'Okay. Judith Tormey, Niall Tormey's wife, was on here, did she get you?'

'No, she didn't.' Marilyn went quiet.

'She wanted to thank you for helping Frank Whelan's wife. They're good friends.'

Are they now? Marilyn went off to find Sean, who came straight into the house with her, forgetting to disinfect his feet.

'You have to call him now. If she knows where you are, then he does too. They're in cahoots these two. Do everything together.'

She dialled Niall's number.

32

'It's not that I don't want to see you at all, anywhere else, but I've taken a couple of things on,' Elizabeth apologised to Tony. She didn't want lifts home any more. 'And please, take the taxi red-alert brigade off me.'

'Don't lie for his sake. You're not a liar,' Tony said. He was right, the lies were mounting up. 'He's no good for you, Elizabeth. He's too tight with his wife to ever give you what you deserve.'

'That's politics.'

'That's not you.'

'I know that too,' she said in a voice that told him she couldn't help feeling for Niall Tormey as much as he couldn't help loving her.

'He's a swine if that's all he's offering you.'

'And what about me? Considering it's all I want, I'm a bigger one,' Elizabeth said. 'Will you still come and see us? I know it's horrible and selfish of me to ask, but I don't think we can do without you. And like I said before, all Brigid wants is to see me with you.'

'Have you told her about Niall?'

'No. I hope to God I'll never have to.'

'Then I'm not going to be a part of it.'

'I'm sorry, I shouldn't have asked.'

On her way to see Niall, at the usual place – now a flat of his own, rather than a friend's – she wondered just how she'd let it get to the stage where she was meeting him again. She suspected the unfinished nature of business had a lot to do with it. As long as there was a 'what if?' to them, she'd be drawn in, at least to find out why she couldn't move on with anyone else. It wasn't his power; that had only caused her to suffer.

'You don't even take me to the apartment you live in all the time,' she mentioned.

'Do you want to go there?'

'No. This time I have as much desire not to be caught as you have.'

'It's not that way with me any more,' Niall shifted.

'It is that.'

'No, it's changed now.'

'How?'

'I took this move to save face. I wasn't prepared to let them humiliate me like that.' He looked almost broken. 'I'll never get there now, Elizabeth.'

'Is the top the only place that would have done?'

'Yes, you know that. You know what I gave up for it.' He took her hand.

'Don't kid me, I know there were plenty more after me.'

'None as good,' he said plainly. It was a new thing for him, to be so open. She liked the man he was now better for it. 'I don't have to tell you why.'

'I've come to pity you for it. There are more interesting routes, and you ignored them all.'

'I had a lot to offer – I still might – with the new party,' he went on, ignoring her.

'In this Ireland, one party is the same as another.'

'Why is it that everyone outside politics thinks they know what it's like inside?' He poured a glass of wine and handed it to her, thinking of his conversation with the taxi driver. He knew now that the man followed her around like a puppy, doing her bidding.

'Because we elect you to represent us, and we're told we

know you. Nowadays you're accountable, we're told.' She sipped the wine and sighed; it was always too good.

'Ah,' Niall laughed, and she felt the race in it and in her as an answer. He had the pull for her, still, always. 'That'll never catch on as practice. What we really need in this republic is a monarchy, of the mediaeval sort. Behead the dissenters. You need that kind of single-mindedness to move the country on.'

'Most of us feel like we live in a dictatorship.'

'Well, if you lived in one, I would have known our daughter. Isn't that what democracy's all about, free will and speech?'

'You were willing to take away mine.'

'If there's anything I'm sorry for, it's that.' He was genuine, which was another new thing. 'I would have tried to give her the best life I could as her father, and I thought at the time it was with me rather than you.'

'So it would never have been with us,' she said, tilting her head. He was making her a salad. When they'd first started seeing each other, all those years ago, he wouldn't have boiled her an egg. Men had changed and he had moved with them.

'If I answered yes to that, you'd know I was lying. But I'll tell you one thing . . .' He trailed off so she had to ask, and he knew in asking that she was pulled in again, had all the interest she'd had over thirty years ago. 'I wouldn't make the same mistake now. Hindsight is for failures and fools, of which I'm one. We both lost the one thing that could have made us happy.'

It was only later that she would look back and realise he hadn't meant that was the same thing for both of them. For her it was a family life with him. For him it was the chance to run the country.

'I was happy, watching Marilyn grow up.'

'I'd like to have seen that. Her.'

'Don't you mean love rather than like?'

'Love, Elizabeth, is for women. They understand what it's for. Men need lessons. Preferably from women like you. I would like one from you.'

'For that, Niall, you're going to have to wait a long time.'

'Why? You feel the same way I do.'

'Unlike you, I need to trust someone for that to happen.'

'So why are you here?'

'Because I can't be otherwise. We have unfinished business.'

'We have.'

They had dinner. Afterwards, her smile was tired, but the energy she'd had in once knowing him was already beginning to return, and she'd lived so long without it that she reached for it, and him, with her eyes.

'Why don't you ask me about Marilyn?' she asked.

'You don't volunteer, and I made it my business to find out a certain amount.'

'In other words, everything,' Elizabeth snorted.

'No, just the basics. I'll find out more soon. She phoned me today. I'm going to Wexford, to see her, tomorrow.'

'Oh my God.' Elizabeth stared at him. 'Shouldn't that have been the first thing you said? Since she found out you were her father, she hasn't even spoken to me.'

'I'm sorry. I know how hard it was for you and I feel responsible for it, so I didn't want to spoil your evening.'

The first shutter came down in her.

'I see. Which must mean you're about as ready to be a father as I am to be a politician.'

'Don't, you know what I am. No one's forcing you to be here.'

'No,' she sighed and stood up, 'and no one's forcing me

to stay.' She left, wishing for a moment that Tony would be outside, waiting for her. She made sure she hailed down another company to his, as if she was betraying him.

Each evening, as soon as he woke, Tony thought of her and went to check on the seed trays.

He had bought cornflower seeds instead of the whiskey, back when Elizabeth had told him how it would be between them. And there were days when it had been his saving grace. Particularly the first one, when he'd gone to the garden centre, armed with information from the Internet, and within minutes the kind old man who ran it realised he was a novice.

'I have all the instructions.' Tony showed the man, who said, 'They look like good ones. Since you're buying all this to go with them, the buttons will come up good for you.'

'What did you call them?'

'Buttons, bachelor's buttons. That's what I've called them all my life.'

'Where does the name come from?' The man could see that Tony's interest in cornflowers wasn't that of a gardener, but of a pilgrim. There was nothing he didn't want to know.

'Well, they last well in a buttonhole, they keep their colour. That's why they're so good for drying, and years ago the young men used to wear them out on their dates. It was a way of telling when a man was on his way to finding the girl he would marry, most likely. I take it from the look on your face that that's what you're after here?'

Tony smiled at the man. His need for that to be the case was apparent.

'You know, if you want, I can help plant them with you. They're an easy thing and you can do it yourself if I supervise.'

'I do. I need them to be perfect,' Tony said.

'We can do it here and you can take them home in the

314

boot of your car, I have all the things you mightn't have thought of, or found in your computer. I've got a sieve, compost of my own making and some old seed trays that have never failed me yet. Boxwood they are, better than the new plastic, but the price drove them out. I never sell them these days, but I'll give them to you. If it's love you're interested in, that's worth helping. The cornflower's kind to men who need a long-lasting buttonhole and a wife.'

Tony learned as he worked under Peter Devon's tutelage that his wife Catriona had lived to see their fiftieth wedding anniversary, but not their fifty-first. 'Eight years ago, that was. But I'm not lonely. And I've three daughters who are the cut of her and who never leave me alone, so it's like she never left me, you see? I'd say she's watching us from the basket chair, where she spent her last few months.'

To secure the interests of his heart, Tony filled the first of four boxwood seed trays and pressed in the compost, firming it in with fingertips, which Peter encouraged him to think were made for gardening. The finest nozzle was put on the watering can and Tony sprayed the soil carefully, as if each drop should matter, and did. He took Peter's old pencil and dibbed holes for each of the large seeds.

'You need twice the depth of the seed now, Mr Devereux, to cover it.' Peter had a formal nature and believed in the old-fashioned custom of using last names before first ones. 'For the best results, which we're after here.

'Sieve the compost now so that each of the holes is filled, careful, that's right, check all the time now, Mr Devereux, that all the holes are filled right. And write your label now. Use my china graph pencil, it'll never wash away, no matter what rains on it. Write the date of sowing, and the seed, though in this case there'll be no doubt about it. It's only the blue cornflower you want, is it, Mr Devereux? For we've fine pink and even white varieties. No, say nothing, I can see by your face blue's the one for you.

'Now do all of this in two weeks' time and repeat it every two weeks and you'll have cornflowers from May through to September.' Peter went off to bring back sheets of glass. 'Give the soil a final watering and cover it with one of these. I had them hand-cut, to fit the old boxwood. And come back and see me when the first lot comes up. Six weeks it'll be, no more, and we'll have a glass to the success of your first bit of gardening. It'll not be your last.

'When they're one and a half inches tall, you'll do something called pricking out and you'll lift them out of the boxwood and into the pots. You'll need pots to transfer them into. You won't want to transfer them all, of course.'

'Oh, I will,' Tony insisted. 'I need at least one pot for each week from May to September.'

'Where will the young lady put them all?'

Tony smiled at the use of the word 'young', then realised that to Peter they would both appear young – he looked like he was in his nineties.

'She loves them,' Tony said.

'She loves them that much?'

'Well,' Tony faltered, 'I'm also trying to get a message across that I won't give up.'

'In that case, do it every week, and with it give her a message. I'll give you my old china graph pencil to write them with, for your calling card. And I've got pots for you – at six months, I estimate that's twenty-five pots. She can give one to all her friends.'

'Will she think I'm stalking her?'

'Not if the message is right. In my opinion, it should always start with "Should you decide not to love me, then all you need to do is leave one pot on the doorstep, and you'll never get another." That way you give her a choice.'

'And I'm doing watercolours, of different plants from the *Modern Botanical*.'

'The best of all books, Mr Devereux. Can I give you one more? It was given to me by my father.' He produced an old leather-bound book with written instructions for a more ambitious project. 'You should begin this come autumn, all going well. You've given me a lovely day, Mr Devereux. A day when I brought someone new to the magic of flowers. There should be no charge for that privilege. Were it not that my daughters need the business kept going, there'd be none.'

They shook hands, and promised that the meeting would not be the last. The old man shuffled in through the wooden gate that had marked the boundary of his world for the eight years since the death of his wife, without venturing outside into Tony's.

Six weeks later, when his seeds sprouted, Tony drove over to Peter Devon's Garden Centre to find that he had died in his sleep the night he showed Tony what to do. He sat outside in his taxi, crying like a child, and when he finished he whispered, 'Watch over my seeds, Peter Devon, and watch over me.'

33

Marilyn phoned Niall Tormey's office twice, but the same unfriendly female voice answered.

'Leave a name and number. If he doesn't return a call to Marilyn Monroe, who will he ever return a call to? And you have to go back to Dublin anyway,' Sean suggested.

'No, I don't.'

'You have to, Marilyn. Your grandmother is ill and missing you.'

She felt a stab of anger, then had to admit that playing house on a Wexford farm wasn't going to get her anywhere. Sean was sacrificing a lot in letting her go back to Dublin. Two horses had placed in races recently and Delaney was coming on in leaps and bounds. Even his helpers, the two Mikes, were less shy with her, saying she was good luck for the yard and its owner.

'Yes,' Sean agreed with them, 'but the good luck's got to go back to Dublin sometime. She's got herself to sort out. She can't be helping out the likes of us with all that brain in her head.'

'You don't mean that?' one of the Mikes questioned. 'Sure she loves it here.'

'That's right,' the other agreed. 'When she first came here she was a tense little mouse. Look at the cut of her now. All glow she is.'

'But she wouldn't stay glowing, lads' – Sean spoke to himself as much as them – 'if she saw what state the yard is in. I won't let her near the books, in case she passes out.'

'Ah, a few wins will sort that out and that little Delaney's the one to give them to us.' A Mike clapped him on the back. But he couldn't feel as cheerful.

His eldest sister Nuala, the one who reminded him most of his mother, called round unannounced one day when Marilyn was in town shopping.

'She has this place like a new pin, Sean. Just like Ma had. It's a relief to us all you met someone like her, I can tell you.'

'It's a relief to me, Nuala, but I've nothing to offer her at present, other than a stack of bills. She has a good life in Dublin.'

'You may say that, but the first time I set eyes on her she didn't look half as happy or relaxed as she does now.'

'She's living in a bubble, Nuala, this is a holiday for her, while she gets her strength up to go back to Dublin. Her own family needs her now, more than me.'

'I don't believe that, Sean! I'd say you need her more than you've ever needed anybody. I have to admit when I first heard she was staying with you for the six weeks I wondered at you two rushing things, particularly when you've always been a snail with women. But seeing you both together it's clear you're carved out of each other. It's like she was made for that place in the crook of your arm.' Nuala was horrified to see him fill up with tears. 'Oh, I'm sorry, love, I had no wish to upset you.'

'Don't be sorry, it's true that I'm all for her, and she's all for me. I just never thought I'd find it is all. And I want something safe for her, not a bankrupt stables.'

'Sean Monroe, it's you and what's inside you is the safety for that girl.' Nuala put her hand on his. 'And I want you to come over to my house on your own tomorrow, I have something to give you for when the time is right.'

Sean thought of this conversation, and what Nuala had given him, as he watched Marilyn pick up the phone and dial for the third time. This time she left her name and number. This will take her from me, back to Dublin. I might never get her back. I shouldn't be encouraging her so much to go. Then he couldn't not. He knew from his last conversation with Elizabeth that things were bad with Brigid. Marilyn wouldn't forgive herself if she didn't resolve things with her grandmother at least.

'His secretary took it all down,' Marilyn said. 'She'll never give it to him. Probably thinks it's a big joke, a prank call with a name like mine.'

'I think he'll phone the minute the message is put in his hand.' Sean couldn't stop his voice from sounding sad. 'I know I wouldn't want to miss an opportunity to meet any child of mine.'

'But you'd never let any child of yours grow up fatherless.' She put a palm to the side of his face and stroked it. 'You're the most caring man in the world.'

He smiled. He hoped one day they would have their children together. Then the pain hit him that he couldn't even support himself right now, much less a family.

The following day he dropped in on Nuala, who gladly gave him another lecture.

'I've thought about little else since I left you yesterday,' she said. 'And it struck me: Marilyn has the business brain you lack. You have the business she lacks. Together you have something big to offer each other, for the financial future as well as the rest of it. You're mad if you don't pull at this chance by the nose, Sean. I know it's a wet day since you met her. But don't let a dry one pass without getting her to agree to marry you. Right now she's full of love potion. I can tell you now that wears off when the first electricity bill comes in, isn't that right, Murray?' she yelled into the sitting room where her own faithful husband was glued to the snooker, after a day tarmacing drives. 'Marriage is the glue. Romance isn't worth a curse after a while.'

Sean smiled to himself as he made the journey home: it had been like hearing his mother talk all over again. As he walked in the front door, the phone rang.

She spoke to Niall Tormey seventeen minutes after she left a name and number. She checked her watch, it was 4.43 p.m. He said he was coming to meet her, tomorrow, first thing.

They arranged the Newcross House Hotel as a meeting point. Sean drove her.

But she went in alone. Before she had a chance to speak, the woman at the reception desk asked, 'Are you Marilyn?' She nodded. 'Mr Tormey says to go on up to his suite.'

Suite, not room. She was aware he wasn't considering her in this arrangement, but his own high profile. She walked up the stairs to meet the father she had never met, having been aware of him all her adult life. The newspaper pictures and television appearances gave her a sense of him, but no life-size impression. His days as Minister of Sport should have given them plenty of opportunities to meet. They might have seen each other across a crowded hospitality suite, recognised each other instantly as blood relatives.

Which is what they did not do when he opened the door. They were complete strangers and acted as such.

'Good morning,' he nodded to her, never taking his eyes from her face. 'You have your mother's eyes, but blue, an amazing blue if I may say so.'

'You have my nose.' She pointed.

'I think you've got mine, can I have it back, please?' His grin was copyrighted. It had seen him out of any number of situations. Not this one.

He was dapper – no bad jumpers here. His clothes were important to him and he'd had help in choosing them. That came from a woman – two mistresses after her mother. He was slight in build and fit for sixty-one years, with no extra weight despite all the government dinners and lunches, a discipline she was capable of. She took after him in stature. He was about five seven.

He showed her to a chair and then took one opposite. She noticed that he put her in the lower one, a trick she had used more than once in her life. They shared one expression – guarded. Then, at the same instant, they each put one hand to the side of their face. It was what made him laugh after a long silence, in which she came to terms with a profound sense of anticlimax. All she could think was, I should be feeling more.

This should be exciting, why does it feel so awful? she asked herself.

Because years have been lost, and opportunities with them, the answer came, not in her own voice, but in that of her own imaginary father, whom she missed.

'I waited a lot of years for this, Marilyn.' He used a tone that sounded almost professional. He dealt with strangers all the time, and his long-lost daughter was one of those. 'I'm glad to know your name at last. Your mother didn't wait long enough after you were born for me to get there to name you together. I suggested Ursula.'

'For the first time in my life, then, I'm actually grateful to be called what I am. I don't look like an Ursula.'

'On the contrary, you're the spit of what she is, or was. She was my mother.'

'I'm sorry.'

'Don't be, I have a lot more to be forgiven for.'

'You do.' Marilyn's mind raced. Elizabeth hadn't trusted him, even after she gave birth, since she'd named her the minute she was born. 'My birth certificate says that you're unknown. You could hardly be described as that.' She was using her own business voice, able to fence off what was uncomfortable.

Elizabeth was right, he thought, she can take care of herself.

'There were reasons, which I'm sure your mother went into.'

'My mother went into nothing but that she was afraid of you.'

'I'm not going to lie, Marilyn. I was in a better position to look after you, so I fought to get you, with all I had at my disposal.' He put his hands together and pressed his fingertips together. Her mother's habit. He must have been remembering her, because he said, 'You're her and me. It's quite incredible. You have my build and her eyes and mouth. The brilliance of colour is your own—'

'No' – she stared at him – 'that came from my mother's father.'

'I see. You're—'

'Don't say I'm beautiful or I'll know you're being insincere.'

'You're like she was, well able for me.'

'She wasn't well able for you. She was a child. You got her pregnant and left her destitute.'

'I spent a long time trying to find her. I put a lot of resources into trying.'

'You had them,' she threw back. 'And she did try, when I turned eighteen. You failed to show interest.'

'At the time I was at a crucial stage.'

'The leap to cabinet big gun? The numbers man?'

'Yes, I'm afraid so. I thought it was a set-up.'

'I'm a numbers woman, did you know that? And I know what you say doesn't add up. If you really thought it was a set-up, you'd have contacted Elizabeth and got the measure of her. You knew she wasn't the sort to shop.'

'Marilyn, after what I did to her, I didn't know what sort she was. But you're right. I have to acknowledge that at the time it wasn't appropriate . . .'

'An unexplained daughter, I know, very inappropriate. Weren't you even curious?'

'I was curious enough to try to get the name and address behind the box number.'

'She falsified them, didn't she?'

'Yes.'

'So she knew what you were like.'

'I can see now, sixteen years later, how I was wasn't the way to be.'

'You should have seen that thirty-two years ago. I'm not giving you an inch, Niall Tormey. You're someone who'll make a mile with it.'

'Well,' he laughed, 'all I can say is, have you considered politics?'

'To tell you the truth, all I considered was a career that wouldn't make me a burden on my single parent.'

He put the tip of his tongue on his bottom lip. 'If you would care to believe me, and I don't expect you to, she's the only woman I ever cared for enough to say I loved.'

'You've been married happily – or is it successfully? – to someone else for almost forty years. She's rung my office looking for me.'

'She did? Well, she won't be doing that again.' For a fraction of a second he appeared surprised. 'I apologise for that. She's a politician, in all but the running for election.'

'Have you apologised to her? For my existence? You must have given her a dog's life as well.'

'Like I said, Marilyn, she's suited to political life. She has her own situations.'

'Not like my mother?'

'No, your mother would have hated it. Trust me on that, if nothing else.'

All her life she had waited for this. She'd bought him presents and had daily conversations with who she imagined him to be. He wasn't anything like she imagined. In her gut, she didn't respond to this man.

But that changed when he admitted, 'Do you know how many times I've set foot in my own home in the past two years? Five times. On the way down here, I counted them. I think that makes me just about homeless. I stay in a Dublin apartment and I work all the hours God sends, because I don't know what else to do. Your mother did well not being married to me. Look what Judith ended up with. Childless and moving to a new place just before her sixtieth birthday. Your mother's just got her exams, you'll be pleased to hear. The conferring is in June—'

'So you're in contact with her?' Marilyn interrupted.

'Yes, we contacted each other to discuss you.'

'Who contacted whom?'

'I got in touch with her, just as she was trying to get in touch with me. You know, when I first met her she worked in a department store, and now she's just qualified and has her own business, all without anyone's assistance.'

'Department store? My mother never worked in one of those.'

'She did when I knew her. She worked in the best one – Switzer's, it was, now it's Brown Thomas – and she was the very picture of style. She could have been a model.'

'It's not my mother who contacted you for this meeting. It was me.'

'Marilyn, I want to know every last little thing about you – where you went to school, who your friends are, what your interests are, who you're going out with, where you live. I want to know my own daughter and I particularly want to find a way to spend time with you. I won't be fool enough to think I can make up for what I missed, but I wasn't the only one who made you miss out.'

'No, I have to give you that.' She took his mobile number and promised to call him again. The number was a new one he had given only to Marilyn and Elizabeth.

'Look, I'm going to stay here overnight, and I'd like to see you tomorrow. I'll cancel all my business if that suits you.' For a minute she felt uncomfortable, because she was needed by him, she could sense, and she didn't know him. It made her want to go.

'I'll call you tomorrow, if I feel up to meeting you. If not you'll have to wait until I am, if you still want to.' She rose.

'I'll always want to, Marilyn. You're the daughter I never had. I'll always want to know that you're in my life from now on.'

After she left he looked in the mirror and said to himself, 'You have a daughter called Marilyn Monroe. Now there's newspaper copy.'

The receptionist nodded in a formal way as she left. Marilyn realised she thought she was his mistress. Marilyn checked the suite windows to make sure her father wasn't looking out of them. He wasn't visible because he stood well back from the window to watch her. She got into Sean's Land Rover.

'I'm not sure, before you ask. I'm not sure how I feel or what I think of him.'

'That'll take a while to figure out.'

'I knew with you immediately.'

'We had no history, no secrets,' he said, then thought, None that you know about.

'He says he wants me to be in his life. He didn't say he wanted to be in mine, Sean. It was the other way around. That gives me a good idea of what he's like and how I figure into it. I think he's been so single-minded that he's ended up with only himself for company.'

326

'A sad affair, that.'

'Not as sad as the one he had with my mother.'

'Are you going to meet again?'

'Tomorrow, if I want.'

There wouldn't be a tomorrow. The phone rang just as Sean went out to the horses. Marilyn had no option but to pick it up. Theresa's voice said, 'Your mother is here beside me, she needs to speak to you.'

'No, I can't talk to her just at the moment. I will soon.'

'You will now, Marilyn.' Theresa was firm. 'This is very important.'

Sean drove her up to Dublin straight away. The two Mikes agreed to hold the fort for a few days.

When they pulled onto Verbena Avenue after only two months away, it was like she had never lived there. It felt too small for a place that had been her only world. And then there was the fact that a six-foot-one Greek man with a battered felt hat was walking down the road, carrying a railway sleeper across his shoulders, like Atlas holding up the sky to stop it from crushing the Monroes.

34

Theresa pulled up in her van as Sean parked.

'The sleeper wouldn't fit in it, so Nikolas carried it all the way from the builders' providers. They weren't going to deliver it until next Tuesday. I've got the rest of the stuff in the back.' She saw Marilyn's blotched face and stopped. It was clear she'd been crying all the way up from Wexford, a two-hour journey.

'What's it for?' Marilyn croaked.

'You'll have to see. Now wash your face in my house before you go and see her, there's a good girl. Sean, an extra pair of hands would be very welcome.'

Marilyn went home fifteen minutes later. It was no use. As soon as she saw Brigid lying on the living room couch, propped up with pillows, her mouth cracked and sore, her hair almost entirely gone, her body all bones under the blanket and a drip in her arm, she got down on her knees. Brigid put her hand on Marilyn's head.

'I can't believe I've been so selfish, to be gone for this length of time.'

In the kitchen they were working as quietly as possible. Even so there was a lot of noise, but Brigid was past caring. All she could do was smile at Marilyn's return. She didn't have the energy to write. She continued smiling even after she dropped off to sleep.

'She's going to die, isn't she, Grace?'

'No one can answer that but her, and she's not capable of

answering anyone right now.' Grace was preparing dinner for the workmen. The patio doors were down and the foundations for a new sunroom were laid. Sean and Nikolas lifted the railway sleeper into position to act as a main supporting beam for the sheets of glass positioned between slats of wood, which Nikolas had cut grooves into using Theresa's tools and assistance.

'They build them like this in Greece,' Theresa said. 'It's single-glazed glass, but he hand-cuts a groove into the wood and slides it in. It's exactly to size, so there's going to be no draught, and we'll put a patio heater into it, for now. Maybe we'll run a pipe for central heating later.' Theresa was practical and strong, but you could see the project was holding her together, to get this finished before Brigid was.

'Your mother's at the shops,' Grace whispered to Marilyn. 'Be kind when she gets back, please.'

Marilyn nodded. There was no need to ask her to be. Her mobile rang. It was Niall Tormey, not yet her father. She went out to the hall to answer it.

'I hope I'm not intruding, I'm still here and wondered if you were up to meeting me again tomorrow. It's a transitional time at work, I need to get back if you can't make it.'

'I could say the same myself. I can't meet you right now,' Marilyn whispered.

As she hung up, the door opened and Elizabeth came in, carrying a cornflower plant in a pot and an A5-sized envelope. She put both down as soon as she saw Marilyn sitting on the bottom step. Outside Marilyn could see six bags of supermarket shopping. She squeezed past Elizabeth to pick them up.

'You met him?' Elizabeth's voice was brittle; she was thin enough to snap.

Marilyn nodded. 'Just this morning. He says you've seen him.'

'Not since last week. I'm sorry it was the day you got this news. She got so bad overnight. We just couldn't hold off telling you any longer.'

'I know.' Marilyn's eyes were full of tears. 'I should never have stayed away so long.'

'We told you she was fine.'

'Yes. You did.'

'She wanted you to have your happiness, Marilyn, it was a gift to you, I hope you see that. You have so much to deal with, and a lot of it is down to me. This isn't something you should be angry about as well.' Elizabeth was gentle, but firm.

'Fill me in, then,' Marilyn whispered.

Brigid had just had the last of six sessions of chemotherapy. Each one made her progressively sicker, but the news was that the cancer had greatly reduced – two of the three lumps had been eradicated. The problem was that now her immune system was so low, but the last lump, right on the vocal cords, would need surgery, and she wasn't fit for it.

'She hasn't been able to eat or drink anything for a week; the drip keeps her alive.' By the time Elizabeth finished telling Marilyn everything they were sitting on the bottom step together. 'She doesn't know I met up with Niall either. It's not the right time for her to hear that.'

'I don't think any time would be,' Marilyn agreed.

'How did you find him?' Elizabeth asked and put a hand on her shoulder. Marilyn didn't discourage it.

'I can't say yet. Where's Tony?'

'He was around,' Elizabeth smiled. 'We'd have been lost without him. He runs us to the hospital and back. He was even picking me up from work at one time.'

'Until my father made himself available, in the most limited way?'

'Yes.' It was a relief not to lie. 'Tony knows all about Niall. I told him. He said he wasn't prepared to be part of that kind of situation.'

'Fair play to him. May the best man win. And I know that's not the one I inherited genes from.' Marilyn nailed her colours to the mast from the word go.

'Well, as a reaction, it's a lot more diluted than I expected,' Elizabeth smiled.

'I suppose I'm learning to live and let live. Finally. I've already forced my best friend out of the picture by being so judgemental. I don't want that to happen to you as well, especially now.'

'Marilyn' – Elizabeth held her – 'you'll always have me. Even if you tried to murder me.'

'I know that. It just took me a bit of time to figure out. And I hope you get smarter about him. He's not for you, Ma, you're cut from too different a cloth.'

'I know. I don't know why, but it's only him I've ever wanted. It seems I'm the kind of woman who doesn't know what's best for her.'

'You knew what was best for me.'

'You believe that?'

'Yes.' Marilyn's cornflower eyes were shining with emotion, as if the sun had come through the stained glass after long years of being blocked out. 'I believe that now.'

At midnight they finished the sunroom. Brigid was sound asleep as they moved around the house as quietly as Persuasion, putting in furniture, a single hospital trolley on wheels and plants, including the potted cornflower.

'Who's it from?' Marilyn asked. 'As if I didn't know.'

'I thought it was you left it there as a peace offering! I haven't got a clue. I didn't even open the envelope. It's in the sitting room, come on.'

She and Marilyn went into the kitchen to open it. Inside was a watercolour of the cornflower with a calligraphic title, done by hand in ink. Underneath was an inscription:

The expressed juice of the petals makes a good blue ink; if mixed with alum-water, it may be used in water-colour drawing.

'So the ink has been made from an actual cornflower. The inscription's from the *Modern Botanical*, a famous book about plants,' Elizabeth breathed. 'I don't think I've ever seen anything more beautiful.'

She flipped open a small card and read it, then nodded silent confirmation.

'What's it say, then?' Marilyn was impatient. The others, in the kitchen drinking tea and admiring their handiwork, were occupied.

'"Should you decide not to love me, then all you need to do is leave this pot on the doorstep, and you'll never get another. Congratulations on passing your exams, after seven years of hard work. It's a credit to you, in the light of what you're going through. Tony",' Elizabeth read aloud.

'I'm sorry, I totally forgot to say the same, and I'm your daughter. Just shows how selfish I can be.' Marilyn shook her head. 'Niall Tormey told me.' She still couldn't call him by anything other than his full name.

'Stop it. I can't say I'm not amazed I got through them. But I did. You only just met your father and then you got the news that Brigid was in bad shape. Is it any wonder?' Elizabeth reassured her. Then she got back to the business of dealing with the message. 'So there's going to be more than one cornflower! This is too much, Mari, I'll have to leave the one in the sunroom out on the step now.'

'No, it's not too much. It's just what you need. This is a contest. You don't want anyone else because no one's worked hard enough to persuade you. He's taking on Niall Tormey. You have to admire him for that. And the best part of his free

332

time is spent planting, drawing and writing with ink from your emblem flower. That's time he normally devotes to recovering addicts. You've got to go with this, Ma, then Brigid can go on happy, to that strict Catholic heaven she's booked a place in.'

Elizabeth listened. 'I heard every word of that, and every word is true.'

She took the card to her room.

When they walked back into the kitchen to view the finished conservatory, it occurred to Marilyn that the men hadn't come armed into the Monroe house, as Grace had prophesied. They'd come in nicely through the front door, and built an extension. The sunroom was ready for Brigid Monroe the next morning. If she saw it. Nikolas was smiling at them all like there wasn't a problem in the world. Theresa told them about Nyphi, and how he'd already been through this. She didn't reveal her sister's visions, knowing how much Brigid wanted to keep those a secret. That was a story for when Brigid was gone, a reality Theresa couldn't as yet contemplate. Each day Grace watched her exhaust herself in an effort of tasks.

'If you're not careful, you'll make yourself ill,' Grace warned her.

'I know, I can't stop. I can't imagine life without her. I love you, but she's my yardstick. I measured myself against her and with her against everyone else from the day I set eyes on her. When she's gone, so is my life before you. No one else was there.'

'Theresa, she has Nikolas. And I need you. You'll have to let her go.'

'Yes, he's the man for the job.' Theresa stood and left without warning, Grace following just behind.

★

When Nikolas carried Brigid into the sunroom she leaned into his shoulder, afraid to look at such a beautiful space. Don't be doing this kind of thing, her eyes said, you know it's too much for me.

She lay on the bed and looked up at the clouds rolling by. The late-spring sun beat in through the windows and made it a furnace for anyone whose white blood cell count wasn't dangerously low. Marilyn was surprised to see Elizabeth dressed for work, but then she realised that Nikolas was all the company Brigid wanted. Theirs was a young love, holding hands, sharing looks. When she drifted off to sleep he picked up his hat and put it over his eyes, sleeping in the chair beside her. As soon as she woke, he was awake. He sang to her in a whisper, he played his bouzouki softly and talked the same way. The sunroom allowed them to feel like they were right in the heart of Elizabeth's garden, maintained now with Grace's help.

Sean spent the morning with Marilyn. They had breakfast, went for a walk, tidied the house and made lunch. By that time she realised she was extraneous to the proceedings, even an intruder. 'You need to get back, Sean. I need to stay here.'

'I can't leave you here with all of this going on.'

'Sean, you've known me just eighteen weeks. During that time I've found my father, disowned my mother, reclaimed her, gone Awol from work indefinitely after an entire career without so much as a sick day, and found out my granny, who half reared me, is terminally ill. I lost my best friend, who found you, and I came to live with you to recover. You have huge responsibilities and you've done enough. I'm going back to work myself tomorrow. Brigid needs privacy and you said yourself I need time. I'm going to try and see a bit of my father. And I also need to see how this turns out. Ma and I need to speak. There's a lot that needs straightening out. That's a lot to take on, considering your own plate was already full. Thank you, I love you, go home.'

She was fine until he drove away, then she sat on the bottom step and wept. Her Greek grandfather came out, scooped her up like a baby and twirled her around before depositing her beside Brigid, who whispered, 'It will all be all right.'

And it was, for a while.

35

Marilyn went back to work the following day, to find that Tommy had taken root in her office.

'Yours is down the hall, where mine was,' he said.

She stormed in to his father. 'He left coffee-cup rings all over my walnut desk. The carpet's got red wine stains. He's been smoking in there! The walls are yellow and the linen blind won't pull up or down any more. How could you let him!'

'It's been a fair while since you've been in, Marilyn, how were we to know you were coming back?' Larry looked up from his paperwork. A lot of it, she could see, was stuff she did.

'I said I was, and you know I never lie.'

'True, but if it wasn't for Geraldine and Sean advising me, I have to say now that I—'

'Don't give me that, Larry. Sean and Geraldine might have talked to you, but you know no one does the job better than I can, including your son, otherwise you wouldn't be filling in my returns. And as it happens, I'm going to be better at it again because of my experience in Sean's yard. And if you don't hire someone to rectify the damage in my office, I'll go off again for another week.'

A smile had spread across his face, then quickly dropped again. 'I'll go and have a word with him. In the meantime, use my office and get on with what you're good at instead of giving me guff I'd never take from anyone else.'

There was a lot of shouting from the bottom corridor and the sound of a door slamming. Tommy caught her in the corridor.

'I'll have you.'

'Have what for me? A new plant for the one you let die, in a nice pot, please? And here, I've got something for you – a rollicking for the state of the last bets. A monkey could have computed those odds, the losses are beyond belief.'

'No one could have predicted some of those big winners.'

'Yes, they could have, if they were doing it right, which you can't.'

Elizabeth found it hard to settle to work but forced herself not to make a snap decision. She did a full day and then an extra hour before she wrote him a note.

Thank you for the beautiful gift, the most beautiful, thoughtful gift I have ever received. Marilyn is back, and tells me that I have to allow you this. I don't like any blood sports, least of all ones that harm people. So can I say I appreciate the manner in which you've put your feelings forward? It would be wonderful if everyone could be so refreshingly honest. Hearts wouldn't get broken half as much, would they? Again, Tony, I have to repeat what I said to you that night. You frighten me with the intensity of your feelings and I must again say I do not reciprocate them. I'm afraid, though, that I can't bear to part with your plant, it's in my mother's new sunroom. So I have to use the words 'as yet'. Niall and I are sorting out what was left hanging all those years ago. I expect you know this. I have to do this with him, for now, and I completely understand if you wish to bow out. But this is signed, with great affection, Elizabeth.

She put a stamp on it, then decided she was going to deliver it by hand to his address, which was printed on the top of his cornflower card. The cab came at seven, fifteen minutes after she'd phoned for it. The driver was Tony.

'The controller called me at home. I hope I'm not intruding.'

'No,' she surprised herself by saying, 'you're not.'

They sat in her office until almost nine, talking. She handed him the card first. His face lit up. 'I'm a selective reader, Elizabeth, so I'm afraid this only encourages me. As for Niall, it looks to me like it's all you can afford to feel.'

'What makes you say that?' She was sharp with him, which didn't throw him; he knew he had reason to stand by what he said.

'He's someone who absorbs love as his right, and does little to earn it. I don't hate anyone, not even my ex-wife. But I will kill him if he hurts you again. If he makes you happy, I'll shake his hand. He'll never make you that as a mistress.'

She nodded. 'I think it would be silly to go to jail over someone like him, when all you say is true. It would be much better to carry on as you are. Prisons are awkward places to continue relationships.'

'Is that what we're having?'

'Yes, but it's not a fair one for you.'

'It's honest.' Tony touched the side of her face. 'I still take honesty every time over a lie, no matter how kind the lie is.'

'Do you know, I said that once, in a manner of speaking, and I still say it.'

When Brigid saw Tony she put energy in her smile. Elizabeth gave Tony's arm a thank-you squeeze, for being there, for showing no shock at Brigid's appearance. Marilyn was busy in the kitchen, but as soon as she saw Tony she came across and hugged him, which took everyone by surprise. In the corner of the new conservatory, which Tony admired and Nikolas took a bow for, he saw the cornflower and thanked it for the bud of hope it offered him.

Marilyn covered all the silences with busy, cheerful talk about her first day back at work and her victory over Tommy.

'Will you stay for dinner with us? I'm afraid I've cooked,'

she offered. Grace had taken Theresa away, since she was having trouble resting around her sister.

'I will, but I just have to nip home first, there's something I think Brigid could do with,' Tony said, then left.

And the questions began.

'I'm answering nothing,' Elizabeth said, 'until I have answers.'

Tony came back with a tincture made with cornflower petals, which he gave to Nikolas, who dabbed it on cotton wool and put it to Brigid's lips.

The juice put into fresh or green wounds doth quickly solder up the lips of them together, and is very effectual to heal all ulcers and sores in the mouth.

'I don't know anything about healing herbs, but I got this out of—' Tony began before Elizabeth interrupted him.

'*Modern Botanical.* I know it well. Your house must be awash with cornflowers, Tony.'

He smiled at her. 'I had a man called Peter Devon's help with this. A plant man. I think he's turned me into one. It's like when I learned to cook, I could only do the one dish. I can only do the one flower, but I'll branch out soon enough.'

'Nikolas rubs olive oil into her skin every morning, with a blend of fresh-cut rosemary and lavender,' Elizabeth said. 'She says it takes away every ache. But they all come back again.'

They ate frozen pizza and pre-packed salad. Everyone kept going on about how delicious it was. Nikolas kept rubbing his stomach, rolling his eyes, patting Marilyn's head, so Marilyn knew it tasted foul. From her sunroom bed Brigid could be part of mealtimes.

I'm going to live to enjoy this, Brigid thought. For the first and only time Nyphi appeared in the same room as Nikolas and disappeared just as quickly.

*

The weeks passed. There was one brutal night when they thought they were going to lose her to a high fever, which proved to be the turning point.

'If she has a fever, then still she has an immune system. Her body is fighting back,' Elizabeth kept whispering to Marilyn.

Nikolas stayed beside her day and night. Occasionally they saw him look at the garden, wistful for his own, but most of his time, thought and energy was trained on her. When the fever broke, she began to take fluids orally. Her aches stayed away longer between Nikolas's massages. The garden grew well as spring suggested a fine summer to come.

Marilyn discovered she liked being needed at work, knowing her cleaning only drove Sean and the Mikes to distraction. She couldn't get to Wexford for more than a night, not wanting to be far away from Brigid, whose next hospital appointment was in early June. The time away from Sean was killing her, but it was giving her a perspective she had lost when she fell head over heels for him.

'You never say you miss me,' she said to him one night. After a hard day working the yard, they had promised to go straight to sleep, and had tried to, but without success. No matter how tired they were, or how troubled, lovemaking had to happen.

'And how will that help things if I say that?'

'If you don't say, I don't know. And I assume.'

'You can assume, Marilyn Monroe' – it was the first time he'd ever said her name in full – 'that with each breath I leave out of me, there's missing you in it. And with each breath I take in, there's longing. So go to sleep now.'

*

Sundays had a new shape to them. She spent them out walking in the Wicklow mountains, with her father.

It had been Niall's suggestion. 'There's been a lot of fuss, since the move.'

She wasn't as fit as he was, so he did a lot of the talking as they went uphill. He talked about his work, what it was like, the endless demands of it, the new party, how one was the same as another.

She stopped for breath, since they were climbing a steep gradient, looked at him and tersely said, 'I've been a member of your new party for longer than you, since I was eighteen. I'd consider there to be big differences between the parties.'

'Then you take politics at face value, which is always a very bad thing to do. Your mother, is she still a member, then?'

'No, she's never been.'

'On the contrary, that's how I met her.'

'You're telling me something else I didn't know.'

'Okay . . .' He drew back and looked at her, hard. 'Do you want to know?'

'Yes.'

'Is that why you agreed to meet like this? You want to know what she was like then?'

'That's one of the reasons. I know it's the same for you.' She looked at him squarely. 'We're both trying to understand her, I'd say. I know you're seeing her, and before you ask, I don't approve.' She didn't mention that Tony was the reason why. 'But there's little chance of me stopping it. She was prevented from doing a lot with her life. She can live it how she wants now. So let's trade.'

He described a woman who even at seventeen had the kind of beauty that lends sophistication. 'Of course she lied about her age, told me she was nearly twenty. She got away with it, too, she had an air about her that made her feel older ...' He described her quickly and with a businesslike manner. It was like listening to herself, before Sean came and Julie left and Brigid got sick. He was driven to do rather than feel, and when it came to anything more than a sketchy outline, he had little detail; he captured very little of Elizabeth's essence in his descriptions. Compared to Tony's analysis, it was like a wren lighting in an eagle's nest. Funny how life saw them the opposite way around.

Marilyn saw that her mother would have to hand herself to him on a plate. At seventeen that's not a hard thing to. At fifty-two it would be excruciating. She thanked heaven for Sean, for how he tried to know her without expectation. And she wondered about herself, about what she was doing there. It wasn't that she had nothing in common with Niall; the trouble was what they did have in common. Their measure of drive would never make her happy in life.

'Okay, enough about Elizabeth,' she interrupted him in a way she could see he wasn't used to. 'The other thing I'm here for is because I want to know what you're like, so I can figure out the bits of me that have always been missing. That's what children of single parents feel like – half of a whole.'

He nodded and resumed the pace.

'If she had contacted you when I was a child rather than when I was eighteen, what would you have done?'

'More is the short answer. And I don't think I would have tried to take you. You'd have been established as her own by then. I saw that soon after I lost you both.' She noted him saying 'both'. 'I looked for you because I would have set your mother up and seen you both when I could. I would have provided.'

'And I'd have felt three-quarters whole, instead of half. Lucky me, and her.'

'Look.' Niall stopped and rested his hands on his knees.

His was the kind of face that lined easily; he wouldn't hold on to being handsome, as her mother was doing to her beauty. 'You asked for the truth. I'm telling you what I would have done, not what I should have done. I should have given up politics and gone into business.'

'But you were tipped for Taoiseach at one stage, I remember.'

'That's politics. They're always giving the wrong jobs to the wrong man.'

'Note you didn't say woman.'

'Well now, Marilyn, it'll be twenty years before we see a female leader of the country. At the moment they just want to dress them up nice and send them off as heads of state to places. That's equality for you.' His laugh was sharp; he didn't consider himself to have been treated equally either.

'Women grow up with that feeling,' she said, looking at him. He didn't look back, and pressed on.

They were coming out of the forest and she could see an overhanging rock at the crest of a hill, a natural shelter and viewpoint. He was heading straight for it like he knew every rut and hole on the track. Lithe and wiry, a goat. Not a bear. Again she missed Sean.

'I come here all the time,' he said as they settled underneath the overhang. 'I look out at the city and at the sea and wish I could take that ferry leaving the harbour to a different country and be a completely different person. A better one.'

'You had the chance of being that here.'

'"Had" is the operative word. I get the impression there's no chance now. Did you tell your mother you were coming here today?'

'I did.'

'Can I ask what her reaction was?'

'She didn't have one.'

'You're right not to tell me.'

'Don't hurt her,' she warned him, suddenly. 'She's going through enough. My grandmother's very sick.'

'Marilyn, my feelings for your mother haven't changed, I've said that.'

'My mother is over thirty years older now. She's middle-aged.'

'You think I don't know that?' It was his turn to snap. 'You think it's young ones I'm interested in? I've had young ones.'

'I'm sure you have,' Marilyn nodded. 'I'm sure Judith's had a miserable life.'

'Don't talk to me about my wife, you don't know the first thing.' He spoke calmly, but she knew it was only anger he felt. It frightened her, as it had once done her mother, more than if he'd shouted.

'Niall? Why are you seeing Elizabeth again? What can you gain from it?'

'I would have thought you'd know – the opportunity to be loved for myself, instead of what I do.'

'Good answer,' she had to admit, 'but not good enough if you don't want all she has to offer. Don't think you can keep her hidden again.'

'We're not having an affair, we're meeting to talk, if that's what you mean.'

'I think that'll have a lot more to do with how she wants it than you. And please, like any child, I don't want to know the gory details,' was Marilyn's parting shot as she headed back down the hill.

He caught up with her. 'Will we see each other next Sunday?'

She knew he needed this as much as she did. It felt right.

On subsequent Sundays, two contained people struggled to

reveal themselves on wet Irish hillsides, father and daughter with no way of being that to each other as yet. The truths came out, slowly.

He stopped speaking in Morse code and told her in more depth what her mother was like. She was beautiful, intelligent, trusting and open. For a time he hated her because of the threat she posed to his career, and for a time he was glad when she disappeared. Then it began to come to him, what he had missed.

'It didn't change me, Marilyn. I drove myself harder, was prepared to compromise more of myself, to get what I wanted. Then I didn't get it. After I lost the official leadership race they took me out of maths and shoved me into PE. They left me kicking a football around and put an idiot in my place. Then I realised they were all idiots, about to lose the next election, so I put myself forward as leader again. And got caught to force an election, a leadership one. They gave me a job scraping chewing gum off the back benches. So I switched to the other side, who now love me after thirty-nine years spent hating me.'

She told him, among other things, that she should never have given up piano.

'Then why did you?'

'I couldn't take the pressure of loving something that much. It was so risky. What if I didn't make it? I hated the uncertainty. I've always liked knowing where I am with things.'

'If I'd been around I'd have made bloody sure you kept it up, went for it.'

'But would you have been able for me if I didn't get it? You don't seem to manage your own failures too well,' she laughed at him.

'They hurt now, but in a few years' time I'll be glad I tried all I could to get where I wanted to go. You know what they say about deathbed regrets. I'll need a king-size one as it is,' he said, then laughed at himself.

After five Sundays out walking, Marilyn and Niall had enough to begin to know each other, and a suggestion that they might like to.

She drove home with his words in her head, and promised herself never to let Sean and her go the same way because of ambition, to have a family with the man she loved and to do whatever she could to make it happen. If her father couldn't be a father to her, he could still be a grandfather.

All of a sudden she couldn't wait for it to happen. She knew this was the reservation she had felt back when Geraldine Leahy had first hinted at her upcoming super-woman position. She wanted to be a mother, and Sean to be the father. As if he heard her thoughts, Sean called her on the mobile.

'I'm just back from the gallop. Delaney ran her best time ever, Marilyn, and Noble was nowhere in sight. One of the Mikes was on her back. She's there, Marilyn. I'm thinking six weeks and I'll start her off racing.'

There was a silence at the end of the phone, then he heard a sniff.

'For the love of God! Why are you crying? We're over the moon here!'

'I'm happy.' She laughed through a sheet of tears. 'I think I just started to really believe in fate, that's all. Before I've always seen it as a kind of giant abacus, with all the wooden counters on someone else's side. But it looks like they're swinging over to ours, aren't they, Sean?'

'It looks like it, Marilyn. It looks like.' He was laughing too. 'I wish you were here now, I'd swing you off your feet and carry you out to see her. She's all pleased with herself in her little stable.'

Marilyn giggled. For a moment there she had thought he wanted to swing her off her feet and take her to bed. But this was an honest-to-God countryman. As far away as you could get from the urbane, smooth-talking Niall Tormey.

This was the man she wanted. The feeling was mutual. Once that horse won her race, she knew he would be asking her, in a clumsy way full of his big heart, to marry him.

'If I have to be the jockey myself that's going to happen,' she vowed.

36

June. The garden was at its most glorious. Elizabeth, Grace and Nikolas were all tending it and Brigid felt part of it, watching all the work from such close quarters in the sunroom. The weeks passed and Brigid pulled back from the brink.

Elizabeth's conferring was a moment she didn't have to miss. Both Marilyn and Brigid, along with Tony, Nikolas, Theresa and Grace, were present for it. Niall sent flowers, an architectural arrangement that was not to Elizabeth's taste. The cornflower plants were still arriving weekly and she'd begun to anticipate them.

Brigid's voice was stronger each day, as she was. When Elizabeth joined the rest of her class on stage Brigid asked Marilyn, 'So who sent the flowers this morning?'

'Who do you think?' Marilyn didn't want to lie.

'I know I don't think much of him.'

'He's not that bad.'

'For a man who ruined her life.'

'Well, she's got it back again.' Marilyn began to clap as the scroll was put into Elizabeth's hand. 'What she does with it is up to her, Brigid.' Theresa, sitting beside them, nodded at this. Tony, sitting on the other side of Nikolas, heard every word. His joy at being invited to this occasion was spliced with a fear that he was being offered a glimpse of what might be possible but, against a man like Tormey, was not probable.

'Don't think like that, my darling, he hasn't got your understanding of her,' Grace, who was sitting beside him, whispered as she picked up his hand and held it. For a reason

Grace could reveal to no one else but Theresa, she had a warm heart for Tony, apart from holding a similar view to everyone else that he was the right man for Elizabeth.

'Thanks.' He gave her hand a squeeze and suddenly it was okay to hope again. It wasn't foolish. It was brave.

They went for lunch and the biggest cause for celebration was that Brigid managed to drink an entire bowl of soup. Marilyn phoned Sean to let him know, there and then, and they could all hear the cheer at the other end.

'So, who's going to make a speech?' Tony asked.

All eyes turned to Brigid, who, although weak, stood up, supported at the elbow by Nikolas. 'I have to be honest and say, there's a part of me ashamed today, that I never gave Elizabeth the credit she deserved. I think in my day and position in life, having brains was a luxury we couldn't afford.' Theresa nodded at this. 'We had to get on with working. Too much thought made too much trouble. Life was hard. I was hard on Elizabeth, but she knew about the beautiful things and she found them, despite all my efforts to stop her. And then she had Marilyn, who's twice as brainy as Einstein. I saw then, when Marilyn was doing her schooling, the importance of education. What it does for a person. The doors it opens. I have to say I was afraid for you, Marilyn, you were a little thing, I thought you'd be trampled so I went tough on you as well.

'Now, I know that you and your mother, with your brains to burn, have hearts to match. The way you've all looked out for me in the past months' – by this stage Brigid's voice was giving out, with effort and emotion – 'persuades me I don't deserve any of you. All me life I chewed altar rails and never really understood what God meant or stands for. Well, I know now, looking at my daughter, He stands for compassion and strength in the one breath. And she has the gift of both. The people who will be helped now, because of her learning, will be grateful and looked after. You couldn't get a more proud mother than me today.'

She sat down and Nikolas immediately put his arms around her. He hadn't understood the words, but their delivery, which had brought the table and Brigid to tears, was impossible to miss. As he held his wife, Elizabeth stood and toasted Brigid.

'To my mother. I hope next week brings us the news she deserves.'

Brigid's hospital appointment would establish whether she was strong enough now for the surgery. She was eating a little, walking around, drinking well and her voice was back, if still weak. They were all too frightened to say or even think the word 'recovery'.

Elizabeth took her to the hospital, at Brigid's request. She didn't want anyone else there. This didn't upset Marilyn. Elizabeth was head of the family now; Brigid had abdicated.

The Friday evening before the conferring, and a fortnight before the hospital appointment, Tony had called around with a cornflower pot. Elizabeth now had five of them.

'Thanks, this one can be for my office,' she smiled. 'You don't have to bring any more of them!'

'I want to, unless you want me to stop, and if that's the case you know what to do.' As usual the inscribed card said so. But he had stopped declaring his love on it, knowing how heavy it weighed on Elizabeth, and it was obvious what his feelings were.

He also had two gift-wrapped boxes. 'One for Elizabeth to say congratulations, one for Marilyn,' he smiled. 'Happy birthday, Marilyn.'

She was thirty-three that day. Sean was coming up so they could go to dinner, but her birthday no longer mattered. It was a birthday like she could never remember, full of magic, full of surprise. Childhood revisited, except that in her childhood she hadn't been a child.

At 8.00 a.m. Grace had knocked on the door to present her with chocolate cake. She blew out three candles with the wish for Brigid to be better, and ate it for breakfast. Her first ever birthday card from her father had dropped onto the mat, though inside it he called himself Niall. There was a voucher for a thousand euros – 'for a lot of lost birthdays'. Elizabeth gave her a summer cotton shawl and a single pearl set into a gold claw for around her neck.

'Your father gave it to me for my birthday, the first one I had with him.' Her voice didn't carry a trace of resentment. This was the first time she had even referred to him, outside of their initial conversation, allowing Marilyn total privacy to the point where Marilyn felt she didn't want to know.

'I can't take this from you.'

'You can and you will. I kept it for you. I wanted you to have something of his. It suits you better than it ever did me. And I know you don't believe in this kind of thing, but I had it cleansed of all the old energies, so that it's a clear path from you to him. I'm glad you know your father. You should have known him sooner.'

'And how well do you know him by now?' Marilyn took the opportunity to ask.

'I can't say, except that he hasn't changed as much as I would have hoped. But he's everything I once loved,' Elizabeth revealed.

'And what about Tony?'

'Tony is more than I could hope or imagine any man to be.'

'You can't keep stringing them both along.'

'I don't plan to. I'm not now.'

'So, Niall knows?'

'No, because he has no need to know.' Elizabeth was firm.

'Don't use Tony as a pawn, Ma, it's not his fault Niall's professionally married to Judith.'

'That's not what I meant. I meant that Niall's at arm's length until I decide otherwise. He may be your father, but he's also a hard man to manage if you give him too much information.'

'And Tony?'

'You can trust Tony, with anything.'

Marilyn turned away from the conversation, smiling.

Sean's present was getting Delaney ready for her first race. The traditional route for a racehorse is to start off point-to-pointing, which Delaney had always performed well at. But her first proper races were where her problems began. All horses are a year old from January first, even when they're born in December. January-born Delaney had been the oldest girl in the class, but the worst behaved. Not any more.

'I've even got her loaded up without trouble, then I take her on a tour of the roads so she's used to the box on racing day. And I've got the two Mikes out there banging bin lids and shouting so as to get her used to the noise. I even borrowed a loudspeaker, to remind her of the tannoy. The two Mikes were rolling around listening to me shouting "winner all right" at the top of my voice. I think you could put her in the middle of the dual carriageway and race her down the grass verge and she wouldn't bat. She's come on, so she has.'

It never occurred to Marilyn to be annoyed at him for taking up so much conversation with Delaney; she was as involved as he was in her progress. Sean was hoping, all going well, to run her in June's meeting in Wexford, in the maiden race.

'When I told the lads in entries and declarations, they laughed. They remember Delaney, say she's no maiden, more an old biddy. I got angry with that, for our little horse. I said she's only coming to form now and has a lot to learn. The way she's going, she'll be the best filly to come out of any stable this year. Anyway, it's good that her reputation goes before her. If she's known for her nonsense, her first proper race will be all the better received. Wait till you see her, Marilyn,' he said. 'I'm talking a lot on your birthday, and it's the first thing out of my mouth, I know, but I wanted to be the first to say it to you, love. And I love you. Is there any chance you could tell me what you'd like as a present?'

'Your presence, for dinner, how about that?'

'Sounds reasonable to me. You aren't going to do the female thing of being all disappointed when there's nothing else?'

'Oh, there will be something else.' She looked at the chart of her cycle. She was getting very good at throwing caution to the winds, and with her numerical skill she had no doubt her birthday night was ovulation night.

Sean was smiling on the other end of the line.

Tony's present was a linen scarf dyed cornflower-blue by his own hand. Her mother had a wrap in the same shade. Inside each box was another card with a *Modern Botanical* excerpt: 'It dyes linen a beautiful blue, but the colour is not permanent.'

'Sorry, Marilyn, I had this made for your mother before I heard it was your birthday and I had a bit left over, to make the scarf with. And you've read the washing instructions.'

'Tony, it's just gorgeous and I love it.' She gave him a kiss. Elizabeth was staring at the cloth, shaking her head.

'This must have taken you ages.'

'Not really, I've got a supplier for cornflowers now, apart from my own stock.'

'You can stop at any time, Tony. This is so much work.'

'The man likes working,' Brigid intervened. 'Be gracious in your thanks. He'll do what he wants, won't you, Tony?'

'I will, Brigid, and you're getting better each day, I notice.'

'I am, and Nikolas gets worse. Will you look at him planting an olive tree in our garden, beside the fig from last week? Are you two trying to outdo each other in romantic gestures?'

There was a shade in her voice too, as she watched Nikolas. He was spending more of his time in the garden now that she was feeling better, and less time in the house. In the house he seemed too big, restless, pacing.

'Can you give me a slice of that cake for tomorrow?' Tony asked Marilyn, quietly, but in a house full of women, everyone hears everything.

'What age are you, then?'

'Forty-eight, time for my eyesight to start failing, Elizabeth says.'

'Ma,' Marilyn yelled across the table, 'he's a toy boy! Only forty-eight tomorrow.'

'You never said! You never gave me any time to get you a present,' Elizabeth said. 'What would you like?'

Tony looked at her. 'A walk with you, if you have the time.'

'Take him on your usual, Elizabeth, he'd like that,' Brigid ordered in the old Brigid voice there was no arguing with.

Five and a half years after first seeing her on the Vico Road, Tony Devereux got the chance to walk beside Elizabeth Monroe on his birthday. They sat on the bench he watched her sit on, and she gave him a present – her own copy of the *Modern Botanical*. He had told her he didn't have a copy of his own.

'Please,' she stressed, 'I want you to have it, for all your kindness and your understanding. You're part of the reason my mother is doing so well.'

Tony was looking at her, wondering if he should say just how much and how often he had wished for this moment, but it wasn't the moment he'd wished for. She was here as his friend, not the woman he was to marry.

It wasn't enough, he knew with a sinking heart. And it didn't look like it was ever going to be more.

Then she did something that took him by surprise.

'I think you're a big part of why I'm so happy too. Niall Tormey never gave more than half of himself. I think I've always been scared of someone giving me more. You see, I barely remember my father, and what I remember was that he was exciting, and I was afraid of him. The look in his eyes, when he left – I saw that in Niall's.'

'And what was that?' Tony asked.

'The look of wanting more than this. I've never been enough for anyone, Tony – not my daughter, my father, my mother, my lover or myself.'

'Well, that's not the case with me.' He looked at her, though she wasn't looking at him. 'You're more than I ever imagine I can have.'

She smiled. 'If you weren't so sincere, I'd think you were a born flatterer. Will you drop us to the hospital when Brigid has her next appointment?'

She knew she didn't need to ask.

Nuala Brady held the stick in her hand, pointed to the light box the X-ray was pinned to and said it three times before it began to sink in.

'I told you, Brigid, you don't need the surgery. You don't have to have the surgery. Your cancer is in remission.'

'What's that?'

'Remission.'

'Yes, I heard you the first time, but what is it?'

'Surely your last consultant used the word? Remission

means it has reduced, and in fact, appears to have disappeared. The treatment was successful.'

'And the care she got,' Elizabeth said, her voice full of tears.

'That's the truth, I got the best care I could have hoped for. Which is why I could swallow my dinner the past two days. Thank God I never have to see that Complan stuff again. You wouldn't feed it to a dog.'

'Exactly, Brigid. We're surprised, to say the least. For the prognosis for a cancer such as yours, especially a second reoccurrence, has, up to now, been fairly certain.'

'Have you ever been smudged?' Brigid asked Nuala.

'No, I can't say I have.'

'Then take my advice and get a wild lad called Leon up here to the patients in your care and then get them all to have a sunroom, and a lovely new husband, and they'll get better too.'

'Well now, Brigid, we might just do that. Can I just put a note of warning into this? The fact that you've had two primary cancers may well dispose you to metastases—'

'Are you saying I'm not well again entirely?'

'I have to say this. For the moment you are, but we're reluctant to say recovered, which is why we say remission.'

'So, remission is like intermission, like the cinema in the old days?'

'You've got it, Brigid.' The specialist couldn't stop herself from smiling.

'I'm glad you managed one of those,' Brigid said, also smiling. 'You give a woman great news and you look like it's bad.'

'I'm sorry, we're just confused, we can't explain it. Because we gave you a decreased life expectancy you may think we were in error originally, which isn't the case.'

'I know that, but you could be a bit more jolly about the whole thing, could you not?'

'It's very jolly, Brigid.'

'That's better.' Brigid sat back and reached for her daughter's hand. Elizabeth was beyond saying anything.

'Can you tell me something now? What are the chances of it not coming back?'

'I can only say that they have to be better than the chances of it disappearing were, and it has disappeared. But you must realise what the reality is.'

'I'm glad, and I'm glad there's a chance it might come back.' Brigid gripped Elizabeth's hand harder.

The specialist shook her head. 'I'm not following you there.'

'If you didn't think I had any chance of getting better, then you weren't the one who cured me, so I know what did. And if I don't carry on with it, the weakness will come back. Are you following me now, Doctor? No? Then they ought to send the lot of you back to college. I was brought up to think the likes of you knew everything. But you don't know the basics.'

'What my mother is saying is that she has a chance that you weren't giving her before,' Elizabeth interpreted.

'Yes, and these days are ones I wasn't supposed to have. I'm going to fill them.'

Tony was outside with the taxi, but he couldn't drive either when he heard the news. They had a cry in the car park and then made the journey to 51 Verbena Avenue, where everyone was waiting. The cheer was heard up at the other end of the street when the outcome was known.

'Tony, I hope you'll drive myself and Nikolas to the airport at the earliest opportunity. He has to go home, or he'll be getting sick, and I tell you one thing. I'm not being parted from him again. You're the woman of the house now, Elizabeth,' Brigid said later that evening, when the celebration had died down.

'Will you make Greece your home, then?' Theresa asked the question they were all afraid to ask.

'Nikolas is my home,' Brigid said in a level voice, 'for however long I have left. But this is my house and I won't be without it or my family for too long at a time. Now we'll stop the soft talk, thank you, and get on with living.'

Brigid and Nikolas were gone by the end of June. Marilyn and Elizabeth were left. It was a comfortable arrangement, peppered with visits from Sean and Tony, but not Niall.

'You know, if you do believe in Grace's reading, then you'll know my father's not the one. He's not coming to our house for you. His publicity machine won't allow,' Marilyn pointed out.

'Yes,' Elizabeth agreed, 'but the question is, can I ever leave it? There's no need for me to live here any more, and I find it's not only my home, but a home I miss my mother in.'

The vacuum of Brigid's departure was always felt; every part of 51 held her as a memory. Even the garden had traces of her now, the pleasure she had taken in it from her sunroom, watching flowers bud, unfurl, bloom, die, to be replaced by new living, new life.

'Don't be lifting up my lovely carpet,' she warned in more than one letter.

'How could we,' Elizabeth wrote back, 'when every time we walk on it, or see it, it reminds us of you?'

37

'The odds for Wexford this Friday – anything you can tell us, Mari?' Larry was back to treating her as his right-hand woman.

'Nothing spectacular according to my calculations,' she said coolly, 'though I know Sean has a great prospect, so we might consider shortening the odds on her.'

'What's that? Reunion Anthem in the sixth? She's near the end of her time, not the start of it.'

'No. Delicia Heartly in the second race.' Marilyn used Delaney's official name.

'That one!' Tommy spat. 'She bit the arse off her own groom last time out and threw the jockey. Sean Monroe bought her in a trailer outside Goff's Sales, the whole place laughing at him. The only form that one shows is that she'll make good chunks in Chum.' They laughed at this.

'We'll leave the odds where they are on this one. Sorry, Mari. Long is too short for that one, our money's safe on any bet we take.' Larry was gentle, but his voice carried caution – it's your head we employ you for.

She sat back in her chair and thought, You wait for Friday.

She left the office early to miss the traffic and to collect Elizabeth, who was due to come to the race with her. But Elizabeth reverted to a form that had almost been forgotten, it hadn't happened in so long – she came home an hour late. Marilyn was fired up. Delaney was running in the second, which started at six.

'All we need now is for the Saab to break down,' Marilyn was peppering behind the wheel.

'Take it easy, love,' Elizabeth tried to calm her.

'Easy? You can't even drive!' was the last thing Marilyn said before she ran into the car in front of them. She got out, offered her insurance details, took the abuse, offered another thousand on top of the damage and the driver in front became suddenly accepting. She got into the Saab to set off again, but it wouldn't start.

Marilyn phoned Tony. Grace and Theresa had gone away for another few days. They were doing a lot of that lately, unravelling themselves from constant involvement in number 51, getting back to the more enclosed world of number 45.

'Please don't,' Elizabeth asked when she realised who Marilyn was phoning.

'Look, I'm going to pay him!'

'It's not that. I just don't want to see him right now.'

'Well, tough. I need to see him. He's someone I can rely on!'

'Marilyn, you're taking this too far. I was late for a good reason.'

'Okay, then tell me what it was.'

'It's confidential, between myself and a client.'

'You know how important it was to Sean and me, to see this together.'

'Marilyn, I did not crash your car!'

'You're too wrapped up playing girlfriend to two men. One's not good enough for you, is that it? You can have Tony hook, line and sinker. Instead you're waiting around for Mr Powerful to come along on his white horse. Only he doesn't own one, does he? And my boyfriend is the owner of a brown horse who I'm going to miss in her first race since he bought her almost a year ago! Because of you!'

'I can see we're not going to get anywhere with this. I'll take a walk.'

'No, I'll do that.'

Half an hour later, Tony came along in his taxi to pick them up. Marilyn was sitting at the side of the road and crying openly. It was four-thirty. She was never going to make it.

'Come on, love.' Tony sat down on the kerb and put his arm around her. 'Where's your mam?'

'In what's left of my car.'

'Look,' Tony said as Elizabeth sat in his car, knowing that even the sight of her was making Marilyn worse, 'you won't get the race, but if we leave now they'll still be celebrating.'

'Will you drive us? I'll pay you.'

'You will do no such thing.' She could see she'd touched a raw nerve. 'This is my car and I'm my own boss. If I decide to go to Wexford for the evening, I go. We'll move this into the car park over there and we'll get you there by six-thirty.'

Elizabeth sat in the back seat. Marilyn was in the front, stone-faced. Tony found Elizabeth's eyes in the rear-view mirror and winked. She managed a small smile. At six they were still sitting in traffic in the town of Gorey, well north of Wexford. Marilyn was willing Delaney to start well. Sean called her at five past six.

'Three lengths,' he said.

'She won by?'

'She lost the rest of the field by. Only after interfering with the rest of the field on the first turn; she ran sideways, she did. Ciaran's an experienced jockey and he said it was like being on a bronco. He couldn't get a hold of her. There's a steward's enquiry. I only managed to walk around the parade ring once with her. She used up most of her energy on that. I had Ciaran on her three times at home and she went around like a puppy for him.'

'I'm not far away, I'm in Gorey.'

The anteroom beside the steward's office was little more

than a cubicle, with nothing to look at. Sean waited outside like a bear in a cage, for Ciaran, who had to face the panel. He put his head in his hands. By the time Ciaran came out, he felt physically sick.

'I was done for careless riding. Only a caution. I was lucky to get that.' Sean knew from Ciaran's face that he wouldn't ride Delaney again.

There was nowhere to park. Cars were pulled up on either side of the road for a mile on either side of the course. Tony dropped Marilyn outside and she pulled her small overnight bag out.

'Where are you going?' she asked them. 'You could pull up at the hotel up the road. We'll meet you afterwards.'

Elizabeth shook her head, and Tony said, 'No. We'll head back to Dublin, you two need time on your own.'

'Thanks, Tony, thanks for taking me, and Elizabeth, thanks for taking the abuse.'

'Look, she's keyed up,' Tony reasoned after Marilyn had raced off.

'I know my own daughter,' Elizabeth snapped.

'Sorry.' Tony flinched.

Five minutes later she apologised. 'I was late, and this was so important to her. The trouble is, I can't tell her why. Niall came to see me today. He says that, all things considered, he thinks it would be best if he and Judith called it a day. He says he thinks he needs to spend time with his family, try to make up for it. He wants me to consider what it would be like if a member of government went through a public divorce to marry his former mistress, but he promises it won't come out about me being his former mistress. He told me why. The reason is awful, sad, and is a fact; it can never come out.'

Tony had pulled over by then. They were parked at a

viewpoint overlooking mudflats and a river estuary, where wading birds fished the silt banks. The water level was low.

'Have you asked yourself what's at the back of this?' Tony asked.

'I have, and I don't know, which I know means I don't trust him. But I suspect that he's got a bit more trouble ahead of him, and knows even his new party is uncertain about him. I suspect he may be covering his bets, in case he has no future with or in politics. He could even be bluffing me, to get me into his bed. That, I'm afraid to say, makes me a cynic. But it doesn't rule out that I have feelings for him, based on what, I can't say.' Elizabeth rubbed the back of her neck and looked out at a heron fishing a shallow shoreline of the estuary, wishing for patience, wishing for answers. 'You're not saying anything, Tony.'

Tony watched the same heron. He didn't want to watch the estuary or the evening sun on the mud flats turning them copper. He didn't want to see anything beautiful. Something beautiful was coming to an end.

'You're going to try it, aren't you?'

'He says he still loves me.'

'I don't doubt that's true, even for a second,' Tony whispered to her.

Elizabeth touched his shoulder.

'Thank you for saying that.'

'And I have to say this too. I know you're the best kind of person, and that if you choose him over me, you'll have everything you want. But in the worst kind of man.'

'Men change. You did.'

'Does this mean you're closing the door on us?'

'No, I don't know what it means, right now. I wanted to wait a few days before seeing you. Marilyn called you.'

'Your family has always wanted me more than you did. Let me close the door for you, Elizabeth. I've hung on by my fingernails, I've pursued, I've proven my feelings at every point, and still you're considering someone who has never even given you a fraction of what he could have.'

'You're right, it's like he wants this, for us to stop seeing each other, but he's never even met you. From the minute I met you I wasn't fair to you. I've treated you like he treated me, in a way. You deserve better.'

'Why do women always say that when they're going to break your heart? Mind you, I lied myself. I told you if he was good to you I'd shake his hand. But I want to break it.'

They drove back to Dublin in silence. He dropped her off and watched her go through the door of 51.

He worked all night until his last drop-off at dawn – a cornflower plant, with a letter asking her please not to do this, without more consideration.

There was another plant pot, outside, waiting, and a note: *I will never forget you.*

Inside, Elizabeth, awake all night, heard him drive away, both pots gone with him.

'Thank God Brigid's not here,' she whispered to herself. Persuasion curled into her.

'I only wish Brigid were here,' Tony whispered to himself. In his conservatory were trays of cornflower seedlings and pots in various stages of budding and flowering. He saw himself smashing every one of them, then saw Peter Devon's face. Besides, he couldn't bear to part from them. They were all he had now.

'Was it worth it?' he asked himself. He thought of the Vico Road walk, and said yes, even for that single afternoon, yes.

It symbolised the whole experience of Elizabeth Monroe. Incredible happiness and loss in the one breath. Now at least he had something to let go of, having tried.

38

Marilyn found herself in the stable, looking at Delaney for the first time. The horse was standing stock-still, her inner ear turned towards Marilyn. Sean had always told her that if the horse has its ear on you, it has its eye and is observing everything you're doing, so make sure you're doing it right.

Marilyn chose a motherly tone, and a Brigid phrase. 'Don't be trying to put me off from what I'm going to say to you, young lady. You had Sean cautioned yesterday for your carry-on at the racecourse. Now I know you're not fond of the places, and you've had terrible things happen to you, but so have all of us. If we went on like you do, no one would get up at all in the morning. He's in the house now, too depressed to come into the yard, doing his accounts to depress him even more. And I'm here having a woman-to-woman talk with you.'

Delaney's ears twitched. 'If life was perfect, my granny would be living with John Joe Monroe and my aunt would be living with a man and Grace wouldn't exist in our lives. My mother would see Tony for an angel and stay well clear of my father, or else my father would be helping her in the garden of our own house. My friend wouldn't have absconded after a passing feather and I wouldn't be, fingers crossed, hopefully pregnant by a broke horse trainer. But that's what makes life interesting, isn't it? We're all the result and product of mistakes that somehow come right. That's how through science, love and maths the planet advances. Fluke! Now, get some sleep and tomorrow let's decide what we're going to do about this.'

One of the Mikes came in. They'd both got over their shyness with Marilyn, to the extent they could now speak.

'Hiya,' she smiled at him, 'which one are you?'

'I'm the other one,' he said, their stock answer. 'The luck's back with us in you, Marilyn. We needed it badly yesterday. You'd swear we'd never done a day's work on her, the way it went. How's Sean this morning?'

'He's not slept much. I gave him some breakfast, which could have poisoned him, and came out here to muck out for him. I was waiting for you to deal with the horses, you know what I'm like.'

He grinned. The Mikes called her the best horsewoman that never touched a horse. He opened the stable door and clipped the long lead rope onto Delaney, who was being led out now without question. Noble went after her.

'How do you feel, after putting so much energy into her?'

He gave her the stock countryman's response to disappointment – 'Ah,' then a shrug of the shoulders. 'You end up switching off. There's only so many times your heart can be broken. Losing your nerve in this game is normal, but Sean's never lost his temper before. He was roaring and shouting in his truck, hitting the dashboard. He had it all pinned to this, which is a bad thing in the horse game. You might talk to him.'

'I already have.'

They were joined by Mike Two, or maybe it was Mike One.

'Well, Marilyn, if I was him I'd marry you. But that'd be a problem for you, wouldn't it? You'd be known as Marilyn Monroe then.'

'A small price to pay, Mike, for a good man.'

Marilyn headed for the house. She saw them bring Delaney up to the field. She wasn't working today, and she wasn't playing either. She stood underneath a tree, close to Noble, and didn't even graze. No one who knows horses can question their intelligence or their nobility in deciding to work with humans. All they want is to be understood. In that moment, watching that little horse hiding from a world she didn't understand, Marilyn decided it was time to make her decision, and Sean's, for him.

Sean was in the house. He looked up from a sheaf of papers that all said the same thing. He was close to ruin.

'Please, let me look at those,' she said, taking them from him. He let her.

After about four hours she came to the conclusion that Sean's figures added up to the following: each of his twenty horses cost eight hundred a month to stable. The owners only contributed five hundred of this cost. The two Mikes were working for a song, but Sean couldn't even afford a verse. In the past six months he'd won only twenty thousand in prize money, of which he received half. He was going broke, fast.

She made a list of his owners' telephone numbers and got ready to phone them to tell them their stabling and training fees were going up by one hundred and fifty euros.

'You can't do that,' Sean said.

'I can and I will. The Mikes tell me that most trainers have costs covered by owners. If that's the case, you're not charging what you should be. You have buildings and facilities to keep up.'

'That's because I'm only starting out, I have to get the reputation first.'

'Sean, you've been in business five years, and your reputation is made. If the owners didn't get you to take the horses, they'd be put down. The money I'm putting your fees up by – and I'll do it, not you – is a compromise. Then by the end of this year they'll be paying the full amount or they'll be taking their horses elsewhere.'

'If Delaney only ran the way she does at home, we'd be laughing, Marilyn.'

'You wouldn't be laughing, you'd be surviving. Look at the figures. She'd need to win every race between now and next year just to cover the losses. That's too much pressure on one little animal.' He smiled at that, seeing her transition to horse-lover. 'You need less horses and more winners as far as I can see. You need to get rid of the five worst performers.'

'Of which she's one,' Sean interrupted.

'She won't be forever, I'll see to that.'

'Oh' – Sean pulled back – 'will you now? Is it my job you want as well?'

'No, I'd hate it. But Delaney is female, small, a fighter. I know her. We only take on the challenges we're sure of winning, or we want to win so much we'll do anything. So somehow you have to persuade the racecourse officials to let her have a training session at the track before her next race.'

'It won't be Wexford.'

'Oh, it will be Wexford.'

'You mean school her there, Marilyn? I couldn't face that again.'

'It won't happen again. Do you know the story of Signorinetta?'

Sean nodded vaguely.

'I think Delaney's got that in her. In fact let's call her Signorinetta!'

'That's it . . . Delaney Signorinetta, and we'll get someone, anyone, to agree to let us give her the run of the course, with no one around. Once she's galloped around it once, she'll do it again. And a crowd, we have to organise a crowd to come here, to get her used to the spectacle of a race day. And a jockey, she needs a female jockey.'

Sean lifted his eyes from the floor, where they'd been for most of the conversation. 'Hang on now. You know as well as

I do, you have to enter the horse's registered name, otherwise how could they keep track of handicaps and that? And Signorinetta, how do you know about Signorinetta?'

'I found her story in Leahy's library, a place I never went to for anything other than reference. Now I read for interest, and Delaney's our Signorinetta.'

'So, tell me what you read.' Sean put his hand over Marilyn's.

Signorinetta was the product of a mating between a stallion and mare who passed each other each day. Her Italian owner, breeder and trainer, Cavaliere Eduardo Ginistrelli, who came to England from Italy, noticed that Signorina, who had been a good race mare in her day, replied with longing to the stallion Chaleureux's call. In the ten previous seasons she had only produced one foal, Signorino, a half-decent colt who was third in the Derby.

Her fancy for Chaleureux, an unfashionable stallion, would have been written off by most breeders since he was so mediocre. But Mr Ginistrelli was Italian, and he knew 'the boundless laws of sympathy and love', so he paid nine guineas to give his mare her wish. And she rewarded him with Signorinetta, who won the Derby at a hundred to one odds. 'Not if I'd been the bookmaker, but there you are,' Marilyn said. Two days later in the Oaks she won again. Mr Ginistrelli, ridiculed in racing circles, was a witness to the second win, in the Royal box, in the company of the king.

'Delaney's the product of a love match. Delaney is even more of a love match because her sire jumped the fence to be with her dam. We've got to observe the "boundless laws of sympathy and love" because they brought us together, and they'll get Delaney around to being a winner.'

Before she was finished, Marilyn believed herself.

*

The clerk of the course, Joe Meagan, watched Sean Monroe's face. 'Sean, I know you well and your father before you. You're racing people. Yourself more so even than he was. What are you at?'

'I'm not looking to run her in the point to point.'

'You're looking for her to have a *look* at the point to point? I'm confused. Sean, why are you at this? She was sweating up even around the paddock last time.'

'Istabraq used to sweat up. He got some prizes for sweating, Joe.'

'Most don't.' Joe was curt. 'Istabraq was an example, but your horse is an example of a different kind. I don't know why you saddled yourself, or her.'

'She'll be worth the effort.'

'What kind of ground does she like? The going was firm last time, maybe you should take her someplace softer.'

'Wexford's where she's run before, and Wexford's soft after rain, same as any course. Any kind you like, she likes. She's light-footed and strong-hearted. Give her, and me, the chance and I'll give you the bet of your life. The odds on her will be so long you'd build runways with them.'

'You know I never bet. It's not like you to be promising things like that without them being true.'

'Come out to the yard and see her at work, then.'

'I've never had anyone ask me to let a horse *pretend* to take part.'

'Not until now.'

'But why, Sean. She's racing already. If you could call it that. There shouldn't even be a point to point on this late in the year.'

'As well there is, Joe. Bad weather cancellation did a good turn for me.'

'Can you just tell me, Sean. What for?'

'She's skittish in a strange setting. But once she's familiar with it, she'll go right for me.'

'With the form I saw last Friday, Sean, I don't know that I agree.'

'If you let her run on the actual course, instead of outside the railings, I'll show you.'

'You know the ground is sensitive here. We can't do it.'

'She's not getting going. I reined her in for all her training, so she's got used to not getting going. But I'm getting her used to it now. Let her run on the course. You haven't seen her, in her right way and form.'

'You can't run her around the course here, Sean, so stop asking. The other trainers would just kick up.'

'Can I show her around? The yard, the stables, give her a shower here? She loves water. Take her around the parade ring, let her see the stands? She doesn't have to run – but surely to God they won't stop me letting her see the place?'

'Okay, okay. Just get here on Friday, late afternoon. If you get here even an hour beforehand, then she can have the look of the place before any horse arrives, will that do? Once the session's over, she might even have a gallop on the outside of the railings, like the point-to-pointers.'

'Thanks, Joe.' Sean sighed. Point-to-points were famous for taking over five to six hours to finish up.

'Don't thank me in that tone of voice, Sean Monroe, or expect it to be easy after that carry-on. And tell me this – one of the Mikes says you're strong with a lady out of Larry Leahy's empire?'

'I'm telling you nothing, Joe Meagan, until I know myself,' Sean laughed.

'You can't keep a secret like that in Wexford town.'

'I'll tell you a secret, then – you get me a run of this horse here, and I'll be asking that woman to marry me, eventually.

I have to have something to offer her. Right now it's a skin of debts.'

Joe Meagan looked at him. As a breeder he had seen previously shrewd businessmen throw money at stock that mostly depreciated and rarely, if ever, granted a return. A return on a high-bred horse would mean the horse would have to keep winning all season, in races with bigger pots than Wexford gave out. Delaney wasn't even high bred, but Sean had high-bred hopes for her.

'The money's in the betting end, Sean. Surely the lady has it of her own?'

'She does, and it's not hers I want, it's my own.' Sean humbled himself, a thing Joe had never known him or his father before him to do. The Monroes were known for admirable decency and foolish pride.

'I'll see what I can do, so, if a romance depends on it. Get her in here Friday early on and we'll give her a good look around, and a stable to see the carry-on.'

Marilyn rang Sean from the office on Friday, and he sounded cheerful. Delaney was stabled at the track. 'She's even been in to see the course vet, who had a good look at her, so she won't have that to get used to either. She's got her ears cocked and her head over the half-door looking at all the goings-on. She's as calm as if she was at home, and I have Helen with me for the evening ride. She even popped in after work, to say hello.'

Helen Ferguson was the best amateur jockey in the county and a friend of Sean's. When she came to the stables at Sean's request to ride out for him, Delaney had taken to her instantly, and Sean insisted it was because Helen resembled Marilyn.

'She has the look of you, Marilyn, same height and hair.

If we could only persuade you to get up on a horse, we'd definitely have a winner in Delaney.'

'I'd have to book a funeral beforehand,' Marilyn laughed. But she was flattered, and insecure about Helen. 'I'll be down soon anyway to see for myself.'

The point-to-point finished at nine-thirty and by ten everyone had left, but for Delaney, Helen, Sean, Marilyn and Joe Meagan. Delaney should have been well asleep, but as soon as she was led out, in the last of the evening light, she came alive, knowing what she was there to do. Sean walked her out for a tour around the parade ring. Her head carriage was high and her ears pricked up, pointing inwards, jig-jogging a little, which made Marilyn nervous. Joe said, 'Don't worry about that, that's a horse on good terms with himself.'

'Herself,' she corrected him.

Sean legged Helen up. Delaney was tired after a full day's work, as they all were, and Helen rode her out. The course was rutted from all the activity and Marilyn could see Joe shaking his head.

'It's not ground I'd run an unreliable horse on, but then, that's Sean's business.'

'She's light-footed,' Marilyn informed him. 'So Sean tells me. And she's more than reliable, in the right circumstances.'

Delaney strode out well. Helen was riding her to the other side of the course, where she had started from last week.

'That's a tidy, loose stride,' Joe said, watching intently, 'not the horse I saw racing last week. Look at that flowing motion, she's taking the outside turf like it was a fairway. I was going to suggest blinkers to Sean, but some say they can suggest an ungenuine horse.'

Delaney was approaching the start point as Sean came up to them in the observation platform. 'She doesn't need them, she needs to see what's going on. She's too smart a horse not to want to know.'

Even as he spoke, Helen was up out of the saddle and Delaney was off.

For the next five minutes, no one said a word.

'She didn't need to be told! She took the fences like they were puddles! I wasn't even working her, she was driving herself!' Helen hadn't stopped for breath since she'd finally managed to pull Delaney in. 'I thought she must be running too free, but she's on the bridle all the way.' Helen patted Delaney's neck. They were a match.

'I think your only worry now is whether the extra weight will hold her back when she wins. She's a small thing.' Joe went to give her a rub, and immediately Delaney's ears flattened. He knew to move off.

'She had me on her little back, and a bad back it was too.' Sean was calm, holding on to Delaney's bridle, rubbing her nose in the way she loved. 'Weight is no problem.'

'I'd keep Helen in your silks, Sean, she's made to ride her. That's a horse-and-jockey fit if ever I saw one. It's as well we have the ladies, changing room now at Wexford.' They knew then he was going to help her get her race. Sean's long day and his long faith in the little chestnut were proving worth it.

'A cubicle with a curtain is all it is, Marilyn,' Helen smiled. 'But the curtain's pink. It's thanks to the course secretary we have that. Otherwise it's the ladies' toilet for us.'

'How do you cope with the sexism?' she asked Helen as they walked to the ladies' changing room. She was so bright, so chatty and so knowledgeable – Marilyn thanked God she wasn't available.

'Ah, if it's sexist, I don't realise it. I'm only looking at the horses.'

'And what about your boyfriend?'

'He's a nurse, never sat on a seaside donkey. Thinks horses are for cowboys. We're getting married next year,' she nudged.

On the way home Sean reached out to hold her hand as he was driving.

'You did this, Marilyn. You got me going on her again, when I was ready to give up. We have our future there behind us.'

She turned around. 'Our future's asleep.' Like a baby – maybe like our baby, Marilyn thought.

That night she got her period. She spent fifteen minutes in the bathroom, mopping up silent tears.

Nature was taking its course in London. Julie was struggling through a last trimester and an existence which was friend-less but for a next-door neighbour who made her look like Maria von Trapp. Magenta was her saving grace, dragging her into her flat for cups of tea and long chats that included a lot of sexual activity and disappointment in men.

'I have a thing you might want to try,' Julie smiled. 'My friend gave it to me, and it worked for her.' She gave Magenta a copy of The Scale in the hope that the man who fathered her fourth child might stay with her.

Magenta regarded The Scale as she described her children's three fathers with a practised irony. 'Number One, he went as fast as he came and he always came quickly, you can trust me on that. Number Two, he was nice, but his wife wasn't. Number Three, I married him, and we had James. And he went to Saudi to earn big money for us all, and I haven't heard from him since. James is five now, still gets birthday cards. The husband hasn't sent me any divorce papers, but then he doesn't send any money either. Me and men, Julie, I love them but I don't like them very much. But you, Julie, you've got something special, and you make it your business to use it properly. Don't waste it, pick someone who can give you what you want.'

'I tried, I only ever picked as well as you did, but for this baby's father' – Julie rubbed her belly, the kicks were insistent now – 'then I gave him to my best friend.'

'Fool.' Magenta shook her head. 'Get him back.'

'No. He wasn't for me. And believe it or not I like standing on my own two feet, even though they're swollen beyond recognition right now.'

'Okay, you know yourself. Find another one. And you be cautious with him, Julie, don't give it all at once. You just have to look at the way the rest of the block of flats looks at you.'

Julie laughed. 'Yeah, the size of me, you mean!'

'No, I don't mean that, though you've got a big baby in there, missus, no doubting it. You have looks like the rest of us want. You just don't have the confidence at the back of them. But if men are looking at you like that and you nearly due a baby then you've got to think about what you're going to do with those looks. There's not many women with your kind of class, as nice as you.'

'Class!' Julie laughed. 'You think I have class. My friend, the one who invented The Scale – she'd laugh in your face.'

'Then she's no friend,' Magenta said softly. 'Class is what you have, to the bone. You got no confidence is all. When that baby comes out of you, you got to act like you have that. Remember, you're strong, Julie, you've done for yourself over here, it's not easy. If you try and make everyone like you, you're only going to come last every time. Now labour's going to be good for that. You can't afford to be nice to no one in labour.' Magenta had agreed to be Julie's birth partner. 'They lay a finger on and you don't like it, you bite it off! They can't sue you. You were in labour! And when that child comes out of you, you're going to be changed. It happened me and it happens any woman who gets to be a mother. That's a lucky thing to be.'

Okay, Julie agreed inside herself. I'll act when I don't feel up to the world. I won't be ashamed of who I am any more.

Delaney won the two-mile hurdle at Wexford's next meet at thirty-three-to-one odds with nine stone ten on her back. She encouraged Joe Meagan to break a life rule. He placed a bet. Marilyn was in the stand with the two Mikes, making noise.

Delaney won again at Wexford, in a low-handicap hurdle with ten stone four on her back at fifteen-to-one odds. Marilyn was there with Elizabeth. And Niall Tormey. He hadn't left Judith. Elizabeth hadn't given him a answer. But he was prepared to be seen in public with her. The local papers took photographs, asked what had brought him here.

'Sean Monroe invited me,' he said without missing a beat, having not even met him. 'This is his partner, Marilyn.'

'And her second name?' A journalist asked.

'Monroe,' Marilyn said with the kind of sigh that knows what's coming next. Elizabeth had moved aside. Niall was pursuing her as aggressively as if she were a top job, though they were never seen out in public alone.

The photographer filed the picture to the nationals, since the caption was so good: 'Ex-Minister at Wexford with Marilyn Monroe'. A couple of the social diaries would pick up on it. As would Judith Tormey.

When Delaney won, Niall thumped Sean between his shoulders. 'Well done, Sean.'

Sean, with his arm round Marilyn, said, 'It's her you should thank. She's a little miracle, so she is, just like the horse.'

'I couldn't agree more,' Niall nodded, then said slowly, 'I

know a few lads who would have horses that would do well coming here. How much room have you got?'

'It's not the room, it's the price,' Marilyn interrupted before Sean could speak. 'It's a thousand a month, for stabling a problem horse, and they pay more the worse that horse is. If they want someone like Sean, they pay.'

That night Niall drove Elizabeth back to Dublin. He was smiling. 'That girl of ours would sell the Pope condoms. She's made for business.'

'Do you think so? I think it's love made her do that. She wants that man to have everything.'

'I want you to have everything, Elizabeth, everything I should have given you the first time around.' She knew he was telling the truth, because he had the note in his voice Tony had, when he spoke of how he felt about her. 'Will you come back to my flat?' he asked.

'No, I have to get back home.'

'Will I come to your house?'

'No again. Sorry, I'm just in need of my own company.'

'So long as it's not a taxi-man's.'

'How did you know about that? And don't speak about him like he's something beneath you.'

'I won't be made a fool of, Elizabeth.'

'You know what, Niall? It's him I made the fool of. You do a good enough job of making yourself one.'

'Are you seeing him?'

'No, I'm not, and I won't be again.'

'Good, we're getting somewhere.'

'If you think that, we're getting nowhere. Good night,' she said as she got out of his car. He didn't stay until she put her key in the lock. Tony always did.

★

Delaney won again, at ten-to-one odds and again with ten stone seven, as race favourite. Then Sean took her out of Wexford, and she lost form. She came fifth at Gowran Park, a contentious fourth in Tipperary. At both courses' next meets she was there, at unremarkable odds, finishing first and second. The horse was none the worse for wear, despite running seven races in a short time. But Sean took the decision to rest her for two months.

Delaney won wherever Delaney went, once she wanted to. Familiarity always gave her heart. With Helen on her back she took everything coming to her. But if it was a new course, she wouldn't co-operate, even with Helen. On the two occasions Helen didn't ride her, Delaney came last.

The routine was set – she was raced when and where Helen was available. She was always the first horse to arrive at the racecourse and the last to leave.

It worked. If she got to race there a second time, her form would see dramatic improvement. She still needed constant handling, but that seemed to be why the crowd took to her. She began to get write-ups and her personality attracted attention. The racing journalists like a horse to define itself, and Delaney was pure definition. Everything was on her terms or no terms.

Larry questioned Marilyn after the third win about their odds. 'You know more than market forces. You tell us what to set in the future. You know all the circumstances.'

'You haven't trusted me up till now.'

'That's because up till now you wouldn't have known the back end of a horse from the front. But you're a fast learner.'

Delaney was the kind of horse no formula could contain, and Marilyn knew her heart. So she joined the rest of them in the boardroom, discussing equine zeitgeist, defining the indefinable. She was lost to it all and Larry watched her with narrowed eyes as she spoke. She was no longer the woman she had been at her job. She was even better. Everyone had more time for her, except his son. Tommy was fully aware he had lost. But none of them knew how Marilyn felt, and she felt trapped. Each time Larry pulled her into a corner, she pulled herself out of it.

Until September. The decision was made for her. He took her out for afternoon tea and told her she wouldn't be going back to the office, that they had something they needed to discuss in depth. What she hadn't realised was that Geraldine would be there, tea and buns and smiles, waiting.

'We're after the woman side of the business,' Larry began.

'He means the female side,' Geraldine interrupted.

'I mean what I say, and what I say is this. Women bet on the lottery and lucky numbers, the highest margin for the bookie, as you know. Punters win more on the horses than anything else. Now, I started off on the horses, Mari, and I'll never be out of the backing of horses, but it's my aim to get going in other areas.'

'Diversify, it's called,' Geraldine said, tapping him on the shoulder. Marilyn smiled. Larry Leahy knew exactly what it was called and exactly what his plans were, for his company and for her. She knew this was going to be a serious offer, a directorship, and felt her heart sink. This was going to be a hard one to turn down. What she didn't anticipate, because she was a numbers woman lacking in vision, was how much of a temptation it would be.

'You know the figures – six per cent margin on horses, lucky numbers fifteen per cent, football up around the twenty per cent margin. It makes sense to push the boat out into other areas. I knew the minute you joined us over three years ago that you were the woman to help us. I'm looking at the woman side, and that's leisure. It's bingo halls, it's casinos

– that's a real couple thing to do – amusements, hotels, leisure complexes. I have the backers, and we're looking at the premises. Until you met Sean Monroe, I would have said that you were the one person guaranteed to be excited about this development, away from just the horses and the dogs. Now, I'm not so sure.'

Both of them were looking at her, not hiding behind their lovely-old-couple disguise. The buns sat on the table, the tea grew cold.

'You want me to help you set this up?'

'We do, we do, but we need your commitment to be to us, and I know you've been having a few personal developments recently,' Larry began.

'Ah, be quiet, Larry, before you make a hames of it.' Geraldine could have been Brigid. 'Everyone is entitled to fall in love. Sure, she'll be over that by next year – not over him, I mean, but settled into it, just like we were, when we were young.'

'I don't think you're making any better a fist than I was, Geraldine,' Larry said, shaking his head. 'We can't do it without you.' He held his hands up. 'You have all the skills to make it happen. You're the lynchpin. And that's why we want you to commit to giving us three years before you set up home and start a family.'

'It's against regulations to offer someone a promotion and then demand she doesn't have children,' Marilyn pointed out.

'I'm not offering you a promotion,' he snapped, 'I'm offering you a share of our business. I want to give you a stake in our company, and in return I don't just want your help to set up the other side. We want you to be the one setting it up. I call the shots only on the locations and finance, the rest is up to you – how it's done, what way it's done.'

He talked on, mostly of the specifics, then Geraldine

rounded it up. 'You have to be careful with this, Mari. Tommy isn't pleased. We had to tell him, he's our son. It should be him doing this, but he'd lose all Larry and I have built. I'm sixty-three, Larry's going on sixty-five and we want to secure all our kids' futures, and grandchildren's. Tommy wouldn't do this right. We're asking you to put off your own family plans and then, when it's done, you can sit back, have your own children, take your share and watch life from a comfortable place.'

'Your share will be worth just over a million initially.' Larry took over to talk the numbers. 'That's before your salary, which will more than double, because your workload will more than double. But just for a while. The expansion is well underway. When I show you the names of the backers, you'll be happy, more than. It's a who's who, Mari. And then there's the sites. We've got four bought already for the big complexes and at least ten places we're looking at acquiring this year, from country bingo halls to city sport stadiums. Sean Monroe will be buying horses with millions rather than buttons.' Geraldine winced at the way Larry put it. 'He won't just be at little winners like Delaney.'

'Firstly, Sean will never buy horses with money other than his own,' Marilyn said. 'Secondly, I've been going out with him only since the new year. It's too early to tell whether we'll get married or not.'

'So he hasn't asked you yet, then,' Larry said. 'But he will. As far as I can recall, and I knew his father, he wasn't much in the way of girlfriends. He was lucky to get you.'

'I was lucky. Which is why I have to think about this, instead of treating it like the golden opportunity it is.'

'I hope we haven't fallen at the first here, Mari.' Larry was cowed, and Geraldine nodded agreement.

'Not at all. I realise what you're offering would require total dedication for a very high return in a very short space of time. I wasn't even in the office for two months of this year, and you're still offering me this.'

'Let's be honest now, Larry.' Geraldine spoke. 'The girl's under enough pressure.'

'We're offering you this, instead of just a directorship, because I saw you slipping away from the firm, off down to Wexford, if I wasn't careful. Let's just say I'm happy for you to work down there for part of the week, if it's feasible.'

'You know it won't be. You know I'll be driving around sites lashing builders, planners, architects, accountants and anyone else who isn't doing their job. I'll be working out margins and costs that'll make me go grey. This is a risk for you, Larry. This kind of expansion takes you out of everything you've ever known, into an entirely new area. No backer will let Tommy near this as a right-hand person, but someone like me is what you need.'

'Now' – Larry leaned forward – 'if you're fishing for more, young lady!'

'I'm not fishing for more, I'm fishing for less. What I'm really trying to say is that I don't even have to think about this. I was saying that to be courteous. You'll get another me, both of you. I'll help you get another me. But I don't want to be her, the lynchpin. I wish to God I did, because it would be just so fantastic to have all that opportunity and money and challenge and status. But the fact is, the only opportunity that's going to make me happy is Sean. Sorry, with great respect, and with a blind sense of panic, I have to say no.'

She left them to gather their thoughts and to empty hers, which were all focused on how mad she was, how pointless the whole first part of her life had been if this was what she did with its culmination – throwing it all over for a man who hadn't committed to her in any way but with his heart and eyes. It terrified her how much she wanted to walk away from everything. If she ever told Niall Tormey anything about this, and she never would, he'd have told her that most people have to do dishonest things for that kind of money.

Marilyn had visions of Nikolas rubbing lavender and rosemary oil into her grandmother's skin, Tony growing cornflowers for Elizabeth, Sean sitting in a shed in January holding her hand and Grace and Theresa unable to hold hands for almost fifty years. She knew you can only afford to have one obsessive professional in a relationship that has children as part of it. She knew she wasn't as dedicated to money as Sean was to horses. She phoned him and by the end of the conversation he was insisting.

'You don't have to do it, we can wait the three years, till it's all up and running.'

'It'd be longer. We'd never see each other. It's the way it is, Sean – good opportunities have come along for both of us at the same time. We've got to take the one that makes us happy most.'

'But that could mean,' he said, sounding almost angry, 'that I could give up this for the while and be your husband.'

'You can't clean, you can't cook, you can't pay bills. What kind of husband would that be for me?' she laughed.

'I could book myself into classes for the cooking, the cleaning I'd get the hang of and after the three years we can do what we want, with money to do it.'

'We can do what we want now, Sean, without the money. We don't have to endure thirty-six months – longer – of misery to get to this point all over again. It's more of a risk this way, granted, but if we muck in together, I can run the business side of your place and you can get Delaney going properly. She could do more if she had your undivided attention. You'll get more horses coming to you.'

'So you're suggesting we go into the business together?'

'No, I'm suggesting more than that. I think we should get married. You already offered to be my househusband. I'm sorry, but if I wait for you to ask me, I'll have to wait until you're out of debt, and without my help you'll never be. I'm ready now, if you are.'

'Marilyn, I have nothing to offer you.'

'You have yourself, and I want that. Please, Sean, don't make me wait for something that we could create together if you'll only let me.'

'It's me should have been asking you.'

'Well, be a gentleman then, and say yes.'

'I will. In six months, if you'll still have me, and I hope to be more for you.'

Neither of them could speak, adjusting to what had just been decided.

'I suppose I could drive up to you?' he offered, after a long silence.

'I could come down to you.'

'No, I want to do the right thing by you, go down on a knee and that, in the shed if we can arrange it.'

'You don't have a ring.'

'Oh, I do. I have my mother's ring. My sister gave it to me when I told her of my intentions.'

'And when was that?'

'February.' The month after he'd met her.

'And I thought I'd turned into a fast mover! Thanks, Sean, for loving me.' If she'd had doubts, they were dissolved. The world would think her mad, but she had never been more sane.

She needed to walk away from all she had ever known, towards everything that was more than worth it. Larry had been right – she couldn't go back to the office, there was a touch of the Lot's wife temptation to it. She went home, sure she would have the house to herself.

Her father was coming out of the gate as she pulled into the street. Elizabeth must be home, then. She could tell both her parents, together, that she was getting married, like she had a normal life. He didn't look up even when she beeped her horn, just got into his car and drove away fast enough to bring attention to himself, attention he was always paranoid about avoiding.

'He must be used to ignoring people,' she told herself, and went in to see her mother. Elizabeth was in the kitchen. Crying.

'What's going on? Don't bother.' Marilyn held her hand up. 'No, sorry, do bother. What did he do to you? Did he dump you again?'

Elizabeth rose out of her seat. 'Everyone always seems to want immediate answers from me, and I'm not good at giving them. Do you mind if I don't talk about it for a while? What are you doing home?'

'Great. The brush-off from both parents in the space of one minute. I don't think you want to hear about it, really.'

'No.' Elizabeth sat upright. 'I want to hear right now much more than I want to talk. Come on.'

Marilyn told her about the offer, about the proposal of her own, about what was going to happen next. 'I'm moving to Wexford. To live.'

'Well, it's fortunate two out of three of our family made the right choice when they fell in love.' Elizabeth was smiling.

'Look, Granny didn't the first time around, so there's no reason why you're stuck with the choice. He's my father, I feel something for him, but I'll tell you something, Ma. If you told me Tony Devereux was walking you down the aisle at four this afternoon, on a whim, I'd be happier.'

'Marilyn, please, not right now. I'm older than you. I get to things slower. And at the present moment I'm older and

386

confused. I have no idea what choices are ahead of me. Now what about yours?'

'We're getting married in April. By then I'll have the house how I want it, and a party in one of the barns. Nothing fancy, we can't afford it.'

'So, it's just me staying in 51,' Elizabeth thought aloud.

So, Marilyn thought, he did dump her, the shite. I'll phone him later.

'You could go as well. Brigid would have no problem.'

'No, I'm fine with it, it's my home. It's not the one I chose, but it's the one I made for myself.'

39

That night, Sean was in bed beside Marilyn, his mother's solitaire on her thumb. Nuala had given it to him that day he had called to see her. 'It should be yours, to pass on to your future wife,' she had said. He hadn't yet got the hang of ring sizes. A woman he was modelled on was bound to have a larger measurement. The phone rang at close to midnight.

Everyone came onto the landing to answer it, knowing it could only be one person. Brigid called from the *platia* on Skyros. Elizabeth had phoned Kristos, who had phoned the island police, who had told Nikolas, who had passed the news on to Brigid. Grace and Theresa, who were there on a visit, were with her in the phone box, shouting in the background with Nikolas.

'*Kalispera*, love! Congratulations! I hope you'll be as happy as you deserve for the rest of your lives!'

'Thanks, Brigid.'

'Don't "Brigid" me, I'm your granny. A good choice he is, I'll be home for the wedding, and Christmas before that. Grace says she wants to do the arrangements, but over my dead body, I told her.'

'I think Elizabeth's going to do all that. She is the bride's mother,' Marilyn said, planting the flag before anyone could assume territory. 'It's going to be a down-home affair in Sean's yard, all minstrels and fiddles and fairy lights. She'll love it. How is it there, Granny?'

Sean and Elizabeth wandered into the kitchen.

'It's beautiful, child, now when it's raining again it's even more beautiful.' There was a note in Brigid's voice that told

Marilyn that it wasn't home. Anyone who misses rain while living on the shores of the Mediterranean has to be a born and bred Irishwoman. There was a note in Marilyn's voice that made Brigid ask if she was all right.

'Of course, I'm getting married, why wouldn't I be?'

'You just don't sound as excited as I thought you'd be.'

'Do I sound like I turned down a million quid?'

'Did you?'

'Yes.'

'Well, my dear, take it from me, it's only money. What you have with him is worth two.'

'I turned down two.'

'You still did the right thing. Only slightly, though.'

'Brigid! You just made a joke!'

'Did I? I'll bring up a serious subject, then. How's Tony? Elizabeth doesn't mention him.'

'He's around.' Marilyn crossed her fingers.

'And your father?'

'He's around too. I mean, I see him now and then. Elizabeth's here, in the kitchen, if you want to ask her.'

'Ah, where would it get me? That one locks her secrets away in a strongbox. Do you have any liking for him, Marilyn?'

'Yes, we get on well, once you consider him for who he is, and he never stops doing that.' Marilyn looked directly at Elizabeth in saying it, and Elizabeth nodded her agreement. 'But you know what I'm like, I'm cautious. Unless I'm picking husbands,' she said, thinking silently, Then I turn down golden offers and propose to near-bankrupts over the phone.

'I do and it's a good trait, encourage it in your mother. She's got a weakness where that individual is concerned.'

They went back to bed after everyone said congratulations to everyone else. After the excitement, Marilyn couldn't sleep for thinking of all that had happened. She couldn't imagine her near-death-experience bedroom not being her sanctuary any more. She wished she could get in touch with Julie, get her home; she could have her room now and keep Elizabeth company and keep her abreast of what was going on between Elizabeth and Niall. For some reason, she couldn't get Julie out of her head. She wanted to share her news, to have her be part of it.

In those same minutes before midnight, Julie was holding Rose in her arms. A long, thin baby, and a beautiful one.

'No adoption now, surely?' Magenta asked, knowing she was still considering her options. 'Besides,' she whispered, 'you'd lose the flat.'

Julie inclined her head to show she was listening, but her eyes were on Rose, on her delicate features and fine skin, and the soft, faint birthmark at the top of her arm, petal-like.

'No matter what I have to do, I'll keep you,' Julie whispered to her child. 'Even if we were to end up on the side of the road.'

'After that labour, you're not having another one for a long time.' Magenta squeezed her hand. The midwife who had assisted Julie had all her digits intact, but Magenta had bitten the head off her a few times. Magenta was right, Julie had learned something from the labour about strength, about resources. The birth was only just over, and with it came the death of her insecurity. If she could produce this wonder, she could do anything.

The controller asked Tony to call in to the office.

'I didn't want to tell you this over the radio or mobile. Niall Tormey and his missus were just seen off Wicklow Street, hand in hand. Then they headed into that posh restaurant.'

'Thanks, but what would it mean to me?' Tony looked at him.

'Nothing, except I put it together, your interest in Elizabeth' – the controller still called her by her first name – 'and in him, like. I didn't add the sum, but I think I can guess the situation.'

'Thanks, but that situation's none of my concern any more.'

'Okay, Tony, thought you should know, and I'll say no more.'

Tony waited on the taxi rank outside. He saw Niall leave Leinster House and hailed him. Niall came over to him immediately.

'Get in.'

'Excuse me?'

'For Elizabeth, get in.'

Niall Tormey's second drive around the streets of Dublin with Tony at the wheel was free of charge.

'If she comes to suffer, I don't mind making you suffer, Mr Tormey. It would be something I had to do. And I'm speaking for the rest of her family too.'

'I'll never let her be hurt. I love her as much as you do.'

Tony got angry, and the anger of soft men has a sharp blade, rarely used. 'You have no idea what this kind of love feels like. If you did, you wouldn't be next or near her. You still won't be seen with her in public alone.'

'I would have been, after I was divorced and when I was re-elected. When my position was clear. That I can promise you.'

'You've never kept any promise you made to anyone, not even yourself. You left your wife, Elizabeth, your daughter and your government. You left your scruples a long way back, so don't talk to me about promises, even Elizabeth knows you don't keep those. She has the misfortune to be the only person who's ever loved you. And she still isn't good enough.'

'Did you notice, Mr Devereux – that's your name, isn't it? – that I said "would have"?'

'Sorry?' Tony looked at him in the rear-view mirror.

'I said "would have been". Elizabeth has decided against involvement with me, on any level, other than through Marilyn. Now drop me back to the House and make it your business never to cross my path again, or I'll keep this promise – you will be sorry.'

Tony watched him retreat. 'She hasn't called you, you have to wait. Even if it never happens,' he said to himself.

He knew this was right, so much so that he got Colin and Mick to act as his sponsors in the arrangement, telling him daily to stick to his guns.

Just before his taxi ride with Tony, Niall had phoned Marilyn from his office.

'Yes?' She was harassed at work, since Larry was still in denial about her leaving. Several interviews had taken place in which they tried to find the perfect replacement, most of whom she found suitable. He wasn't interested. 'What do you want?'

'Nothing, just wanted to see how you are.'

'Oh, lovely, I'm grand, thanks. And you?' Elizabeth had told her she'd finished the relationship.

'I know what it was now, Marilyn,' Elizabeth had said. 'I knew when I met him that he was on the way to becoming someone. There was all that anticipation. Then he became it. But the way he went about it, he lost all the power he might have had, as a person. He's broken, Marilyn. I feel sympathy for him, and it's good to feel that after what he did to me.'

'But how did you realise it?'

'When he offered me an open life with him, I didn't trust his motives. Without trust, you can't love.'

'How did he react?'

'Badly. You know enough about him now to know why. He said I'd shamed him, made him lose to a taxi driver.'

'And has he lost to Tony?'

'I couldn't believe Tony had made it his business to meet Niall. I wasn't happy about it at first, but now I see that he was doing anything he could to help me, not himself. That's the difference between them. For the moment I just want to be by myself, love's too hard a subject right now. Divorce is more my area.'

Marilyn knew Niall was at a loss. He told her in the way he phoned for no reason, not a Niall thing to do. It was often enough for her to know he needed her.

'How are the election plans gearing up?' She tried to provide the purpose she could hear was missing.

'Judith and I will be looking for a house in Offaly, by the looks of it. It seems a shoo-in, if you can have those in this game.'

'I hope this is a private line you're talking on.'

'Ultra-private. Would you be about on Sunday?'

'No, sorry, I'm getting organised for the move. Hey, you ready to give me away next April?' She was joking, knowing the position it would put him in, just before the polls.

'I'll be there, if you'll have me, as a member of the congregation. I'm sure your mother is giving you away. I certainly hope Tony the Taxi isn't.' At least he could laugh at his bitterness.

'Of course she is, and of course we'll have you.' Marilyn avoided the subject of Tony. 'Now get back to buggering up the country. I'm off to chase Larry down the corridor and persuade him no one's as indispensable as he's making me. And Niall?'

'Yes?'

'Thanks for the call. Keep your spirits up.'

He put the phone down, with the knowledge that he'd lost his chance. 'At least I'm like any other ageing father who hasn't seen enough of his kids. A nuisance.'

He picked up the phone again and found himself calling Judith.

'I wonder if you'd like to go out to dinner again tonight? My diary's empty.'

'Niall' – Judith spoke with the bitterness he felt about Tony – 'in all the years I've known you, I've never seen you two nights on the trot. That diary made you do other things.'

'Do you want to or not? We can have a stroll around, like we did last time.'

'Maybe the photographers will snap us this time, isn't that it? We're too old to be interesting.'

He smiled at that. 'Nothing I can't handle.'

She surprised him by saying yes.

'Why? Why are none of these women suitable, Larry?'

'Because they're not you.'

'They're as well qualified, in some cases twice as.'

'I can get people with your knowledge, Mari, but not your honesty. Now you're going to have to bide your time and give me the time I need.'

'I'm giving you until Christmas, and then I have to be on my way. I would be delighted to work as a consultant, but I might not have anything to consult to if you don't appoint a replacement and keep your backers happy.'

Marilyn was still preoccupied when she got home. She felt that Larry was delaying her move elsewhere until he was sure he couldn't hang on to her. And looking at Sean's books, the offer became more tempting with each passing day. She needed another push to get her out of her cosy world, so she was still trying to get pregnant. It still wasn't happening.

'I must be barren,' she told her reflection as she opened the tampon box.

You've only been trying a few months and your period is like the rest of you – clockwork. You just have to calm down about it, it said back.

'If you dare say "let nature take its course" again' – she pointed at her reflection – 'I won't be responsible for what I do to you. Stop being so practical.'

Why don't you let Sean in on this? Maybe his sperm would co-operate a little more if he was conscious of what they were trying to do? Maybe he'd will them on.

'Quiet. If we had to wait on him to decide, it'd be interminable. I had to ask him to marry me. Imagine how much rumination it would take to persuade him that a child is a good thing. He hasn't the price of a foal in his pocket.'

2 December. Grace called up with another eight a.m. chocolate cake, wanting to catch Elizabeth before work.

'Happy birthday, darling,' she said as she handed over her present as well. 'Are we having dinner later?'

'To be honest, Grace, I'm not up to it. Marilyn's gone to Wexford and Brigid's not here. It won't be the same.'

'Come to us for supper, then. Is that your cup I see in the sink?'

'I had coffee.'

'Maybe you'll have tea later.' Grace went in and took the cup. 'I'll have this washed and ready.'

'Okay then, Grace, after that delicious food I have to have some tea. I know you want to do a reading.' Theresa grinned.

Elizabeth had come a long way from craving prophecy via routes like this.

Grace squinted and tilted the cup towards Elizabeth.

'Lots going on. Nothing you can't handle, but lots going on.'

The doorbell went, as did the phone.

'My goodness, this house is like 51, we're normally so quiet.' Grace ran to answer the door and Theresa went for the phone.

Marilyn was outside. 'I got back early, I wanted to see her on her birthday.'

Brigid was on the phone. 'Well, what did the leaves say?' Theresa put Elizabeth on. Marilyn came over to listen too.

'Nothing much.' Elizabeth found she was disappointed. 'It looks like the men have moved on to another house. They've finished with us and they've left me.'

'Nonsense,' Greece and Ireland said simultaneously, as if they shared the same mind, which of course Brigid and Marilyn always did.

40

Julie's eyes ached with sleep deprivation. She was in front of the mirror trying to achieve the impossible with make-up. Her shift at the pub started in half an hour and the baby had been changed, the milk expressed and sitting in two bottles for Magenta to give her.

'Come on, Magenta,' she whispered, 'knock.'

As if she heard, Magenta appeared at the door.

'Okay, okay, I see. You're so tired you can't speak. Off your feet, girl, on the sofa and I'll give you a foot rub.'

Rose was only two and a half months old. Since she was six weeks old Julie had been working six to midnight at Turner's bar, serving customers who spent more on one bottle of wine than she got paid in a night.

'To think I wanted to be one of those idiots. They're too pissed to know what it tastes like.'

'Are they tipping you the same way?' Julie nodded. 'Then don't complain. And it's cash in hand. You've got your social, your flat and your Rose.'

'I have everything I want, then.'

'No.' Magenta eyed her. 'You have to think of the girl. She needs more out of life, and with your looks you've got more to get her.'

Julie laughed with Magenta, feeling a freedom and lack of judgement that she had never felt with Marilyn.

'I've tried. It doesn't seem to work for me.'

'It'll work now. You're not gullible, like you were once. That wears off after the first child.' Magenta rubbed Julie's feet with peppermint lotion as she talked, preparing her for a night's work standing up on them.

'Yes, but I know now that I want someone who knows what's going on inside me. Or has an interest in it, at least. The package isn't as good as the wrapping.'

'Don't you believe that crap. That crap means your girl will grow up to think the same of herself, and that will get her in the messes you and I got into.'

'Sometimes, Magenta, I feel like you're the coach in the corner, sending me out into the ring. I never imagined getting pregnant and having to run away would be the best thing that ever happened to me.'

'Well, it is, because you have me to tell you where the pitfalls are. And that's exactly what I'm doing, sending you out into the ring.' Magenta's voice was tired, but she smiled as she pushed Julie out the door. 'Just box better than I did. Box clever. The dad's around. Get him to start coughing up. Even just enough so you don't have to do this work.'

'If I did, Magenta, I'd ruin two people's lives.'

'Rose's matters more.'

Almost as if they heard Magenta, the Missing Persons Bureau sent round a policeman and a social worker again.

'I already told you—' Julie began to say.

'We've got a message from your mother. She needs you to call home. Your father isn't very well. Here's the number—'

'I have the number.' She hadn't expected to feel this shocked; she rarely thought of her parents now.

'And here's a letter from your mother, she asked us to forward it on.'

Julie opened it and read:

Dear Julie,
    I know this will come as a surprise, and I'm not even going

to pretend I want to write this, but you should know your father's very unwell. He has Alzheimer's, we just got the diagnosis after a few months of persuading him to go to see the doctor.

The day you called he was in a condition I would rather you didn't have to see him in. He has his pride. Things are so bad here, Julie, he doesn't even know me half the time. I just can't manage. He should go into a home but he point-blank refuses, you know what he's like. I'd be lost without someone in the house, I'm no good on my own.

I was wondering – if I were to sign the house over to you, would you come and care for him? As a job? I know you're not fond of either him or me, but there's something in it for you. I can do this, our solicitor has arranged for me to have the authority to act without his signature.

Again, you might not find this good enough, but in explanation for how things were for you, growing up here, you might want to know that your father married me and lost all his relatives because of it, plus a very valuable inheritance. I wasn't what his family expected of him at all. You get your looks from his side, and you reminded him of what he'd given up.

I was so grateful to him that I did what my generation did. I became his servant. That was no good for him, or me, and especially not for you.

My heartfelt apologies
Margaret

'She didn't even sign it "Mum",' Julie said, passing the letter to Magenta. She scanned it quickly.

'You've got your chance now. A nice house, all paid for, for you and Rose,' she said.

'They don't know about Rose.'

'Then you don't tell 'em until she signs on the dotted line. The way they treated you, you do the same.'

'I can't. I'll have to phone and tell her.'

Mrs Purcell wept, recovered, then said, 'It'll be just like Marilyn's family, except for your father being here. But he's not here half the time in his head. Please, Julie, please come and help me, I'll do anything.'

'You've got power of attorney, you could sign him into a home. When he is in his head, he'll go ballistic when he sees baby stuff all over the place.'

'Well,' her mother sighed, 'he'll have to see that having you and his grandchild here is better than being in a home.'

'How'd it go?' Magenta was waiting to hear.

'She's still on for it.' Julie almost couldn't believe she was saying it.

'Great!'

'Not really,' Julie sighed. 'She's as self-centred as ever. She never even asked me who the father was. Or what her name was.'

'So, you going or not?'

41

On St Stephen's Day, Marilyn was back at the corporate suite at Leopardstown racecourse, with Sean, Brigid and Nikolas this time.

'One year to the day after having not met me.' Sean hugged her. For her there was no place safer than that hug.

Geraldine and Larry were happy with their new replacement, a woman with a background in hotel and catering management and a head for figures that rivalled Einstein's. And she was grateful for Marilyn's expanded job, which she got for Marilyn's old salary, with a promise of profit share. Larry and Geraldine had saved themselves two million euros, thanks to looking elsewhere.

Everyone was getting everything they wanted. Brigid was home for Christmas, as promised, with Nikolas, eating Grace's plum pudding (suet-free) and calling it 'fair enough'. She was the picture of health.

Marilyn hadn't put nine months into planning her presents, but everyone had seemed just as happy with their gifts on the previous day. She had one package sitting in the locker upstairs, for Niall. What do you get the man who has everything? She had looked through all her old gifts, and decided none of them were really for him. So she got him a special compass for his hill-walking, and a note with it: 'A good navigation tool, for all those difficult twists and turns.'

She hadn't seen him in the past few months. Something had always come up and they were both too busy. His

Sundays were for going down to the new future constituency, to make new friends.

Brigid had given Elizabeth the photo hidden in her bedside locker for fifty years.

'Life's never like the picture, but I promise you, we were all happy at Trabolgan. Even him, the louser.' They had laughed, because she said it with affection. She could afford to be affectionate now.

'I remember the waves there. Where did he end up, Mother?' Elizabeth asked as she traced the line of his face.

'A doss-house somewhere. A graveyard by now, I'm sure.'

'Was it him I let in when Marilyn was thirteen? Was it him I was running the bath for?'

'It was, and I didn't know what else to do but railroad him out. He was full of the look of drink, and I couldn't let Marilyn grow up seeing it. Then she went off and worked for a bookmaker, the ones who took all his money.'

'If it wasn't Larry, it would be someone else taking money off him. He seems that kind of man.' Sean spoke his mind, a thing he didn't normally do, but whenever Marilyn was even vaguely criticised, he intervened.

'Seconded,' Theresa said tersely.

'Don't you worry, you two' – Brigid eyed them both – 'I see that now. Now, to strike another controversial note, any chance of seeing Marilyn's father this Christmas?'

Elizabeth and Marilyn shook their heads.

'He's steering well clear of you, Granny.' Marilyn tried to break the ice, but it was the kind that sank the *Titanic*.

'And what of Tony Devereux, the good friend to this family he's been?'

'He sent me a card,' Marilyn surprised everyone by saying. Even Elizabeth hadn't seen it. 'It's a dried cornflower pattern. He wishes us all well.'

'Where did you put it?' Brigid asked.

'In my room.'

'I must phone him,' Elizabeth said softly, 'though I'm sure he'd rather hear from anyone than me, after all my dithering.'

'Well, don't leave it as long as you did last time,' Brigid snapped, in her old manner. 'He's been messed around enough by you, if you want my view.'

'That's it, Brigid,' Marilyn sighed. 'Really, show her some encouragement.'

'Sorry. I was made for plain speaking, wasn't I, Nikolas?' Even though they were picking up words of each other's language, it hadn't progressed far. Two old dogs trying to learn new tricks, as Brigid put it. But he nodded emphatically at the mention of the name Tony.

Elizabeth went off on her Stephen's Day walk, though she'd been invited dozens of times to go to the races.

'It's important I do this by myself. I'm going to be on my own for the first time in my life, I need to prepare for it.'

They watched her set off down the road with her green velvet notebook, full of intentions for each coming year. Marilyn was moving in a few days, and Elizabeth had managed to smile and participate in the excitement. The only time that was lost was when she asked if she could take the piano.

'Of course. That piano belongs with you, always did.'

'I'll play when you're around, Ma, I promise. And you can be around as often as you like.'

'I'll be down as often as I'm welcome.'

Leopardstown was Marilyn's swan song, saying goodbye to Leahy's, hello to her new life. She would be living in Wexford on 1 January.

Delaney was running in the third race, her last race as a

filly. On 1 January all horses age by one year, and she was going to be five, a mare. She hadn't put a hoof wrong since late September. She'd had four wins and a second on the bridle, in a class field. Today was an important race. At the parade ring, Nikolas was beside himself with excitement to see so many beautiful horses in one spot.

'They're twice the size of his,' Brigid said as she held on to his arm as he watched them being led round. Nikolas pointed to the tote with longing, but the look in Brigid's eyes said there would be no betting.

They went upstairs to hospitality, where Brigid and Geraldine Leahy made a beeline for each other and the tea urn, getting stuck into a conversation full of nods, inclinations, raised eyes and 'I know's'. Their husbands stood side by side, whiskeys in hand, sharing the same language, if not being able to speak in it. Sean took Nikolas to the balcony to watch the first race.

Marilyn thought of Julie and what had happened there the previous year, wondering what might happen by the next. Her period was four days late. She no longer needed pregnancy as an excuse to cut the ties from Leahy's. It didn't make her any less excited. She pictured her mother on Vico Road, writing up her New Year intentions, and hoped she wrote down 'becoming a grandmother' with her usual psychic intuition. She'd need something. Brigid was going back to Greece on New Year's Day. Marilyn was moving to Wexford on New Year's Eve, paying double time to the removal company because she wanted to spend every last minute with her grandmother, but also wanted to see midnight in her new home. The van was full of appliances and home décor items from her Christmas list, and Sean had cleared a space for the piano in the living room.

It was a crisp, clear winter day, cloudless, just above freezing. Leahy's had Delaney as the favourite and every other bookmaker had her at longer odds. They didn't have an inside track, but were basing it on her performance the last time out at Leopardstown. Sean left them to go down to her after the first race. She was in the third.

She trotted around the parade ring like a prayer, her inside ear twitching at Sean's instructions. Her edge was obvious. It might have marked her down in most punters' eyes, but Marilyn knew her by now; she was full of excitement. As time went on she was beginning to enjoy herself. She knew what it was all about and wanted to be there.

Helen hopped into the saddle, and Scan and Marilyn headed down to the terraces with Brigid and Nikolas, to be with the punters for the race.

Delaney took the rest of the field round the track from the off. It was a brave try full of the guts Marilyn and Sean knew she had. But she ran too free and found herself being shaded out of winning at the post, by less than a nose.

'By a nostril!' as Larry Leahy put it. 'Still, a second in a race like this pays well, you'll have no need of our money, will she, Ger?'

Geraldine rolled her eyes.

They weren't too disappointed, especially when they saw Brigid sneak off to the tote to collect her winnings.

'An each-way bet, Granny? Would you not have backed her to win?'

'I'm a realist.'

They trooped back up the stairs. The first person Marilyn saw when she walked in wasn't her father, but Judith. Marilyn gripped Sean's hand and his grip answered. Behind her, Brigid put a hand on her back.

'You have to face this,' she whispered. 'Go on in and smile like they're doing. You're the one who belongs in this room, not them.'

Judith glanced over at her, then stopped as the face clicked. But she wasn't expecting Marilyn to hold her eyes and walk over to her and introduce herself.

'This is my fiancé, Sean,' Marilyn went on. By this stage Niall was right beside Judith, the look on his face telling Marilyn that Judith had demanded this meeting. 'My grandmother, Brigid, and her husband, Nikolas.'

'I'm pleased to meet you all.' Judith was looking at her, judging resemblances in the same way Niall and Marilyn had done with each other at the first meeting. 'And this is my husband, Niall Tormey.' She reached around and pulled him to her side. 'As you know. I believe you met at Wexford, had your picture taken together? Having all the fun. Same horse on show, as I recall.'

'So, Marilyn,' Niall struggled for something to say, 'Larry says you're off to pastures new?'

Judith was watching her. 'I also hear you're getting married. I don't seem to have been invited. I know Niall plans to go. It was in his diary.'

Marilyn was aware of some force outside herself dealing with this. 'Niall is a friend of our family. It's a small wedding. Not all partners are being invited.'

Brigid stepped forward.

'A word, Mr Tormey, please, on your own.' Judith was thrown, intimidated by the way Brigid steered Niall Tormey off into a corner for a quiet chat. Nikolas went with her, sensing that nothing about this situation was comfortable for anyone in it.

Sean and Marilyn faced Judith.

'I'd like to talk alone too, Sean.'

'If you wanted to meet me, you could have picked a better place,' Marilyn said.

'I'm sorry, I had no idea your grandmother would be here too.'

'And my mother?'

'I've already met her. I don't need to meet her again. I want you to know how inappropriate it is that Niall attend your wedding. In fact, it's crucial he doesn't. Just before an election.'

'Is that it?' Marilyn saw that her coldness had more to do with loss than success. She felt sorry for her, more sorry than she could ever have imagined feeling for someone who had planned to expose her.

'And I wanted to see you' – Judith paused – 'for myself. I could have been your mother.'

'No.' Marilyn's voice was as quiet as she could make it, but there was no mistaking the tone. 'If you had become my mother, that would have been stealing. If Niall decides to come to my wedding, it will be as someone who wishes me well, which you obviously don't.'

'I—'

'I had no choice in who my father was. I had no father growing up, and your husband is still little more than an acquaintance to me. I never did you any harm, and I don't intend to.'

'But you do it now, in keeping in touch with him. We're attempting a full reconciliation, leaving our pasts behind us. You're a part of that. I won't allow it.'

'You can't disallow it. If he wishes to speak to me, or see me, then I'm not going to stop him. I understand my mother betrayed you, but she was seventeen when she met him. I understand he was a bastard to you, and also to her. If he's willing to live with his regrets and make amends, then I've no right to judge him, and no wish to stop contacting him. I'll never reveal who he is, just as you won't. So don't use it as an excuse to come and threaten me or intimidate my family.

We are close-knit, good people. He doesn't want to be here, and neither do you, really. And I don't want you here. Please go.'

Marilyn watched Judith pull Niall out of a corner and leave. Brigid had had time enough to say what she needed to. They stayed on until the last race, knowing that leaving early would give all the wrong signs. On the balconies Marilyn saw them; they were popping into all the parties, 'like hopping fleas', as Brigid put it.

'Are you all right to stay, child?' Brigid asked. Sean had taken Larry and Nikolas down to see Delaney.

'I wouldn't be your grandchild if I wasn't.' Marilyn's knees were weak but she refused brandy. 'I'm not running away.'

'No, but he is,' Brigid whispered.

'What did you say to him?'

'Nothing you haven't. He apologised for bringing her here, but she would have come herself. A troublemaker, that one.'

'I gathered that.'

'He tells me your mother wants nothing more to do with him. That tells me she was having something more than she should to do with him. Poor Tony.'

'Brigid, it was something she had to see through.' For the first time, Marilyn found herself able to see her mother's motivation and to explain it to her grandmother.

'It's as well,' Brigid nodded. 'Families are messy things, and he's not equipped for that.'

'I'm not so sure.' They watched horses round the home bend. This was supposed to be a day for Delaney, for celebration, but she had come second and so had Marilyn. 'When I first met him, he was never done asking about her, talking about her. I think she appealed to the best side of him. I've seen it.'

'Never let him gloss over the truth. That's in his nature too, and because I've been around longer than you, I'll say this. Look at the way he put in a visit to the other high folk, after the shock they've given us! It takes a steel neck.'

They were only just home when Niall phoned to apologise.

'I couldn't persuade her against it. It won't happen again. Whatever you said sank in with her.'

Marilyn went out of the room to speak to him. Her voice was raised upstairs, but no one could make out what she said.

No one mentioned it to Elizabeth, who also didn't mention who she had spent the afternoon with. Where there was a Monroe, there was still more than one secret.

Elizabeth was glad of the winter sunshine, but at the same time wishing fewer people were about. It seemed the world was out, walking off their Christmas indulgence. It was difficult to write this year, to know what to expect. Somehow she only had three lines, where she normally wrote pages:

Help Marilyn to have a wonderful wedding, but don't intrude.

Learn how to become a grandmother (?)

Phone Tony.

Work was taking care of itself. She was going to move office to the ground floor soon and employ a junior who didn't mind doubling up as a secretary. And for the first time since she was seventeen years old, Niall was no longer an issue.

She thought of Tony. She told herself she didn't need a full-time relationship, with a practice getting busier all the time. She told herself that because she knew she was never going to get one. Looking at all the families and the couples who were out made her feel lost. Christmas was a time for grouping, and she felt more alone than she ever had. Past times had carried more terror, more responsibility, but they had always had Marilyn in them, or Brigid; now both were gone. And she knew she had thrown away the opportunity to know and love a more than good man.

'Do you mind if I join you, or is this a private bench?' he asked.

'Please do. I'd be delighted.' She held out her intentions for him to read, to reveal how true it was. 'I'm so glad to have your company, if I can still be considered your friend after what I've done to you in the past year. There are times when I have absolutely no one I can talk to who would understand what I'm truly saying. Those are the times I think of you and our conversations.'

'I echo that, Elizabeth.'

'I see you have a notebook.'

'I came to write some intentions, as I know you do. To be honest, I thought you wouldn't be here until later. I hadn't planned to bump into you. When I saw you I thought, Ah well, give fate one more chance.'

'Well, I had no distractions, so I got out a couple of hours earlier than usual. Thank fate for me, when you're speaking to her.'

'I have only one intention,' he admitted. 'To see you.'

'Niall is gone,' she said.

'I know.' He looked at the ground.

She picked up his hand and held it. 'Don't tell me, the taxi mafia informed you.'

'No, he did. I went to make sure he was looking after you. He told me you'd done the best thing to look after yourself, in leaving him. Are you angry at me?'

'For interfering in my personal life? I heard you had visited him, and I was put out, but then, you're a rescuer. You were rescuing Phoebe when I met you here six years ago. Would you care to watch me drink a hot whiskey?'

They talked all afternoon, and it went as quickly as it always did when they spent time together.

'Would you mind,' she said softly to him as he walked her to the end of her road, 'if we didn't tell anyone about renewing our acquaintance, just for a while? I'd like a little bit of privacy where you're concerned.'

On New Year's Eve, Marilyn moved out of her lifelong home in the early hours of the morning.

'It's a good thing,' she told Sean through her tears.

'Sure, with the changes you made to the place, it's your home as much as Verbena Avenue ever was,' Sean assured her, 'and if you don't get carried over my threshold Nuala will kill me, along with the other sisters. They've been cleaning nonstop. Helping me move furniture around.'

'Oh.' Marilyn was worried. 'I wanted to do that.'

'They had a good reason to, you'll see.'

The four Monroe sisters had left a full fridge for them. There was a casserole in the oven and the table was set. But in the living room was the greatest welcome: a roaring fire and a space cleared by the wall.

'It's for the piano. I told the girls and they said it would be the best spot.'

'That's exactly where I saw it.' Marilyn smiled.

She held her tongue until the stroke of midnight. As soon as the last strike on the grandfather clock had sounded, she asked him if he would like a baby.

'Yes.' He pulled her into the place under his shoulder that was meant for her. 'In the fullness of time.'

'How about September?'

He stared at the fire for what she counted, by the ticking of the grandfather clock, as four minutes. She wanted to burst in but knew if she didn't wait for his response she'd never get the truth. Have I ruined everything? she thought.

'Are you sure?' he said finally.

'Not yet.'

'I thought you were looking after things there.'

'I was, and then I decided I wanted to look after them in a different way.'

'Meaning?'

'I know this will sound like a huge presumption. I thought it would never happen, that you'd hang off until we were secure, and we mightn't ever be, Sean, so I just went ahead.'

'And didn't consult me.' His gaze was steady, but his voice wasn't.

'I thought you might like one. If you're as good with children as you are with animals . . . And I thought after your parents dying like that, in such an awful way, this would be nice for you. And for me, Sean. I want to be a mother, more than I've ever wanted anything.'

'Will we ever do anything together, instead of you running a mile ahead of me with plans?'

She shrugged her shoulders. 'I don't know, I think it's one of the ways we work. I've always worked hard all my life, had goals; this is just my new one. It sounds a bit Thatcherite, but it's because I love you. And I don't know what to do with that sometimes. I have a big problem trusting anyone, especially people I love. It comes from a space inside me where a father should have been, and an overcompensating family to the point of suffocation. I'm going to long lengths to explain myself here. Please help me.'

'Okay, Marilyn Monroe, I'll help you. If you are pregnant, well, I've wanted to be a father for the past ten years, but I never whispered a word of it. I put all my fathering into horses. You're going to see some good come of that. You're going to see the kind of father mine was to me, before he was taken from me. I'm just sorry my own parents won't be here to see it.' His voice was cut with emotion.

'I take it that you're extremely happy, then?'

'You take it right, with one proviso.' He held a finger up. 'I want to be in on the next life decision, I don't want to be led around on a chain. Okay?'

'Okay,' she whispered. 'I mightn't be, you know. I'm over a week late, though, and I'm usually on the button. We can do the test together, now. I've brought one with me.'

He put his arms around her and she ignored the discomfort of the sideways hug, because he needed it more than her.

The test confirmed what Marilyn knew in her heart. 'It's very early days. Can we keep it to ourselves for a while?' she asked him. 'I don't want to disappoint anyone if it's not the case.'

He said, 'Everything starts from here.'

And on New Year's Day, Tony came to take Brigid and Nikolas to the airport, a surprise arranged by Elizabeth.

Brigid, Nikolas, Theresa and Grace greeted him like a long-lost son.

42

After all the noise of departure, the house was unnaturally quiet. Silence is only a good thing when wanted; Elizabeth realised she didn't when the doorbell went. Tony was outside.

'I hope I'm not intruding. I just thought the end would be too loose after all the family. Was I right? Let's have a pot of tea, a cure-all in Ireland.'

'Even for coffee drinkers?' She had the beginnings of a smile.

They sat in the living room and spoke quietly, until the phone went in the hall.

'Just calling to see how you are,' Niall Tormey said, 'with all the comings and goings.' Marilyn had told him she was moving on New Year's Eve.

'Managing,' Elizabeth said to herself as much as to him.

'There's a function in Offaly, but I could come up after it. Once they ring in the new year, I'm free to go.' She knew he'd spent the season in the way she had when she was his mistress – thinking only of the one he couldn't have.

'No. But thank you for calling. I do miss her, she was great company, especially this past year.'

'I can say the same. I wish I could do it all differently. I wish I had as many years as you have to remember her.'

'She'll be very glad you feel that way. You should tell her that. I'm sorry that I had to take your chance away.'

'Don't be. I took it away for myself. I was afraid of love, Elizabeth.' His voice told her he was still afraid now, at sixty-two, with everything to prove. She came back in to find Tony ready to go, his coat on.

'I know you must be tired.'

414

'No, don't go on my account. Stay a while, please.'

'I can't just now, I have the lads to see the new year in with, they're staying home on my account, thinking I need the company. You could come with me if you want.'

'I'm not big on New Years. They always remind me of the opportunities I've wasted.'

'I'm not a fan myself, but they have to be got through, don't they?'

'See you next year?' she smiled. He smiled back.

Two weeks passed.

Julie knocked on the door of 51. Elizabeth opened it, let out an exclamation of delight, then saw the pram.

'Come in.'

Julie held Rose in her arms. Rose kept reaching out to Elizabeth, in the way a young Elizabeth did in the photograph Brigid had given her.

'She's beautiful, Julie.'

'How can you say that after what I just told you?'

'It's the truth. It might not be the truth everyone wants, but there's no blaming this little creature for that, is there?'

Julie nodded, tears rolling down her face.

'What am I going to do?' she asked Elizabeth in the way she might have asked her own mother. 'I had to give Rose a proper home, but I don't want to wreck their lives.'

'Then don't,' Elizabeth said quietly. 'She'll be married in less than fourteen weeks. After that, we'll have to see.'

Elizabeth went down to number 45, needing help with this burden. Grace and Theresa took the news with their minds open, but they reeled as much as Elizabeth.

'Poor Marilyn,' Grace said, pressing her fingertips to her face.

'I don't know how we'll keep it from her.' Elizabeth was sipping strong sweet tea, which Grace had given her for the shock. 'I thought Julie left because she felt something for Sean she didn't want to feel. I never would have believed they'd slept together and she had his child! What were they doing bringing Marilyn into that?'

'She saw that he was right for her, and she had no idea it would be so right, or that she would be pregnant by him,' Grace reminded her. 'You told us that yourself.'

'I know I told you, but I can't believe they were so stupid, so deceiving.'

'So human,' Theresa intervened. 'You're not a stone-caster, Elizabeth. I know this is awful for you and your daughter, but she's full of Wexford and her arrangements. She won't come up to Dublin for a while. If she does, one of us will make sure to keep Julie out of the way.'

'Is it the right thing, keeping it from her until she gets married?'

'It's not the right thing,' Grace insisted, 'but it's the only thing. Marilyn loves Sean. He loves her. Julie has no wish to jeopardise that.'

'But she could still extricate herself, couldn't she?' Elizabeth looked at them. 'If she knows we could have given her the choice, I don't think she'll ever forgive us. I'm so sorry for giving it to you to worry about. I just didn't know what else to do. All her life I've lied to her about her father, then I lie to her about her husband-to-be.'

'On both occasions it's been for her own sake,' Grace said.

'You and Marilyn are like our own daughter and granddaughter, your problems are our problems,' Theresa said. 'While your mother is away, we're your mothers, and we'll share the burden of keeping this from her. What's more, we think it's the only thing to do. Considering how Marilyn is, with a setback like this, she'll never get on with her own life. She's gone too far with Sean to go back.'

'I may as well tell you too, in that case. I think Marilyn is pregnant.'

'How can you be sure?' Grace asked.

'I just sense it.'

'Well, if she is, then we'll find out before she gets married.' Grace started counting months on her hands.

'You know,' Theresa said, reaching for a cigarette, which she lit in the kitchen – she was never allowed to smoke in the house, but this time Grace didn't object – 'Marilyn is a changed person this past year. If she knew the truth, she might be able to handle it.'

'Not this,' Elizabeth sighed, 'not yet. This is the only thing to do if we want her to be happy in the long term. And it will be a risk higher than she ever took bets on in that place.'

43

Three nights after Rose came to live with her grandparents, Julie gave up on the crib her mother, Margaret, had put up in her room and put her back in the bed beside her. It was hypnotic watching her on the pillow, holding her hands across her face, chasing angels.

'Just as you did.' Margaret had come into the room. 'She looks just the same.'

The girl had her mother's soft green eyes and Margaret could see from them that she wouldn't have to grow up to be wise. Rose had wailed for the first two days and nights, but then settled, knowing they weren't going to go back to their familiar surroundings.

'You'll soon like it better there,' Margaret smiled into her granddaughter's face. 'Do you know that your mother kicked up just as much fuss about that crib? After her father making it for her.'

'I never knew he made it.' Julie looked up from her daughter to her mother.

'He was very excited about you, but he did think you were going to be a boy. Then I couldn't have any more. He just didn't know what to do with a girl.'

'Neither did you,' Julie found herself saying, wishing she hadn't. Her mother was thin and exhausted. Her father had been bedridden for some of the time since she'd come home, when he recognised Julie, he had smiled, like he had forgotten all he had done to her. And when he held out his hands for Rose, she could almost forget too.

'Is this Julie?' he asked Margaret.

418

'It is, William. It is.'

'And who's that?' He pointed to Julie.

'That's Julie too.'

'Two of them,' he grinned. Then his mind lapsed again.

Three weeks later, William came out of his reverie long enough to judge the situation with the mind he had once had. He threatened to kill Julie and the baby if they didn't get out at once. He slapped at Margaret: 'Disgusting, you, letting them into our house.'

'It's hers now.' Julie had taken Magenta's advice and waited until Margaret had signed over the house before setting foot in it.

'What?'

'It's hers.' Margaret's voice trembled with the effort of standing up to him. 'She's looked after you night and day these past weeks. She should get something, for taking us both on.'

'She should get out of my sight,' he spat, going purple, 'and take her brat with her.'

Julie was trembling, walking the streets, wondering why she'd agreed to this, then remembered. For Rose. Everything was for Rose. That's when she heard the car pull in beside her and someone get out. She turned her head away.

'I knew it was you!' Marilyn's voice.

There'd been no warning from 51. Julie turned, and Marilyn could see from her face she was going to lie. And because she was a numbers woman, she figured the rest out.

Julie watched her get back into the passenger seat. Sean was driving. He looked stricken, as she was sure she did, as she could see Marilyn was. They drove off. She looked at Rose, who was watching clouds, oblivious.

'We should never have come back.'

Then she heard Magenta's voice: 'You have to think about her now. She's the important one.'

★

'We came up to tell you our news. You're going to be a granny. I didn't want to tell you over the phone, it's too important, isn't it? Important?' Marilyn was in the hallway of 51. Elizabeth couldn't persuade her to sit down. Sean was still in the door-frame.

'I knew. I already knew about Julie, and that's why I'd been trying so hard to get pregnant. Brigid used to say that, didn't she, Elizabeth? "There's no sixth sense, there's only common sense." Now I know – they're one and the same. Since Julie left, I've known. You remember the basque thing, Sean? Catwoman? Ha, you've seen two catwomen. One was only a mongrel stray compared to the real busty, sexy thing. We never mention her,' she said, pointing at Sean. 'I didn't want to know and you didn't want to tell me.'

'Marilyn,' he started to say, 'I had no idea.'

'But you did.' She was sounding so reasonable still, Elizabeth was frightened for her. 'We wrote her out of our story. But before that you fucked her, and got her pregnant. Did you know?' She looked at Elizabeth, who could only nod.

'My own mother knew. Why is she back here?' she whispered to Elizabeth, pleading with her for an interpretation.

'There was no one else to take care of her father. He's sick. And her baby needed a proper home.' Elizabeth was pained in answering.

'What about my baby? I'm supposed to get married. It's going to grow up here, isn't it? I'm chained to this house. I thought I was gone from it.'

Sean was baffled. He still wasn't sure, but was getting there.

They got somehow to the kitchen, sat at the table.

The doorbell rang.

420

'If it's her, don't piss on her if she's on fire,' Marilyn spat.

'It's not, it's Tony.' Elizabeth stood. 'I'll tell him to go away.'

'You won't. We need one truthful person in a roomful of liars. Get Tony, I want Tony.'

When Tony came in he saw three people, all in their own worlds. He didn't want to know why, because the air was full of sadness and loss.

'I think we'll have to go.' Sean stood. 'I can't take this in, Marilyn. We'll go home and come back tomorrow, sort it out.'

'You'll go home, Sean. I'm already here.'

'Marilyn, please, for the love of God, you have to come with me.'

She walked past him as if he wasn't there and did what she always did when she couldn't cope – she went to her bedroom, and waited to die.

44

It was a quiet, grey, late February morning. Julie's head was full of what she would say, and do. No contact from the Monroes meant she had to do something. She had to bring Rose with her, because of how her father was. As it turned out she didn't have to say or do anything. Elizabeth opened the door.

'I don't think it's a good idea for you to come in. I'm sorry, Julie, I wish it could be different.'

Julie knew then that Marilyn was still home and would be watching behind her cream linen blind, which let light in and kept intruders' eyes out.

'I can't be sorry that I had her,' Julie was crying, 'I just can't be. I didn't mean for any of this to happen.'

'I know, and neither did he, but both of you have hurt her more than any person can afford to be hurt.'

'Can you please ask her if I can talk to her? Please?'

'I already have. She hasn't left her room, she wants nothing to do with you. I'm sorry, but you have to understand. If you could both have been honest with her in the beginning, this would never have happened.'

'Yes,' Julie hissed, 'and she'd have stayed in that fucking bedroom until she was Brigid's age. He was meant for her. Why else do you think I went through all I went through? I could have had him, Elizabeth; you said it yourself.'

'Please, Julie, don't upset yourself, and don't get her any more upset. She's my daughter, I have to respect her wishes. I'm wishing you the best, but unless things change, we don't want any more to do with you. Sean wants to be contacted, he left details and a letter with me.'

'Sean doesn't have to be involved in this. I didn't even put him on her birth certificate.'

'That's a mistake, darling. Take it from me.' Elizabeth's voice hardened. 'But you two must do what you want between you. I'm not saying any more. I'm going to close the door now, Julie.'

'I never thought you'd behave like this, Elizabeth.'

'I have to. You're not the person I have to think about. Bye.' She kissed the top of Rose's forehead.

'You tell her, Elizabeth, that she's got to understand – I don't want him and he doesn't want me. He loves her the way I wish someone loved me, so she needs to climb down and see sense. Her days of judging me are over. I was as good a friend to her as she was to me. I just make more mistakes. I'm sorry for them, but I'm not sorry for Rose, no matter how she came about.'

Marilyn heard it all. It was like someone was operating on her without anaesthetic. Thirteen weeks pregnant. It was agonising not to be with him, enjoying it, to wish Julie had got rid of the little girl. That little girl had done nothing to her. Just as she had once been wanted by her single mother, so Rose was wanted now by Julie. It didn't help her.

She watched Julie walk down the road with her, and heard Elizabeth make a call. Tony pulled up twenty minutes later. She heard Elizabeth crying in the hallway, and him soothing her.

'Such a thing to happen. I should never have agreed to hide it from Marilyn. If I'd explained then, there might have been some chance. I have no idea what she looks like, or if she's eating anything I pass in to her. She won't use the bathroom unless I leave the house. It's been three weeks! My God, Tony, I don't think I can stand it.'

'Have you phoned Niall?'

'I doubt he'd manage anything better. He's not used to family life.'

Marilyn remembered Brigid saying something similar.

'They don't need to ring Niall,' she said to herself. 'I've got Dad here, haven't I,. Dad?'

'Yes, Princess,' he said, but he seemed sad to be back.

There was life growing inside her. She had no job or partner. She was fitting, at long last, into the Monroe life pattern.

Julie's father answered the door. He was having a spell where he could get up and about. She couldn't use her key because one time he'd flown at her for letting herself into his home.

'What do you want?' He looked at Rose. 'Come in,' he snapped, 'we figured as much had happened to you, you were born with no sense.' He went into the back room, where she knew that at this time they would be having their breakfast. 'She's at the door, with a baby.'

Always the same breakfast, in the same portions. After it they would once have gone to mass, then on to the shops, then to a café for tea, then home for lunch. Afternoon film, crossword, paperwork, tea, telly, bed. Now they rarely got out of the house.

She heard whispered agitation, then a distinct phrase: 'She lives here now, William, this is her house.'

'Well, if it is, tell her to sort that patio lock, it's sticking.'

'It's not sticking, we have to lock it to keep you in. You keep running out there, taking wet things off the line.'

'Rubbish, you always talk rubbish. Put more milk in my tea.'

She took Rose upstairs and willed her father to deteriorate to the point where he stopped greeting her and Rose as if they'd just turned up. Some days he was the perfect grandparent, other days a bastard from hell.

Her mother knocked on the door. 'Sorry about that,' she apologised as if she too had Alzheimer's, as if she couldn't remember that she had apologised yesterday, in the same way, for the same thing. 'This came for you.' Her mother retreated from the room and Julie opened the letter and read.

. . . I wish, Julie, that you could have told me. I would have looked after you and I certainly would never have taken things so far with Marilyn. She moved everything down to me, gave up everything for me. By now I expect you know she's pregnant.

Julie looked up from the letter. She had never considered this as a possibility; Marilyn wasn't the type to rush these things. It was a worse mess than she had realised. 'No wonder she didn't want to see me,' she whispered to a sleeping Rose.

Julie, I have two children to think of now. Please, let's come to some arrangement whereby I can support this little girl. And you, naturally. It's the right thing, having thought about it. The circumstances were beyond all our control, after that night. We should have thought more about them. The worst crime is mine. When it comes down to it, I'm like all men, visiting where I shouldn't. Don't be guilty for your girl, Julie, she's a blessing. I'm the curse.

He was willing to take the blame on his shoulders. She picked up the phone. 'Before you suggest it, I'm not a farm sort of woman. I have trouble cutting grass.'

45

Niall and Elizabeth were in the front room, on either side of the fireplace. The mantel was crowded with photographs of Marilyn. He had been unable to get hold of Marilyn on her mobile. Then, as the wedding day loomed, he had decided to phone Elizabeth.

'Marilyn's very depressed. She's back here living with me. I can't explain over the phone.'

'Is this big trouble? Yes? Then I'm coming up.'

'What about the campaign?'

'It'll be here tomorrow. I'll be there with you tomorrow.'

He didn't keep his word, but he got there by the weekend, the weekend that should have been Marilyn's wedding. It was Sunday afternoon when he rang the bell of 51.

'I don't understand. She was offered a share in Leahy's and turned it down? Sean got someone else pregnant? Marilyn's friend, the one Frank was trying to screw when his wife knifed him? This is ridiculous, this is insane.'

For six weeks Marilyn had closeted herself away, never leaving the house, refusing all contact with the outside world. The day her wedding should have taken place on had passed unmentioned and on everyone's mind.

'I didn't tell you to let you stand in judgement over her, Niall. I want you to help her. Who do you know who might offer her some work?'

'Ah, you're clutching at straws now! She's halfway through a pregnancy, Elizabeth. I think it would be best to wait until she's had the child?'

'She's lost everything. What are we going to do?'

'Losing everything's a choice. The girl's got to see sense. Her life isn't over, it's derailed. She's tough, she'll pick herself up, though I don't think much of the choices she made. Why did she not just take the partnership, then set up with him later?'

'Because the partnership was a pair of red shoes, Niall,' Elizabeth said into the fire.

'What's that? What do you mean?'

'The legend of the red shoes. A woman who gives up her wildness for gilded confinement, perceived success, and ends up dancing perpetually until the shoes are cut from her feet, and she's left crippled.'

'Look, now' – Niall pointed at her – 'Success is no bad thing, it's a good thing. She's got to get out of the room. Can I go up and at least try?'

'It's time you went. It's late enough. She could be sleeping.' Elizabeth was almost impatient with him. 'There's nobody outside on the street, and you can get a good night's sleep before you head for Offaly. The campaign trail awaits. Only weeks to go, Niall.'

'Fuck the campaign trail. I'll give talking to her one go, and if it's useless then you can add it to a long list.'

Elizabeth smiled.

'Marilyn? It's Niall. Let us in, will you?'

No answer.

'Look, let us in, please? Otherwise I'll have to shout in from the landing the things I don't want your next-door neighbours or even your mother to know.'

He sat on the edge of the bed, as her imaginary father did, and he told her in a way that was far from fatherly what loneliness in late middle age was like.

'You end up in a palace of dreams, with no one to share

427

it with. You have money to spend and no one to spend it with. You have professional friends, professional family even. You wish someone, anyone, could tell your middle-thirties self just where he was going wrong. But it's too late. The woman you love is downstairs, and she threw you over for a taxi driver.' He looked at her.

'Stop fishing, Niall, I don't know either if she's with him now. You're such a politician,' Marilyn smiled, turning her face back from the wall.

'Ah well, old habits never die in my case. Let me carry on talking about sixty-odd eejits who lose all the best things in life. The woman you live with had an abortion to get rid of another man's child, which left her unable to have children with you. The daughter you're a stranger to lies on her bed, not even returning your calls, when she should be phoning you with her troubles.'

'You don't act like a father. That's why.'

'Because I never was one. And I'll tell you another thing, it's as well you weren't born a man.'

She looked up from her pillow. He was shocked to see how thin she was, how frail, when she should be looking after herself.

'Why?'

'Because then you wouldn't be having a baby to help prevent you from making the biggest mistake of your life.'

'He has a baby already, by my best friend. The fact I'm carrying his makes it as big a mistake as I could have made.'

'No. Your mother made that in getting pregnant by a fool like me. Sean was going to marry you. He wanted to give you everything he had.'

'I had more before I met him and I'd have been a millionaire now if it hadn't been for him.'

'I know, I can't believe you turned that down. But then,' he said quickly, 'you know where my advice will get you. Here's some that's out of character: he did the best he could.

428

He'll love you until you die and he made the mistake of lying to you once. He's not likely to do it again. Ever. So get up, dry your face and get downstairs, at least to make your poor mother feel better. I've got to go back to Offaly now and make new friends. Which is hard, because everybody hates me, and I don't blame them. The lad the party got rid of was much better at being an Offaly man than me. He even liked it.'

'Can I show you something?' She sat up. 'The only things I left in this room are in this locker. The rest is all in Wexford.' She took a key from under the bedclothes. 'You can have them all.'

After five minutes of looking, Niall whispered, 'If I needed any further knowledge of what a mistake I made, I've got it. I can't take any of these. I haven't earned them. Give one of them to me next Christmas, or my birthday – that's 9 November – if I do well in the meantime. Now I have to go, I'm no use at all at this. Goodnight, Princess, mind yourself. You're on my mind. Not that I'll show it much, I'm a Tormey. We weren't brought up like you Monroes. You're an emotional crowd.'

'Leave the door open when you go out,' Marilyn said through her tears. 'Thanks for coming, Niall, it means a lot to me.'

'Ah, too little too late, but I'll be here, Princess, should the shit ever hit that fan. Whenever it does, you call that number I gave you. I'll come.'

'Please, a little less of the fatherhood!' She was smiling for the second time in six weeks.

Elizabeth came up with some hot milk and toast.

'Niall's right,' she whispered. 'I'm a Monroe, not a Tormey. He thinks I was nuts to turn down the Leahy offer.'

'He's like a bull in a china shop. Heroism is in caring,

Marilyn, and you chose caring at the expense of success. I watched you love Sean and I know he's hurting like you do, only worse. He's lost more than you, he's lost your baby. A child he wanted.'

'Don't. How can I miss someone like I miss him, like I've had a limb cut off, and then hate the thought of him at the same time?'

'He betrayed you. It doesn't make him a terrible person. He's a fine man who did a terrible thing. I've betrayed people – Judith Tormey. You. For starters. Do you think I'm undeserving of forgiveness?' Marilyn shook her head. 'Then your father is right. You have to get on, with forgiving, and see what you can salvage of yourself and Sean. He's going to be your baby's daddy, and you know what it was like to grow up without one.'

'I can't get past it. My heart won't let me.'

'It hasn't had enough time.' Elizabeth spoke with sorrow. 'You're just going to have to get through the days until enough have passed for you to think differently.'

The phone went, and both would have ignored it, but somehow they knew it had to be answered. Elizabeth ran down the stairs. It was Brigid. She was aware of Marilyn's situation, but had listened to Marilyn begging her not to come home.

'Please, it's just about the only happiness I have that you're out there, enjoying yourself. I'm too miserable to cope with making you miserable too.'

'How's the child?' Brigid asked, referring to Marilyn.

'She's better than she was and still not good. What's up?' Marilyn was at the top of the stairs again. The instinct was rising in both of them, and it proved right.

Brigid wanted to come home, for good, and Nikolas with her. The shadow had landed again, almost a year after recovery.

*

Things had changed. She was full, plump, this time. And she wouldn't have enough time to vanish.

'At least I'm going with meat on my bones, not a scrawny skeleton. I want to go out a woman,' she advised them from her sunroom throne.

Nuala Brady, her consultant, came to visit her at home, since in Brigid's words she had 'no truck with hospitals, flecking sick places'. The only treatment she would accept was for the pain. Morphine and cups of tea, mountain or Lyons.

'That coffee stuff, it was only a fad with me.'

It was as before – Elizabeth going to work, Grace making meals and Theresa fixing things, since Nikolas was all for Brigid.

The only difference was Marilyn, rounder by the minute.

'I'll tell you one thing, I'll be around to see my great-grandson. Whether I'm alive or not, I'll be here to see him.'

'How do you know it's not a daughter? Especially in this family?'

'I have my sources.' Brigid looked beyond Marilyn. After only two days in the house, she had pushed Marilyn out of it, for a walk, saying, 'You can't refuse the request of a dying woman.' Especially one like Brigid.

'I hope you don't mind a bit of death in a house that's going to have a young life soon?' They weren't allowed to hide from this. The order was to face it, line up for the charge. She held on to Marilyn's arm and made it as far as the end of the road before they had to turn back.

'No, Brigid.' Marilyn was strong for her, not soft. 'It's great having you home, though I know that's an awful thing to say.'

'That's not awful,' Brigid laughed, 'it's natural what's happening. The old die off, the young get born. Don't think

I won't be around. That's my great-grandchild to be looked after. He's a first since John Joe, a male Monroe.'

Marilyn was sure it was a boy also. 'I'm so in tune with myself these days I could play fiddle as well as piano,' she laughed to Brigid.

'Well, at least you and that piano are together again.' It had been in Wexford, along with all of Marilyn's things. Sean had offered to send them back up, but hadn't heard from the house for weeks. Weeks in which he hadn't the heart to be without them. He sat each night at Marilyn's piano, playing single notes of his own loss. If it hadn't been for the horses he wouldn't have left the house. The Mikes and his sisters brought him food, knowing he wouldn't eat for himself. Then he got the call, from Elizabeth, that everything was to be returned. He stopped eating even what the Mikes and his sisters brought him.

Brigid and Marilyn didn't tell anyone else. It was their secret, in a family that was good at keeping them. They knew, and the others didn't, that she wouldn't last long enough to see him born.

'Get them to lay me out at home,' she instructed as they walked back to the house. 'I don't want a night in any cold chapel. I'll go straight from my sunroom to my grave. With my old hot water bottle, please. I don't care for cold. And the cheapest coffin you can get. I can't stand overdone, it's no class to it, has it, Nikolas, love?' She was referring to him even when he wasn't there.

Back at the house, Theresa noticed that Nikolas nodded, as if he was in a conversation. But the two of them were alone.

'Did you learn any English out of Brigid?' Theresa asked him. They were fixing a faucet together.

Nikolas nodded, looked at her seriously, and said, 'Howya, Tereesa.'

Theresa laughed until the faucet leaked again.

'I bet she learned how to nag you in Greek. She tells me Manos, the lad you got to teach her, used to slap her wrists if she got it wrong, until she smacked his face. Is that right?'

'Manos!' Nikolas looked at Theresa and smacked his own face. 'Howya!'

In a rare quiet moment, Elizabeth took the opportunity to tell her mother her news.

'I think this is it for me, Mother. I go to say something and he says it before me. I think it and I know he's thinking it too. I can't not love him. He's the part of me I never thought I'd find.'

'Oh, he's that all right, is Tony. I'll let the fixers in heaven know when I get there, if it's there I'm going.' Brigid embraced her daughter with what strength was left in her tired body. 'You've given me my dying wish. There's nothing else I want.'

'What about Marilyn and Sean?'

'That's one will be solved once I get to where I'm going. I need a good word with God about that one.' Brigid chuckled faintly.

Elizabeth watched the face of the woman she'd been at loggerheads with for most of her life. There wasn't a line on it she didn't love, there wasn't a part of her mother she didn't want to hold on to.

'What am I going to do without you?'

'You are going to be happy with him. No more soft, now, this is a good time. I have to go and you have to let me.'

Every day Marilyn went with Brigid, to walk to the end of the road. They made it less and less far, until the walk was only to the gate and back.

'I don't know which's worse, you or me,' Brigid abbreviated, wheezing.

Then she couldn't come with Marilyn any more. Marilyn was told it would be bad manners not to continue, so each day she ended up getting Tony to drop her to the Vico viewpoint. Watching the sea, wondering what Julie was up to, two streets away, and what Sean was doing with himself, two hours down the coast.

Elizabeth was right – the hurt was fading, but only just enough so she could breathe, and breathing was a problem. She was small and was carrying a big baby, right under her rib cage, which kept knocking the breath out of her.

It was coming into summer, and she read that Delaney was winning. She read that Niall Tormey was on the crest of the campaign wave. It was going well for him. There were pictures of him in his new Offaly residence, leaning over a fence, looking at the midlands countryside, Judith at his side. Forty years married. Brigid's words came to Marilyn: 'Life's never like the picture.'

Delaney won at the Kilbeggan Races. Sean was there, and so was Niall. The papers reported that Sean refused to be photographed with the canvasser, but they were seen deep in conversation. Marilyn almost felt left out, but she egged on the little horse, still felt her victories over everything life had thrown at her.

Sean had written to her most days, when it became clear she would accept no calls. They had been apart for three months. He wrote that if he had it all back he would still have tried for her, but been more truthful with it. They were his own words, clumsily put, but she could feel the love and loss in them. Rose had come down to the farm, was a grand baby by anyone's standards. She had his mother's mouth, but otherwise he could detect no trace of his family. He didn't mention Julie.

It ripped her in two to think of Julie's child in the yard her son should have been running around in in a few years' time.

'Why are you telling me this?' she asked the letter, then realised he was telling her that honesty would be the only way from then on. Even when the truth hurt her, he would tell it. He'd decided not to tell it, once, and it had hurt her more than anything had before.

'This is what you've decided,' she had to remind herself. 'If Julie and Sean get together to raise Rose . . .' She couldn't finish the thought.

'Please, Marilyn,' he still wrote every time, 'please reconsider.' Then, as the weeks went on, he wrote, 'Please allow me to be part of the child's life, I want to be a father to it. Not absent as I am to Rose.' 'Please' was his most frequently used word.

He knew nothing about Brigid. Only Tony and Grace knew from outside the family.

51 Verbena Avenue was full of coming and going, if not with life, then with tasks. Brigid's voice was going, the first part of her to leave. She said to Marilyn, 'Every woman wants to be loved. Every Monroe is, nowadays. What we do about it is up to us.'

Marilyn whispered the name she had chosen in her ear and Brigid nodded with approval. Each day as Marilyn walked she talked to the child growing inside her. She also played at every opportunity. Her piano was back from Wexford, removed by a specialist firm Sean had employed at a cost he couldn't afford.

She played for her child, each day, so that he would grow to know and love music and her with it, since it was such an essential part of her soul, missing for so long, brought back to her by love, chance and all its consequences.

She would never play to concert halls, but would always play for family gatherings. And receive the same joy from that.

The house was empty – Marilyn was out walking, Elizabeth

working, Theresa and Grace at their own affairs – when Brigid died.

Nikolas told them, through Kristos, who had come to be there for the last days, to say goodbye to a woman he regarded as a second mother. But the women already knew it had happened. When they came home to 51, the air was filled with a quiet peace that comes only from good passing, to a better place.

'Nikolas, tea.' She wrote the words he had come to learn. 'Lyons' and 'strong' were two more. He came back with a pot and brought the cup to her lips. She managed two or three sips, which was two or three more than the day before. He smiled, looked into her eyes, knew.

Carry me upstairs, please, to my bed. She pointed to convey the wish and he knew how to obey it.

He climbed into the bed beside her and lifted her into his arms, so that his body took up the hollow carved by life, and filled it. She lay in the crook of his arm, and he sang, in a whisper, along the line to the other side. She closed her eyes, and the door to him, since it was not his time.

Marilyn played a requiem at the funeral. They had worried she might not be able to, but she played as she had never played, putting all her loss and yearning into the space between notes. Putting all of her heart.

At the burial Elizabeth saw Sean, behind a tree, a ghost of himself. He walked away before it was over. She could see it pained him not to be comforting her. Elena had also come over, for a simple service, without demonstration, just as Brigid wished for. But there was a crowd. You can't have a character like Brigid Monroe and not have hordes attending. The house was full of her, stories, snapshots from the minds and hearts of other people. Marilyn could almost hear her saying, 'Gawkers, the lot of them, coming to my house to get a look. Well, let them look elsewhere, tell them nothing.' But it would have filled her with secret pleasure, to have so many respect her.

In the days after they bombarded Kristos with questions for his father, from whom they took their cue. Nikolas was full of cheer. Brigid in her strength had given him what Nyphi had failed to in her timidity – the ability to face death and grieve with a torn heart and a full smile.

Niall phoned to express condolences.

'I wish I could be there for you. She was a grand woman,' he said, having only met her the once.

He had topped the polls, as only he knew how to. He was more Offaly than the Offaly people themselves. The opposition formed a coalition government, and he found himself in charge of fisheries. You might as well have slapped him in the face with a fresh-caught cod.

46

A week passed in which Elena kept smiling and patting Marilyn's bump, which Marilyn had to come to terms with, being a touch-phobic Irishwoman. By the end of the week, everyone felt they had a pass to touch the bump, celebrating the new life due on the planet in just a few months. Elena patted her own stomach, crossed her fingers, pointed to her watch, sighed.

'We have two years trying, nothing.' Kristos was sad, but his father spoke sharply to him in Greek, admonishing. They were all alarmed at the naked way in which the Faltaitses displayed their emotions, but it was good for the grief in number 51. They were either shouting at one another, or laughing, or discussing things in tones loud enough for the neighbours to hear.

'My father says two years is nothing, he and my mother waiting seven for me, and when I came I was too big to be a baby. He says you will have a big child, he says start thanking God for it. There is no sadness, only surprise, we must have faith,' Kristos explained.

They had seven days of the Faltaitses and then Tony drove them to the airport in a borrowed seven-seater, with promises that the link would not be broken.

Nikolas spoke frantically to Kristos, pointing at the driver.

'My father says you must come with your Elizabeth before there is another summer, to Skyros. He will arrange your wedding, in the little church in the rock, where he brought Brigid.' Kristos's eyes were shining. Elizabeth and

Tony couldn't look at each other. But Marilyn was grinning at Nikolas and giving him a thumbs up. She stopped grinning after Kristos translated for his father again:

'Marilyn, you are a small woman with a big wall around your body. You must open the way for the big man Sean, who is your protection in this life, and put his problem in your past. My father is talking Brigid's wish. Bye, my sister,' Kristos said as he embraced Marilyn. 'We will not be strangers.' Nikolas placed a great hand over her belly, and a kiss on her head. He went home a Lyons tea convert. Brigid had begun the conversion in Greece.

Before he left, Elizabeth pressed a package into his hand. Inside it was Brigid's chipped china cup. No one, not even Theresa, could remember her drinking from anything else. Nikolas would drink from it each day, until his own death.

Theresa and Grace were not at the airport. Theresa became the silent one now. The loss of her sister had passed her over to a place she had never been before – after an active, strong, vigorous life, she felt her age, and let it arrive, defeated by her grief. The Downes sisters' strength had been symbiotic. Grace never left her side.

June came again, and Marilyn's birthday. Niall didn't remember. He was preoccupied with keeping other trawlers out of Irish waters, fishing quotas and Offaly affairs. She phoned him to give out, in a playful way.

'Sorry, Princess, expect something soon.'

'I want to know when I'll expect you.'

'You'll see me before the grandchild, hopefully.' Life was full for him again, he didn't have a trace of his earlier emptiness. His need for Elizabeth had been a transient thing, a physical representation of all he had lost, which he now had back again. Fisheries was a busy place to be.

Sean sent a card. Inside was an open ticket to the

Wexford Opera Festival in November. Not bad for a man not good with presents. A wish expressed that he might accompany her. Or at least babysit.

Elizabeth gave her sessions with an osteopath to sort out her aching back before birth. At the time, to Marilyn, it was worth as much as the deal she'd turned down with Leahy's.

Elizabeth got an unexpected visitor to her office in that week. It was their next-door neighbour, with the Humpty husband.

'I'm sorry about your mother,' Fiona Sharp said in a manner close to her surname.

'Thank you, Fiona, though you could have told me this at home. You're always welcome to knock.'

'No, I'm here on business too. I need advice myself. Michael left me for a lap dancer. I always thought he had a fancy to you, that's why I kept him out of your house. Now it's full of men. Your bad luck travelled next door. He wasn't as choosy as to pick someone like you. A tart's better than me.'

With eight weeks to go, Marilyn was finding it hard to motivate herself to do anything. Theresa had taken her on as her project, to alleviate her grief. For the first time in her life she needed Marilyn's support and Marilyn was giving it to her, in the form of a bitten lip at worse bossing than Brigid had ever dished out.

'You need to have Brigid's room for a start, if you're planning to sleep in the same room as the baby, and I hope you will. I'm not for farming children into the next room. That's a cold, modern way of carrying on.'

'Whatever you think,' Marilyn sighed. She could only think of 1 September, her due date. It was like entering a tunnel. The dread of the birth, the excitement of the baby coming, the terror that Sean wasn't going to be there. She said so to Theresa, but she was in no mood to indulge.

'Ah, don't be soft, that's your choice you're making, and I may as well tell you, none of us agree with it. You're too much like Brigid in that respect. No going back on decisions, even the wrong ones.'

Grace came to Marilyn's room, where she had retreated. They could hear Theresa still thumping about in Brigid's room, taking measurements, trying to get over her guilt at saying the right thing, if in the wrong way.

'She's taking Brigid's death badly, as we all know. And her own mortality's to be faced. Neither of us is getting any younger. We're likely to be the next to go, and we've our own mistakes to consider.' Grace's hands were crossed in her lap.

'You always look so flawless to me,' Marilyn said, watching her.

'Oh, you think that, do you? It's good I'm able to hide it. I'm terrified at the prospect of dying. Always have been. And losing Theresa. Only one thing can hurt more than that. I have something to tell you, Marilyn.'

Grace's husband had said, 'If you leave me, you'll never see your son again.'

'I can't believe you're telling me this.' Marilyn felt the baby kick against her, leaving her short of breath. The shock of hearing Grace had been married, had a child, was almost too much.

'He wasn't in love with me, but he had no desire to be related to scandal. He wanted my money. My father had been a very rich man, a baron, if you can believe that.' Marilyn could. 'I tried to deny who I was and it didn't work. Theresa came into my life. She was working her way around the country, as a domestic!'

'Did she do an awful job?'

'Yes, but I'd never have let her go, from the moment I saw her. The wealth . . .' Grace smiled. 'I don't miss it. You can have luxury in small things. And gold cages are as awful as rusted ones. I happened to be living in one when I fell in love with your aunt. He found out and wouldn't let me continue the relationship, though he had plenty of his own. Theresa settled into the area, I kept her in the style to which she was accustomed. A Spartan one!'

'How did you continue to see each other?' Marilyn couldn't help asking for details.

'We went to a sympathetic place, and found it wasn't so sympathetic. The police found us, on a tip-off. A terrible way to be found, like it wasn't love, like we were filthy beasts. Theresa and I were charged with mental deficiency. If I hadn't had friends, we would never have made the bail amounts. We had to run away.'

'That's a disgusting thing to do to two human beings! Especially two who feel for each other like you two do.' Marilyn's outrage didn't faze Grace, who had long since passed beyond that emotion. She continued with her story.

'If it weren't for the same friends, we would never have had a penny. They lent me money my own husband took from me. Then he settled on a pittance, once I signed over all my shares to him, or else he would have made sure I faced prosecution wherever I was. He would find me. That was the law then, men still had the say, on financial and property rights. Anyway, that money bought this house and ours.'

As Marilyn's baby kicked again, she had to ask: 'What happened to your son?'

'I never saw him again, until his father died I made myself known to him. We met once. He is very like Tony, physically. But Tony has all the attributes my son has grown up without. He is a pauper compared to Tony. Don't get me wrong – he's a rich man now. But he grew up without his mother, into what he is. He has prejudice he wouldn't have had if he'd been under my influence. I don't like him, and I

442

still love him. He doesn't love me and he certainly hasn't any desire to see me. He met me once to tell me to my face what he thought of me.

'And you, my dear, may wonder why I'm telling you all of this, when you're so low yourself. It's because you are depriving yourself, and your child, of happiness. If he doesn't know both parents, he'll grow up slanted, perhaps. Though not a bigot.'

Marilyn couldn't not answer this. The air was charged. Like the diplomat she had been all of her life, Grace brought the conversation to a close.

'Did you know that my and Theresa's initials are G and T? Just like the drink, we were made for each other. All my life she took care of me and now I have to look after her in the same way, now that Brigid's gone and she's lost herself. But for many years I looked at your great-aunt and it reminded me of what I had lost. There were occasions when I wished I had never met her. The love of your life, darling, can't be that every minute of every day. There are times when what you had disappears entirely. Then the genie finds its way back out of the bottle. Anyway, that's quite enough of that.'

Grace didn't linger. She called Brigid on her way out, then corrected herself to call Theresa.

Within a week they had her grandmother's room made into one suitable for both of them. Everything was new, but for the bed, which had a new mattress. What Grace had said ran round in Marilyn's head. 'I wonder if we'll live here as long as Elizabeth did with me,' she said to her child. The thought came, unbidden: I hope not.

47

Late July. Marilyn sat watching the Galway races, envying svelte women in architectural hats. The weather was right for them, and wrong for being heavily pregnant.

Delaney, now a mare, had got into the Galway Hurdle, on the basis of some fine performances and press coverage. Crowds loved her, but didn't fancy her odds in this race.

She didn't have an architectural hat's chance of winning, according to the bookies, at forty-eight to one odds. The field was pure class, as you'd expect from a feature race, the race of the season for her. Elizabeth was on two weeks' holiday, having left the office to her junior, for a break.

Elizabeth handed her daughter yet another cup of raspberry-leaf tea. She was drinking it round the clock in the hope it would bring on contractions and give her a quicker birth. Her fearful, numerical side, long latent, had begun to reappear and told her this was like pissing in the wind and to book an epidural at the hospital in advance, in case all the anaesthetists were out playing golf when she began. August seemed to make everyone want to go on holiday.

Elizabeth rubbed Vitamin E cream into Marilyn's bump with soothing motions. The baby was going to be born with a beard at this rate. Elizabeth was her birth partner and she was urging her on to labour, alarmed at her growing size. Tony was on twenty-four-hour alert.

'I feel like I'm going to be a granddad,' he confided in Marilyn.

'That's because you are, this child needs you!' Marilyn hugged him.

Elizabeth, listening, blew him a kiss, an unexpressed thanks for his statement.

'I think the last period must have been your show, Marilyn. Your dates have to be wrong. This baby is coming any minute, surely?' She could see Marilyn wasn't listening, her eyes glued to the television screen. 'What about Sean? I know you're looking for him in that crowd.'

'He can see the child as much as he likes.' She'd decided that after hearing Grace's story, and Niall's input, of which there'd been none since he came to power. But then, there was a cod war in the North Sea, which had nothing to do with him, but he was being a mediator to warring Icelandic, Nordic, Irish, Scottish and English fishermen. 'But he's not going to be present at the birth. I couldn't handle him and all that pain at once.'

Then Sean was there, on television, the first she had seen of him, parading Delaney around the ring. He had no weight on his big bones and his eyes were the size of saucers. Marilyn put her hands to her face. He didn't look involved with anything, and leaned against Delaney.

'That, Marilyn, is what someone looks like when they've lost everything they care about,' Elizabeth whispered.

'I had no idea. I thought he had the horses to keep him going.'

Almost as she said it, the commentary team were talking about Sean Monroe, and how he had cut his horses down to a handful.

'He's concentrating on Delicia Heartly, grooming her to be a possible champion, but she's skittish, as we know, and the odds are never sure on her. Her recent streak, great form, good wins, made her something to be looked at. The ground's her ground today, a big-hearted horse, she is. And the go in her might make her a choice bet, but don't put all the money on it.' The betting man wagged his finger.

'What are you talking about?' Marilyn screeched. 'She's the most reliable thing on four legs. Didn't you mention her heart? She's got the biggest heart there! She'll win this.'

'Marilyn, don't upset yourself.'

'How can I not be? He looks terrible. Why didn't someone tell me?'

'None of us see him.'

'I mean the two Mikes, they could have called.'

'Marilyn, we've all been telling you, nothing's worked.'

Delaney was boxed at the back. Helen was driving her on, but with nowhere to go. Then Marilyn heard the commentator say, 'There's always a gap at Galway, if they can hang on up the big hill.'

Marilyn knew what Delaney was like going up big hills. It was like the waters parting for Moses – she came through, her jockey practically over her head. They were all neck and neck, but her little neck got there first.

The crowd's roar could be heard on the other side of the country, without the benefit of broadcast. Delaney was the heroine of the hour and Sean Monroe was the toast of trainers and owners, the new good-luck story. But the bigger story was Helen, the first female jockey to have won the race. Never mind the little backward mare from Wexford.

Sean was quiet at the interview, which he was known for, but not known for his intention – he announced he would sell her at the next big sales.

'Well, she's selling at the top of her form,' they said, trying to pad out their commentary since his interview had only lasted a minute before he walked away. 'He'll make more money than he's ever had.'

'A trainer not known for his love of it, he's always been into his horses, and brought this one on from the very back.'

They went back to Helen, but Marilyn wasn't listening.

★

'Why didn't I listen to Grace?' Marilyn berated herself.

'Why didn't you listen to any of us?' Elizabeth felt obliged to say.

'Because I'm still a stubborn wretch. Right, that's it' – she got up from the couch with effort – 'I'm off to see him.'

'We can't travel all that way, with you the way you are,' Elizabeth was protesting.

'Then I'll drive myself, Ma, but I'm going. I want to be there when he gets home, sort his woolly head out for him.'

'You know that I haven't driven for years. And I never passed a test.'

'Then phone Tony.'

Tony turned up, but not for an hour. He was on the other side of the city when he got the call.

'Sorry,' Elizabeth said as she opened the door. 'If you lived here you'd be better off.'

'Is that an offer?' he quipped. Elizabeth averted her eyes, making him wish he hadn't.

Elizabeth had dinner on the table for him, insisting that he have some before he took them to Wexford. Marilyn noticed it was her terrine, which took hours to make and was frozen in batches. The food of special occasions and honoured guests. Elizabeth went upstairs. Marilyn looked at him as he dug in.

'Read the papers recently?'

'Sure have,' he grinned.

'At home with the Tormeys, round their new log fire. Wait until it starts to smoke. Well, what are you going to do about it? She's freer than Nelson Mandela.'

'It's all going around in here.' He tapped his forehead. 'I just need to make sure I'm wanted.'

'You know what I think? She wants you too much to say,'

Marilyn mused. Then Elizabeth was back, and they were on the road, driving carefully, avoiding all bumps but the one in the back seat.

They got to the stables just as one of the Mikes was leaving.

'Which one are you?' Marilyn asked.

'The other one,' he half whispered, not knowing what to say or where to put himself. 'Come in, come in to the house. You saw the win? A great win, a great win. Come in, I'll make tea, or do you want to, Marilyn?' Then he checked the size of her and stuttered on, 'I'll make it, I'll make it, grand tea I'll make, and I'll butter bread. He won't be long himself, he's on the road, come in, come in.'

'Ma, Tony, do you mind if I wait on my own?' she asked them.

'He's selling her to pay for all the babies,' Mike said, eyeing her belly. 'It's you he thinks of, though you'd never get him saying it. He's ruined himself drinking, and his manner is ruined with it. I'm only here because I wouldn't leave him. The other Mike took work elsewhere. Who'd have thought it of him, never a woman in all those years, then two babies both his? Who'd have thought it of him, the quietest man in the county?'

'I need you to do two things for me,' Marilyn asked. 'Clean out that sink of the stuff growing in it. And go home. I want to see him on my own.'

It was eight o'clock before the Land Rover and box came into the yard. He didn't come into the house. She heard him unload Delaney and put her to bed, still in the stall beside Noble. They were two of only a handful of horses left.

Odds-setting is an odd business, named after what it is – putting numbers on the indefinable, quantifying chance. It's pernicious and that's why so many of its terms have found their way into the modern language.

Like the phrase 'horses for courses'. It refers to the fact that an animal can go out and win one day and come last the next. Why? They're breathing. It's as simple as that. Anyone breathing can change their mind, and heart.

The going has to be soft. Sometimes. It's enough to make you go soft, dealing with such whimsy. But that's where the promise lies. If you can avoid definition and embrace chance enough, you can set odds that turn out even, or well, in your favour. That's why Marilyn loved numbers – in a way, still, they could make anything work. Even what doesn't exist. Like trust.

What were the odds of her realising she had to go back to him, after ignoring Grace? Niall? Brigid? Elizabeth? Julie? Herself? A million to one? A hundred to one? Hunch came into its own. The sight of him spurred instinct. They would find the trust again, the hunch said. But if she'd waited, he would be lost. It was a notion she would have sniffed at, said 'so what' to, at age thirty-two.

At thirty-four she was pregnant by a man who loved her, which was a starting point. Going forward still meant him, the man who made her friend pregnant before her, who fathered two children within the space of a year – children who lived two roads away from each other – a man who would never rescue her from her surname, but would consign her to it forever.

She found Sean in with Delaney, rubbing her down, talking to her with the same tone of voice he used with her, the same loving and understanding, creating safety and encouragement. She stood back, watching them, waiting. He finished a few minutes later. The way he turned showed her he knew she'd been there.

'You shouldn't be out, Marilyn. I take it you saw the television. That's why I got off it quick. Don't come back out of sympathy.'

'You win the race of the season, with the outsider, and you think you need sympathy? I've no sympathy to give, I'm starting with an order. You're not selling our little horse. She's our luck. And the best of our business. Where are we going to be without her? And we'll get the stables filled up, once I empty your head of nonsense. And tomorrow you get over to where the other Mike is working, whichever one he is, and get down on bended knee and get him back. Ask for forgiveness.'

'Do I need to do the same for you?' He was trembling now, trying to hide his emotions, not sure where they belonged.

She knew she'd already brought him to his knees. Julie had been right – she had never understood people making mistakes. And she'd made the biggest mess of all, expecting perfection from a real world.

'It's a lot to live with, but I'd rather live with it than without,' she said. She wanted him to hold her so much she could feel her arms rise of their own volition.

He had the sense to walk into them.

Sean told Elizabeth and Tony he would drive Marilyn back once she'd had a good night's rest.

'No woman coming up to nine months gets a good rest. I'm just afraid she'll start down here, Sean, that's all,' Elizabeth said.

'I won't start, I promise,' Marilyn advised. 'I'm too knackered. I'll be there tomorrow.'

He had clean sheets for the bed, most likely because he hadn't changed them since she'd moved out, so he still had the ones she'd left in the hot press.

'Mike says you've been drinking a lot.'

'Ah. I started on the wedding day that should have been ours. That's when I knew the horses had to go, I couldn't look after them properly. I only kept Delaney on for money.'

'I don't believe you.'

'It's true, or I think it is. I need to look out for the kids. I still need to see Rose, Marilyn. She's a grand little thing. I know it will be hard for you.'

'I can't pretend it won't. But I admire you for doing it, and at least I know each child will know its father, which is more than I did. But I can't marry you until everything settles. Is that okay with you?'

'I understand, even if you never do. I understand, so long as you know my mother's ring and the offer is there. Nuala had it altered to your ring size. She swore blind you'd come back to me.' His voice quivered. 'It was three sisters against one in that regard, I have to say.'

'I like those odds.' Marilyn stroked his cheek and looked into his eyes, which were sunk into the back of his head. 'I'll have to get her to teach me to cook. You can't go starving yourself like that again. I'm not having your sisters round here all the time, fixing our meals.'

Tony drove Elizabeth home, and on the way, she kept a hand resting on his thigh.

'I would love it if you would please stay in my house tonight,' she asked him.

Marilyn Monroe's Scale was reduced now to three things: weathered face, kind eyes and big heart. Sean had them all, and he was her choice, her antidote to loneliness in a lumpy old bed – that had been her grandmother's life.

'What if it doesn't work, Brigid? I've given all the heart.'

'Don't "Brigid" me. Get on with it.'

Whether the reply was real or imagined, it had an effect. Using her mother's intuition, Marilyn could run the risk of being wrong.

She'd had back pain during the night, so they set off first thing in the morning, stopping only so Sean could talk to the second Mike and Marilyn could see them shake hands, once without ceremony, after a bit of talk.

They were only a half-hour out of the house. The contractions began, faint, and she knew not to panic him. You win the Galway Hurdle and get your pregnant fiancée back in one day, have a baby the next. Anyone would need a drink. And it was the last thing she wanted him to have.

At number 51 she had a quiet word in her mother's ear. It was ten in the morning. Tony was in her mother's teal dressing gown and had odd socks on. He seemed not to care, or mind, to be caught in this manner, and Elizabeth seemed the same.

Then Marilyn stopped being so quiet. Sean went to take her out of the door, straight to hospital, but then she crouched down, the Axminster got a soaking, and he knew it was too late, as did Elizabeth.

She was in good hands. One had had a child and the other had birthed calves and foals enough to know the basics of mammalian birth. His direct involvement and Elizabeth's great efficiency kept it calm.

At twenty minutes past eleven, on 31 July, Daniel was born on the same bed his great-grandmother had died in. His first breath, her last. A circle of life completed. He was delivered into his father's hands, hands that would hold him all his life.

'You must have done the first stage through the night. We'll have to ring the hospital, get you checked out, but the afterbirth is all here,' Sean was able to report, after a while. 'You don't look torn.'

'Lovely,' Marilyn winced. 'There were things I didn't want you to know about me. But I'm glad you have the knowledge to tell me.'

'Well, I'd say you're a walking advertisement for natural childbirth and raspberry-leaf tea,' Elizabeth smiled as Marilyn put Daniel to her breast for the first time.

48

Elizabeth, home alone, found the autumn hard to get through. Tony was on hand. They spent most evenings together before he went to work, but he still lived in Loughlin's Wood, with Colin and Mick. She needed to be sure, since she couldn't bear to break such a good man's heart.

One evening, Tony said to her, almost as an aside, 'I'm going away to Europe for a few weeks. I want to see the Bay of Naples for myself, compare it to Vico.'

She was silent. She couldn't think what to say, and wondered why he hadn't invited her.

'I think you need a little more time, Elizabeth. It's been a lot to adjust to – your mother going, your aunt not well, your daughter moving away, Rose and Julie. Not to mention Niall and me.'

He would be back in time for Christmas. She was disappointed and wanted to say she didn't need any more time. Then it came to her – he was the one who needed it.

'Please, don't let him not love me. Not after having found how much I love him,' she found herself praying that night to her picture that she kissed each night as her mother had.

She had hoped he would be there for her birthday meal, which they hadn't bothered with the previous year, since Brigid and Marilyn hadn't been around. This year she wanted to resurrect tradition, with Theresa and Grace, in the hope of finding familiarity.

★

She helped Fiona Sharp, her neighbour and most recent friend, clear out the house. It had been sold.

They had a cup of tea together, sitting on the last of the boxes. It was funny for Elizabeth to see a house just like hers empty of all life and involvement. Is this what mine is like without all the people in it? Have I lost him? she couldn't help thinking to herself. Fiona's voice distracted her thoughts.

'I saw him, leaving your house.'

'Who?'

'The government minister. Don't worry. I won't breathe a word. She's the cut of him.'

'Who?'

'Your daughter.'

'Is she? I'm afraid I can't comment on that.'

'You don't have to!' Fiona laughed. 'To think for years I was worried you were after Humpty!' To cheer her up, Elizabeth had revealed what they called her philandering ex-husband. 'Your standards were a lot higher.'

'Fiona, I'll say this. What you saw coming or going wasn't any better. Now I've a daughter to think about, so I won't say any more. So, who's moving in?'

'I can't say, don't know anything about them.'

'I hope they're happier here than you were, and that you're happier elsewhere. Enjoy going round the world, lucky cow.' Elizabeth grinned as she spoke.

'Oh, I know they will, be happy, the ones who move in here!' Fiona grinned back. 'They've got an ideal neighbour in you!'

On the morning of her birthday Elizabeth woke up alone and the wish to speak to him was so powerful that she called his house to ask for the number of his hotel. He hadn't bothered to give it to her. A strange voice answered.

'Is that you, Mick, Colin?' she asked.

'No, this is Brian. They aren't living here any more. We bought the house last month.'

Tony had sold up and moved out in recent weeks. His belongings were in storage, and his post was going to a PO Box. She replaced the receiver.

'What do you expect?' she asked her reflection. 'He waited almost two years for a definite response from you, with no guarantee. You can't blame him for anything other than he didn't have the guts to tell you face to face.'

At dinner, Sean and Marilyn made an unexpected appearance. This lifted Elizabeth out of an all-day sadness. They were happy but for the fact that Daniel, named after Sean's father, was waking up three times a night for milk he didn't need since he was the size of a small schoolchild.

'Blame his father,' Marilyn smiled at Sean, who was returning to himself, having all that he wanted in his life, again. The horses were retuning to the yard, as did the second Mike, whichever one he was. 'They both eat for Ireland.'

Marilyn was going to cookery classes in a neighbour's house to prevent bankruptcy as a result of ready-made meals. In the living room before dinner, Marilyn whispered to Elizabeth that Sean had seen Rose earlier. Julie had a partner.

'Maybe someday you and her can meet up again,' Elizabeth said.

'Someday is a long time away yet.'

'How's Niall?' Elizabeth asked, changing the subject. 'Especially with all this?'

The first mention of Judith Tormey, together with an as yet unnamed associate, in connection with accounts in the name of Magpie Holdings, had happened in November.

Speculation was mounting. The dates matched her husband's time in office. The Tormeys were not looking forward to a quiet Christmas.

'He's been down to see us a couple of times. He says he's after nothing but free time, but he can't let Daniel out of his arms. I can see he's worried. The scut. He had the brains to earn it in the right way. We have to be there for him.'

'You don't,' Elizabeth reminded her.

'Then it must mean I want to be. Now don't talk any more about this depressing stuff. We'll handle it when the time comes, won't we, Elizabeth? Happy birthday to you. Danny has just filled his nappy, to confirm the greeting. Do the cake, then I'll take him up.'

Elizabeth sat down to her birthday cake and blew out the candles. Daniel watched the flames and wailed when the candles were snuffed out. Grace offered to read Elizabeth's tea leaves. Marilyn took the baby out of the room to change him. In Brigid's room she advised him, 'This is where you were born, little man.' As she said it, she could feel her, watching, disapproving of how she changed Danny. 'They don't use Sudo any more, Brigid! It's like putting tar on the baby's skin. And I am tying it the right way. At least I'm a clothie, not polluting the environment with disposables. Yes, he is gorgeous.' Marilyn had no problem with speaking to her. 'Did I tell you, Brigid, I'm doing an online course in numerology? Could you get on to God and see if I'm a heretic? It's just for fun, really, but I'm trying to work out when we should run the horses, for optimum results. It's fascinating. It seems to work!'

Sean and Theresa excused themselves for a smoke, leaving only two in the kitchen. Grace smiled as she examined Elizabeth's tea leaves.

'The men are on the way to the Monroe house. Armed.'

'Not again!' Elizabeth sighed. She told Grace about Tony moving out of his house and going away. 'The one I want believes in non-violence. I don't think he'll be back. Travelling will suit him.'

'As it does you, darling. Happy fifty-fourth birthday. A spring chicken.'

Elizabeth smiled, then started at what sounded like a fence panel collapsing in the back garden. 'I knew one was loose, but there's no wind. Sean!'

'He's out the front smoking,' Grace reminded her.

'I don't know why they didn't go out the back as usual.'

'You gave out to them for putting out their butts on your patio . . .'

A male voice cut across them. 'I'm a brickie, not a designer! I did the paving in the middle of the night, for one of your notions. Now I'm after burning the hand off myself.'

'Someone's breaking in.' Elizabeth leapt up. 'Grace, get Sean. Make sure the baby is safe.' She flicked on the patio lights from the inside switch. Out of the corner of her eye she noticed that Grace hadn't moved an inch and appeared to be smiling.

'What's wrong with you. All right, I'll do it myself.' She stormed through the sunroom. That's when she saw the path. It was lined with cornflower pots and tea-lights. It led right up to the fence panel that had come down. That's when she knew the panel had been loosened deliberately, some days ago. Marilyn appeared in the kitchen. She and Grace were smiling together now, as was Daniel.

'I can't,' Elizabeth whispered.

'You can.' They said it in unison.

She walked along the path which led from her garden into what had been Fiona Sharp's. Tony Devereux had come for the last of the Monroe women by laying a path to her door. She stepped through the gap in the fence and found him waiting on the other side, in a tuxedo.

'We had planned some music, but Mick gave the game away after burning his hand on the candles. He's very sorry for almost spoiling it, and he's inside. What I want to know is: will you come in too, Elizabeth?'

She nodded but couldn't speak. The joy of seeing him robbed her of anything but a smile.

'Happy birthday, Elizabeth, and many happy returns. But not, I hope, of these.'

He handed her two packages. One ring-sized, the other book-sized. The ring was a sapphire, cornflower-blue. The book was Peter Devon's gift to him almost a year previously: *How to Make a Wildflower Meadow*.

'I'm offering you my new garden, for you to make a meadow in.' He smiled, and she was given to tears. 'Will you have me as a neighbour? And my two lads, if that's okay.'

'Of course I'll have you,' Elizabeth smiled. 'On condition you and your crew put up a proper gate. No builder gets paid otherwise. That's my mother coming out in me.'

In the summertime of the following year, there was to be a wildflower meadow in suburbia. If you had a bird's-eye view of Verbena Avenue, you would be lucky.

Also in the summertime of the following year, Delicia Heartly's winning streak would end, and Marilyn would remind Sean why.

'She's Signorinetta, don't forget. She wants to foal. But we'll have to pick the right stallion, or she'll do nothing.'

Delaney liked the look of Dunbrody. They chose him for his handsomeness, lineage and fine call to her. She answered him like she'd been answering all her life.

The first letter addressed to Marilyn arrived in Wexford that same month. They were normally addressed to Sean and had a photo of Rose, which Marilyn looked at, with interest.

'Please,' Julie wrote to Sean, 'send one back. I'd love to see him.' Marilyn always refused.

'I'm not going to play happy extended family.'

'Isn't that what you have?' Sean reminded her. 'In 50 and 45 and 51 Verbena? Isn't your family taking over the whole street? Julie's round the corner, she misses the bones of you, Marilyn. From the word go she was clear with me that she'd never have us live together to rear Rose. "I'm no farm girl," she says to me. And you are. So give up on being bitter. Give me a puck now and again when the hurt rises, and take it off her.'

Marilyn found she wanted to, but didn't know how.

The letter, which came just before Daniel's birthday, didn't start 'Dear Marilyn'. Julie was never one for formality.

> *'Hey, did you ever try dunking a potato chip in champagne? It's real crazy!'* —Seven Year Itch
>
> *I gave up the booze, so I won't be getting pregnant by any other friend's boyfriend. Plus now I have my own. And I'm worried. His name is Mick and he lives next door to your mother and Tony. He's also Tony's foster-son. Please write indicating disapproval/approval.*
>
> *Love,*
> *Julie*

Julie's father had finally become unmanageable to the point where Margaret said, 'He'll have to go into a home. We can't have him around Rose.'

They picked one close by, where they could see him every day. Julie went to her first AA meeting, having met Tony down the shops and complained there was nothing to do but go to pubs in the evening.

'I've done enough to myself in drink and through it,' she revealed. Her first meeting was all old ladies and men. Her second had Mick in it.

'Well' – he stood – 'my name's Mick and I'm a recovering drug and alcohol addict. I saw a beautiful woman coming in here and I decided to turn left instead of right and go to AA instead of NA tonight. This love-at-first-sight thing wrecks your head. Me da's all for it, though.' Some laughed, some disapproved. Julie glowed.

Marilyn wrote back:

Carry on. Here's a picture of Daniel. Rose is beautiful, like her mother. I like the Marilyn line.

Five months later, Julie sent another letter.

'You wouldn't marry a girl just because she's pretty, but my goodness, doesn't it help?'—Gentlemen Prefer Blondes

He's asked me. He's ten years younger than me. He looks like an ugly boxer. His teeth require surgery. He's an ex-con and junkie. Likes Sylvester Stallone films and period telly dramas make him cry! Scores zilch on the Scale. Rose thinks he's God. My mother the same. And me. He could move in with us at our house. Colin could be best man. You could be bridesmaid. Please indicate approval/disapproval.

I love you,
Julie.

Marilyn wrote back:

I hope you're very, very happy and I'm sorry that I can't be bridesmaid. But invite who you like, and that does mean Tony and my mother.

On Christmas Eve of 2003 Julie and Mick went off with Rose and Margaret, Colin and Tony to a registry office. It wasn't what Mick wanted for her, but Julie insisted.

'I'm not putting Marilyn through any more endurance tests. The less fuss about this, the better.'

461

*

Sean came in from the yard to find suitcases in the hall. 'What? I thought we weren't going up? I thought that's why your mother was down.'

Elizabeth was behind Marilyn, carrying Daniel. Marilyn was frantically putting stuff into plastic bags. He was confused, still not used to his partner always charging ahead, miffed that he was expected to follow. Then she spoke.

'I have a wedding to get to. My best friend is getting married at two o'clock. I'd like to be there.'

He softened. 'Marilyn, are you absolutely sure about this?'

'Yes. Can you drive us safely and get us there on time?'

They had planned to sit quietly at the back of the room. But Daniel kicked up a stink. Julie turned around to see Marilyn about to feed him. Marilyn's face apologised for the noise and begged Julie not to make a fuss. Julie knew this, because she knew Marilyn. Because she knew Marilyn she knew how much effort had gone into this appearance. It didn't make her day perfect. It made her life perfect. Mick gave a thumbs up and a broad grin. Tony and Colin came over to Marilyn and sat on either side of her, Elizabeth and Sean.

'We all belong,' Marilyn, greasy-haired and not dressed for a wedding, whispered to Sean. He held her hand. All of her was glad she had done this. When Daniel had finished feeding there was a noise outside. A stranger came in with a toddler demanding to see her mother. The stranger was Magenta, who had flown over and was babysitting. But Rose wouldn't wait any more. She ran up the centre aisle and straight into her father's arms. Mick put his forehead on his daughter's and Julie put her arms round both of them. They were a family as much as Sean, Marilyn and Daniel were.

As soon as the ceremony was complete, Julie walked past

everyone to Marilyn. They embraced. Daniel, on his grand-mother's lap now, reached out his arms for Tony.

'Will you come for the meal?' Julie asked with a longing Marilyn couldn't refuse, and didn't want to. 'We won't be out late. I know how knackered you must be. That was me only a few months ago. Still is.'

They walked out together, comparing notes on mothering and sleep deprivation. Mick and Sean walked behind them.

'It's like them two got married instead of us!' Mick complained. 'Women.'

At the restaurant Marilyn announced to Sean that she'd like them all to stay at 51 that night. 'I'm not making promises. You should see Rose for Christmas. You're feeling a bit left out since Mick took out the adoption papers.'

Tony excused himself early. He was going out to taxi, working hard so he could take Elizabeth for a surprise visit to Skyros at Easter. He went home first to change out of his suit. Home was now 51. Colin and his girlfriend lived in 50.

He was waiting for the others to come back to say goodbye, knowing they wouldn't be much longer. The doorbell went.

'They must have forgotten their keys.' He answered it.

Outside stood a tramp.

'Is the lady of the house here?'

'She's at work,' Tony said.

'She normally gives me dinner and a few bob, round the Christmas. A grand woman, she is, from the old days, before people got mean with their money.'

'I think you must mean Brigid?'

'Indeed.'

'Brigid died, eighteen months ago. I don't think we saw you last Christmas.'

'Oh, I move round, shuffle round, a bit. A woman like that dying, so sorry to hear it, a grand woman like that.'

'She went well, surrounded by family.'

'Pass on my sympathies.' The man was filthy, but dignified in his offering. Tony took it for what it was, knowing that it was only luck that kept him on this side of the threshold.

'I've no dinner, but here's a few bob. Happy Christmas,' Tony said, watching him put it away with a sniff. Brigid must have given more.

'Thanks for your trouble. I wouldn't normally knock, unless the lady of the house is there. The best, she was.'

'Her daughter's as grand,' Tony smiled. 'Call next year.' She might be more generous than me, he thought.

He watched the tramp wander out the gate, in a manner that said he was unaware of what he had become. By the spring in his step, he saw himself as a gentleman caller, and the whiskey on his breath helped him keep the illusion alive.

Marilyn and Sean pulled in just at that point, with Elizabeth and Daniel in the back.

The tramp looked at the Monroe family in the Saab, saw the baby seat, tipped his hat to Daniel in the back, and wandered on. Elizabeth was preoccupied with picking up his rattle, which he insisted on dropping every five seconds. Her back ached, she wanted to see Tony, before he went out. The tramp had moved on in the opposite direction before she got a look at him.

'I hope he's got somewhere to go tomorrow, they do a Christmas dinner at the Mansion House,' Tony said to himself, feeling guilty for looking forward so much to his own Christmas, his second with Elizabeth Monroe. He pulled on his coat and headed out in the cold to help bring in the bags. Elizabeth came down the path, carrying her grandson in her arms.

Marilyn and Sean were bickering behind them, over something that showed they loved each other.

Tony forgot about the tramp, who was never seen again at 51.

The noise of family carried down Verbena to the tramp's ears.

'Well, Brigid,' John Joe whispered, 'the men got back in at last. After too long away.'

Acknowledgements

The biggest acknowledgement has to go to Ciara Considine, publisher at Hodder Headline Ireland, for a magnificent editing job. The rest of the team at HHI – Breda Purdue, Claire Rourke and Ruth Shern – have my gratitude also. And thanks are due to Kristin Jensen for a painstaking copy-edit.

The back up at home is second to none. Albie, Rory and Finn, my parents James and Marina and my sister Amanda have all put themselves out to let me do this work.

In the horse-racing world, Mary Ballantyne of Wexford race course threw open their stables and imbued me with an enthusiasm that now makes me a member of the course Supporter's Club.

Tom Foley, Danoli's trainer, is a true horse knower and lover, as is Sally Bolger, resident of West Cork and the world. They know their stuff and they love their work. I couldn't have gained the insight I did without them.

Mary Fitzgerald, PR and horse-racing aficionado, pointed me in all the right directions. Above all thanks to patient, kind Louise Kane of *Horse Racing Ireland*, who put up with my compulsion to call her Elaine and gave me great assistance.

To Marian Keyes, as always, my respect and gratitude.

Thanks to David Godwin, my agent, for support above the call of any duty, enthusiasm and honesty. And to the team at DGA – Rowan, Sarah, Heather, Katya, Kirsty.

May I point out that any mistakes made are mine, nothing to do with the sources and experts I consulted.